HIS FORBIDDEN
DIAMOND

SUSAN STEPHENS

Susan Stephens was a professional singer before meeting her husband on the Mediterranean island of Malta. In true Modern Romance style they met on Monday, became engaged on Friday and married three months later. Susan enjoys entertaining, travel and going to the theatre. To relax she reads, cooks and plays the piano, and when she's had enough of relaxing she throws herself off mountains on skis, or gallops through the countryside singing loudly.

CHAPTER ONE

TYR SKAVANGA IS HOME!

THE HEADLINE BLARED at him. His sister Britt had placed the newspaper on her desk, where she knew he couldn't fail to see it. Britt was trying to tell him in her usual no-nonsense way how much he'd been missed, and how words could never express his three sisters' happiness now he'd returned. The photograph beneath the headline showed Britt, Eva and Leila, hugging each other, their faces wreathed in smiles of joy.

Because of him.

Turning, he went to stare out of Britt's office window, where snow drifted from a black sky like frozen sighs. Everything outside the building was pristine white and unspoiled, while inside, reflected in the window, was a killer's face, *his face,* and he couldn't hide from that.

He had no wish to, Tyr thought grimly. He was back in Skavanga, the small mining town that bore his family's name, to reboot himself amongst people he loved. He'd stayed away for too long after leaving the army, to protect his sisters and friends from a man who was vastly changed. Britt, his eldest sister, had never given up on him, never ceased trying to contact him whether he replied to her messages or not. *Not being the usual response from him.* Britt was one of the few people who could reach him through her husband, Sheikh Sharif. Sharif was one of Tyr's closest friends and had remained loyal throughout, refusing to reveal Tyr's whereabouts, or what he was doing while he was away, even to his wife, Britt.

In the end it was a child who had pricked his conscience and brought him back. He had carried the little girl from the war zone to reunite her with her family in a refugee camp, and when the tears of joy subsided she had turned to him to ask, with all the concern a child of seven who'd seen too much could muster:

'Don't you have a family, Mr Tyr?'

The little girl's question had shamed him, shattered him. It had broken through his armour, forcing him to think about those he'd left behind. Yes, he had a family and he loved them very much, he had explained to her. No one in the girl's family had commented when his eyes filled with tears. They'd seen everything. They were reunited. They were alive. That was all they asked for. When he'd left the camp to return to the desert to begin rebuilding, he'd worked until his strength gave out, and all the time he was there the little girl's comment about his family nagged at him, made him realise how lucky he was to have people who loved him. He knew then he had to go home, though he had dreaded confronting his sisters, who would see through the shell in an instant to this new and much changed man.

He had been of inestimable value to Special Forces, a senior officer had told him as he pinned a medal on Tyr's chest, but that wasn't something Tyr wanted carved on his tombstone. He wanted to be remembered for what he'd built, and not for what he'd destroyed. He'd encountered three types of soldier in battle: those who enjoyed their job, those who went about their duty with unfailing courage and loyalty to comrades and country, and those who would never recover from what they'd seen, physically, mentally, or both. He had no excuse. He was strong. He had the love of a good family, and somehow he had managed, not just to stay alive, but to remain relatively unharmed, at least outwardly. And now it was up to him to complete the healing process so he could be of some use to those less fortunate than himself.

'Tyr!'

'Britt.' He swung round just in time for his beautiful sister to throw herself into his arms. Britt's face was ecstatic, but she was full of questions. Flight good? Journey good?

'You look great, Tyr.'

His mouth quirked. 'Liar.'

His eldest sister took a step back to take a proper look at him. 'Okay, so your clothes look great.'

'Better,' he said dryly as they shared a laugh. 'I stopped off in Milan, knowing if I was coming to a party hosted by my glamorous sisters, I had better look the part.'

Britt's face grew concerned. 'You know, you don't have to do anything you don't want to, Tyr.'

'But I want to be here. I wanted to come home and see you.'

'So, you're ready to face the music?' Britt enquired, glancing across the road to the town's smartest hotel, where she had arranged a welcome home party for him.

'I am if you are.'

'I only wish we had longer to talk, but you've never been one to ease yourself into a situation by degrees, have you, Tyr?'

'Full immersion,' he confirmed, determined to keep the tone upbeat. 'It's the only way I know.'

Britt gave a disbelieving hum. 'If you say so.'

'I do say so.' He gestured towards the hotel, where they could see cars arriving. 'And thank you for going to all this trouble for me.'

She laughed. 'It's nice to have the chance. And if I can't welcome the town's hero home…'

'Just welcome your brother home. That's all I want.'

'I'd go to the ends of the earth for you, Tyr—and almost had to,' Britt reminded him wryly.

'Those emails kept coming,' he agreed.

'And you kept ignoring them.'

'But I saved you a trip in the end,' he pointed out.

'Tyr, you never change.' Britt was laughing but her eyes were sad behind the fixed smile because they both knew that was a lie. He'd changed a whole lot.

'This quiet time in my office has been good for you, though, hasn't it, Tyr?'

'This quiet time has been perfect. Thank you, Britt.'

Aside from shopping for some essentials, which meant ditching the desert boots and safari shirts in favour of city clothes, Tyr hadn't suffered any human contact since leaving the sandbox. After the silence of the desert even street noise was deafening. But when could Britt not face anything that came her way? he reflected as he gazed into the eyes of a most admirable woman. Even if she hadn't been his sister, he would have placed Britt on a pedestal a mile high.

'Well, you've had your moment,' she told him briskly. 'I want a few words alone with you, and then we'll go.'

He frowned. 'This sounds serious.'

'There's a lot to tell you, Tyr. You've been away for such a long time. Leila's had twins—'

'This I know—you already told me.'

'I told you when they were born,' Britt agreed. 'They're

practically school age now, yet you still haven't seen them.'

He acknowledged this with a regretful dip of his head.

'And Leila's pregnant again—'

'What?' This was news to him. 'Raffa doesn't waste any time.'

'Stop with the dinosaur spiel. Those two adore each other. They want a football team, according to Leila. And if you will go off radar the world isn't going to stand still until you decide to come back.'

Where he'd been there was no communication with the outside world—not until he set that communication up and moved on, leaving others to go about the business of contacting loved ones. For a long time he'd been too beat up inside to even think about inflicting himself on his sisters.

'You're not going to tell me where you were, are you, Tyr?'

'Need-to-know basis only.' He made light of it and shrugged. His work was important to him. It was the only way he knew to make reparation. He didn't want to talk about that work to anyone, not even to Britt. He didn't want praise for putting right the wrong he'd done. He just wanted to get on with the job.

Britt shook her head at him. 'Well, I give up. But just wait until you see Leila. She looks—'

'Huge?' he suggested, ducking as Britt aimed a swipe at him.

And just like that they were back to the happy days, the carefree days. 'So, what else is going on I should know about?'

'Jazz is here.'

Electricity coursed through him. 'Jazz. I haven't seen Jazz for years.' Just the mention of Sharif's younger sister's name took him back to wild school holidays, when he could ride himself into the ground and swim until his arms ached, and think of nothing more but the next harmless adventure with his two friends from Kareshi. But beneath Britt's matter-of-fact tone, he sensed something more. 'So?' He shrugged. 'What's happening with Jazz?' He was fairly confident Sharif would have told him if anything serious had happened to his Jazz—Princess Jasmina of Kareshi, as Jazz was better known to the world. 'Jazz is okay, isn't she?'

'Of course she is.'

'But?' He played it down, but his heart had stopped at the thought of harm coming to Jazz. They'd known each other since Sharif had first invited Tyr to spend his school holidays in Kareshi, where Jazz teased him unmercifully for his lack of desert lore. He'd shrugged the irritating kid sister off, but surprised himself by always being pleased to see her. A type of camaraderie had grown between them, and the thought of Jazz sick, or injured— His stomach churned. He'd seen too much of that.

'But nothing, Tyr,' Britt insisted. 'I'd tell you if there was anything wrong.'

He searched Britt's eyes, knowing that wasn't the whole story.

'She's coming tonight, Tyr.'

'Great.' It would be good to see Jazz, though Sharif's sister could see through everyone, and he wasn't sure how he felt about that.

'She's changed, Tyr,' Britt said quietly.

He looked up.

'Like the rest of us, Tyr, Jazz has grown up.'

What was his sister trying to tell him? He shrugged, picturing Jazz with braces and pigtails. How much could one person change? He glanced at his reflection in the window, where he got his answer to that.

'What's wrong, Tyr?'

He slanted a smile. 'Nothing. Absolutely nothing's wrong.'

'We've all changed,' Britt said, reading him easily, 'but at least you're smiling now. Thinking of Jazz?'

He hummed and shrugged Britt's question off, but he was thinking about Jazz, who, all those years back, had used to refer to him as the guy from the frozen north with the funny name. Sharif, Jazz and he had been an oddball team. Jazz started out the most unwanted member of that team, but she was also the most determined, and could ride him and Sharif into the ground. And she knew the shifting patterns of the desert like the back of her hand. There had been no getting away from Jazz Kareshi, so in the end they'd given up.

'Don't look so worried, Britt. I can handle Jazz,' he said with confidence.

'Just don't tease her, Tyr.'

'Don't tease Jazz?' He frowned. Jazz had always been the butt of their humour, and Jazz had always given back as good as she got.

'Jazz has only agreed to come tonight because this is such a big family occasion. And I'm here to chaperone her,' Britt added with a meaningful look. 'Me and Sharif, that is.'

He frowned. 'This is all sounding terribly formal and not a bit like Jazz.'

'Like I said, Tyr, Jazz is all grown up, and unmarried sisters of the ruling sheikh in Kareshi don't share our freedoms.'

'Is Sharif penning her in?'

'Don't be silly. You know Sharif is a big advocate for

progress. This is Jazz's decision, and we have to respect her for her beliefs. It shows a quiet strength and lots of courage, in my opinion. Jazz has stood by Sharif's side throughout as he's coaxed Kareshi into the twenty-first century, and now she doesn't want to do anything to rock the boat, let alone give the traditionalists in Kareshi an excuse to criticise Sharif for implementing progress too quickly.'

'So Jazz sacrifices herself?' he demanded, outraged. 'Jazz shuts herself away?'

'Not exactly, but Jazz has become quite conservative, so for her sake, Tyr, just tone it down when you see her, okay?'

'What do you think I'm going to do? We've been friends for most of our lives, Britt. I'm hardly going to leap on her.'

'Just cool the friendship, and stay clear of Jazz, except for the most perfunctory greeting. Okay?'

He raked his hair. 'I can't believe you're serious. Is anyone allowed to approach the royal presence?'

'Don't mock her, Tyr. Of course they are.' Britt fired a warning glance across his bows for making light of something that was obviously a great concern to her. 'Jazz lives a near normal life in Kareshi. Sharif broke all the traditionalists' rules by giving Jazz a job at his racing stables, where she's excelled in management, but, more importantly, this has opened the floodgates for all the women of Kareshi to work, if they choose to do so.'

'But?' he prompted, homing in on Britt's brief hesitation.

'But it's made Jazz more determined than ever to uphold tradition in other areas of her life, so that no one can find fault with Sharif's decision to allow her to work.'

'What does "upholding tradition" mean exactly?'

'It means that Jazz believes Kareshi can only take one small step at a time, and if by staying in the shadows it means every woman in Kareshi has the right to work, she's prepared to do that. We should admire her for that sacrifice.'

'Her *sacrifice*?'

'Kareshi has to be coaxed, not bullied, Tyr. Jazz understands this as I do. Freedom for women to work is the first big step. Freedom for unmarried women to mix openly with men without being shunned by society is the next. Kareshi will take that step, but Jazz is devoted to her people, and I think we can safely trust Jazz to know what's best in this instance.'

'To know what's best for her, or for Kareshi?'

'Don't get so heated, Tyr. For both, of course. And please don't scowl at me like that.'

'You're right, and I apologise.' Britt had done too much for him for him to sound off at her like that. 'I'm still trying to get my head around the feisty girl I knew becoming some sort of reclusive woman.'

'So you didn't shut yourself away from those who loved you?'

Trust Britt to point that out. He forced a smile over his concern for Jazz. 'Point taken.'

'Be happy for her, Tyr. Jazz is a wonderful young woman with the strongest sense of duty where Kareshi is concerned, something I know you can relate to. It makes sense that she doesn't want to cause ripples on the pond.'

'It makes sense to you maybe,' he agreed, 'but Jazz is my friend, and I'm going to see a lot of friends tonight and I'm going to treat them all the same.'

'Then there's nothing to worry about, is there?' Taking his face between her hands, Britt stood on tiptoes to kiss him on both cheeks. 'Now, there are some people outside that door who have waited a long time to give you a big, sloppy welcome without the rest of the world looking on.'

His spirits soared with expectation. 'Eva and Leila are here?'

'With their husbands—I didn't think you'd mind, seeing as Roman and Raffa are your closest friends?'

'I don't mind at all.' He was looking forward to it, and his cynical self reassured him that if he kept it light they wouldn't see anything in his eyes except the happiness a reunion like this would bring.

His middle sister, Eva, was the first into the room, changing the dynamics completely. Eva lived up to her bright red hair with the sharpest tongue this side of a scalpel, and the long space of time since they'd seen each other hadn't dulled Eva's approach. Standing back, she weighed him up. 'You look every bit as formidable as I remember, warrior-boy.'

'I could crush you with one finger, squirt.'

Fists raised, they squared up for a mock fight, and then, bursting into tears, Eva launched herself at him. Pummelling him with her tiny fists, she raged in a shaking voice, 'Don't you ever do that to me again. Do you hear me, Tyr?' Pulling back, she stared at him with furious eyes. 'Don't you *ever* disappear out of my life again without at least having the courtesy to leave me the keys to your muscle car.'

Laughing, he embraced her. 'Promise,' he murmured softly as he kissed the top of her head.

Eyes softened with tears, Eva pulled back to stare at him. 'You've no idea how we've missed you, Tyr.'

'I've missed you too.' How much, they'd never know. 'I can't imagine how I survived all that time without the three of you nagging me.'

As Eva roared with pretended fury, Britt walked to the

door and swung it wide. 'Leila!' He was ready to catch his youngest sister and swing her round. Thankfully he stopped in time. 'Wow. You *are* pregnant.'

'Bowling-ball pregnant,' Leila confirmed, laughing and crying all at the same time as they embraced.

'But you look as beautiful as Britt warned me you would.'

Leila huffed a laugh as she stood back. 'If you like waddling hippos, I'm your gal.' She stared at him intently for a moment. 'I can't believe you've come back to us.' His sister's eyes filled with love and concern. 'But life's taken a bite out of you.'

'Enough.' He straightened his jacket. 'We're going to a party, aren't we?'

'We mustn't keep our guests waiting,' Britt agreed, exchanging a look with him as she held the door.

Linking arms with his two younger sisters, he urged them out of the room.

For the first time Jazz could remember, Sharif hadn't shown impatience with her when she wasn't ready to leave for the party at the same time as him and Britt. 'No hurry,' he'd soothed with a smile. 'Just call me when you're ready and I'll come back for you.'

At the time she'd been flapping over what to wear. This might seem like a storm in a teacup to the average bystander, but, when you chose not to socialise in mixed company, it was hard to know what high society in a bustling mining town like Skavanga would expect of a very conservative princess of Kareshi.

'Your smile,' Britt had told Jazz in her usual down-to-earth way, insisting Jazz must show her face on this occasion. 'You don't have to take the traditions of Kareshi to the nth degree when you're staying with us in the frozen north.'

'But if I were photographed—'

'The people of Kareshi could only be proud of their princess. Seeing you with your brother, surrounded by a family who loves you both so much, how could they not be proud of you, Jazz?'

Britt was always hard to argue with, and on that occasion impossible, though Jazz had had to wrestle with her inner demons before she could agree to showing her face in public. Her parents had abused their privilege and neglected their people, leaving Sharif and Jazz in the care of a succession of nannies while their mother had flaunted her beauty on a world stage. Sharif and Jazz had grown up sensitive to the rumblings of discontent in their country, so that when the time came for Sharif to inherit the throne he had moved as quickly as he could to turn the super-tanker round and establish a fair rule so he could make their country safe. Sharif was good and strong and kind and wise, but their troubled childhood in a land of absentee rulers and rampant corruption had left Jazz determined not to cause any more upset, so, however free her spirit, in appearance she was always careful not to offend.

'You should get out of Kareshi more,' Britt had insisted when they had discussed what Jazz would wear for the party. 'It would be good for your people, and good for you.'

Jazz agreed, but Kareshi was steeped in millennia of tradition. Sharif had already given her a job at his racing stables, which had opened the floodgates for every woman in Kareshi to work, should they choose to do so, and Jazz wasn't about to risk their freedom by pushing the traditionalists too far. And it was much easier hiding behind a veil than facing up to a night like this. Staring into the mirror, she wished her heart would stop pounding. Her brother had already left with Britt, so Britt could enjoy a private reunion with her sisters and their long-lost brother, Tyr, at the Skavanga Mining company offices.

Tyr.

Jazz's throat dried. She had always been excited to see the big Viking.

But things were different now, Jazz told herself firmly. She was an adult with responsibilities, not a child who had plagued the life out of her brother's closest friend. She had to guard her feelings.

But Tyr was someone she could always depend on.

Or he had been, until he'd disappeared.

How she'd worried about him—wondered about him— prayed for him to be safe.

And now he was back.

What would he think of her? She was so changed, so solemn and so silent. She wouldn't be playing any tricks on him today.

And she wouldn't be going to the party if she didn't calm down.

Taking a few steadying breaths, she closed her eyes and tried her hardest not to think about Tyr Skavanga. After a few moments, she gave up.

Tyr paused at the entrance to the hotel ballroom and smiled. 'This is beautiful, Britt.'

'No welcome banners,' Eva complained, staring around.

'No. It's all very Britt,' Leila commented approvingly, echoing his own thoughts. 'It's a really classy setting.'

'For a warrior's return,' Eva said proudly, putting her hand on his arm.

'For a homecoming,' he argued gently.

There was no doubt Britt had gone to a lot of trouble. The flowers in the tall vases flanking the easel to one side of the grand double doors were classic and white. The photograph of him Britt had chosen to prop up on the easel showed him laughing and relaxed before he'd entered the theatre of war, where his life had changed completely.

'You look about twenty years older in real life,' Eva informed him helpfully to a chorus of disapproval from their sisters.

'Watch it, shrimp,' he warned playfully, feeling his spirits lift to the point where he thought he might actually enjoy the evening. 'Roman's out of earshot, so you could be heading for a soaking in the chocolate fountain.'

Eva gave a theatrical sigh. 'Death by chocolate suits me.'

'Come on, you two, stop squabbling,' Britt insisted, pulling the big-sister card on both of them.

He walked ahead of his sisters into the lavishly decorated ballroom with its Gothic curlicues and massive, glittering chandeliers, and the first thing he saw when he entered the room was Jazz.

CHAPTER TWO

HOLY CRAP!

Tyr's heart banged in his chest when Jazz turned to look at him. It was as if some invisible electrical cord connected them. What was it he'd said so confidently to Britt only minutes before? *I'm going to see a lot of friends tonight and I'm going to treat them all the same.*

Seriously?

No one else stood a chance of top billing with Princess Jasmina of Kareshi in the room. Britt had been derelict in her description of this new version of the tomboy Jazz, who hadn't just grown up, but who had blossomed like an exotic flower into the most beautiful woman he'd ever seen. Jazz's new air of serenity intrigued him. It was as if she had created a role for herself that she was determined to play out to the full.

He dismissed the new role Jazz had slotted herself into with a disapproving huff. She was avoiding the truth.

A bit like him, then?

Not a bit like him!

Swiping his hair back, he turned his mind to the flash of fire he'd seen in her eyes when Jazz had first spotted him entering the ballroom. It reminded him of the days when Her Royal Cheekiness had used to goad him on every possible occasion. Level calm had returned to her eyes now that Jazz was concentrating on the group of women surrounding her.

'Tyr?'

He turned to look at Britt.

'She's beautiful, isn't she?'

There was always more to Britt's questions than at first appeared, so he replied with caution. 'I guess.' His world was private. He'd lived alone for too long to share his personal feelings with anyone, even Britt. He should have known his sister didn't need any conversational pointers to read him.

'Don't shake her up, Tyr,' Britt implored. 'Be mild-mannered around her. Don't pull the marauding Viking act. Jazz is trying her hardest to play the conservative card, so that traditionalists aren't rattled when Sharif makes sweeping changes for good in Kareshi.' Britt shook her head for emphasis. 'This evening is really hard for her, Tyr. Being out in mixed company, I mean. But Jazz needs this. She has such a free spirit—but you know that.' Britt frowned. 'She's sacrificed more than we know for Kareshi.'

'Her freedom?' he cut in.

'Tyr, please. Don't make it any harder for her,' Britt begged him with a restraining hand on his arm. 'You, of all people, can surely appreciate the value of sacrifice. So just say hello, be polite and then back off. All right?'

'Thanks for writing the script for me, sis.' He raised an amused brow.

'Just don't mess with Jazz. She's got enough to contend with.'

'I've no intention of messing with Jazz, as you put it, but I'd have to be wood from the neck up not to respond to such a beautiful woman.'

'Just keep your feelings under wraps, Tyr. Spare Jazz

the heartache. She's always been half in love with you. And you've been alone a long time, remember.'

'Relax, Britt. I'm not that desperate. I haven't exactly been a saint while I've been away.'

'You can find love in all sorts of unexpected places,' Britt agreed, 'but I don't think Jazz is looking for the type of love you're offering.'

He gave his sister an amused look. 'I hope she isn't looking for love at all.'

'Why, Tyr?' Britt's stare pierced him. 'Would you be jealous?'

'Of Jazz's suitors?' He laughed that off. Offering Britt his arm, he led his sister deeper into the crowded room.

'There are too many alphas in this room,' Britt commented wryly as his sisters' husbands Raffa and Roman waylaid him for a brisk man hug. 'I may drown in testosterone.'

'Don't worry. I'll save you,' Tyr offered as the men broke away to claim their wives.

'That's what I'm afraid of,' Britt murmured.

When they drew closer to Jazz, Britt gave him a warning look and he squeezed her arm to reassure her. 'I remember what you said. I respect Jazz. Always have, always will.'

He didn't hear Britt's reply. The hubbub of excited guests rolled over him like white noise as he kept his gaze fixed on Jazz. Bathed in light beneath a huge chandelier, she was chatting animatedly to an admiring group of women.

'No, Tyr.'

He paused mid-stride with Britt at his elbow.

'Don't you remember what I said? Jazz is going to be heavily chaperoned tonight, and I won't thank you for interfering.'

The corner of his mouth kicked up. 'You still think I'm going to leap on her?'

'I know that look in your eyes. When Jazz marries she's stated her intention to be pure.'

He frowned. 'What are you suggesting?'

'You don't put her in a compromising position. Go easy on her, Tyr. Jazz has barely left Kareshi since the day she was born. Coming to Skavanga is a big adventure for her.'

'I've got no intention of spoiling anything for Jazz. If she has chosen to live her life according to the traditions of Kareshi, then I respect that.'

'Good, because you might be the brother I adore, but if you hurt Jazz—'

'You don't have to say it, Britt.'

'Don't I?' Britt followed his stare straight ahead to the slim, straight-backed girl wearing the long, concealing robes of Kareshi.

So much for her intention to live a chaste and pure life! Jazz's intentions hadn't changed, but her body was rebelling like you wouldn't believe. Hyper-arousal was an involuntary reaction to a threat, and one glimpse of Tyr Skavanga was all it took to give her all the symptoms. Her muscles were primed for action, while she was tense and ready. Her heart was racing, and her breathing was hectic as adrenalin raced through her system, putting every nerve ending she possessed in super-receptive mode. The flight-or-fight mechanism common to all human beings, whether they were autocratic sheikhs, powerful Scandinavian warriors like Tyr or the highly protected sister of the ruling Sheikh Sharif of Kareshi, could not be controlled by force of will.

But it must be controlled, Jazz determined, glancing

at her brother to make sure Sharif had not noticed her response to Tyr.

It wasn't *fear* of Tyr Skavanga raising Jazz's heartbeat as she continued to chat with the group of women surrounding her, but the excitement of rekindling a lifelong friendship with him that was as close to love as it could get. But they weren't children any longer, and Jazz was an unmarried princess of Kareshi, which meant that to love a man outside the family, however innocent that love might be, was absolutely forbidden by the traditionalists in Kareshi. Sharif was a progressive ruler, but Jazz believed that things could only move so fast in a country mired in tradition, and only the fact that tonight was an unmissable family event had ensured her attendance at this party.

She had spent so many years thinking about Tyr, however, that it was impossible to put him out of her mind now he was practically within touching distance. No one knew where Tyr had been for all these years, except perhaps for Sharif, who had been his closest friend since school, and who was as annoyingly silent as the Sphinx on the subject of Tyr Skavanga. They had both attended an elite military college, that much she knew, and then they had both joined Special Forces, where Tyr had been decorated for his courage, but then he'd disappeared. 'Into the desert,' Sharif had told her vaguely. Sharif would never betray a friend's confidence, but had explained that Tyr was working on rebuilding and repairing infrastructure that had been damaged during the years of conflict before Sharif ascended the throne.

Tyr's life experiences had changed him, Jazz realised as she stared at him. There were shadows behind his eyes and deep lines furrowing Tyr's strong face. Whatever her pledge regarding friendships with men outside the family, her heart went out to him.

And bounced when Tyr glanced at her.

It was as if he could feel her interest.

Her cheeks burned as she turned away. Surely Sharif had explained to Tyr that she might be working, and have all the outward appearance of being an independent woman, but she was bound by her duty to Kareshi, and was only marking time until her brother could arrange an advantageous marriage for her—advantageous for Kareshi, that was.

'Skavanga is so glamorous these days, isn't it?'

Thankful to be distracted, she turned to smile at the elderly woman standing next to her. 'This is my first time in Skavanga,' she admitted, 'so I only know what my brother has told me about a place he's come to love.'

'Before diamonds were discovered in the family mine,' the same woman continued, 'Skavanga was just a tiny mining town beyond the Arctic Circle, scratching a living as best it could, but now our town glitters as brightly as the precious stones your brother mines. We have Sheikh Sharif to thank for playing a major role in the consortium that saved us.'

'You're very kind, but my sister-in-law, Britt, Sharif's wife, has always been the driving force behind the Skavanga mining company.'

The older woman stared at Jazz approvingly as she stood on tiptoe to confide, 'I'm surprised those three powerful men didn't run Britt Skavanga out of town.'

Jazz laughed with all the other women at this reference to the three ambitious men who had formed the consortium that saved the mine. 'I hardly think my brother would run his wife out of town. He adores Britt. And though it's true the consortium provided the funds to mine the diamonds—without Britt?' Jazz shrugged.

'Britt Skavanga has always been a brilliant business-woman,' another woman confirmed, smiling at Jazz.

'And now the brand Skavanga Diamonds is an inter-national household name,' the first woman supplied with admiration in her voice.

'How can you all bear to talk business when Tyr Ska-vanga's home?'

Jazz stared at the pretty young woman who had just spoken up, and couldn't help noticing that the girl was staring at Tyr.

'You must be as excited as I am,' the girl said as she glanced around their group. 'The marriage market has really opened up again. Don't you agree, Princess Jas-mina? Have you had chance to speak to Tyr Skavanga yet? I know your brother, His Majesty, and Tyr used to be close friends.'

'They're still friends.' Jazz confirmed this pleasantly, knowing that it shouldn't grate to such an extent to hear Tyr discussed so openly when he was such a private man. Why couldn't she accept the interest of these women and agree with them?

'Is that him over by the door?' another younger woman who had just joined the group demanded.

'How can you mistake him?' the first one exclaimed with affront. 'Tyr Skavanga is easily the best-looking man in this room.'

The latecomer frowned. 'But I thought he was work-ing rough in the desert?'

'I think he might have had a shower since then,' the old lady commented to general amusement.

Jazz couldn't blame the women for being bowled over by Tyr's compelling appearance. Dark and tall, he looked untouchable, yet commanding. Who wouldn't want to know the secrets of a man like that?

'He looks good for someone who's been living like a nomad for so long,' one woman commented.

'Tyr has been working in the desert with the nomadic people,' Jazz felt bound to explain. 'The nomads have a very sophisticated society.'

The same woman feigned a swoon. 'How romantic… billowing Bedouin tents, and long desert nights with a Viking warrior.'

By this time Jazz was tied up in a knot inside. 'Tyr was in the desert building schools and looking for clean water sources.'

When everyone went quiet she could have bitten off her tongue. She hadn't meant to sound preachy and spoil the fun, but to hear people talking about Tyr when they didn't even know him, let alone the valuable work he was doing…

Tyr glanced at her and the world fell away. He would hate to think people were gossiping about him. And she had joined in, Jazz accepted as Tyr's dark stare held hers briefly across the blurring faces of the crowd.

Sharif, who was as sharp as the ceremonial *khanjar*, the curved blade he wore suspended from the jewelled scabbard on his belt, missed nothing, and was instantly at her side. 'Don't you feel well, Jasmina?'

Touching her fingertips to her brow, she used Sharif's reading of the situation to her advantage. 'It is quite noisy, don't you think? Perhaps I won't stay long.'

She wanted to go almost as much as she wanted to stay. She didn't know what she wanted to do.

She should do what was best, which meant staying for as long as politeness dictated and then leaving without drawing attention to herself in any way.

'Just let me know when you're ready to leave, Jasmina,' Sharif said, reading her.

'I will. Thank you.' Gazing up, she touched his sleeve. Beneath his steely exterior Sharif was the kindest and most considerate man she knew.

'And if you're uncomfortable meeting Tyr, just let me know that too.'

'I'm not uncomfortable. We were childhood friends.'

She hated deceiving Sharif, even in her thoughts, and had to take a few deep, steadying breaths. Had she really thought she could handle this?

Sharif's hawk-like gaze flashed from Tyr to her. 'Just so long as you're all right with this, Jasmina?'

'I am. Of course I am.' But her lips felt as stiff as a ventriloquist's doll. She had to face the truth. She couldn't trust her feelings where Tyr Skavanga was concerned.

'Tyr's on his way.'

Sharif's terse warning flashed through her, though she could feel Tyr's approach without needing to turn and look. And then he was in front of them, just inches away.

Jazz remained frozen and stiff as the two men exchanged their customary bunched-fist greeting, then her brother stepped back and she was face-to-face with Tyr Skavanga. For a moment all she could do was study his face and log all the terrible changes, and then she remembered to breathe.

CHAPTER THREE

'HOW WONDERFUL TO see you again, Tyr.'

'And you, Jasmina.'

Wonderful? How inadequate words could be. Her world had been empty and now it was full. The strapping Viking was as fatally compelling as she remembered, but the changes in him were painful to see. Tyr had experienced a lot. Too much, Jazz sensed, and his eyes reflected this. He seemed harder and more cynical, though he was staring down at her with something close to humour in his clear, sharp gaze.

'You've changed, Jazz.'

'So have you.' She said this lightly, but Tyr's essence had changed—frighteningly. The days of teasing him were long gone.

'How are you, Jazz?'

Tyr's sharp gaze pierced her and clearly asked her: *How are you really? Tell me the truth.*

'I'm very well, thank you. And you?'

Her stilted tone brought another flash of amusement to Tyr's dark eyes. 'You look well,' he said.

Heat pooled inside her as he continued to stare down, making a nonsense of her decision to remain aloof from men. And how could she have forgotten the effect of his voice? Tyr's deep, husky tone embraced her like a welcome memory from the past, even as it rang warning bells in her head.

'We must find time to catch up, Jazz.'

She actually gasped at this suggestion. Did Tyr have any idea what he was suggesting? 'Catching up' implied an intimate one-to-one conversation, which was absolutely forbidden. Private time with a man apart from her brother, Sharif, could never happen, but as Sharif was called away to greet some of their other guests she found herself alone with Tyr. Jazz's cheeks flamed red with embarrassment. The connection between them hadn't been lost. If anything, the passage of time had only made it stronger.

Britt saved her. Having organised the event, Britt was easily the busiest woman in the room, but still she had spotted Jazz, who was marooned on her own personal desert island with Tyr, and quickly came across to offer a life raft.

'Jazz, there are some people I think you'd like to meet. Excuse us, please, Tyr.' Smiling briefly at her brother, she whisked Jazz away.

Jazz exhaled shakily as they crossed the ballroom. 'Thank you for rescuing me.'

'From those two dinosaurs?' Britt laughed. 'I could see Sharif's tension a mile off, and when Tyr came over to speak to you I knew it was time to launch a rescue mission.'

Jazz glanced round to find Tyr was still watching her.

'Come on.' Britt squeezed her arm. 'There are lots of great people for you to meet.'

Jazz counted herself lucky to have a sister-in-law like Britt on her side. Britt acted as a sounding board, and, with no other female relatives to confide in, it was reassuring to know she could always talk to Britt. Jazz really valued her growing friendship with the three Skavanga sisters, though doubted they understood her point of view where her chosen lifestyle was concerned, as they came from such a different world.

'I'm going to introduce you to a really nice crowd,' Britt promised, linking arms with Jazz. 'We'll leave the men to brood.'

Jazz blushed. She could feel Tyr's stare on her back, halfway across the room.

'Are you all right?' Britt whispered discreetly during a lull in the conversation with the crowd they'd joined. 'I saw the way you looked at Tyr.'

Britt's eyes were full of compassion. Had everyone noticed? 'I'm fine.' She smiled to reassure Britt. 'I can handle Tyr.'

Britt smiled back, but nothing about that smile convinced Jazz that Britt believed her as they both glanced around at Tyr. 'He cares about you, Jazz. We all do.'

Impulsively, Jazz gave Britt a hug. Britt was the closest thing she had to a sister, but, however much she thought of Britt, nothing could derail Jazz's determination to live a life beyond reproach in service to her country.

Jazz Kareshi was all grown up. Tyr's mouth tugged fractionally at the irony of doing everything in his power to avoid finding his best friend's sister attractive and failing miserably. Jazz had grown into a beautiful woman and he could look at nothing else. He should be grateful to Britt for whisking Jazz away before his interest became more obvious. The fact that Sharif had stood between him and Jazz until Sharif was called away had irritated the hell out of him. He'd known Jazz since she wore pigtails and braces; couldn't they even talk to each other now? They were both powerful men, and used to having their own way, but it seemed there were some things Sharif would like to deny Tyr, like catch-up time with Jazz.

'Jazz seems happy tonight,' he commented when Sharif joined him, determined to find out everything there was to know about Jazz.

'My sister is always happy. Why would she not be?'

'No reason, Sharif.' He returned Sharif's suspicious glance with a level stare. 'Are you trying to keep her away from me? Relax,' he said as Sharif stiffened with affront. 'Jazz is your sister and I respect that. I wouldn't do anything to cause either of you embarrassment.'

'Jasmina has chosen to distance herself from the modern world for her own reasons, not because anyone, least of all me, has tried to confine her.'

He stared into the eyes of a man he'd known and trusted most of his life, and knew instantly that Sharif was telling him the truth.

'Jasmina believes that while I implement change for the better, she must reassure the more conservative groups in our country by remaining a very traditional princess. We will both do anything we can to avoid the chaos of our parents' rule.'

'I understand that, and I respect it,' Tyr assured his friend, following Sharif's stare across the room to where Jazz was standing. Both Sharif and Jazz were determined to do everything they could for their people, even if that meant sacrificing their own happiness.

'Jasmina is finding the party a little overwhelming, I think,' Sharif remarked as if reading his mind.

'It must be a conflict for her—coming out into mixed company, I mean.'

They shared a smile as he remembered the tomboy who had been at the forefront of every adventure, while

Sharif had always had to consider his dignity and look forward to what was best for Kareshi.

'And you, Tyr?' Sharif looked at him with concern. 'How are you enjoying the party?'

'Like Jazz. Mixing with so many people at once is something of an ordeal.' His lips pressed down at this rueful admission, but both he and Jazz had chosen the solitary life, if for very different reasons. 'But I'm grateful to Britt for arranging this party. Britt is right—I need to be back amongst people I love.'

This was true, but there were too many people here and far too much noise. Five minutes alone with Jazz, someone he didn't have to explain every little thing to because they had that long history of friendship behind them, would have been more than enough for him, but he couldn't share that opinion with Sharif.

'Tyr—'

'Over here—'

Another friend. Another photograph.

He should be more gracious. He would try, but the flare of candlelight on crystal was like a barrage of spotlights directed on his face. Everyone wanted to know where he'd been, what he'd done, what he'd seen. Only Jazz shone like a beacon in the midst of all the uproar. She was an oasis in the desert of his life, and his gaze sought her out hungrily.

'I'm guessing you'd rather be back in the desert, Tyr?'

Jolted out of his reverie, he turned to lock stares with Sharif. 'You guessed right.'

It was the silence of the desert that had first imprinted itself on his heart, and Sharif and Jazz were an integral part of the land he loved. He loved their harsh country and the hostile terrain. He loved them. The hardship of his work in the desert soothed him. It distracted him from other things, ugly things in his past. Up to tonight he'd had no wish to rekindle gentle feelings that seemed to have died inside him, but now?

'I wish you the very best of evenings, Tyr.'

He refocused on Sharif.

'But stay away from my sister.'

It took him a moment to realise that he'd been staring at Jazz the whole time they'd been talking.

'Don't make Jazz's life even harder than she makes it for herself, Tyr.'

'I wouldn't do anything to hurt either of you,' he assured his friend.

As he spoke, a group of guests chose that moment to draw Sharif away, leaving Tyr free to gaze at Jazz uninterrupted. Strange to think the happy, carefree girl he remembered would never be truly free again and that the best thing he could do for Jazz was to butt out of her life altogether.

He tried to ignore her. He chatted to some guests, but while Jazz was in the same room as him he couldn't concentrate. Were they supposed to ignore each other for the rest of the night? He was so tense that his expression was fierce as he whirled around when someone touched his arm. He was shocked to see an old lady staring up at him. 'I'm so sorry.' His expression softened instantly. 'Please forgive me.'

'There's no need to apologise,' she said with a smile. 'I just wanted to tell you how good it is to see the Ska-vanga family reunited. And I think it's especially significant to see Sheikh Sharif's sister here. I understand why Princess Jasmina has chosen to live her life the way she has. I was talking to her earlier. It must have been a big step for her to take, and an even bigger one for her to be here tonight. She's obviously courageous. And what a beautiful girl she is. She is so lucky to have a brother who clearly adores her.'

Tyr made polite noises as the charming old lady chatted on, but what he really appreciated was the excuse to stare openly at Jazz. He'd been a prisoner of war for a time, and understood that captivity could be as much a condition of the mind as the body, and his heart went out to Jazz. He would not exchange one moment of his life now for Jazz's confined existence, but he couldn't blame her for her choices when Jazz was as much a servant to duty as he.

As if sensing his interest, Jazz turned to look at him, and for the briefest moment her expression held all the warmth and mischief of the past.

'Well, I mustn't take up all your time.'

Realising he'd been ignoring the old lady, he quickly turned to her. 'You must once more forgive me. I was distracted.'

'By Princess Jasmina?' The old lady smiled up at him. 'I'm not surprised.'

He shrugged with amusement at being caught out. These were good people, all keen to welcome him back, and he should show them more respect. He would. Tonight would go smoothly from now on, if he just could stick to one simple rule: Jazz Kareshi was off-limits.

But within moments a group had formed around him and all they wanted to talk about were his exotic friends from Kareshi. One of the women pointed to Sharif, who even Tyr had to admit looked striking in his flowing robes.

'The sheikh is exactly what I think of when I imagine a desert warrior,' she enthused. 'Tell me, Tyr,' she added with a smile, 'did they hand out handsome pills at your school?'

'No. Cold showers and the birch,' he murmured distractedly, wondering what the crowd of young women around Jazz could have said to make her face light up. Leaving the women around him still exclaiming with outrage on his behalf at his comments about his old school, he made his way towards her. There was only one woman in this room who held his attention and only one woman in the world who could provoke any sort of response in him. He'd clamped down on feelings in order to survive, and had thought he'd lost the knack of feeling anything, until tonight.

Britt was in the same group as Jazz, and smiled as he walked up to them. Sharif's hooded stare followed him across the crowded room. He glanced back to reassure his friend, and to tell him at the same time that they might be as close as brothers, but no one told Tyr how to live his life. But could he risk infecting a bright spirit like Jazz with his darkness? Hadn't Jazz heaped enough pain on herself without him interfering? Freedom was a gift he had always taken for granted, but Jazz was a glaring example that life wasn't always so straightforward. Jazz's boundaries hadn't expanded. When she grew up they had shrunk.

There was another quick look from Jazz that took him right back to the tricks they used to play on each other when they were younger: burrs beneath the saddle, itching powder in their riding boots. Innocent times before the shadows crept in. He'd have a short, polite conversation with her and then move on, he decided. What could be more innocent than that? He'd ask her about the riding stables. Britt had told him how much Jazz enjoyed working there. He wouldn't make a single comment about the remote racing stable being yet another way for Jazz to shut herself off from the world. And he certainly wouldn't tell her about the arousal that lanced through him each time their glances met and held. They were good friends. They would remain good friends. They had always been able to ease their way back into an easy friendship, even after months apart.

That was then and this is now, and now everything has changed.

True, the past could not be recaptured, and the future was not his to command, but seizing the moment was his particular skill and this chance to talk to Jazz was up for grabs.

CHAPTER FOUR

JUST AS TYR came within earshot, Britt whisked Jazz away, explaining that she had arranged the place cards on their table so that Jazz wouldn't have to sit anywhere near Tyr, or any other single man. As Britt smiled reassurance into her eyes, Jazz was reminded again how much she valued their friendship.

'I'm so glad you're here to share Tyr's homecoming. It wouldn't have been the same without you, Jazz.'

'I'm sorry if I seem tense to you.'

'You feel awkward around men?' Britt shrugged. 'That's hardly surprising. You should get out of Kareshi more. I'm going to speak to your brother about it.'

'Please don't give Sharif anything more to worry about. I'm happy in Kareshi. You know how much I love my work, and—'

'And how you live under your own self-imposed guard while you're there? Yes. I know all about that, Jazz—only allowing yourself this briefest of trips outside the country?'

'I know you find the way I live hard to understand, but please believe me, Britt. This is the right thing to do for my country.'

Britt shook her head. 'Locking yourself away can

never be the right thing to do. It would benefit your people *and* you if you travelled more.'

'I can never forget that I'm a princess of Kareshi,' Jazz argued, trying her hardest not to glance at Tyr. 'Or that with that title comes duty and responsibility.'

'But not a ball and chain, surely?'

Britt's expression made Jazz laugh. 'Now you're exaggerating. Anyone would think I was my own jailer.'

'But aren't you?' Britt turned serious. 'Beware of squashing your spirit completely, Jazz. Don't turn yourself into something you're not.'

Jazz's eyes sparkled. 'Like an embittered old shrew, do you mean?'

'There's no chance of that.' Britt laughed. 'And now we've got my brother to contend with.' With a sigh she stood aside as the crowds parted to allow the handsome Viking through.

'Don't look so worried. I can handle Tyr.'

Jazz could only hope her heart was listening.

Tyr paused for a moment to check Sharif was still talking to the ambassador and his wife, before approaching the family table for dinner. He didn't want to cause Jazz a moment's discomfort, but, as if sensing his approach, Sharif called his sister over.

Britt walked over. 'You're looking thoughtful, Tyr.'

'I am thoughtful.'

'But you'll stay and see the evening through?'

'Of course I will. I appreciate everything you've done for me.'

'But you would have preferred something a little more low-key.'

'No, in this you're right,' he admitted. 'Better to see everyone at once.'

Britt cocked her head. 'Get it over with?'

He looked at his sister with amusement. 'I couldn't possibly comment.'

And then the ever-changing pattern of friends re-shaped again, leaving Jazz all alone in a halo of light.

Jazz made her way to the family table, only to find Tyr there ahead of her. Relaxing back on one of the gilt chairs, he was surveying the party with his cool dark gaze. She was about to turn around, to go and find Britt, or her brother, but Tyr was already on his feet, holding out a chair. 'Jazz.'

No man should smile at her like that—so openly—so invitingly.

There was a belief in Kareshi that members of the opposite sex could never stare directly into each other's eyes without there being some form of sexual implication.

'Tyr.' Had she always felt so awkward around him?

She knew the answer to that question. They had never been awkward with each other in the past, but a new tension had entered their relationship and that seemed set to stay. Neither of them was the same person they'd been ten years ago. Britt was right in saying a lot of water had passed under the bridge since then.

It was only when she sat down that Jazz realised Tyr had ignored Britt's carefully arranged place cards completely. Britt had assured her she wasn't going to be sitting anywhere near Tyr, so he must have moved the cards around.

So what was she going to do about it? Make some excuse and move halfway round the table? Wouldn't that seem rude? Wouldn't that be ridiculous, considering they were the only people at the table? Her heart thundered as Tyr's mouth slanted in a smile.

'So, what have you been doing with yourself while I've been away, Jazz?'

She stared into a pair of eyes that had always been able to devastate her nervous system. 'Where to start?' She gave a shaky laugh.

'Jazz?'

Tyr's voice sounded as if it were coming to her from a long way away, down an echoing tunnel. She should not be here. She should not be talking to a man. And this was not just any man, but Tyr Skavanga, a man who demanded every woman's attention, especially Jazz's, and to the point where, having stared into his eyes, she couldn't look away. 'It's been a long time, Tyr.'

Tyr's mouth curved with wry amusement at this comment. And no wonder, when that was probably the lamest thing she could have said. They'd been friends for years and she couldn't think of a single question to ask him? Not even when she was so hungry to know every detail of Tyr's missing life.

Sharing none of her reserve, Tyr continued to study her face as if he would like to record every tiny detail. This made her deeply uncomfortable, though thankfully, Britt was heading towards them at speed. And then out of the blue her courage returned, and, holding Tyr's gaze, she accepted the connection, as she told him with her eyes that things could never be the same between them again, and that he mustn't tease her and flirt with her as if she were still ten years old.

'Tyr?' Britt's voice sounded brittle as she hovered over them. 'Have you changed my place cards around?'

'Would I?' Resting back in his chair, Tyr cast a lazy glance up at his sister, which made Britt huff impatiently, but it was too late for Britt to change them round again as some important guests had arrived and were waiting to be seated.

Neither Sharif nor Tyr could ever be said to have forgotten their manners. They were both round the table in an instant, holding chairs out for their visitors. Sharif even put a restraining hand on Britt's arm when she would have changed places with Jazz. 'The ambassador,' he murmured discreetly.

Damned by etiquette, Jazz thought as Tyr sat down at her side. The ambassador and his wife were Britt's guests of honour tonight, and as Britt and Sharif were hosting the party it was unthinkable that the ambassador would sit next to anyone but Britt.

When everyone was seated and chatting happily, Britt managed a discreet word while Tyr was talking to the ambassador. 'Are you sure you're all right sitting here next to Tyr, Jazz?'

Smiling, Jazz confirmed, 'Of course I am.'

What else could she say?

Was she the only one to feel the tension building around the table? Jazz wondered. She was doing everything she could to ignore Tyr, but he was sitting so close, her whole body was tingling with awareness. How could she remain insensible to his heat, or to the compelling presence of the big Viking at her side? She had forbidden herself every sensual delight reality could offer, and exploring the forbidden in her mind had become a favourite pastime. But not tonight. She must not allow her thoughts to wander tonight. Gathering her robe a little closer, she forced the direction of her thoughts away from the devastating man at her side.

For around five seconds.

'Would you like some water, Jazz?'

Staring into Tyr's eyes made her heart race. 'Yes, please.' She sounded so formal and distant. Which was good, she reminded herself, even if it was directly opposed to what was happening inside her.

'Will you be staying in Skavanga long, Princess Jasmina?'

She turned with relief to the woman sitting on her other side, but even that didn't help, because her mind had taken a photograph of Tyr that meant she could chat intelligently enough, while studying every detail of Tyr in her mind. His hair was thick and tawny, and sun-bleached around his face where it hung in rebel tousles no matter how many times he swept it back. His stubble was sharp and black, and thick, though he must have shaved before he came to the party...and she could smell his cologne. Everything about him spelled danger. Everything about Tyr Skavanga was what she had vowed to avoid. He was wearing black on black tonight, when every other man at the table, apart from Sharif in his ceremonial robes, was dressed in a conventional dinner suit, with a conventional shirt and a conventional tie. Tyr had always bucked the trend, she remembered.

'More water, Princess?' Tyr's gravelly voice shook her round. 'Or something else, perhaps?'

'No, thank you.' How prim she sounded. But those wicked eyes— How dared he look at her like that? Storm-grey and darkening, Tyr's eyes were lit with a disturbing understanding of her inner turmoil. He had always been able to read her mind. It was a skill that had made her mad when she was younger, and which now made her uncomfortably aware. And that firm mouth that she had all too often imagined kissing her.

She must forget that now.

She must!

'Are you sure? No more water?' he prompted.

Her cheeks flamed red. 'Yes, I'm sure.' Frowning, she looked at him with what Jazz realised was the type of black look she would have given him when they were both younger, which was far too intimate a reminder of how close they'd once been.

'Your napkin, Jazz?'

She dragged in a sharp breath as Tyr leaned towards her. Shaking out her napkin, he moved to lay it on her lap. His face was so close to hers, her cheeks were burning. The brush of starched linen against her skin sent shivers of arousal streaking through her. The whisper of its touch against her thigh shocked her to think that she could be so easily seduced. Tyr was a force of nature, Jazz reassured herself. Anyone would feel as she did. She should leave now and have nothing more to do with him.

'You look beautiful tonight, Jazz.'

You can't say that!

But how she wanted to hear it.

Tyr's eyes were warm and amused when she didn't reply. Didn't he know how dangerous this was? Didn't he care?

Eva saved the day, taking control of the conversation around the table. Smiling at her brother proudly, Eva proceeded to tell everyone that Tyr had been born with a map and compass in his hand, and when everyone laughed, Jazz was able to relax as the spotlight swung away from her.

But not for long.

'How do you feel about wanderlust, Jazz?'

Why did Tyr have to ask her that question? Why did he have to speak to her at all? She stared into his eyes. This was her opportunity to make her position clear to him. 'I've always believed there's no place like home, and so far I've had no reason to change my mind.' Unless a marriage organised by Sharif took her to a new country, and a new family, where Jazz had no doubt she would be treasured like one of the hard, blue-white diamonds her brother and Tyr mined. She experienced a chill of apprehension at that thought. And then with everything inside her warning her to leave it, she turned back to Tyr. 'I have never felt your desire to keep moving and searching.'

'Maybe because you've never given yourself that chance,' Tyr cut in, resting his chin on his hand as he stared at her with amusement.

'Tyr's dangerous to know and even more dangerous to love,' Eva confided across the table, laughing as everyone else laughed with her.

Jazz laughed too, thankful to Eva for diluting the tension with a joke. Joining in with the laughter seemed safest, and she thanked her lucky stars she would never be in a position to find out just how dangerous Tyr Skavanga could be.

'We never know when Tyr's going to disappear again,' Eva continued, capturing everyone's attention again. 'He might not be there if I blink.'

More laughter followed this, but Jazz felt a pang of loss as if Tyr had already left them.

'Don't worry. I'm sticking around,' he confided, but why couldn't he say that to the whole table, instead of just to her?

He pretty much kept his promise to leave Jazz alone right up to the moment when Britt mounted the rostrum to deliver her speech of welcome and the lights dimmed. This left Britt alone in the spotlight and the rest of the room in shadow. Sharif had turned his chair around to listen to his wife, encouraging everyone else at the table to do the same.

'What?' Jazz murmured when she felt his interest switch to her. 'Will you please stop staring at me, Tyr?'

'No.'

Jazz's voice was a fierce whisper, his was a lazy drawl, and her little growl of anger could have come straight from the old days, and that made him smile. Then she must have decided that if he was going to provoke her, she was going to lob back some polite and wholly innocuous conversation, and as he continued to study Jazz at his leisure, he was so engrossed he barely heard her question.

When he'd computed it, he frowned. 'Did I manage to bring water to that village?' he repeated. 'Yes, I did. How do you know about that?'

'Don't worry. Sharif didn't betray you. I happened to see the invoice for aqua-cleaning machinery come in, and I knew Sharif didn't have any current projects running, so I put two and two together.'

'And came up with me?'

'I do have some original thoughts that aren't stamped approved by my brother.'

'I'm sure you do. And was that a hint of amusement in your voice I detected, Princess?'

She raised a brow. 'Am I so dull?'

He paused. 'You've changed.'

'Don't mock me, Tyr. I'm not sixteen any longer.'

'This I can see for myself.'

'Then you shouldn't be looking.'

They were silent for some time after that.

The speeches ended and the prizes had all been handed out. The lights went up and Britt returned to their table to be congratulated by Sharif. His friend was a different character when he was with Britt, Tyr noted. Britt was a soothing hand on the warrior brow—something Tyr badly needed.

Anything that could distract him from his feelings for Jazz—feelings that clawed at his senses—would be good.

'You're like a seething volcano of pent-up energy,' Eva commented, picking up on his tension. 'Thor minus the hammer, unless you're keeping that under the table?'

He hummed with amusement as he settled back. Eva knew him too well. She could sense his hunting instinct. He was the wolf. Jazz was the petal in danger of being trampled underfoot. Watching Britt persuade Sharif to dance, he felt his hunting instinct sharpen as one by one the other couples at the table joined them, leaving just one elderly man and woman to chaperone him and Jazz. And as the elderly couple were currently engrossed in their own conversation...

'So, Princess Jasmina.'

Taking a deep breath, Jazz turned to stare at him. 'Can the Sunday title, Tyr. You don't need to pretend with me. You've called me Jazz from the first time we met, and I'm still Jazz to you.'

Mentally, he reeled back with surprise, then rebuked himself for forgetting that Jazz might have changed outwardly, but inwardly she was the same girl. He searched her eyes, but she turned away, then tensed when a group passed by and bowed to her in respect for her rank. 'You can't blame people,' he pointed out as Jazz chewed her lip unhappily. 'You're not the tomboy to them you always were to me. You're a princess.'

'But that's just it, Tyr. I can't buy into the title when I haven't done anything to deserve it.'

'But you will,' he said confidently, relieved that at least they were talking.

'Perhaps you're right,' Jazz admitted with a sigh. 'But I don't feel any different from anyone else. Except...'

'Except?' he prompted, angling his chin to stare into her eyes.

'Except I think you should bow to me.'

She said this with all the old humour and, sitting back, Tyr laughed with relief to think the girl he used to know was still in there somewhere. 'Now, why should I bow to you, Princess?'

'Viking warlords need to be put in their place by a princess of the desert.'

'And what place is that?'

Jazz's cheeks flushed attractively with heat. 'A dungeon, preferably,' she said as if realising that this conversation had already gone too far.

'But I didn't think you were frightened of anything?'

She fixed him with an unwavering gaze. 'You're right. I'm not.'

'So if there's any little service I can offer you, at that time and that time only, I will be sure to bow.'

For once in his life he broke eye contact first. If any other woman had looked at him the way Jazz had so briefly looked at him, he would have anticipated a very different outcome to this evening. High time for a reminder that when it came to the mating game, Jazz was so innocent she didn't know the rules.

But he couldn't ignore her for long. 'You look good, Jazz. Life is obviously treating you well.'

'Very well, thank you,' she said primly. 'You look good too.'

He huffed with amusement. 'There's no need for you to be polite with me.'

As Jazz's eyes clouded with concern, he warned, 'Don't get into it. This is a party, remember?'

'A party in your honour, Tyr, so I'm afraid you have to accept that people care about you. I don't suppose anyone knows how to behave around you when you've been away for so long.'

He sat back. He liked this new Jazz. She was as much of a challenge beneath that prim exterior as she had ever been, but he liked the wild child from the past better. This new version of Jazz was a tightly strung instrument that only played to Jazz's self-imposed restrictive tune.

'It might help if you talked about things that matter to you, Tyr, like the ideals you were fighting for.'

'Like what?' He tensed. She had hit a nerve. It was Jazz that had the problem, not him.

'Like freedom, Tyr,' Jazz said calmly.

'Freedom?' He laughed incredulously as he stared at her. 'And what do you know about that?'

'What do you mean?' she protested. 'I'm free.'

'Are you, Jazz?'

She couldn't meet his eyes, and then she whispered, 'You always represented freedom to me, Tyr.'

'I did?' An invisible hand grabbed his heart. Years of feeling nothing had hit the buffers tonight, he realised, and all thanks to Jazz Kareshi.

'You've always done what you wanted, Tyr,' she explained. 'You could go where you wanted, do what you wanted to do, when you wanted to.'

'You can too,' he insisted, staring hard into Jazz's eyes. 'This is the twenty-first century.'

'Not in Kareshi.' Jazz smiled. 'And we should stop talking like this before someone takes a photograph of us having this conversation.'

'Britt wouldn't allow the paparazzi within a hundred miles of here,' he reassured her as Jazz flashed an anxious gaze around.

'Please don't tease me, Tyr.' There was real concern in her voice. 'You've got no idea what it's like for Sharif in Kareshi. He's doing everything he can to help our people, but a strident minority still continues to rail against progress. I'm doing all I can to reassure that section of our society.'

'Public opinion will do that,' he argued. 'Sacrificing yourself will hardly be noticed in the grand scheme of things, but your life will have been ruined—and all by you.'

'And if I want to do this?'

When he remained silent, Jazz shook her head. 'I should have known you wouldn't understand. You're too like Sharif. He says I'm going too far.'

'Well, aren't you?' he cut in.

'The two of you are as close as brothers,' Jazz said, ignoring his comment. 'You can both do as you like, when you like, and you take that right for granted, but life isn't like that for me, Tyr. I'm a royal princess of Kareshi and I have a duty to uphold certain standards.'

'And what does that entail?' His heart was sinking even as he asked the question, because he knew Jazz's answer would involve more sacrifice, more confinement, more restrictions. Basically a smaller life for Jazz, and, knowing her as he did, that felt like a tragic waste of life to him.

'I'll just have to see what the future holds,' she said. 'Sharif has been approached by the Emir of Qadar.'

He had no idea what that meant, but it didn't sound good.

'It would be a great match for me, Tyr. Our two countries share a boundary.'

'A *match*?' He looked at her disbelievingly. 'As in marriage?'

Jazz blushed. 'This is only the start of negotiations.'

He raised a brow. 'So you're a bargaining counter now?'

'Of course not. Sharif would never marry me off to someone I couldn't get along with.'

'Get along with?' He spat out the words like something nasty in his mouth. 'Aren't you supposed to love the person you marry?'

'Love?' Briefly, Jazz seemed bewildered by the concept. 'I don't even know him.'

'Do you think this is wise?'

'I've *seen* him.'

'You've seen him?' he repeated. 'Oh, well, that's all right, then.'

'Don't mock me, Tyr. This is our way in Kareshi.'

'Freedom to love should be everyone's way in every country of the world.'

'But Sharif has already broken with tradition by allowing me to pursue a career, and sometimes you have to be content. I agree that by staying in Kareshi I could achieve a lot, but if by marrying the emir I can take some of the burden off Sharif's shoulders—'

'Sharif's a grown man,' he cut in, having heard enough. 'Sharif is a proven ruler. What about *your* life, Jazz? What about *you*?'

'Me?'

He didn't know which of them was surprised more by his passionate outburst.

'Kareshi is my life,' Jazz insisted. 'Anything I can do to help my country I'll do gladly.'

'You're repeating yourself, Jazz,' he said. 'And if you really want to help your country, why not stay in Kareshi and work?'

'But the emir... I agreed Sharif could meet with him.'

'And you can stop him doing that in a few words.' He fixed Jazz with a stare, which she avoided.

Heaving a sigh, she glanced around, presumably to see if anyone had noticed this heated discussion. 'I don't want to stop him,' she admitted, leaning close. 'If my marriage to the emir will benefit Kareshi, then that's good enough for me.'

'What you've just suggested is outrageous.' He sat back. Subject closed.

'Fine words, Tyr, but you weren't born into the royal family of Kareshi. You're free to do anything you want and I'm not. It's that simple.'

'Nothing is ever that simple.' As he should know.

Grinding his jaw with frustration, he had to remind himself that this was a party, and that it was better for them both to calm down. At least for now.

CHAPTER FIVE

THERE WAS NO more chance to speak as Britt and Sharif had returned to sit at the table. In spite of his lifelong friendship with Sharif, he couldn't believe his friend was going along with Jazz's crazy idea, or that neither of them could talk Jazz out of the narrow path she had chosen to follow.

'Stop seething, Tyr.'

The sound of Jazz's voice, low and urgent, made him turn to look at her.

'You're making me uncomfortable,' she explained in an undertone, 'and people will notice.'

'You're making me uncomfortable with all this talk of an arranged marriage to a man you don't even know,' he countered. 'What makes you think you've changed that much, Jazz? When you were younger you would have laughed an idea like that out of court.'

'Exactly. We're both older now, and I'm in a position to do something to help my country by making at least one of our borders secure.'

Shaking his head to shut her up, he hit Jazz with a cynical look.

'Allying our two countries will be good for Kareshi,' she insisted.

'But Kareshi is rich, since Sharif took over, and your

brother is a wise ruler. Why the hell would he agree to sacrificing his sister for nothing more than political expediency?'

'If he thinks it makes me happy—'

'Ha! I can't believe Sharif goes along with that.'

'Tyr, please keep your voice down.'

'Whatever you say, Princess, but I don't think you've thought this through.'

'I'm not going to argue with you. I'm saying this is how it's going to be.'

'What happened to the girl I used to know?'

Jazz threw him an accusatory look, but there was something in her eyes that suggested deep down she agreed with him. It was sad to think her stubbornness wouldn't allow Jazz to admit she was wrong so she could put a stop to these crazy marriage plans.

Sensing something was going on between them, Sharif glanced round. Tyr exchanged a brief look with his friend, lips pressed down to express regret at the fact that this was one time when he couldn't help Sharif out. Sharif shrugged. Jazz had always been stubborn. Once she got an idea into her head, they both knew she ran with it until Jazz, or the concept, ran out of steam.

After feeling nothing for so long, Tyr felt this urge to help Jazz overwhelming him. He would like to get very close indeed to Jazz Kareshi.

All the more reason to sit back and ignore her.

This was turning into one hell of an evening.

And it was about to get worse.

As he released a sigh of frustration, Jazz looked at him with something in her eyes that made his senses go into free fall. 'Don't play games with me, Jazz,' he mouthed in an undertone.

'I'm not playing games with you.'

So her eyes were playing games with him—her lips too. And flushed cheeks betrayed her more than any excuses she could give. The laws of attraction took no prisoners. Nor did they show concern for a self-contained warrior who'd had his armour split wide open tonight, or a conservative princess who had just rediscovered her wings.

'Tyr.'

He glanced up with relief to see his sister Britt. Putting one hand on the back of his chair and the other on the back of Jazz's chair, his sister bound them briefly. 'How are you two enjoying the evening so far?'

You two? Should he tell her the truth and ruin Britt's evening after all her hard work on his behalf? He was tense beyond belief, and Jazz was—Jazz. 'I'm having a wonderful time. It's been a great chance to catch up.'

'Do you mean that?' Jazz murmured when his sister had left them to rejoin Sharif.

'I've learned a lot.' Like Jazz's freedom shouldn't depend on some misguided idea of how she could best help her country.

'Why are you staring at me like that, Tyr?'

'Am I staring at you?' He guessed Jazz would have to be contained in a hermetically sealed suit for him not to stare. In a traditional, slim-fitting ankle-length gown in a rich shade of midnight-blue, edged with subtle bronze thread, she was dressed perfectly to suit her character; that was to say, demure with a touch of fire. He'd like to see that spark inside her ignite. What would it take? he wondered. With her waist-length inky-black hair covered with a filmy veil, she looked stunning.

'Tyr,' she warned, staring down at her hands, 'will you please stop staring at me?'

'You can't blame me for looking at the most interesting thing in the room.'

'But I do blame you. I'm not a child, any longer. You can't tease and flirt with me as you used to do.' Jazz shook her head, making her filmy veil shiver. 'Don't you understand anything? Or are you intent on making my life more difficult?'

'That's the last thing I want, Princess, but it is usual to hold a conversation with the person sitting next to you at the dinner table.'

'You're impossible.'

Jazz whipped her head away so fast her veil slipped back. Before she could rearrange it, the soft nape of her neck was revealed as her hair swung to one side. The wave of disappointment that hit him when she quickly pulled the veil forward and that delicate sliver of naked flesh disappeared was a real eye-opener. He really did have it bad. And then Jazz proved his suspicion that the grit was still there when she stood to propose a toast. Raising her glass of juice, she turned to face Britt.

'I would like to propose a toast of thanks to a wonderful woman and a dear friend: my brother's wife, Britt. I want to thank you on behalf of everyone here for the work you've put in to make tonight such a wonderful success. I couldn't love you more if you were my own sister.' Emotion made Jazz pause for a moment as murmurs of approval rose around her. 'The charity we're supporting tonight means a lot to all of us seated round this table, and tonight is also an opportunity for us to welcome Tyr home.'

Tyr tensed as Jazz stared straight at him. This evening would be over soon, but something told him the repercussions from tonight would spread out like ripples on a pond and touch them all.

* * *

Even after a few days, it still felt strange being at home with his sisters after so long away. All four of them together at one time like this was practically unique, but Britt, Eva and Leila had put their husbands out to graze for the day so they could spend time with him—and with Jazz. At least, that was what they'd told him, but for the past half-hour they'd cut him out and talked exclusively to Jazz. And in ever-diminishing whispers that left him super-alert and ultra-suspicious.

'You're not supposed to be listening,' Eva complained when he glanced up. 'Get back to watching sport.'

Yes. He was the token man, allowed to remain in the same room as his sisters and Jazz, providing he took the lid off the nuts and poured the sodas for them. With his feet crossed on the coffee table and a bottle of beer in his hand, he'd been invisible up to this point.

'Could you speak up?' he requested dryly. 'I'm having trouble hearing you.'

'If you must know,' Eva fired at him from her position at the head of the table, 'Jazz is in a fix.'

'A fix? What does that mean?' He swung round to stare at Jazz.

'It's nothing.' Jazz tried to brush this off with an airy sweep of her hand.

'You've started, so you might as well finish,' he observed dryly, noting her cheeks had turned bright red.

'If you must know,' Eva cut in, 'Jazz has today received a formal offer from the Emir of Qadar.'

He groaned inwardly. Time had run out. In the interest of learning more, he acted dumb. 'What kind of offer?'

'Oh, for goodness' sake,' Eva exclaimed, glancing round the table. 'I know you're a man, but you must have some idea?'

He shrugged. 'I'm sure you'll enlighten me.'

Clicking her tongue against the roof of her mouth, Eva—as he had hoped she would—hurried to fill in the details. 'An offer of marriage, dummkopf. And soon.'

Soon? He didn't want to hear another word. He knew his face must be as black as thunder as he appeared to consider this bombshell.

'The Emir of Qadar?' he said at last, lips pressing down as he nodded his head, acting impressed. 'Big country. Important title. That's quite a compliment for Jazz, isn't it?'

Britt put a restraining hand on Eva's arm when she sucked in a breath.

'Well, isn't it?' he said mildly.

Eva scowled, while Leila bit her lip, and Britt looked troubled. Jazz avoided his stare altogether.

'Is anyone going to explain?' he requested mildly, seething inside.

Eva took the bait. 'May I?' she said, looking at Jazz with concern.

Jazz shrugged and appeared resigned. 'Go right ahead. It will soon be public knowledge, so, why not?'

Taking a deep breath, Eva stared into his eyes. She was sending him a strong message of sympathy for Jazz, along with an entreaty for him to do something the heck about it. 'You might not think it such a compliment when I tell you that the emir has insisted on Jazz being a virgin when they marry.'

He exploded out of his seat, then remembered he was supposed to be acting out the concerned friend, rather than overheated would-be lover. Making a calming gesture with his hands, intended for himself as much as anyone, he turned to Jazz. 'Forgive me, Jazz. This is none of my business, but I didn't know men still made that type of demand on a woman. This must be hard for you, impossible to talk about with me around…' He turned for the door, desperate to kick it in, or smash a fist into a block of wood.

'No, stay,' Jazz said quietly. 'You might as well know everything.'

Too right. He leaned back against the door. 'OK.' He remained outwardly calm, while a firestorm of concern for Jazz kicked off inside him. What kind of Neanderthal was she planning to marry? And when had this been settled? Last he'd heard, talks between the emir and Sharif were just getting started.

'Jazz must do what's right for her,' his peacemaking sister Leila insisted. 'None of us has any idea what it takes to be a princess of Kareshi.' Turning to Jazz, she added, 'And we'll support you in whatever you decide to do.'

Jazz stood up too. 'I know you will.' She was clearly moved by their concern. 'Will you all excuse me for a moment?'

'Of course.' The chorus of Skavangas was unanimous.

Tyr stood aside to let Jazz go, but he didn't give his sisters a chance to reinforce the message the three of them were so urgently firing at him. He was going to do something about this, and was on it before Jazz had closed the door.

He closed it for her—with them both on the same side.

'What are you doing?' Jazz gasped, staring up at him in alarm as he shut the door behind them.

He came straight to the point. 'Have you thought this through?'

Jazz stared down at his hands on her arm, and for a very dangerous moment passions ran as high between them as they had way back when. Anything might have happened in those few, potent seconds, but then Jazz drew in a shaky breath and the torment in her eyes made him let her go. As his hands dropped to his side, she whispered, 'Leila's right. I know you don't understand this, but I have to at least consider the emir's offer, because of all the benefits it could bring to Kareshi.'

'Nonsense! I told you before, this isn't right for you, and you know it, Jazz. I can see it on your face.'

'I knew I should have come veiled,' she murmured dryly, the old Jazz peeping through. Somehow that flash of spirit made it all the harder to come to terms with this.

'Don't joke, Jazz. This is your life we're talking about.'

'Exactly, Tyr.' Her chin tipped up. Steel entered her voice. 'This is my life. Now, will you please let me go?'

She stared past him to the bathroom and he stood aside. Grinding his jaw, he watched her go, wondering how he was going to live with himself if he did as Jazz asked—stood back and did nothing.

Jazz left them soon after that, kissing and hugging his sisters goodbye, but barely acknowledging Tyr. She had somewhere to be quite urgently, he gathered. The rest of the afternoon was spent in stormy silence. He turned up the volume on the match, while his sisters talked in undertones at the table. He had no more interest in their conversation. He knew what they were talking about. He knew how he felt about it. And he was damned if was going to share those feelings with anyone.

He didn't move until his mobile phone rang and then he took the call in the other room.

'Sharif? There's nothing wrong, is there?' The line was bad. He was instantly concerned.

'Yes and no. I need you out in Kareshi, Tyr.'

His thought processes raced. Kareshi? Jazz. Yes. *Yes* had to be his answer to Sharif's request.

'Sorry to rush you back there, Tyr—no, there's nothing wrong,' Sharif confirmed to his relief. 'Had to leave unexpectedly. No problem. Just some business to attend to.'

'I understand.' He relaxed. Sharif was obviously travelling where a good line wasn't always a given.

'The Wadi villagers have called for help in getting their Internet connection established, and they need someone to show them how to use it. I wouldn't ask you to go back right away, but I can't send anyone they don't know. They've been so isolated up to now and they trust you.'

He frowned as he remembered his promise to return to Wadi village as soon as he had made his peace with his sisters. 'I won't let them down.'

'Soon?' Sharif asked cryptically.

'Tomorrow soon enough for you?'

'Tomorrow is perfect.'

Britt's face was rigid when he returned to the sitting room. 'Leave it, Tyr.'

'Leave what?' His thoughts were racing with plans for his return to Kareshi, and the chance to see Jazz again, on her home ground, where they could continue this discussion. When Jazz had talked about freedom, she had envisaged the type of freedom everyone in this room took for granted. He couldn't just sit here. He had to do something.

'Leave this business with Jazz alone,' Britt insisted when he stonewalled her with a look. 'And don't tell me you're not thinking about her. I know that look. You seem to think Jazz was forced into making this decision.'

'A decision she hasn't seen through yet,' he pointed

out, 'so there's still time for her to change her mind, and if I see her in Kareshi I will certainly say something.'

'Are you suggesting Sharif would force Jazz into doing something she doesn't want to?' Britt demanded.

As passions between them grew heated, Leila stepped in. 'No, of course Tyr isn't saying that, Britt.' And gradually, like a pan of boiling milk taken off the heat, everyone calmed down again.

Until Eva chipped in with, 'You should tell him, Britt.'

He spun round. 'Tell me what?'

'I know you just spoke to Sharif,' Britt began, haltingly for her, he thought. 'Sharif told me he was going to ring you—'

'And?' he flashed.

'Calm down, Tyr. Give me chance to explain.' Britt's face was white with tension. Nothing about this situation was easy for her. 'Jazz won't be in Kareshi when you get back,' she explained, 'and you'll probably have left the country before she arrives. And, before you ask, she isn't in Skavanga, either.'

'She was here earlier,' he protested.

'And now she's gone,' Britt confirmed.

'Gone? Gone where?'

'Jazz has left Skavanga with Sharif.'

His mind reeled. Just when he thought he might get the chance to talk some sense into Jazz, she had left Skavanga for some destination unknown.

Unless—

'Tell me she hasn't gone to Qadar.' His muscles tensed as he waited for one of his sisters to answer.

'No,' Britt reassured him. 'And before you get angry, I think this might be my fault. Sharif and I talked about getting Jazz out of Kareshi so she can get a fresh perspective on life, so instead of leaving Skavanga for Kareshi as Jazz had planned, Sharif has laid on a treat for her. He's not happy with Jazz falling meekly into line with the traditionalists in Kareshi, either. He doesn't see Jazz as a docile princess. He never has.'

'Jazz—docile?' He grimaced at the thought. 'So where's he taken her?'

'To the fashion shows in Milan.'

'To the fashion shows?' He laughed out loud. No wonder Britt couldn't look at him. 'To the *fashion* shows?' he repeated. 'Does Sharif know anything about his sister?'

Ignoring Britt's protests, he made an angry gesture. 'Since when has Jazz been a front-row fashionista? Jazz is happiest out in the desert, riding free.'

'Tyr.' Leila followed him to the door. 'Don't do anything hasty. It won't help Jazz. Sharif was looking for something to take Jazz's mind off the emir and his proposal. It will at least give her a chance to think things through calmly before she agrees to something she might regret for the rest of her life.'

'But I haven't had a chance to say goodbye to her.'

'You sound so lost,' Leila observed, touching his arm.

And angry, he thought, ashamed he'd sounded off as he stared down at his heavily pregnant sister. 'I'm acting like a bear with a sore head. I just can't get my head around Jazz's crazy life choices. You know I'm never angry with you, Leila.'

'I know that.' Leila smiled in sympathy, then exclaimed, 'Where are you going?' as he moved past her towards the door.

'I'm not sure yet,' he said honestly. 'But I promise to keep in touch this time, okay?'

He had not expected Leila to stand in his way. Drawing her into a reassuring hug, he kissed the top of her head. He hated leaving his sisters like this, but they had husbands to take care of them and Jazz had no one.

No one apart from an army of heavily armed bodyguards sent by Sharif to watch her every move, he guessed. Once again, Jazz would be shielded from reality, and from life itself, so what chance did she stand of making an informed choice about her future?

CHAPTER SIX

SHE'D HAD THIS crazy idea that if she stayed out of the way until the links with Qadar were safely established and the final arrangements for her wedding to the emir were in place, it would be too late for her to do anything about it. The decision would be taken out of her hands. All good for Kareshi. Borders secured for all time through her marriage to the emir.

But when you put three Skavanga sisters into the mix, with Britt's business brain calling foul on the suggested arrangement between a very wealthy Kareshi and a less well-off Qadar, and Eva ranting that no one in their right minds could possibly want to spend the rest of their lives with a man they hadn't even been to bed with, backed up by a chorus of concern from Leila, you were left, not with a melodious chorus of agreement and support for her decision, but with a rowdy chorus of dissent.

And then there was Tyr.

And Sharif.

And the fact that, far from being happy on her tiny gilt chair squashed in between all the heavy hitters and fashion press in the front row of every show in town, Jazz was thoroughly fed up. If she had to watch another unlined, asymmetric rag passing itself off as a work of art, she might have to resort to wearing a hemp sack for her wedding.

Her wedding.

It was definitely time to go back to Kareshi before she lost her nerve to go ahead with what she still stubbornly believed was the best thing she could do for her country. Wedding negotiations between Kareshi and Qadar must be close to complete by now, surely? And even that sounded wrong. How could two countries get married?

She was planning to marry a country?

Heaving a sigh so loud it made Jazz's neighbours on the gilt chairs turn to look at her with surprise, she confronted the marriage plans she'd thought made such sense and realised they were full of holes. How could she help her country if she was stuck away in Qadar? She needed to get away from the flashing lights and loud music to the quiet of the desert, where she could rethink her plans for the future. Bringing out her phone, she was just about to start making travel plans when a message from Eva flashed up.

Tyr is working at Wadi village.

And?

And good morning to you, Princess Prim.

Eva? What do you want me to say???

Is sexual frustration hindering your ability to think straight? If so, please call this helpline now—

EVA!

Just thought you'd like to know. Fashion shows treating you well?

Zzzzzzzzzzz

Why are you still there?

My thoughts exactly.

Jazz paused a moment before asking the question drumming at her mind.

What's Tyr doing in Kareshi?

Not looking for a patsy to perform the dance of the seven veils for him in his harem like the Evil Emu of Qadar, that's for sure.

EVA!!

What good are you to Kareshi if you're trussed up in feather handcuffs?

Not sure the emir would go for that.

Are you prepared to take that chance?

There was a long pause while Jazz digested this and squirmed uncomfortably on her chair.

OK, I give in. *big sigh* Tyr's setting up an Internet connection at Wadi village, so if you hurry…

What's that got to do with me?

He needs fizzers and gum to keep him sane. You can take them with you.

But I'm not going to Wadi village.

Yes, you are.

There was a very long pause and then Jazz tapped in a message.

Miss you, Eva.

Miss you too, brown eyes. See you in Kareshi?

Never say never to a billowing Bedouin tent ☺ xx

She could be part of Eva's world, and part of the new world Sharif was working so hard to build in Kareshi, or she could become Princess Prim—embittered old spinster, twisting around in her own web of gloom, Jazz concluded as she put her phone back in her bag. The alternative was marriage to a man she didn't know. And if the emir did decide to shut her away in his harem, Eva was right: What use would she be to Kareshi then?

The least Eva had done was make her think. Excusing herself politely before the lights went up on the second half of the show, Jazz picked up the hem of her flowing silk robe to brave the hazard of big bags and small feet as she made her escape from fashion fantasy island to the reality she had been avoiding for far too long.

Jazz knew she had made the right decision in coming back to Kareshi the moment the royal helicopter lifted her high above the rolling plain of verdant green immediately surrounding Sharif's principal palace smack bang in the middle of the desert. 'A garden in the desert' was how the world's press described this area, and that was all thanks to her brother's vision.

Sharif was her idol. Her brother was Kareshi's idol, and one day she hoped to equal his achievements.

And she wouldn't do that in Qadar.

But she still had that niggling sense of guilt, because she had always chosen duty over self-indulgence every time, and coming back here to Kareshi seemed like the biggest self-indulgence of all when there was nowhere else on earth she would rather be. But if, by staying in Kareshi as the unmarried sister of the sheikh, she became a burden to Sharif, she would never forgive herself. So, wouldn't it be easier to go along with the emir's plan?

Easy was not an option for Jazz Kareshi, or for her brother, Jazz reminded herself. When Sharif took the throne there had been endless conflict until he proved himself a worthy leader. Their dream was for all the people of Kareshi to live together in harmony, and now Jazz wondered if perhaps she had taken her personal crusade a step too far. Sharif had never asked her to appease the traditionalists by marrying the ultra-conservative Emir of Qadar. When had that idea seemed the only sensible solution? Now she was back in Kareshi, the answer seemed clear. She had to stay here, to work here; this was where she belonged.

As she rested back in her seat to consider this change of plan, the royal helicopter soared high over Wadi village, where Eva had said Tyr was staying.

Tyr.

Tyr had a special affinity with the desert that had brought them together when they were young. Staring down through the always disturbingly see-through Perspex floor beneath her feet, she wondered what he was doing and if he was alone. Tyr shouldn't be alone. The shadows behind his eyes called for friendship and support to remove them. She had to thank Eva for rattling her out of going down the wrong path and bringing her back here. There were people who needed her far more than the Emir of Qadar. People like Tyr, whose soul was wounded, and who had returned to find peace in the vastness of the desert and real purpose in his work. She would like to help him, but would he let her?

Shifting position, Jazz knew she had to stop dreaming about Tyr Skavanga and what he meant to her. They had both moved on, and Tyr had made it clear at the party that he didn't want or need her company. She couldn't save the world—not even her own small part of it, let alone get to the bottom of those shadows behind Tyr's eyes.

But that wouldn't stop her trying, and it wouldn't stop her dreaming, either. And dreams had to be big, or what was the point in having them? If Tyr Skavanga was working at Wadi village, she was bound to see him. She often rode out that way.

As the helicopter came in to land, she accepted that it might be necessary to trim her dreams to fit reality. Even if he were interested, Tyr would want more from a woman than a shrinking virgin, and Jazz dreaded the reality of sex. Somehow marriage to a man she didn't know had held far less fear than any physical association with someone she did know, perhaps because marriage to the emir had always had an air of unreality about it.

While Tyr Skavanga in all his randy, delicious state was all too real.

That evening with Tyr at the party had sent her primal senses rocketing off the scale, because even she could sense that Tyr was a highly sexed hunter in the prime of his life, while she was a virgin who knew nothing about sex, except in theory. And what she'd heard was hardly enticing—except when Eva got started, but then Eva had always liked to shock, so it was never possible to be sure if what Eva said was absolutely true.

'You can take your safety belt off now, Princess Jasmina.'

The pilot's voice sounded shrill and metallic in her headphones as he switched off the engine, and she bit back a smile at the thought of how lucky she was that he couldn't read her thoughts. She'd keep her safety belt well and truly fastened until the day she got married, thank you very much.

Tyr was coated in sand from head to foot after trekking for hours over rugged terrain. There had been a shift in the pattern of the sand dunes since the last storm, meaning the four-wheel drive couldn't take him any closer to the village. He'd radioed to make sure the vehicle could be collected before the next storm closed in, and then he set out on foot. It was a relief to know Jazz was half a world away with this bad storm closing in.

Pausing to shift his backpack into a more comfortable position, he thought back to his schooldays, when Sharif had taken pity on him during the holidays because Tyr had three sisters. But when Tyr had arrived in the desert he had discovered that his troubles had only just begun, because Sharif's one sister had been more aggravation than his three put together. At first he'd thought it would be an easy matter to shake Jazz off when she tagged along, but they hadn't had a horse fast enough to get away from her. They'd devised all sorts of cunning plans, but Jazz had always outrun them. They'd be relaxing beside the oasis while their horses drank their fill when she'd appear round a palm tree to taunt them, until finally they gave in, and their exclusive gang of two became three.

Cresting the dune overlooking Wadi village, he stared down as if he expected to see Jazz waiting for him. Of course she wasn't there. She was in Milan, pretending to be a fashionista. And even if she had been waiting for him, they could never recapture those innocent days. Time had changed them both too much for that. Squinting his eyes against the low-lying rays of a dying sun, he set out on the last leg of his journey.

Had she ever been so happy to tug on riding gear?

Nope, Jazz concluded, not even bothering to check her appearance in the mirror. The sun was up and the grey light of dawn was slowly giving way to a warm buttery glow. It promised to be a fabulous day for riding, if she got out before the sun rose too high, turning everything from comfortably warm into the fiery pit of hell. With her hair tied neatly back, and her close-fitting breeches covered by one of the long, concealing shirts she wore for riding, she only had to pick up her hard hat at the door and she was ready to trial her new stallion. Spear was said to be impossible to ride. She'd see about that. Kindness combined with firmness always won the day with a difficult stallion, and Spear was such a beautiful beast.

Now, why should Tyr Skavanga flash into her mind?

Where beautiful beasts were concerned, Tyr was a prime example, that was why.

Maybe she'd catch sight of Tyr if she rode by Wadi village.

She was a princess with responsibilities—she had to remember that.

Okay, so she wouldn't go that way, not unless the wind blew from the east, in which case she didn't want the sand in her face, and so then she would have no option but to turn in the direction of Wadi village.

Leaving her bedroom, Jazz raced down the stairs and minutes later she was in the stable yard. Crossing to the half-open door, she whispered to Spear and caressed his ears, for which she received a whinnying reply and a good nuzzle as the horse set about searching her pockets for mints. Resting her cheek against his warm, firm muscular neck, she revelled in the stallion's tightly contained strength, and her thoughts flew back to Tyr. What was he doing now? Would he be thinking about her?

Don't be ridiculous!

But there was a chance Tyr might be preparing to ride out. Dawn and dusk had always been his favourite times to ride too, because dawn was so beautifully still and silent, while dusk was cool.

Talking quietly to her horse, Jazz led her magnificent stallion into the yard. 'You are a bad boy,' Jazz breathed as the stallion threw back his head, resisting her attempts to calm him, 'but you're very handsome,' she soothed as she sprang lightly into the saddle. The stallion was impatient for his morning run and skittered sideways until she brought him back under control. Shifting her weight, she coaxed him forward at a controlled canter, rather than the flat-out gallop Spear was aiming for.

Having passed beneath the stone archway that divided the safe, controlled environment of Sharif's racing stables from the desert beyond, they entered the wild, unpredictable frontier, as Jazz always thought of her desert home, and, drawing in a deep breath of joyful anticipation, she lightened her grip and gave Spear his head.

The wind ripped her veil off as she galloped across the dunes. She was at one with the powerful beast as he surged forward, and that was the best sensation in the world. Spear had exceeded all her expectations and anyone who said she couldn't ride him because he was too strong for her was so wrong. She could do anything if she put her mind to it, and Spear was perfection. It was just a pity about the wind. Blowing from the east, it gave her only one option, which was to head in the direction of Wadi village.

She decided to take a short cut. It was a riskier route than going round the dunes, but much quicker. The climb up the final dune was the most testing, but when she reached the top she could see the oasis where she had used to swim with Tyr, and Wadi village, spread out like a twinkling toy city in front of her.

The cold water of the oasis hitting his heated skin was a pleasure Tyr had anticipated since the moment he woke up. There was nowhere else on earth like this; nowhere that assaulted his senses quite so comprehensively with such contrasts of hot and cold, shade and light, and sheer vastness. Everything was extreme in the desert. That was why he liked it. There were no grey areas. There was just constant challenge and danger. Easing his shoulders, he prepared to dive in.

And was stopped by a shriek.

Swinging round, he saw the stallion's legs buckle beneath it as it started the long slide down the dune. It was a relief to see the rider instinctively kick away the stirrups and leap off its back to avoid being crushed beneath half a ton of horse. Recognising the rider, he grabbed a towel and began to run.

'Jazz!'

He powered up the bank of the oasis. The next few seconds passed in a disorientating blur of sand and spinning horse as Jazz and her stallion rocketed down the slope. He jumped clear as the horse skidded past him with its legs pounding uselessly at the air. Jazz took a little longer to arrive, before landing at his feet in an untidy sprawl. Hunkering down, he made a quick assessment. She was winded. She was shocked. She couldn't speak. Apart from that, her colour was good and she was breathing, always a plus.

'Tyr?'

Letting go of her hand, he sat back on his heels.

'My horse?' she gasped out.

'Unharmed.' He glanced at the banks of the oasis, where he could see Jazz's horse sucking in water. 'Are you okay?' He sounded gruff and guessed he was probably more shocked than Jazz. 'Aren't you supposed to be swanning around in Italy, buying next year's thrift-shop donations?'

'Sorry?' She gave him a look that came straight from the old days. 'Did I get off at the wrong stop?'

Hiding a smile, he stared sternly down at her. 'This could have been a really serious accident, and we still don't know if you've been hurt.'

'Only my pride,' she admitted, struggling to get up.

He pressed her down. 'You're not going anywhere until I check you over for injury. And, apologies in advance, but I will have to touch you.'

'No, you won't,' Jazz flashed, doing her best to roll out of reach.

'For purely medical reasons,' he said, patiently bringing her back again. 'Believe me, I have no wish to do this.'

Much. His fingers were on fire at the thought.

CHAPTER SEVEN

JAZZ BRACED HERSELF as she prepared for Tyr to conduct
his examination. Closing her eyes, she turned her head
away, as if to show him that if she must endure this personal invasion, she would do so while distanced from
him in both thought and response. This was something
new for him, and he wasn't sure whether to be offended
or amused by a woman who didn't want him to touch her.
He made the exam swift, gentling his big hands as much
as he could, but Jazz felt so good beneath his touch, he
found it almost impossible to remain clinically objective.

'Is this really necessary?' she demanded at one point
when his fingertips scraped her breast.

'Bruised ribs,' he said tersely, consciously steadying
his breathing. 'I'm checking they're not broken.'

'What about the new medical facility in the village?
Can't I get checked over there?'

The new medical facility he had only recently installed? Now, why hadn't he thought of that? 'I'm just
making sure it's safe to move you first.'

'It's safe.' Jazz's eyes flashed fire. 'And as soon as I've
had chance to catch my breath, I'm standing up.'

'And I'll help you,' he said calmly. Straightening her
shirt, he hunkered back on his heels to wait.

This was not the way she'd planned it. This was supposed to be an innocent morning ride. And, okay, if it had turned into a scouting mission, she hadn't expected such immediate and intimate contact with her target. Having Tyr loom over her while she was lying prone on the ground was having all sorts of odd effects on her body, none of them welcome.

'If that snake hadn't slithered in front of my horse…'

'You'd still be up there, spying on me swimming naked in the oasis?'

'Certainly not!' She tried to get up, but Tyr pushed her down again. 'I didn't even know you were there,' she defended, studiously ignoring his towel-clad frame. She absolutely refused to notice his biceps, or his formidable torso, or any other part of him that was currently brazenly on show. 'I was taking my horse for a drink, and that's all.'

'You certainly picked a safe way down,' Tyr remarked, his voice dripping with irony.

'Past a snake,' she reminded him acidly.

'End result? You're lying in a heap at my feet.'

'A heap? I'll have you know, I'm still in shock.'

'Of course you are.'

'And don't you dare look at me like that.'

'Like what?' Tyr demanded as he unfolded his massive frame.

'As if I'm today's entertainment. And don't stand over me, either.'

'You're right. I'll have to carry you back to the village.'

'What? You can't do that.' Scrambling to her feet, she promptly fell down again.

Luckily, Tyr caught her before she hit the ground. He propped her against the sturdy trunk of a palm and stood back. 'Stay there while I put some clothes on.'

Shivers of awareness raced through her as she closed her eyes.

A pair of snug-fitting jeans, some desert boots and a black top later, Tyr returned. 'Here's what's going to happen, Princess. You may or may not have concussion, so you're not walking back to the village.' He held up his hand when she began to protest. 'You can do what the hell you want once the doctors have checked you over, but until then you're under orders—*my* orders.'

Her jaw dropped with astonishment. Her body might have other ideas, but she wasn't completely mad. 'I forbid you to touch me.'

'You forbid me?' Tyr laughed. Then he swung her into his arms.

At some point she realised that the more she struggled, the more her body approved as it rubbed against Tyr's, so she made herself as stiff as a plank. But this was no longer a game, and the implications of arriving in a conservative village in the arms of a man didn't bear thinking about. 'Tyr. Please. You can't carry me into Wadi village.'

'Watch me.'

'You don't understand. Some of the most conservative people in Kareshi live in Wadi village.'

'I understand everything, Jazz. You forget, I've been working in the village for quite some time.'

'Then please put me down.'

'I won't take that risk with your safety.' Ignoring her increasingly strident protests, Tyr continued on along the bank of the oasis, where he only paused to gather up her horse's reins before turning in the direction of the village.

She made one final attempt to make him change his mind. 'Please, Tyr. Put me down. I can ride back.'

'You're in no fit state to ride back. Look at you. You're shaking.' Halting mid-stride, Tyr blazed a stare into her face, his expression fixed and determined. 'What am I supposed to do? Leave you here to fry?'

'That might be better.' But then she glanced up at the sky, which was rapidly changing from cloudless blue to sun-bleached white. Death was better than disgrace, right? she reasoned frantically—which made her wonder briefly if she did indeed have concussion.

'How would it look to the people of Wadi village if I leave you in the desert to die?' Tyr demanded, distracting her. 'Let me tell you,' he said before she had chance to reply. 'It would look as if the man who has been working with them, the same man the villagers have grown to trust, is nothing but a barbarian who holds life cheap, and who shows total disrespect for their royal family. You've had a fall. We don't know if you're injured yet. At the very least, you've sustained a shock. In the absence of an ambulance rumbling over the dunes, I'm carrying you back to the medical centre, where you can be checked out and treated. Anyone on earth would understand that.'

'My people won't.'

'Your people would rather have you dead?' Tyr shook his head. 'You don't know them, Jazz. They love you. They talk about you and Sharif constantly. Together you've brought stability to Kareshi. You must never take a chance like that again. What if I hadn't planned to swim in the oasis? What if you'd broken your leg and were stranded out here? What if your horse had run away? Are you carrying a satellite phone or a tracking device?'

In her rush to see Tyr, she had remembered none of these things, Jazz realised, but that wasn't something she was about to share with him. 'They must have been lost during the fall.'

'Yeah, right.' He strode on.

Her heart sank. They had almost reached the outskirts of the village, and people were already coming out of their houses to take a look. Smiling grimly as he reassured people in broken Kareshi, Tyr continued on through the crowd. He either didn't know or didn't care that touching her was practically a criminal offence. And she couldn't blame the villagers for their concern. Before Tyr had arrived on the scene, installing the Internet and bringing fresh water to the village, they hadn't met a stranger for goodness knew how long. They led remote, sheltered lives, shielded from the world, with traditions that had remained unchanged for centuries. How long before news of her unconventional arrival flashed around Kareshi? She smiled in an attempt to reassure the veiled women, whose eyes were wide with concern for her, and nodded briefly at the men, who turned away. She was shamed in their eyes, and no excuse could possibly explain her outlandish behaviour.

Pausing only to hand over the reins of her horse to one of the young boys who had been following them, Tyr carried her inside the clinic, where he handed her over to the orderlies like a parcel he was glad to be rid of. There was nothing wrong with his manner towards her. There was nothing but pure concern in his eyes, though Jazz doubted the traditionalists would see it that way.

'I'm going to check on your horse,' he called back as he left the building.

'Thank you.' She was uncomfortably aware of the increasing clamour of the crowd outside the clinic as the people waited for news of their princess.

'I must go to them and explain,' she told the nurse, struggling into a sitting position.

The nurse gently pushed her down again. 'We can do that for you,' she said firmly. 'Forgive me, Princess Jasmina, but you're not going anywhere until the doctor's had chance to take a look at you. You might as well rest back. There's nothing for you to worry about. His Majesty has already been informed.'

Great! Jazz's breath left her body in a shuddering sigh. She could imagine Sharif's reaction. Having had her beg him to arrange a marriage for her, he now discovered she was here with Tyr.

Needless to say, by the time the nurse took her blood pressure, it was sky-high. The nurse peered at her over her spectacles. 'Even if the doctor gives his okay, I'm going to insist that you stay here and rest. This equipment tells me you've been badly shaken up.'

And not just by the fall from her horse, Jazz thought.

Tyr needed space from Jazz and time to think. He still hadn't got over the shock of finding her here in Kareshi, and now there was the sensation he'd caused to deal with on top of that. He wouldn't risk losing the people's trust. Nor did he want to damage his friendship with Sharif. Taking some of the elders aside, he decided to sort it out.

Their reaction threw him.

'No, no, no,' he said, smiling as he shook his head to make his position clear. 'We're not planning to get married.'

'But you must,' the headman said in a tone that brooked no argument.

Tyr was still smiling, still convinced that this couldn't be a serious suggestion on the part of the headman, but his laughing gaze was met by an unwavering stare. 'All right.' Taking it in good part, he clapped the old man on the back. 'We'll sort this out—

'Apparently not,' Tyr murmured as the old man walked away. 'Later,' he called after him.

The headman raised his hand, but only in acknowledgement that he'd heard Tyr, and nothing more.

He got a really bad feeling. That encounter with the headman of the village had suggested that nothing would yield to good humour in this situation. And in truth, fudging an issue wasn't his style. He was straight down the line. So far he'd done nothing to let these people down and he wasn't about to start now.

He placed a call to Sharif, but couldn't get through. Leading his horse out of its stable, he sprang onto its back and headed out of the village. This was a mess that should never have happened. Jazz Kareshi, innocent princess, and the ruthless killing machine? If her people knew his history, would they be so keen to make a match between them? He couldn't do that to Jazz, so the only thing he could do was to leave Kareshi.

And how was he going to do that, when he was tied by his love for the people? His work here wasn't done.

As each insoluble point jabbed at his mind, he spurred his horse on until they were racing at a flat-out gallop. He only reined in when he spotted a Bedouin encampment in the shadow of the dunes. Changing his balance, he slowed the horse. For a while he just let the reins hang loose as he watched the people going about their daily lives. The Bedouin were purposeful and contented. He had always envied the nomadic lifestyle, and it was only recently that he'd lost the urge to move on. He loved the desert, and he wouldn't abandon Jazz, not when he was responsible for the situation she was in. He would stay and see this out, and when everything had settled down again—

He'd turn his back on Jazz and leave?

That was the safest thing to do. Safest for Jazz.

Turning his horse, he headed back to the village. The only thing he could be sure about was that he wasn't going anywhere until this mess was sorted out.

CHAPTER EIGHT

As soon as the doctor said she could go and the nurse released her, Jazz called the palace to arrange for the helicopter to pick her up and for her wilful, snake-shy stallion to be collected. She could have ridden him back if the nurse hadn't mentioned a storm closing in. She wouldn't risk her horse, so it was down to hoping the weather would hold long enough for the helicopter to fly in, and then back again to the palace.

And now she was grateful to the women of the village for being so kind to her. After standing vigil outside the medical facility, they insisted on taking Jazz to the unmarried women's quarters, where they said she'd be safe until the helicopter came to take her home. Having grown up with her brother in the palace, she found it a fascinating experience to be drawn into village life. Everyone was so friendly, and it made her think again how much she had missed female companionship, and how her life could change for the better if she only allowed it to. She'd had the warmth and friendship of the Skavanga sisters since Britt married Sharif, and she could have the friendship of these people too, if she stayed in Kareshi.

Once inside the women's pavilion, it surprised Jazz to see that, along with the more traditional trappings she might have expected, like silken cushions and low brass tables bearing platters of fruit and jugs of freshly squeezed juice, a large space had been allocated to a bank of computer screens faced by no-nonsense office chairs.

'Our benefactor is Tyr Skavanga,' one of the women explained, her sloe eyes warm with admiration behind the traditional veil. 'He bought all the equipment and installed it for us. It's like a miracle. The world comes to us. We can even Internet shop.'

As the women started to laugh, Jazz joined in the fun, but it did make her wonder if she was the only one being left behind where progress was concerned.

'Distance learning,' the same woman explained, jolting Jazz back to the present.

They joined a group of women clustered around a screen. 'We all want to be able to work like you, Princess Jasmina,' a young girl exclaimed, springing up.

'Please, won't you sit down again?' Jazz insisted. 'I'm here to learn all I can from you.'

Reassured, the girl continued, 'Thanks to this link with the outside world, set up by Tyr Skavanga, we can learn to become the teachers of the future.'

Tyr Skavanga...Tyr Skavanga...

And there was so much to do here—so much enthusiasm for progress surrounding her. What was she thinking? Leave Kareshi? Was she mad? What was she so afraid of? Tyr at the party flashed into her head; Tyr rescuing her after the fall from her horse; Tyr—

Just Tyr, Jazz realised, because Tyr represented a time that was lost, and everything she feared about the future. It wasn't Tyr's fault he was so brutally masculine, but, though she was bold in every other area of her life, Jazz had always had a fear of men and sex—Tyr and sex— because all she knew about sex was colourful and sometimes terrifying rumour.

As the women continued to chat easily to her, Jazz knew exactly what she had to do—and it didn't include the Emir of Qadar. Sharif would be mad with her for wasting his time and she couldn't blame him. There would be diplomatic repercussions, but this was where she belonged. She could be of some real help to her brother here.

And then the bombshell dropped.

Another, bolder girl asked Jazz how she had dared to love an outsider.

All the women went quiet as they waited for her answer.

'An outsider?' Jazz queried cautiously.

'Tyr Skavanga,' the women prompted in a laughing chorus, as if this were obvious to everyone except Jazz.

Jazz laughed too. 'I don't love Tyr like that,' she protested, maybe a little too heartily. 'We've been friends since childhood. And, yes, I admire Tyr, but that's as far as it goes.'

The women seemed unconvinced. No wonder, when her cheeks burned red. They were determined to believe she was involved in a runaway romance like the films they'd been able to watch on the Internet, thanks to their benefactor, Tyr Skavanga.

And then one of the older women took her aside. 'Just think of it,' she said. 'You have already proved your worth to your brother, His Majesty, by improving the management of his racing stables. Imagine what you could do for us in Kareshi with Tyr Skavanga organising the various building programmes, while you recruit and manage the staff?'

'What? I—? Oh, no.' But it was a seductive thought, though what Tyr would make of it, she didn't like to think.

* * *

Things couldn't get any worse. Tyr was still miles from the village with a sandstorm coming. All flights were grounded. No one would be flying in or out of Wadi village any time soon to rescue Princess Jasmina. All communication links were down, and no one could predict how long the storm would last. Sensing danger approaching, his horse had started to play up, which was why he was on foot. Having tied his bandana over the animal's eyes, he was coaxing it forward inch by torturous inch, his muscles bulging at the strain of persuading the horse to lift its hooves out of the treacherously shifting sand. He could only hope Jazz was safely housed in the village by now. He was impatient to get back and make sure of it.

The sky was an ominous greenish-yellow by the time he made it back to the village. Having fed and watered his horse, he went to find Jazz. It was his duty to do so, he told himself firmly. He found her in the village hall, where she was taking note of people's concerns. Typical Jazz—no time like the present, even with a sandstorm brewing. She was fully veiled in deference to the traditionalists, but, even with only her expressive eyes on show, he could see enough to want her in a way he was more than certain the elders of the village would not approve of. And then she saw him and her eyes crinkled slightly. The tightening in his groin was immediate, and it was almost a relief when she turned away.

Watching Jazz amongst her people only reinforced his opinion that Jazz was needed right here in Kareshi, not in Qadar. Jazz Kareshi was one of the most valuable resources Kareshi possessed. There wasn't a single doubt in his mind that Jazz belonged with her people.

How much more they could accomplish if they worked together.

Thoughts like that led nowhere. If they saw each other on a regular basis and he infected an innocent young girl like Jazz with his darkness, what then?

As it happened, Jazz took the decision out of his hands by approaching him, and, in spite of all his self-imposed warning, his heart warmed when Jazz stared up at him.

'You're back.'

For a few potent moments she stared into his eyes.

'If you need me, Jazz, you only have to ask.'

'As it happens…'

He followed her gaze to the bank of computers he'd installed, which were currently standing idle.

'While I take a note of everyone's concerns, you could show those who don't know how to use the computers,' she suggested.

'You want me to teach school?'

'Why not?' She gave him a look. 'That's if you're up to it.'

He held her gaze. 'I think I can handle it. Though I'm pretty sure the Internet's down.'

'No excuses, Tyr. You can still show people plenty without it.'

'Whatever you say, Princess.'

Did Tyr have to lower his voice and stare quite so intently into her eyes? Jazz glanced around to make sure no one had noticed.

'There's no point sitting around doing nothing as we wait for the storm to pass,' she pointed out. 'The children are bored, and this is a great opportunity for those who want to benefit from your expertise.'

Her heart raced as Tyr raised a mocking brow. 'Would you like to benefit from my expertise too, Princess? Or are you already a computer expert?'

She let a shaking breath out with relief, and then noticed Tyr's eyes were warm and teasing, as they had used to be when they were kids. 'Just pretend you know what you're doing,' she suggested.

'Oh, I know what I'm doing, Princess.'

There was something in Tyr's tone that made her suck in a fast breath. She pushed it aside by raising her voice so everyone could hear.

'Tyr has offered to help anyone interested in learning more about computers.'

The stampede made him smile. He'd been leaning against the wall with all his attention fixed on Jazz, but she'd stitched him up good and tight. She didn't know how good she was, he reflected as he watched her settling people down in front of the screens. And her spirit had definitely returned in Wadi village. The people loved her, but, more importantly, Jazz was gaining in confidence all the time. The people trusted Jazz, and responded to her. They confided things they would never dream of confiding to a court official, let alone Jazz's brother, Sharif. This was where Jazz belonged, and he could only be thankful that she was beginning to see that for herself.

And how about his pledge to stay away from her?

He glanced outside at the whirling sand. How was he supposed to predict they'd be sharing an enclosed space like this?

'They like you,' Jazz remarked to him when they broke for refreshments.

'Don't sound so surprised. I have been working here in the village for quite some time now.'

'But I am surprised. You're really good at this, Tyr. And here was me, thinking you were a confirmed loner.'

'I am, but we're trapped by the storm,' he pointed out.

Jazz was so enthused, she wasn't even listening. 'What we need is a new school and more teachers. I put that in my last mail to Sharif, so I hope we get an answer from him as soon as this storm eases up a bit. Everyone's so eager to learn.'

He smiled as he listened to Jazz spelling out her plan. His thoughts were somewhat less innocent. There was only one woman in this room he wanted to teach, and those lessons would have nothing to do with computer skills.

He glanced outside at the rapidly darkening sky. 'I'm going to call a halt soon, Jazz,' he said, breaking her off. 'I want everyone safely under cover before this storm gets any worse. It's going to be bad, so I'll see the elderly home, and then come back for you.'

She bridled at that suggestion. 'I'm quite capable of looking after myself, Tyr.'

'Are you? Would that be the same way you looked after yourself when you were out riding?'

Feeling her bristle, he drew the back of his hand down her arm to lighten the atmosphere. He could not have anticipated Jazz's response. To say she recoiled in horror was putting it mildly.

'Haven't you heard a word I've said, Tyr? You *must not* touch me.'

The skin around Jazz's eyes had paled to ivory, but her eyes were almost solid black. He'd seen that same reaction before in a woman, but never in a situation like this. Passions were certainly roused. No one was looking, but anyone would think he had cupped Jazz's breast, or worse. How innocent was she, exactly? Utterly innocent of all things sexual, he concluded as Jazz continued to glare at him.

'I'll see the children home,' she said sharply, and with a swish of her veil she was gone from his side, but before she could round up her flock, the headman called the meeting to order.

Tyr shrugged and threw Jazz a rueful smile when she was forced back into his company.

'No hope of the helicopter arriving to save me from you, I suppose?' she gritted out during a lull in the proceedings.

He held her gaze and saw her eyes grow black. 'Not a chance. The forecast is grim. Nothing's coming in or out of here today.'

Including us, Jazz's worried eyes seemed to say. 'Did you manage to speak to Sharif?' she asked.

'No. Did you get hold of him?'

Jazz shook her head. 'Everything's down. Does anyone know how long this storm will last?'

'If I could get the Internet up, maybe I could tell you. Best guess?' He shrugged. 'It's set in for a while. I shot off an email to Sharif earlier on today to let him know you took a tumble, no harm done. I also reassured him that the women of the village are taking good care of you. I just can't be sure the mail got through before the connection went down.'

'So we're stranded?'

'Looks like it. Nothing's changed for me, Jazz. I work here.'

But everything had changed for Jazz, her eyes behind the veil told him.

Then, remembering who she was and where her duty lay, and that she should not be holding his stare like this, she looked away as the headman began to speak.

'Don't worry, Jazz,' Tyr murmured discreetly. 'I won't let any harm come to you.'

'I can look after myself, Tyr,' she murmured back. 'Storms in the desert are nothing new to me.'

Something told him Jazz wasn't referring to the weather conditions.

By the time things got under way, the searing heat of afternoon had faded to a comfortable warmth, while the sand flurries outside the windows had bathed everything inside the hall in a deceptively muted glow. Tyr gradually edged his way to the back of the crowd, where he could observe without being observed. As expected, there were speeches from several of the village elders, but then a group of old men ushered him forward until he found himself standing next to Jazz at the foot of an improvised stage.

'This won't last long,' Jazz reassured him, knowing his dislike of being in the spotlight. 'Just a formal vote of thanks for helping out, I think, and then you can leave.'

He hummed, wishing he felt as confident as Jazz. There was an air of anticipation surrounding them that he couldn't account for, and when he glanced around, people smiled back at him as if they were sharing a great piece of news. The villagers' initial shock at Jazz's unconventional arrival at the village in his arms must have faded, he guessed, but was that it?

'I told you things would soon return to normal,' Jazz said confidently.

'I hope you're right,' he replied with less enthusiasm, remembering his bizarre conversation with the headman.

'I am right,' Jazz assured him as the speeches continued on.

He was soon distracted by some alluring scent she was wearing and the seductive rustle of her robe. Jazz was certainly playing the traditional card now, and had dressed for this session in the village hall in a plain black robe with only her expressive eyes on show. Eyes and tiny feet, he noted, telling himself not to be so ridiculous as to be affected by the sight of a set of shell-pink toenails.

'Excuse me.'

Careful not to touch him, she moved past him to stand with the elders who had invited Jazz to join them on the stage. Gesturing for quiet, she began to speak. He couldn't understand every word in Kareshi, but he knew enough to raise his hands in a signal that he had done no more than his job when Jazz praised him and everyone turned to face him and applaud. Then the headman beckoned for him to join Jazz on the stage and the smiling crowd parted for him.

'The headman's just explained that we'll be working together as a team,' Jazz translated, leaning forward as the headman took up his position between them.

Blood rushed to his temples as the headman began to speak, but good manners forced him to remain silent until the old man had finished. He didn't need an interpreter to judge the mood of the crowd. They were jubilant. Some of the men started clapping him on the back. He turned to Jazz, who said something in Kareshi, and the cheers grew louder.

'What did you say?' he demanded, but the headman distracted her and she turned away.

'What did you say?' he repeated when Jazz started waving to the crowd.

Jazz was like a fire burning too bright, in danger of consuming everything around her, including him. What was she keeping from him? It wasn't enough for her to smile and nod her head in his direction, when not once had she held his gaze.

And now the headman stepped forward to speak again.

'If there's something I should know, you'd better tell me now, Jazz,' he warned in an urgent undertone.

Putting a finger over her mouth beneath the veil, Jazz shook her head as the headman cleared his throat and began to speak. He was brandishing a sheet of paper, which Tyr guessed must be an email that had arrived when the Internet was still up. Who could possibly evoke this level of response simply by sending an email? Only one name sprang to mind, and that was his friend Sharif. 'What the hell is going on, Jazz?'

'I'm sure there's nothing to worry about. The headman says it's very good news.'

For whom? he wondered.

'I'm hoping it's a reply to the mail I sent to Sharif, requesting more funding for the school,' Jazz explained.

'So what is he saying now?' he demanded as the headman waved his arms and called for silence. A cold blade of dread sliced through him as Jazz paled and swayed. She looked as if she was about to faint. 'What is it, Jazz? What is he saying?'

'We've got the money for the school.'

'Aren't you happy about that?'

'Of course I am. And the headman has just explained that we will both be staying on to supervise the setting up of the school.'

'Both?' He frowned.

'Tyr—I don't know what to say— Everything's out of control— This is all going too fast—'

'What is?' he demanded.

'The headman just confirmed that Sharif has also agreed to his request that when I do get married it will be here in the village.'

A storm of emotion hit him as cheers rose around them. 'Not to the emir, I hope?'

'Not to the emir,' Jazz confirmed to his relief, but the tears in her eyes did nothing to reassure him.

'Then to whom?' he demanded, the punch in his gut delivering the answer before Jazz had chance to speak.

'The headman's somehow got the idea that I'll be marrying you,' Jazz told him faintly above the roar of the crowd.

CHAPTER NINE

'WE NEED TO TALK, Jazz.'

'We certainly do,' she agreed, all business now, 'but not here and not now. These people deserve everything we can do for them, but the one thing they don't need is our problems on their shoulders.'

The meeting was breaking up. 'We've got work to do. You go and round up the children, while I make sure everyone gets home safely.'

'And then we'll talk,' Jazz assured him tensely.

'You bet we will. I'll come and find you.'

'Tell me you're not thinking of coming round to check out my accommodation?'

'The headman's little speech has changed nothing, Jazz. I still owe it to your brother to keep you safe, so, however much of a pain in the backside you are, that's exactly what I'm going to do.'

'I've lived in the desert all my life, Tyr.'

'In a palace, Jazz.'

'Have you forgotten our camp-outs when we were younger?'

How could he ever forget? Worms in his bed? Stones in his boots?

'Back off, Tyr. Just leave me to work this out, will you?'

'I'd love to,' he assured her, 'but something tells me

it's going to take a concerted effort to solve this one. And right now, I have bigger concerns, like making sure you're safe. One thing I do know is that Sharif would never forgive me if any harm came to you. More importantly, I would never forgive myself.'

Straightening up, Jazz pulled the regal card. 'My people will make sure I'm safe. And now, if you will excuse me?'

He almost bowed mockingly, but he was all out of humour and confined himself to watching from the door as Jazz shepherded the children home through swirls of sand until finally she was lost to sight.

By the time he'd delivered the last older person safely home, the storm had the village in its vicious grip. The roar of sand driven at speed by gale-force winds was deafening and his only concern now was for Jazz. Fighting against the power of the wind with one arm over his face and his bandana tied over his nose and mouth, he finally reached the large guest pavilion nestling against the cliff. His feelings lurched from concern to relief when he spotted the hurricane ropes connected to the cliff face, which Jazz had already secured across the entrance.

'Jazz?' Shaking the brass bell, he yelled her name again. He wanted to check the struts holding the pavilion before the wind really got up.

'I'm coming in.'

'Don't let me stop you,' she yelled from somewhere deep inside the tent.

'You should have stayed in the hall until I came back with you to check everything was safe.'

'How many times, Tyr?' Jazz demanded as he closed the roar of the storm out behind him. 'There's no need for you to come and check up on me. Why risk your life for no reason?'

'Maybe I disagree with you about there being no reason for me being here?'

He went about doing the job he'd come for, shaking poles and checking roof beams. 'Move aside, Jazz. I need to make sure this structure's safe.'

She stalked round after him. 'Do you really think the Wadi people don't know how to build a structure that can weather a storm?'

'Like your brother, Jazz, I have only survived this long because I never take anything for granted.'

'Are you satisfied now?' she demanded, when he stood back to take one last long look around.

'Not nearly,' he said. 'How long do you think you might be confined here? Do you have enough water? Enough to eat?'

'Look around, Tyr.'

He dragged his gaze reluctantly from Jazz to take in the platters set out on low brass tables. They were laden with sweetmeats and fruit. 'Jazz.'

'And don't *Jazz* me. I'm not a child,' she snapped. 'Well? Are you satisfied now? Oh, and there's an underground stream running through the back of the tent, should I start to get thirsty.'

He glared back at her.

'So, what are you going to do now, Tyr? Stroll back to your place in the village—get knocked off your feet and killed?'

'Hopefully not.' Jazz sounded belligerent, but her expression was both wounded and touchingly concerned for him. This had to be embarrassing for Jazz. According to the headman, they were destined to be married, though not a word of romance had passed between them.

Jazz didn't know how to handle it, and for once he had no advice to offer her. 'I'm satisfied you're safe in here,' he said to break the tension.

'The pavilion is well insulated, thanks to its outer skin of camel hide,' Jazz confirmed with a dry throat, clearly relieved to seize the distraction lifeline he'd offered her.

'And you're right, saying no one is safe outside in a storm like this,' he agreed for the sake of encouraging Jazz to use her sensible head, rather than the turbulent emotion he could sense bubbling so close to the surface. 'Not even me.'

'Well, that's something, I suppose.' And then she fell silent. 'You should never have come here,' she said at last in a strained voice.

'I'm supposed to pretend nothing happened back there?' He jerked his head in the general direction of the village hall.

'Can't you see how bad you're making things look by coming here, Tyr?'

'Your safety comes first. And considering you weren't supposed to be here when I arrived, that's rich, coming from you. But we are where we are, Jazz, and it's no use looking back.'

'If you'd left me on that dune as I asked you to, this wouldn't have happened.'

'If I'd left you on that dune, you'd be dead. And if one of my sisters was stranded in the middle of a sandstorm when Sharif was close by, I would expect him to do exactly what I'm doing for you.'

'But this is different, Tyr.'

'Why? Because you're a princess of Kareshi? You're also a human being, aren't you?'

'I'm alone with a man.'

'Who is here to make sure you're safe, and for no other reason, Jasmina.'

'You can't even call me Jazz now?'

'You're a princess,' he reminded her coldly.

But there was more to it than that. Jazz was the woman he wanted to take to bed, while Princess Jasmina was the innocent sister of his closest friend, and therefore untouchable. Princess Jasmina had nothing to worry about where Tyr Skavanga was concerned. Another tense silence hung between them. And just like the old days, neither one of them was prepared to back down first.

'Well, I might as well be hung for a sheep as for a lamb,' Jazz said finally. 'You're here, and, as you say, we're in this situation, so I might as well offer you a drink.'

He slanted a wry smile at her. 'Charmed, I'm sure.'

'Juice?'

'Thank you.'

While Jazz was arranging things, he took the chance to stare around at all the rich hangings and the jewel-coloured rugs. The Wadi people had really pushed out the boat to show their love for Jazz by offering her the best of everything they had. The smell of precious incense rose from brass burners, while a honeyed light shone from intricately pierced brass lanterns, which were almost certainly centuries old. And there were enough sumptuous throws and hand-sewn silk cushions to make up ten beds.

'It's beautiful, isn't it?' she commented, seeing his interest and perhaps relieved for another chance to move onto safer ground. 'Though you forgot to secure the storm sheet when you came in.'

Surprised, he glanced around.

'You were too busy lecturing me,' Jazz observed dryly as he corrected his mistake.

As he returned and tugged off his jacket, he noticed Jazz staring at him. It occurred to him that in Jazz's ultra-protected world even the flash of a naked biceps would be disturbing. She was staring now at the tattoo that wound around his arm, which was a brutal reminder of his proud Viking heritage and another warning of the many differences between them.

What on earth had persuaded her to allow Tyr Ska-vanga inside the pavilion? When he'd touched her lightly on the arm with his hand at the meeting, it had felt as if the voltage of the entire national grid had shot through her body. And now she was in lock-down with him? She couldn't allow him to risk his life outside. That was the only reason this was happening, Jazz told herself firmly. But Tyr filled the tent. His aura of power and command surrounded her. He was so brazenly male and so fright-eningly virile.

No one could be this close to Tyr and feel nothing, Jazz reasoned sensibly. The ferocity of the storm had unsettled her, but that wasn't an excuse for her imagination to run riot. They were stuck here. They hadn't chosen to be here.

But to be alone with Tyr, when she was never alone with any man apart from her brother? She didn't know where to look, how to act, where to sit.

Look anywhere except at this man mountain, Jazz con-cluded. *Don't stare at Tyr's hard muscled body covered in scars, and wonder how he came by them. Just accept Tyr for who he is, and what he was when you were both younger and could call him a good friend. Don't stare into Tyr's shadowed eyes and ache to know his past. Don't even begin to think of how it felt when he touched you. Concentrate on practical matters instead, like lock-ing down the pavilion together in preparation for the storm, and everything else will sort itself out.* She hoped.

It was a relief to have something practical to concentrate on, Jazz reflected as she started to move anything breakable out of danger as the wind battered the sides of the pavilion. She was an observer, and a fantasist who had dreamed about Tyr constantly since she was a teen.

But having him here, brutally male and frighteningly close—

'Would you mind if I have a piece of fruit to go with my drink, Jazz?'

Well, that sounded like a threat—not. 'Of course I don't mind. Help yourself.'

Just because Tyr was worldly and she wasn't, it didn't mean he expected anything from her. She'd known him half her life, and Tyr had never done anyone any harm.

Until he became a trained soldier.

Under orders, Jazz reminded herself as she refilled Tyr's goblet and handed it back to him. She blinked when he reached for the dagger at his belt. She remembered exactly when Sharif had given him the dagger. It was the same deadly curving *khanjar* her brother wore hanging from his belt. Sharif had said the gift of a dagger bound Tyr and he as close as brothers, and there was no one in the world he trusted more. As if hypnotised, she watched Tyr slice the fruit into slim pieces with that same lethal blade and put some on a plate to tempt her.

'We could be here for hours, Jazz. You should eat something.'

Hours? One crucial word broke through. How was she going to remain calm and sensible for hours alone with Tyr when her heart was already going crazy?

Jazz accepting the plate of fruit was a turning point. It was a small but significant step towards her relaxing around him. If she couldn't do that, this was going to be a long night for both of them.

'Good?' he prompted as she lifted a sliver of fruit to her lips.

'Thank you.'

She was so prim, so tense, so frightened of him. This was a new Jazz indeed, though her black eyes and perfectly sculpted features had never seemed more beautiful to him.

'Why are you staring at me?' she demanded suspiciously.

'Am I staring?'

'You know you are.'

She blushed and turned away, then moved at the same moment he did for a second piece of fruit. As their arms brushed, she took in a swift gulp of air. The jolt to his own senses stunned him. This was crazy. Sheltering from the storm had become an exercise in restraint he hadn't expected.

Only when Jazz had put half a pavilion's distance between them did she start talking to him again. 'I'm glad you're back, Tyr.'

He stabbed another piece of fruit. 'Glad I'm back from my travels?' he enquired, biting the succulent fruit from the tip of the knife. 'Or glad I'm here?'

'Both,' Jazz admitted frankly, hugging herself tight as the wind threatened to tear the roof off the pavilion.

'So, what do you suggest we do now?'

'What do you mean?' Her eyes widened as she stared at him.

He gave a short laugh, but there was no humour in it. 'Do you tell the emir we spent the night together, or do I?'

'Do you mind if we talk about something else?'

He shrugged as he refilled his goblet with juice. 'Whatever you like.'

He began to pace. Inactivity didn't suit him, but wherever his strides took him in this confined space, it could never be far enough away from Jazz. Wanting her was like a slow burn eating him up inside. 'Why don't we start with your plans for the future?' he suggested.

'My plans?'

He was instantly alert at the touch of steel in Jazz's voice. 'I'm going to continue working at my brother's racing stables, and I'm going to extend my work with our people. My brother has always wanted me to work for Kareshi. Don't look at me like that, Tyr. Sharif has always known where my future lay. It just took me a little longer to see the light.'

'And now you have it all worked out.'

'Men make plans. Women improve them.'

'Was I part of your plan?'

'No,' she exclaimed, sounding genuinely shocked. 'And if you think for one moment that I manufactured this insane wedding idea, you're completely wrong.'

'All right,' he placated her. 'So we know the people of Kareshi love and respect you, and you are right in saying this is where you belong. I'm just not sure that I do long-term, Jazz.'

She was silent for a moment. 'Do you believe in fate, Tyr?'

He shrugged. 'Where the hell is this leading us, Jazz?'

'Bear with me for a moment, Tyr. It's quite simple. Do you think things happen for a reason? You must do,' Jazz argued before he could say a word. 'Look at the evidence. The fall brought me to Wadi village. The storm kept me here. And now—'

'And now?' he prompted.

'And now, apart from the fact that the events of the past couple of days have woken me up so I can see clearly where my future lies, it's also given me chance to talk to you.'

'What about?' He was in no mood for an inquisition, and barriers had snapped around him before he had even finished asking Jazz the question.

'We're stuck here, Tyr. You've been away a long time. We have lots to talk about.'

Nothing could ever keep Jazz down for long, he remembered. Jazz Kareshi was as complicated as the politics of her country. She had grown up surrounded by intrigue and danger. Forced to negotiate pitfalls and double-dealing since she'd been a very small child, she knew how to survive pretty much anything; even a surprise wedding announcement, it turned out.

'All right, I'll start,' she said. 'I'm going to live here in Wadi village. At least for the time being.'

'You're going to live here?'

'Why not? I can commute to the stables.'

'What about your home at the palace?'

'What's the point of living in a palace distanced from my people, when I can be here where I can see their problems for myself?'

He couldn't argue with that. 'I don't think Sharif will have any trouble accepting that decision. You know as well as I do that as far as Sharif is concerned, all the pomp and ceremony surrounding his position is just a necessary part of the job. It's the people of Kareshi that matter most to both of you.'

'And I can be quite determined when I put my mind to something.'

'You don't say,' he murmured dryly.

'Where are you going?' Jazz asked as he turned to go.

'Back to my own place. And don't look so worried. I'll make it safely.'

'I'm not worried, but it's your turn now. This is an opportunity for us to catch up, Tyr.'

'I've been here long enough, Jazz. Your reputation is already in tatters.'

'My reputation is shot,' she argued. 'You couldn't have caused more of a sensation if you kissed me in public.'

He paused with his hand on storm cloth over the entrance. 'Now, why didn't I think of that?

'Tyr.'

'Next time I'll leave you where I find you,' he vowed before Jazz could get started.

'No. You'd never do that. You always were the white knight, Tyr.'

Their eyes met and held a dangerous beat too long. 'Not many people would call me that.'

'No,' she agreed, 'they'd call you a hero.'

'Leave it, Jazz—'

'No. I won't leave it.' Her voice was every bit as loud and angry as his. Standing up, all five feet two of her bristling with pent-up frustration, she stood between him and the only way out. 'One day you will tell me why you always avoid talking about the past.'

'My past is none of your business.'

'It is my business,' Jazz said fiercely, 'because, like my brother, I care for you, and I refuse to watch you suffer on your own.'

'Maybe I want to be on my own,' he fired back. 'Believe me, Jazz, you don't want to go where I've been, and you certainly don't want to see what I've seen—not even in your head.'

CHAPTER TEN

IT WAS HIS turn to tense up when Jazz put her hand in his. 'That's where you're wrong,' she said. 'You underestimate me, Tyr. You can tell me anything. *Anything*,' she stressed.

'Some things are best left unsaid, Jazz.'

'I don't agree.' She shook her head and walked away a little distance. 'If you keep all those ugly thoughts inside you they'll just fester until they make you ill. Everything has to be faced at some point, Tyr. Look at me. I've made a mess of things, and now I've got to put them right. I haven't a clue where I'm going to begin with this marriage nonsense, but I'll sort it somehow.' She sighed, but her compassion was all for him. 'I can't pretend to understand the enormity of the memories you're avoiding.'

He said nothing.

'And I can't imagine what you've seen.'

Thank God for that.

Jazz's gaze was unswerving. 'I'm not going to stand by and see a friend in trouble without trying to help.'

'I'm not in trouble.' And he wasn't into spilling the past as Jazz had suggested he should, but as she continued on he had a great sense of the girl he used to know returning, and that was the only news that mattered to him. The strong, practical, sometimes crazy, always feisty, dangerously impulsive girl he used to know was back, while the prim contrivance Jazz had turned herself into in the hope of reassuring one small sector of Kareshi's population that not everything in their country was changing at breakneck speed had been forced to take a back seat. Great.

'And as for that...' She paused and bit her lip.

'Marriage nonsense?' he suggested.

'You might not want to hear this, Tyr, but physical contact between a man and a woman in Kareshi can only mean one thing.'

He refocused on Jazz's concerned face. 'But there's nothing going on between us, so everyone's wrong.'

Jazz shook her head. 'We can't sort this out as easily as that. Whatever we know to be the case, those who would seize on anything in order to destabilise Sharif's peaceful rule will refuse to be convinced. It doesn't suit them. Can't you see that?'

'So, what are you suggesting?'

Taking a deep breath, Jazz braced herself. 'It's too late to save my reputation and I won't risk either of us losing the trust of my people.'

'We know that.'

'So, it's simple,' she said. 'We'll get married, just like the headman said.'

He almost laughed. 'That's insane.'

'No, it isn't,' Jazz argued. 'It's a practical solution. And don't look so horrified. We won't be living as man and wife. There'll be no passion involved. And we can still be friends.'

While he was still absorbing this ill-advised plan, Jazz came up to him and, standing on tiptoe, she brushed her lips against his cheek. 'Friends?' she whispered.

Her touch scorched him. Taking hold of her arms, he moved her back. 'Don't,' he warned.

Needless to say, Jazz refused to be put off. 'I promise I won't tie you down, Tyr. You can leave Kareshi any time you want, and we'll get divorced quietly at some point in the future when all the fuss has died down.'

'Love's young dream?' He shook his head disbelievingly. 'Jazz, you've come up with some madcap plans in the past, but this one is heading for the history books.'

'No, it isn't,' she argued firmly. 'We both trust each other to do what's right, so this is the perfect solution. Don't look at me like that. I have to do something, and this is the best I can come up with. The best for both of us. You don't want to lose the people's trust any more than I do. No one needs to know how we live out our private lives, and this way we can still live in Kareshi and work together.'

Holding up his hands, he stopped her. 'I can't believe you're serious about this.'

'I've never been more serious in my life. Can you think of a better solution?'

'You bet I can. I leave now. And you leave the moment the storm passes over and the helicopter can get here to take you home. You get on with your life, and I get on with mine. Separately.'

'I'm not leaving my people. And as far as we're concerned, in their eyes the damage is already done.'

'All I can see is you panicking, and proposing to go ahead with some mockery of a ceremony that's supposed to convince your brother, my sisters *and* your people into believing you and I are intending to spend the rest of our lives together. I've backed some of your crazy ideas in the past, Jazz, but this is way beyond reasonable.'

'Tyr. Come back here! Please, listen to me.'

He stared down at Jazz's hand on his arm and she quickly removed it.

'What do you suggest?' Her voice was quiet, but her eyes were direct and unflinching.

He pulled away. 'I don't have to suggest anything. Nothing's changed, as far as I'm concerned. The people of Wadi village accept me for who I am. They always have.' Which was one of the reasons he'd stayed so long. No one asked him any questions.

'But that will change now,' Jazz assured him tensely. 'You will never be able to work here again, because if you don't marry me after spending so much time alone with me, the people you care so much about will shun you.'

'Why would they do that, Jazz?'

'Because in their eyes you will have disgraced their princess.'

With a laugh, he shook his head. 'You make a great case, but I'm not going for it.'

She went rigid. 'A great case? I hope you're not sticking with the idea that I'm trying to trick you into marriage, because nothing could be further from the truth.'

'I just know this crazy idea of yours is going no further. *I* will explain to the people of Wadi village that our relationship is nothing more than a friendship of long standing, and Sharif will understand.'

'If we were in Skavanga, I might agree with you, but this is Kareshi and you have no idea how wrong you are.'

Firming his jaw, he turned away from her. 'This conversation is over, Jazz.'

'Don't you dare,' she warned with all the old spirit. 'Don't you dare mistake me for some spineless pawn who accepts whatever scrap you care to throw at me. I'm trying to do the best I can to repair the damage *I've* done. And, yes, I can stand up for myself and I don't need your help, but you're involved in this whether you like it or not and you can't just walk away. These are my people and you're in danger of offending them, and no one loves these people more than I do. Yes, they're flawed, but so am I. We all are. We're human, Tyr, and flaws come with that territory. No one understands the people of Kareshi better than me. All I'm asking is the chance to continue working with them. I can see now that my idea to marry the emir to strengthen our borders and appease the traditionalists was a terrible mistake, but I'm not going to allow a second terrible mistake to ruin my chances of helping my people.'

'Jazz, you need to sit down and think through things calmly,' he advised, but even he knew it was too late for that.

'I shouldn't have been up there on the dune,' she said, shaking her head. 'If only I'd ridden a different way, none of this would have happened.'

'So don't pile another mistake on top of that one.'

'How fortunate you are to be exempt from the shortcomings that afflict the rest of the human race,' she called after him as he started to unbuckle the storm cloth.

The wind howled in and nearly knocked her over. He reached out to save her and Jazz grabbed hold of his arm. She was pulling at him with all her strength to keep him in the tent, and yelling at him above the ear-splitting howl of the storm. 'Are you mad? You'll be killed out there.'

'So, what do you want me to do, Jazz? Spend the night with the forbidden princess? Will that help your cause? Well?' he demanded, shouting in her face.

Jazz's tears shocked him rigid. He'd done so many things that haunted him, and in the process had changed, or so he had believed, into another, callous and more dangerous person. He was a trained killer, a dangerous man, but right now he was only aware of a pressing need to reach out and help Jazz in every way he could.

'Please don't leave me, Tyr.'

Jazz's voice was small and made the impulse to drag her close unendurable. Her quiet strength reached out to touch some hidden part of him. Relaxing his grip so the cover fell back into place, he secured it firmly, then, taking her hand as if Jazz were a child again, and he the youth who had always looked out for her, he led her back into the heart of the pavilion.

'We will find a solution to this marriage problem,' he promised, wondering for the first time in his life if he could keep his promise to Jazz. He had never let her down before, but this time maybe he would. She'd gone without so much in her young life, compared to the camaraderie he'd enjoyed with his sisters, and then, to all intents and purposes, he'd come along and stolen her brother away. 'I owe you,' he murmured, thinking back.

'More juice?' she suggested, her lips slanting in a small smile.

Her hands were shaking, he noticed, but she clasped them tightly round the goblet in the hope he wouldn't see. He watched her gather herself in a way Jazz used to do as a child. She had always had a backbone of steel.

'I owe you an apology, Tyr,' she stated levelly, not disappointing him. Raising her head, she looked straight at him. 'I got us into this mess and I couldn't regret it more. I just get so frustrated sometimes, and I know I come up with some wild ideas—'

'Wild?' He relaxed. 'You can't go round kissing men and proposing to them.'

Jazz's cheeks flamed red. 'Yes, I know. I feel embarrassed about that. If I'd had my choice you'd have been a long way down the queue.'

He laughed, relieved to see her relaxing at least a little. 'You're a beautiful woman, Jazz. You don't need to do any of that. And I'm not just talking about what the world sees. You're beautiful inside, and you deserve better.'

'Than you?'

'Much better than me. And better than some emir you don't even know. You'll fall in love one day, and when that day comes you won't want baggage. Believe me, I know all about that.'

'You're not married, are you?' Her smile vanished.

'Me? No. The women I meet have got more sense.'

'I think you'd be a good catch,' Jazz argued.

'Do you?' Once again they were staring at each other and all sorts of wicked thoughts were flying through his head, but best of all was the fact that maybe their friendship could move on now.

'Why don't you tell me about the baggage, Tyr?'

It had always been a mistake to relax around Jazz.

She stared at him in silence for a moment. 'It's another of those things you don't want to talk about, isn't it, Tyr?'

He shrugged. 'You've known me most of your life, Jazz, but people change over time.'

'So I'll get to know you all over again.' She met his stare steadily. 'I don't see anything different, Tyr. I just see you. And I'm not afraid of anything you have to tell me, but I think you are.'

'Where are we going with this?'

'If you point-blank refuse to tell me about your past, then all that's left to talk about is you agreeing to marry me.'

She said this lightly as he raked his hair with frustration. 'I thought you'd agreed we would forget that.'

'You're not making this easy for me, Tyr.'

'Easy?' He laughed. 'Nothing about this situation is easy, Jazz.'

She huffed a smile. 'Bet marriage was the last thing on your mind when you heaved me out of that sand drift.'

He slanted her an amused glance. 'You could say.'

'And now if you don't marry me, I will be known to one and all as the disgraced princess of Kareshi. My people will never forgive you for that,' she said, growing serious, 'and neither will Sharif. He might be a forward-thinking leader, but he would never do anything to risk losing the hard-won trust of our people. I'm sorry, Tyr, but there really is no alternative—for either of us.'

'Do you know how mad that sounds?'

'Not mad,' Jazz said sadly, 'realistic. The emir won't have me now, and neither would any other man in our world. I could run away and live somewhere else, I suppose, but I wouldn't be much use to my people.'

For once he was lost for words. Finally, he said tensely, 'Can you hear that?'

Jazz frowned. 'Hear what, Tyr?'

'Exactly.' The wind had dropped. 'The storm has passed over. People will be on their way round to check up on you very soon and you don't want me here when that happens.'

'It's too late to worry about that, Tyr,' Jazz assured him with a rueful smile.

Freeing the storm sheet, he stepped outside. Unfortunately, Jazz was right. He stopped short on the threshold of the pavilion as a group of villagers came up to him, wanting to know their princess was safe. He saw the exchange of glances when he tried to reassure them, then realised they assumed Jazz was safe because he had been with her throughout the storm. How could he betray these good people? He couldn't indulge his wanderlust any more than Jazz could run away. He was definitely going to stay and see this out.

As he walked away, he could feel the villagers' stares on his back. They weren't hostile—quite the contrary. They seemed delighted by the developing relationship between him and Jazz. There was just one thing wrong with that. He didn't want a wife, and the last person on earth he'd risk sweeping into his dark world was Jazz, though he could still feel the brush of her lips against his cheek, and the softness of her body beneath his hands. He would never forget how she'd trembled when he'd barely touched her, or her delicious scent that wound round his senses. He wanted Jazz in every way that a man could want a woman, but would he be forced into marrying her? That was too crazy to contemplate, and it wasn't going to happen. There had to be a way out of this for both of them. And whatever that way was, he would find it.

CHAPTER ELEVEN

He spent a restless night and was out before dawn the next day. He had to get out and think. He had to drive himself hard until the right idea came to him. The chill of night was still in the air he rode into the echoing canyon. An underground stream surfaced and ran from here to feed the oasis. It deepened into a small lake or wadi, from which the nearby village took its name. This was where he usually stopped to let his horse drink.

Easing back in the saddle, he allowed his mount to pick out a safe path down the steep embankment to the water, where he dismounted. Stretching, he turned to run up his stirrups and make the horse comfortable. Loosening its girth, he secured the reins and gave it an encouraging slap on the neck, though after their fast gallop here his horse needed no encouragement to drink. Stripping off his shirt and jeans, he dived into the icy water. It cleared his mind and soothed him as he worked out where to go from here.

He needed space from Jazz to figure out how to leave without ruining her. It was too late to regret what had happened. He had to find a solution that would work for both of them. Jazz had led a sheltered life, but that hadn't stopped her dreams being big. He could relate to that. Now she was old enough, she was putting those dreams to good use on behalf of her people. He could relate to that too. The sister of his closest friend, a woman he found dangerously attractive, should have been the perfect match for him—would have been perfect, if he hadn't had so many ghosts dogging his footsteps.

He took out his frustration in a powerful freestyle stroke that took him within sight of the dunes at the far end of the wadi. Swimming back, he waded out and shook the water off himself like a wolf. Reaching for his jeans, he tugged them on and shut his eyes, as if that would close out the image of Jazz.

Then his horse whinnied, and, shading his eyes, he saw her riding flat out. He would have known her anywhere. No other woman rode with Jazz's grace and elegance, or with such confidence. Silhouetted against the pale sapphire sky of dawn, with her hair flying loose like a banner, she was leaning low over her horse's neck. He followed her progress with admiration, and then she spotted him. Goodness knew how she knew exactly where he was standing travelling at that speed, but she reined in and rode directly towards him. Something twisted inside him as she approached. Jazz belonged here, just as he did. She was in her element riding free in the desert, but as a deserted wife she would never be free again in Kareshi, at least not free as he understood the term.

He barely had chance to turn around and act nonchalant as she came clattering towards him across the stony ground. Sitting back in the saddle, she smiled at him as she slapped her stallion's neck. 'So I found you.' Kicking her feet out of the stirrups, she jumped down. Having drawn the reins over her stallion's head, she turned to give him one of her slant-mouthed smiles.

'I'll take him,' he offered as her stallion pranced impatiently on the spot.

'No need,' she insisted.

'There is need,' he argued. 'Sometimes even you have to accept help, Jazz.' He took charge of the horse and led both their mounts down to the shallows to drink.

As she battled to rule her veil and put it back in place after her hectic ride, Jazz realised she had hoped she would find Tyr at the wadi. She'd been thinking about him all night. Thinking about his past, and everything Sharif had told her about Tyr's time in the army, which wasn't nearly enough. Sharif had been discreet in the extreme, she suspected, filling in only a few of the gaps for her. Tyr had stayed behind after the conflict to rebuild where he could, but what had happened to him before that? This was her chance to ask him, but somehow as she stared at Tyr's strong back when he took their horses down to the water, the right words refused to form. Perhaps she was afraid of being stonewalled again, because that would be just one more sign of how far they'd grown apart, but she had to set some things straight.

'You would never leave Kareshi because of what's happened, would you, Tyr? Not when the village needs you.'

'The longer I stay at Wadi village, the more people will talk. If I don't leave, then you should, Jazz.'

'Why should I leave when the damage is already done?'

Catching hold of her arms, Tyr brought her in front of him. 'Will you stop arguing for once?' he demanded, staring fiercely into her eyes.

She was ready for anything, but not that. The touch of Tyr's hands on her body was electrifying. But Tyr felt nothing, Jazz concluded as his stern gaze drilled into hers.

'I'm thinking of you, Jazz. The villagers are getting

used to seeing us together and if we stay on they will get carried away by this idea of a marriage between us. If that happens I will have ruined you. As you say, you'll never be able to marry.'

'Do you seriously think I'd want to after this?' She confronted Tyr's stormy gaze with amusement. 'How do you expect me to feel, Tyr? I don't like this any more than you do.'

So the thought of marrying Tyr has never occurred to you?

'I'm still trying to find you a way out of it, Jazz.'

'There is no way out of this.' She stared out across the water. 'Shall we swim the horses while we're here?'

'If you like.'

She exhaled with relief. They had used to swim the horses in the wadi when they were kids. It was a great way to ease tension, and there had never been a better time to reinstate that tradition.

Their horses plunged forward, heading in the direction of a sandbank where they could find solid ground. Once they were safely out of the water, Jazz turned her face to the brightening sky and smiled as she dragged in a lungful of air. Just this one last time, she wanted to escape reality and feast on the innocent pleasures of Kareshi. 'Can you smell the desert, Tyr?'

'Camel dung and heat?'

'You're such a savage. That's Arabian jasmine and desert lavender. The scent is so intense, because our horses' hooves have crushed the flowers.'

'If you say so.'

Romance was clearly the last thing on Tyr's mind this morning. She could hardly blame him, Jazz thought as he sprang down. Preparing to dismount, she held out her hand so Tyr could steady her on the slippery bank, but he bypassed her hand and gripped her round the waist to lower her gently to the ground. The touch of his hands was everything she had ever dreamed of, but the instant her feet were firmly planted, he stepped away. Shading his eyes, he stared across the tranquil water.

'I should be getting back, Jazz.'

'But this is our chance to talk about you. You got away with it last time, but I won't let you get away with it twice.'

He turned to look at her. 'So what do you want to know about me?'

'Everything,' she said softly.

'A princess of Kareshi might be entitled to many things, but those privileges don't extend to me, Jazz.'

'So I'm not allowed to know anything about the man who used to be my friend. And still is my friend, I hope?'

'I don't know what you want me to say.'

Jazz shrank inside. There was nothing in Tyr's voice for her, nothing at all. She'd tried to reach him and she'd failed. The tiny amount of progress they'd made while they were swimming their horses and relaxing in each other's company had vanished. Closing her eyes, she knew with certainty she didn't want to travel another yard with a man who didn't want her, but she also knew she would never stop trying to reach Tyr, if there was even the smallest chance she could help him.

'Come on, Jazz. Make a decision,' he prompted. 'I've got to get back.'

'I had intended to take a quick look at the caves.'

'Why?'

Because this was her last-ditch attempt to re-establish contact with him. There were prehistoric paintings in the caves, to which, on one memorable occasion, Jazz had added her own childish daub. Sharif had been furious and had ordered her painting removed. Tyr had defended her, insisting Sharif needn't worry as the rainy season would soon see to that. And it had, washing away Jazz's painting, leaving the art of prehistory untouched. They had explored the caves endlessly when they were younger. Maybe revisiting them would light that spark again, she hoped.

'What are you playing at, Jazz?' Tyr called after her as she set off.

'Nothing.' She shrugged as she quickened her stride. 'Just progressing our catch-up plan.'

'*Your* catch-up plan.'

Jazz looked so appealing in pale, figure-hugging riding britches, with the long, concealing shirt she wore over them rippling in the breeze. A flowing dark veil completed the picture, and, whether this was sensible or not, Jazz was the best thing he'd seen since he last saw her the previous night.

'I'm going to ask Sharif if we can open the caves to the public,' she explained, slowing to view the cliff path ahead of them. 'We should share the history of Kareshi. All we'd need to do is to build a proper path with handrails up this cliff and train some guides.'

We, we, we. As Jazz continued to ride her enthusiasm, he wondered if he was guilty of overreacting, or if Jazz still imagined they could live together here? Surely she'd had time to think about it, and had realised what a bad match they were?

It seemed not, and as Jazz started up the cliff, he brushed away a twist of unease and followed her.

'Be careful when you come up here, Tyr. This scree is treacherous.'

'Jazz!'

His heart stopped as she wobbled precariously on the edge of a narrow ledge. Bounding up, he dragged her to safety, and for a few intense moments they just stared at each other, and then, conscious he was still holding on to her, he lifted his hands away.

'Don't make such a fuss, Tyr.' Jazz was straightening her shirt as she spoke. 'I know this terrain like the back of my hand.'

'Terrain changes over time, and just as sand can slip away beneath your horse's hooves, these small loose stones are deadly underfoot. You could have gone over the edge.'

'But I trust you to save me.'

He flinched as she touched his arm. 'Then you're mad.' He turned away before the urge to unloop Jazz's veil and kiss the life out of her overwhelmed him.

And that was all they had time for before Jazz's riding boot hit a patch of loose stones and she started to slide away from him. Yanking her back, he stared into the face of a woman he wanted, a woman who, judging by the look on her face, badly wanted to be kissed. He didn't need any encouragement. Removing her veil, he looped it around her neck and drew her close. Her breathing quickened and her lips parted. 'What are you doing?' she whispered.

His answer was to dip his head and brush his lips against hers. Jazz responded as he'd hoped she would, melting against him as she reached up to link her hands behind his neck. He pulled away, cursing himself for the loss of control when he felt her trembling. 'And now we really should be getting back.'

'You're right,' she agreed, swallowing deep. 'Do you mind if I take hold of your hand for the rest of the way down?'

'Be my guest.'

By the time they reached level ground, reason had

thankfully re-entered his thinking. 'You're going to ride into the village ahead of me.'

A frisson of concern tore through Jazz. The tone of Tyr's voice had changed so completely. He'd kissed her. Tyr had kissed her. But in the short time it had taken them to walk down the cliff path together, he had grown distant again. The fact that Tyr could cut himself off so completely, and in so short a space of time, frightened her. There was so much she didn't know about him, and it distressed her to think things were so messed up between them she was in real danger of losing the friendship of a man she had loved since she was a child.

As they mounted up in silence, Jazz reflected that if the past few weeks had taught her anything, it was that she couldn't write the script for a perfect life, because everyone had different aspirations. Tyr's dream was to rebuild, then move on to the next project, while hers was to stay and develop what she started. His kiss had been a fleeting reminder of what might have been, but Tyr obviously thought the kiss was a mistake. The time she'd spent with him had been an unexpected gift, but it was over now. Urging her mount into a brisk trot, she watched Tyr turn his horse around and head in the opposite direction as he took the long way back to the village.

Disbelief racked Tyr. He'd kissed Jazz? What the hell was he thinking? He'd been back at the village for just under an hour when she came to tell him the news. She found him at the village hall, where he was fine-tuning the Internet connection, which he'd managed to get back up.

'I thought you should know,' she said.

'That's putting it mildly. Why don't you start at the beginning and tell me everything in Sharif's mail.'

'You know what email's like. You write one thing

and the person at the other end reads something else. I mailed Sharif to explain that we can sort this mix-up out between us, but what I didn't know was that the headman had already mailed Sharif to tell him how happy everyone is at the prospect of us staying on here, once we are married. Please don't be angry, Tyr. This is just a terrible misunderstanding.'

'This is like a sandstorm from hell,' he argued.

Closing down the computer, he steered Jazz outside. The time for worrying what people thought when they saw them together was long past, but Jazz was right in saying it was too late for recriminations. 'When is this ridiculous ceremony supposed to take place?'

'Tomorrow.'

'What?'

'I'm sorry, Tyr, but there's no such thing as a long engagement here.'

His face turned thunderous. 'No kidding.'

Tyr had every right to be angry, Jazz conceded as he marched her down the dusty village street towards her pavilion. He left her at the door without a backward glance. He was mad and she didn't blame him. There was no way out of this now, for either of them, unless Tyr was prepared to risk his friendship with Sharif, and she doubted he would ever risk that. She had hoped for enough time to plan a way forward together, but there was no time, and now they were further apart than they had ever been, which meant she was faced by the bitter prospect of a loveless marriage to a friend she'd lost for ever.

No! No! No! His mind was splintering into a thousand pieces, all of them emblazoned with the same word: No. Did he want this sham marriage? Did he want to deceive the people he'd come to care for in Kareshi? Did he want to subject Jazz to a farce on a grand scale? No again.

Jazz was innocent, and the people of Wadi village were only guilty of wanting to share their princess's happiness. Having a princess of Kareshi marry in their village was a dream come true for them. How could he walk away from that? And now he'd spoken to Sharif he had confirmation that if he walked away from this, Jazz would never be able to lift her head in Kareshi again. He had to give Sharif credit for remaining strictly neutral throughout a very difficult conversation: 'You're my friend and Jazz is my sister,' Sharif had said. 'I trust you to work this out between you.'

He didn't sleep that night. How could he sleep with Jazz lying half naked in a bed close by? Jazz with her storm cloud of jet-black hair drifting round her shoulders and that sweet mouth begging to be kissed.

He should never have kissed her. He should have stayed away from her.

It was too late to worry about that now. Staring into the darkness, he thought about the irony of Sharif finishing their conversation by begging him to be kind to Jazz when he didn't know any other way to be with her. But Sharif had only seen him at his most brutal recently, Tyr reflected. They might call him a hero and pin a medal on his chest, but he could never imagine bringing new life into such a violent world, and Jazz deserved children.

Swinging out of bed, he paced the floor. Who was he to ruin Jazz's life? He had asked Sharif this same question, only to have Sharif insist that marriage to Jazz might turn out to be the best thing that had ever happened to him, if Tyr would give it only half a chance. But he couldn't bear to see the hurt in her eyes when Jazz finally understood how easy it was for him to close off from all human emotion. And if he were ever selfish enough to wrap his arms around her, he would never let her go.

Right now he'd settled for the easy friendship they used to share, though it seemed to him that any type of relationship with Jazz beyond a formal contract of marriage had finally slipped out of his grasp.

In spite of all her misgivings, Jazz couldn't help but be touched by the amount of effort the villagers were putting into making her wedding day special. She was hyperventilating most of the time at the thought of becoming Tyr's bride. It was amazing how she could cut out all the bits about this being a forced wedding and just think about being married to Tyr. Not that this fantasy version of events was something she could share with him. Fortunately, she didn't have to, as Tyr was careful to keep his distance. There wasn't much time before Sharif arrived to give his blessing, so everyone was rushing to put everything in place.

There was just one spoiler. As she toyed with a veil of the finest Chantilly lace, Jazz shivered as she thought about her wedding night with Tyr.

And Tyr? How must he be feeling?

Probably repulsed at the thought of sleeping with her?

She would almost prefer that, Jazz realised. It would lift her most pressing concern away: *the wedding night*. Perhaps they could come to some sort of mutual arrangement. Separate beds? Sleeping with a friend was totally weird by any standards. Surely Tyr would agree with that? She had a total blind spot when it came to sex. She didn't have a clue, except for what she'd read or overheard. Vowing to remain chaste until marriage hadn't been too big a sacrifice when she only had hair-raising gossip about *the wedding night* to go on. She'd always been chaste and had had no plans to change the status quo.

Until now.

Putting the veil aside before she ruined it, she took a deep breath. *Calm down!* If she carried on like this she would be a gibbering wreck by the time she stood beside Tyr at the ceremony.

Would he even turn up?

The thought that he might not chilled her. The thought that he would led immediately back to their wedding night. She had to try to concentrate on the fact that Sharif and Tyr's sisters and their husbands would be arriving soon, or she would never be able to go through with this. Sharif had delivered his itinerary in one of his customarily brusque texts:

Prepare for full contingent of family members arriving to celebrate with Wadi villagers tomorrow night.

Sharif hadn't mentioned celebrating with his sister. Jazz gathered that Sharif had nothing to say to her of a celebratory nature. And who could blame him? She'd pressed for marriage negotiations with the Emir of Qadar and then she'd changed her mind, only to hit him with the bombshell that she was going to marry Tyr Skavanga. All in all, Sharif was being quite restrained.

For now.

CHAPTER TWELVE

JAZZ WAS OUT of bed at dawn and pacing restlessly. Her wedding day. Her marriage to Tyr! She couldn't believe it. She wasn't sure she wanted to believe it. Britt had texted to confirm the Skavanga sisters were on their way, so that was a relief at least. Having the Skavanga sisters onside equalled having the best support team ever in her corner. She had nothing to worry about, Jazz told herself firmly.

Except her wedding night tonight with Tyr.

Tonight was a long way off.

And Sharif?

She wasn't going to think about her brother now.

And if Tyr didn't turn up?

What if he left her to stew with all the wedding arrangements made and her family arriving? How many people would she let down then? And her heart would break. She loved Tyr. She had always loved Tyr, and even if this wedding was a sham, she was as excited at the prospect as any bride. She could weave a thousand fantasies about marrying Tyr Skavanga, but nothing could compare with the real thing, just so long as she didn't think too much about the future. But would he turn up? Tyr was an adventurer by nature, always seeking the next horizon. Maybe he'd already left Kareshi. Tyr was loyal to her brother, but he was his own man—and, as Tyr had said, did she really know him now? The days of reading him easily were long gone.

The women of the village distracted her from her mixed-up thoughts. She could hear them gathering outside the pavilion, waiting impatiently for the moment when she invited them in so they could prepare her for her wedding day. It was hard not to be swept away by their enthusiasm as they crowded into the pavilion.

She could do this! So long as she stuck to her original plan to ask nothing of Tyr.

But what would he ask of her?

Apprehension fluttered through Jazz at the thought that whatever Tyr expected on their wedding night, she could only disappoint him. But when she tried to imagine Tyr touching her, Tyr's hands on her body, Tyr, the master of pleasure…

Something of this excitement must have shown on her flushed face. The women had started giggling behind their hands, as if they knew what she was thinking. It was a relief to submit to the beauty treatments they had prepared for her and hope they would soon drop the subject, but it wasn't long before they returned to their favourite topic.

'But it won't be a proper wedding night,' Jazz was horrified to hear herself blurt out.

'Who says it won't be a proper wedding night?'

'Britt!'

Leaping off the cushions, she threw her arms around all three Skavanga sisters as they moved in for a group hug. Now she felt better. And worse. Better because three women she was coming to love had arrived, and worse because she hated deceiving them.

'Why are you crying?' Eva demanded in her no-nonsense way. 'Do you want red, puffy eyes? This is supposed to be a happy time.' This was followed by a big sigh and worried glances Eva exchanged with her sisters.

If her eyes weren't puffy before, they were now. Jazz bit back a laugh as Eva mopped her face vigorously with the sleeve of her rough cambric shirt.

'Enough!' Leila winked at Jazz. 'We're not here to administer exfoliation. We're here to act as cheerleaders for the bride.'

Having nudged Eva out of the way, Leila put her arm around Jazz's shoulders. 'Everyone gets emotional on their wedding day, and we couldn't be happier that you are taking our brother off our hands. So don't worry about it, because we're all here to help.'

But nothing got past Tyr's oldest sister. Britt was staring at Jazz with concern, having sensed in a nanosecond that all was not well with the blushing bride, though to her credit, Britt kept those thoughts to herself.

The sun was already blazing like a merciless brand in a cloudless blue sky as they got down to some serious wedding preparations. Why did time pass so quickly when you wanted it to drag? She wanted this. She didn't want this. She was far too tense to enjoy the moment. She longed to confess everything to Tyr's sisters and seek advice, but she could hardly do that. She couldn't even be certain that she hadn't driven Tyr away again. And how would his sisters feel about that, when they'd only just got him back?

They would never forgive her, and she would never forgive herself.

'So, you're nervous about the wedding night?'

'Eva, do you have to be so blunt?' Leila reprimanded her.

'Yes, I think I do,' Eva insisted, circling Jazz like a mother hen.

Jazz blenched at the thought of revealing her ignorance where matters between a man and a woman were concerned to the three Skavanga sisters, but the women of the village had left the tent to bring Jazz the precious wedding jewels they wanted her to wear, so there was nothing to stop Eva continuing her interrogation.

'It's a simple question.' Eva paused. 'I take it from your public announcement that you're still a virgin, Jazz?'

'And what a question.' Leila showed her outrage on Jazz's behalf. 'Jazz, you don't have to answer that.'

Jazz forced a confident smile. 'Don't worry. I'm not going to.' She added a laugh. But Eva was right. She was scared out of her skin. She didn't have any sexual experience, and, with only old wives' tales to go on, her expectations were hardly encouraging. So here was her dilemma: if Tyr did turn up, she would be afraid of the thought of their wedding night. If he didn't turn up, it would be an unmitigated disaster all round, as well as a tragedy for his sisters, who had only just got used to having him around again. And she would be the cause of that disaster.

'Well, she either is a virgin or she isn't,' Eva insisted stubbornly, without the slightest hint of remorse as she helped herself to a giant-sized lump of honeyed halva. 'There is no in-between. And if the answer's yes, then all I'm saying is that I'm prepared to offer a few useful tips.'

Britt responded calmly. 'Thank you for that insightful comment, Eva, but I really don't think this is the moment for a session of your helpful hints.'

'Eva, can't you remember how you begged us for peace and quiet on your wedding day?' Leila asked. 'Don't you remember how hard it is to remain calm while everyone's adding their own piece of advice? If you must pace up and down the tent munching and scowling, why don't you at least make yourself useful? You could go and find the henna lady to find out how long she's going to be.'

Eva's face fell and she stopped pacing immediately. 'Jazz, I'm sorry. I wasn't thinking.'

Leaping up, Jazz gave Eva a hug. How she longed to ask Eva for some much-needed help so she could get through the ordeal of the marriage night ahead of her, but how could she admit to being a virgin, let alone explain that she was likely to remain a virgin long after tonight?

'I'll go with Eva to help find the henna lady,' Leila offered tactfully, sensing Britt would like some time alone with Jazz.

The moment the cover was over the entrance, Britt asked Jazz the one question she'd been dreading. 'What's wrong, Jazz? Can you tell me?'

Jazz heaved a long sigh. It was so tempting to tell Britt everything. She had often longed for a sister to confide in, but Britt ran a company and had Sharif to consider. Did Britt need anything else to worry about? 'It's nothing. Just pre-wedding nerves.'

'Well, they're understandable,' Britt agreed, and then she smiled. 'I saw the connection between you two at the party, so I'm not really surprised. But I have to admit I didn't see this coming. Not so fast, anyway.'

No wonder! 'Neither did I,' Jazz admitted truthfully, feeling ten times worse at having to hold things back from Britt.

'I hate to think of you having an accident, but if that tumble from your horse got you two together, it certainly saved a lot of time.' Britt laughed, and then grew serious again. 'If anyone can get my brother to stay in one place, it's you, Jazz. So thank you. I really mean that. And, if it helps, I think you two were made for each other.'

'Do you?'

'Yes,' Britt insisted. 'Fate clearly brought you two together.'

How temptingly close that fantasy version of events seemed now.

'Where is Tyr? Have you seen him?' The anxious words spilled out of Jazz's mouth before she could stop them.

Britt reassured her with a smile. 'Don't look so worried. Tyr's riding with Sharif. The way you look, anyone would think you expect him to leave you standing at the altar.'

I couldn't blame him, Jazz thought as she forced a laugh. 'Was he in a good mood?' She asked the question casually.

'What do you think?' Britt arched a brow.

Good question.

If Tyr and Sharif were riding together, they must be concocting some sort of plan to get Tyr out of this, Jazz concluded.

'Jazz?'

Hearing the note of concern in Britt's voice, she refocused. 'Wedding nerves. I must stop fretting.'

'Indeed you must,' Britt agreed, throwing a thoughtful look her way.

Could it possibly have been a more beautiful evening? Jazz wondered as she stood outside the pavilion with Britt, waiting for everyone to return. The great bowl of the sky provided a violet backdrop for the moon, which was hanging like an ivory swing suspended on moonbeams surrounded by stars. Lifting her face, she closed her eyes and told herself she was going to marry Tyr Skavanga. Now, if that wasn't the stuff of dreams—

Except this had the potential to turn into a nightmare.

An hour or so later, and the wedding party with Jazz at the head of it was ready to leave the pavilion. The front entrance had been opened up, and a vast, jostling crowd had gathered outside to throw petals that had been brought all the way from Skavanga in Jazz's path. Nothing about this celebration smacked of a rushed wedding. Quite the contrary. Thanks to the hard work of Britt, Eva and Leila, together with all the women of the village, she was going to have the fairy-tale wedding she'd always dreamed of, and one Jazz guessed would be remembered for generations to come in Wadi village.

Lifting the hem of her floating chiffon skirt, she could hardly believe she was on her way to marry Tyr. Her heart was singing even if her hands were trembling. She led the way out of the pavilion, followed by Britt, Eva and Leila, who were acting as her bridesmaids. She whispered her thanks as Britt pressed a bouquet of Arctic roses into her hands. She wanted to tell all three of Tyr's sisters that she couldn't remember a time when she hadn't loved their brother, but she couldn't say something that would paint a false picture of this wedding. She had never been more grateful for a veil to hide her mixed and tumultuous feelings. Secured with a glittering diamond tiara studded with the now famous blue-white diamonds mined exclusively at the Skavanga diamond mine, her veil was a fall of Chantilly lace, sprinkled with diamonds and seed pearls that flashed in the light of a thousand torches as she walked along the sandy path to the man she had loved all her life.

'I've never seen anything more beautiful,' Leila said as she walked behind Jazz.

'Don't worry. We'll deduct the cost from Tyr's next dividend,' Eva joked. 'Why are you shivering, Jazz?' Eva added, catching up with Jazz. 'You're not sickening for something, are you?'

Lovesick? Heartsick? Any one of those would do. 'I'm just not used to such a fuss,' she fudged.

'Then you should be,' Eva insisted. 'You're a princess, after all.'

'Every bride's a princess on her wedding day,' Leila agreed.

Jazz shivered again as she touched the cold white stones in her tiara with her fingertips. 'But here's one bride who doesn't deserve all this attention.'

'Of course you do,' Eva insisted. 'Every bride deserves a fuss on her wedding day. And you can always give the tiara back when you're finished with it,' Eva joked. 'In fact, you can give it to me.'

'For goodness' sake, Eva, will you stop teasing Jazz?' Leila cautioned as she came up on Jazz's other side. 'Can't you see she's not in the mood?'

The crowd fell back as they sat Jazz on a camel that had been specially shampooed for the occasion. It was caparisoned with handwoven wedding finery, heavily embroidered with silver thread and tinkling bells, and its swaying gait would announce Jazz's arrival long before Tyr could see her. A collective sigh rippled through the waiting crowd as Jazz drew close to the wedding arbour, which had been decorated with colourful desert flowers. Some of the villagers had climbed up the palm trees to catch a better view of her, and she waved and smiled to them, wishing she could live out their fantasies for her with Tyr.

Tyr. Surely he'd turned up, or someone would have stopped the wedding procession, wouldn't they?

Her gaze found him immediately and relief flooded through her, swiftly followed by the most excitement yet. Dressed in a plain white robe that outlined his impressive frame, Tyr was the only person not looking at her when she arrived. He didn't even glance her way when the boy leading her camel gave it the instruction to kneel, and then helped her to dismount. Perhaps Tyr had persuaded himself that if he didn't look at her, he could preserve the illusion that this was just a bad dream.

And then he turned and it was as if the air had been sucked from her lungs. The look he gave her was devastating. She could almost convince herself that Tyr really did want to marry her.

A great roar rose from the crowd as Sharif left Tyr's side to escort Jazz under the wedding arbour.

'Brother.' Dipping into a low curtsy brought on another loud cheer.

'You look very beautiful, Jasmina,' Sharif commented as he brought her to her feet in front of him.

Jazz met her brother's keen stare steadily. Everything was going to be all right. She had to believe that, though she couldn't help wondering what the two men had been discussing during their ride. It was too late to ask Sharif now, and she could only be grateful to Britt for smiling reassurance at her as Sharif gave Jazz's hand into Tyr's keeping.

CHAPTER THIRTEEN

SOMETHING HAPPENED WHILE she was standing beneath the wedding arbour alongside Tyr. The turmoil inside her settled and she was filled with a deep sense of calm. Tyr was so strong and true, it was hard not to react that way to him. And he was as passionate and as committed to Kareshi as she was. And though he hadn't wanted this marriage, she had been a fool to doubt he would turn up. Tyr would never flinch from duty any more than she would.

But forget duty. She loved him. She loved Tyr with all her heart, Jazz thought as she stared up at the magnificent Viking at her side. She had always loved Tyr and she always would.

'Do you take this man...?'

'Yes.' Her answer was unhesitating.

'Do you take this woman...?'

'I do.'

Tyr's voice was firm and low and measured. It was the type of voice that inspired confidence. And it did, inside her. Was she fooling herself? She hoped not, for, against all the odds, she sensed they both knew that what they were doing was right.

Loveless, maybe, but right, Jazz told herself as the formal

part of the ceremony drew to a respectful close, and Tyr, who was now her husband, led her carefully down the steps.

Could anything be more romantic? If the night sky had been magical, surely the setting for their wedding feast could not have been more beautiful!? The temperature was perfect with just the slightest breeze to play with Jazz's veil. She was seated alongside Tyr on a bank of silken cushions arranged on a priceless rug. They were seated well apart in accordance with tradition, and they hadn't spoken a word to each other since exchanging their vows. This was the expected behaviour of a new bride and groom in Kareshi, but Tyr had certainly taken to the detachment with ease. He was unemotional to a fault, his expression composed, but distant. Until he turned to her and her stomach lurched.

'Would you care for some fruit, or some Arabian coffee?'

She tried to detect some warmth in his voice, but it was the same neutral tone Tyr had used throughout the wedding ceremony. Theirs was a marriage of convenience, Jazz reminded herself, every bit as much as any marriage she might have made to a stranger. She accepted fruit and coffee, knowing she'd taste neither. A young boy stood beside her, waiting to peel the fruit for the bride, should she wish him to, but neither he nor Tyr spoke another word to her, not even when she thanked the boy for filling her jewelled goblet with juice.

She was invisible. She should have been used to this public treatment of a royal princess of Kareshi, but her country's traditions had never seemed quite so draconian before. Because she had dreamed of laughter and intimate glances on her wedding day, secret smiles and potent stares connecting. She'd been to weddings where the fingertips of the bride and groom had touched briefly. Accidentally on purpose, Jazz had always thought, and the air around the newly married couple had sizzled with expectation and suppressed passion. That was what she had dreamed of for her wedding day.

Was it a dream too far? she wondered, risking a glance at Tyr. For all the attention this groom was paying his bride, she might as well have married the Emir of Qadar.

No!

This was nothing like marrying the Emir of Qadar. If she'd married the emir, she would only ever have been able to look at Kareshi over her shoulder. This was infinitely preferable to that. And Tyr was a prince in every respect. Tyr inspired people. Tyr got things done. Tyr was the love of her life. If only this could have been the fairy-tale wedding of her dreams, they might have accomplished so much together.

This was not a fairy-tale wedding and she would not deceive herself into believing it was. She hated deceiving everyone else, for as lovely as they'd made this evening for her, she couldn't wait for it to end so she could be alone with Tyr, and they could sort this out.

Alone with Tyr?

Jazz's mouth dried at the prospect as she glanced at the mountain of muscle beside her. Did she really want to be alone with Tyr? *Alone in bed with him?*

Alone in bed with both of them naked?

'Did you say something?'

She looked up as Tyr spoke. Her cheeks flamed with heat when she realised that she must have exclaimed out loud with apprehension.

'No. Nothing.'

She pinned a small smile to her face to reassure him. How could she admit that she was terrified at the thought of being alone with him when they'd known each other all their lives?

Anxiously, she began to twist the simple platinum wedding band Tyr had placed on her finger. How disappointing he would find her. Tyr was so vital and masculine, while she knew nothing about physical love between a man and a woman. She had hoped the first time would be special, and not painful, as she'd been told it could be, but beyond that—

'Do you like it?'

'I'm sorry?'

'The ring?' Tyr prompted. 'Do you like it?'

Her eyes must have been wide with dread, Jazz realised. 'I love it.' This was the truth. She loved the simplicity of the Scandinavian design. If she had chosen it herself she couldn't have picked a ring she liked better. But it was sad to think that the ring wasn't a love token, but only the ink to seal the deal. 'How did you find such a lovely ring at such short notice?'

'Britt bought it for me.'

Of course. Tyr would have contacted Britt, who had chosen something she thought Jazz would like. The thought of Britt doing that for her made Jazz feel emotional. She didn't deserve such good people in her life, and she longed to tell Britt the truth.

Tyr stopped her with his hand on her arm as she started to get up to go and find his sister. 'Where are you going?'

'To speak to Britt. I have to explain that this wedding is a sham.'

'You'll do nothing of the sort.' Tyr's voice was low, but insistent. 'Not unless you want to upset everyone who's come here to wish us well.'

'That's the last thing I want, but—'

'Not now, Jazz,' Tyr murmured as the speeches began.

Tyr didn't ask her to translate for him. He'd heard enough, Jazz guessed. There was no eye contact between them, no contact between them at all. Would things improve when they were alone?

'Are you cold?' he asked as she shivered with apprehension.

Before she could answer, Tyr had draped a cashmere blanket round her shoulders, making her remember times when he would have laughed and dragged her into a wholly innocent bear hug to warm her up.

'Cold and tired?' he diagnosed when she heaved a sigh.

'No.' She would be awake all night, pacing the pavilion.

When they finally got up to leave, Jazz felt like a prisoner walking to her doom, rather than a bride eagerly walking at the side of her husband to her marriage bed. The wedding procession took its time to wind its way with some ceremony around the village before it turned in the direction of the bridal accommodation that had been set aside for them on the banks of the oasis.

The wedding pavilion was very grand and had been erected a tactful distance away from the village. When they walked inside, Jazz gasped to see such luxury. Everything had been provided for the comfort of the bride and groom. There was an abundance of fresh food laid out on platters along with jugs of juice and fresh water. There was also the most enormous bed, which she had to try very hard not to look at.

Next there was a ceremony that allowed Tyr and Jazz to thank everyone for such a wonderful day. She could tell Sharif was slightly embarrassed when it came to his turn, while Britt's hug lasted longest of all. 'You'll be all right,' Britt whispered. 'I know Tyr will take good care of you.'

That was what she was afraid of, Jazz realised as she forced her lips into a smile. 'Of course I'll be all right,' she agreed brightly, with absolutely no evidence to back that up. When everyone had left, the two of them remained standing, staring at each other from opposite sides of the pavilion. There would be entertainment for their guests, Jazz registered numbly as the sound of traditional music floated towards them on the balmy air.

This was no way to get her new life started.

She gathered her courage. 'Would you like to bathe first, or shall I?'

'Why don't you go first?' Tyr suggested. 'Would you like me to help you with your gown?'

'No, thank you.'

They both sounded so stiff. They were as remote as two strangers who had been thrown together for the night.

'No, please—I insist,' she said, putting off the moment when she would emerge from behind the curtain a virgin bride. 'I'm happy to wait while you bathe first.'

All night if necessary.

It was a relief when Tyr disappeared into the curtained section of the tent. This was as far from her fantasy wedding night as it was possible to get, Jazz reflected as she paced nervously up and down, waiting for him to return.

When he did come back, Tyr was covered by only a small towel, which he had secured around his waist. She had to remind herself that where Tyr came from same-sex saunas, followed by rolling naked in the snow, was considered a harmless family activity, rather than some intriguing erotic ritual, so walking about half naked in front of her was nothing new for Tyr Skavanga.

She flashed a smile that didn't quite reach her eyes

as Tyr held the curtain leading into the bathing tent for her. This was going to be the longest bathing session in the history of the mountain stream. And now, because she'd been so stubborn in refusing his help, it was going to take her an age to undress. Finally, after much tugging and pulling, she stood naked in the balmy warmth, and, taking the plunge into the stream, she was glad of the shock of the icy water hitting her overheated skin.

'Are you all right in there?' Tyr called out as she exclaimed with shock.

'I'm fine,' she yelled back, sinking low in the water in case he should decide to come and investigate.

Climbing out only when she was in danger of turning into a prune, she grabbed an all-concealing bath sheet and wrapped herself in it like a mummy.

Viewing the various pots of creams and lotions that the women had left for her, Jazz huffed a humourless laugh. The fabled potions of Wadi village were lost on her. These were said not just to smooth the skin but to heighten sensation everywhere they touched. She'd need an industrial bucketful, and a man who showed some interest in applying it.

She took her time to select a nightgown. This wasn't as easy as it sounded, as all the garments the women had left for her seemed to be composed of gossamer-fine silk, and she could see through them quite easily. How was she supposed to face Tyr dressed like that?

This is your one and only chance at marriage. Just for once, can't you allow yourself to want something for you?

Like what? Jazz argued with her inner critic.

Like Tyr making love to you, before your life becomes one of practical solitude.

Allow Tyr to make love to her? He'd have to teach her about sex first.

Why don't you ask him to do just that?

Ask Tyr to teach her about sex? Her cheeks were on fire with embarrassment at that thought. Reaching for a robe, she wrapped it around the flimsy nightgown she had chosen to wear. If Tyr would settle for friendship, then so would she.

No, she wouldn't.

Yes, she would. She might have to.

There was only one way to find out.

She paused and took a deep breath. Her hand was trembling as she gripped the dividing curtain. She had to do this. *She could do this.* She would find a way to reach Tyr and restore communication between them, to clear the air. And then they could talk into the night until they were both so tired they fell asleep.

Coward.

Tyr had made himself comfortable on a bed of cushions as far away from the main bed as possible, Jazz noticed when she returned to the main part of the pavilion. He was resting back with his eyes closed.

Good. Maybe he was asleep.

He closed his eyes as Jazz walked deeper into the pavilion, but he'd seen enough to know she took his breath away. Standing with her back to him, she had begun to brush her hair. The light was behind her, and even though she had thrown a robe over her diaphanous nightgown, he could see her naked form quite clearly. She was easily the most beautiful woman he'd ever seen. As she continued to brush her long, damp hair in smooth, hypnotic strokes, he realised that Jazz had no idea she possessed a magic strong enough to arouse a man who had believed for years he was dead to all but the most primitive feelings. He was painfully aroused now, and emotionally aroused, and all thanks to Jazz Kareshi.

Jazz Skavanga, Tyr amended, smiling to himself as he considered this most surprising of all the recent developments.

Jazz had applied some attractive scent, and the robe she had donned was of some flimsy material in softest coral that picked out the blush in her cheeks. And she was plaiting her hair—

Don't do that. Don't plait your hair. Don't tie it back.

He smiled as he imagined Jazz's reaction to his new-found feelings, but meanwhile frustration was threatening to throttle him. What he needed was another dousing in the freezing-cold stream.

He turned away, feigning sleep as Jazz stood up and turned around to face him. If she had any sense she would go straight to the big marital bed, and then tuck herself in and go straight to sleep. At the very least, she should stay well away from him. He was curious as to what she would do. He'd hunted her down at the party and had wanted her ever since. When she'd fallen from the horse, his heart had stopped beating, and when he'd checked her over for injury, his life had stopped too. He wanted Jazz more than ever now, but though the world might assume he had carte blanche to seduce the woman who was now his wife, Jazz meant more to him that that, and he would never mislead her by promising more than he could deliver.

He breathed a sigh of relief when she turned for the big bed. But would that help him? Having Jazz a few feet away when he had spent most of the wedding ceremony trying to avoid contact with her because the ache of wanting her was so acute? Did he seriously think he was going to make it through the night?

CHAPTER FOURTEEN

IF ACTIONS SPOKE louder than words, then Jazz had no option but to do this. With the prospect of a loveless wedding night ahead of her, what did she have to lose? She stared at Tyr's big, muscular back clad in a black tee. He was wearing black boxers too. She'd sneaked a look.

What a modest bridegroom. What a shameless bride.

When fantasy clashed with reality, all she could think about was Tyr looming over her, magnificent and immense. But if he moved a muscle, she'd probably run a mile.

So was their friendship dead too? Jazz wondered as Tyr remained motionless with his back turned to her. As he continued to ignore her, she wondered if Tyr ever ached for a touch, or a kind word and a warm look, as she did right now. She understood why he'd become hard and self-reliant, but she wanted him to know that she cared, and that this was their wedding night—which terrified her, and challenged her to be more courageous too. Or else, was she doomed to an empty life with a head full of Tyr Skavanga? She gazed at the big, silent Viking, currently stretched out on his bed of cushions just a few yards away. Maybe she should have married the Emir of Qadar.

How lucky was she to have so many choices?

'Jazz?' Tyr murmured her name without opening his eyes. 'Jazz, what are you doing? What the hell!'

'What does it look as if I'm doing?' Having climbed beneath his covers, she pulled them up to her chin. 'I was cold, so I'm joining my husband for our wedding night. The least we can do is share our body heat.'

'No, we can't,' Tyr assured her, putting space between them.

He had tried not to look at Jazz in her diaphanous robe, with her hair streaming round her shoulders, and had failed miserably. The urge to make love to her was overwhelming him. She was lying in his bed, for goodness' sake!

'You'll be more comfortable in the big bed.' He spoke gruffly, closing his mind to a sight that had cracked his heart wide open *and* left him with the worst case of frustration known to man.

'I might be as comfortable in the big bed, but I wouldn't be as warm,' Jazz argued in a voice he'd never heard her use before.

'Jazz, please be sensible.'

'I don't want to be sensible,' she assured him in the same husky tone. 'What are you worried about, Tyr? Do you think I'm going to make a move on you—take advantage of you?' Angling her chin on the pillow, Jazz slanted him a look. He had never seen that look on Jazz's face before. 'Are you concerned I'm going to wear you down, and make you do something you *want* to do?'

'Now you're being ridiculous.' Closing his eyes, he tried to ignore her.

'Ridiculous?' Jazz hummed. 'What am I supposed to think? Am I repulsive? Can't you stand the sight of me?'

'For God's sake, Jazz!' He sat up in his makeshift bed. 'Just leave it, will you? Isn't this situation bad enough?'

'You tell me,' she said softly, showing no sign of going anywhere.

Touching Jazz, let alone making love to her, could only lead to the bond between them tightening, when it was better for both of them if they kept that bond on a really long leash.

'We're married, Tyr. Have you forgotten that?'

'I haven't forgotten anything. Now, will you please go back to your own bed and go to sleep?'

Once again, she didn't move. 'Maybe I'm so irresistible you can't trust yourself to leave me alone once we get started?'

'For goodness' sake, Jazz.'

Swinging his legs over the side of the bed, he turned his back on her and sank his head into his hands. 'We're not kids any longer. And this isn't a game.'

'You've noticed?' she fired back. 'It certainly isn't a game to me, Tyr. I'm a bride and this is my wedding night, but the groom apparently wants to go to sleep.'

Sleep was the last thing on his mind, but Jazz didn't need to know that. 'What do you want from me, Jazz?'

'What any bride wants from her husband on their wedding night: closeness, loyalty, trust, intimacy.'

Not passion, he noted. Even Jazz the eternal optimist couldn't push the boat out that far.

'And friendship.'

He looked up when he heard the break in her voice, and saw her tears, but Jazz had more grit than to fold because he was being cold towards her.

'I want you to make love to me, Tyr,' she said fiercely. Swiping the back of her hand across her eyes, she lifted her chin. 'I want you to teach me everything you know about sex. I want you to show me what to do and how to please you.'

He was so taken aback, he couldn't speak for a moment.

'Tyr, I—'

'I heard what you said, Jazz.'

'So?'

As Jazz waited for him to reply, he could sense her thinking: *What do I have to do to get through to this man?* She had risked everything, her pride, her self-respect. God, what a monster he'd become.

Why should Tyr respond when he was only here acting out the role of groom to get her out of a hole? She had no idea how to handle a rejection as comprehensive as this. She would never take anyone for granted again, Jazz vowed fervently. She had thought she could handle anything Tyr threw at her, but then she had thought she was strong too. Turned out she was wrong on all counts. When you loved someone as she loved Tyr, this was always going to hurt.

'I'm sorry, Tyr. I should never have put you in this position. Of course we should sleep. Sex has to be by mutual consent and not to order. I know that much.'

Lifting his head out of his hands, Tyr straightened up and turned to face her. 'You don't want this, believe me.'

'I'm not frightened of you, Tyr, if that's what you think. And how can you doubt that I want this?'

'Brave words, Jazz.'

'They're not just words.' She stared into his eyes. 'We can't go on like this. What's wrong with you, Tyr? It's not like you to back away from opportunity.'

'I'm not backing away. And this isn't an opportunity, as you put it, Jazz. I'm trying to protect you. Can't you see that?'

'You're trying to protect me by making me feel like

the most undesirable woman on earth? How does that work, Tyr?'

'I'm trying to protect you from me.'

'Why? Are you such a beast in bed?'

'Jazz—'

'You probably are a beast in bed.' Her shoulders lifted in a shrug. 'How would I know?'

'Jazz,' Tyr exclaimed with exasperation. 'Take the big bed and try to get some sleep.'

'I'm not going anywhere until you tell me what you're saving me from, Tyr. And you'd better come up with something good, because right now I'm feeling pretty—'

Tyr's fierce growl of impatience made her reel back as he closed the gap between them. His face was so close. 'OK, I shouldn't goad you.'

'And I shouldn't overreact, *elskling*,' Tyr murmured, his minty breath brushing her skin as he held her suspended in his arms. 'And as for goading me?' Eyes that speared deep into hers lit with a glint of humour. 'Why change the habit of a lifetime?'

That hint of warmth gave her hope. 'I'm not about to,' she flashed with all the old spirit as Tyr steadied her on her feet.

'You know I'd never hurt you, Jazz?'

'I absolutely know that,' she confirmed. 'But as I don't have anywhere else to be tonight…'

Looking away as he raked his hair, Tyr huffed a laugh.

'And, by the way, Tyr, I asked you a question and I'm still waiting for your answer.'

Folding his arms behind his head, Tyr rested back on the pillows, allowing his corded muscles to relax. 'Repeat the question.'

'I want you to make love to me, Tyr. This is our wedding night and I'm a virgin with everything to learn, so

I'm asking you, my husband, to teach me everything you know about sex.'

'In one night?' Tyr raised an amused brow.

'We can make a start,' she suggested.

CHAPTER FIFTEEN

CLOSING HER EYES, Jazz reached out. At first her touch was tentative. Tyr was so firm and warm and vital, but this was the first time she had ever touched a man's naked skin, and it took a little time to gain enough confidence to explore him more thoroughly.

When she did, he was a revelation. Tyr was so packed full of energy, her fingertips tingled. He was so toned and fit, his slightest movement allowed her to feel the shift of muscle beneath her hands. Drawing in a shaking breath, she dipped her head to brush her lips across his chest, where his distinctive clean man scent filled her senses.

Her feelings for Tyr were so strong, she was desperate to please him, but was concerned she might do something he wouldn't like. Should she trace his scars, or ignore them? She kissed them, regretting each terrible and unimaginable incident that had carved them into his bronzed skin. Tyr and she were different in so many ways and she only wished she could put the guilt instilled in her by centuries of tradition aside. Intimacy between a man and a woman was often discussed in a community divided by gender, but never in front of an unmarried girl, so the little Jazz had learned, she knew from eavesdropping and reading, and from various media sources, but nothing could have prepared her for a titan like Tyr Ska-vanga in the flesh.

Instinct told her that what Tyr needed even more than sex right now was tenderness. It was time to forget her hang-ups and think about him. Tyr was still a prisoner in his mind without an outlet for his feelings. Maybe she could help him with that. Reaching her arms around him, she rested her head against his powerful chest and hugged him tight. Tyr instantly grew tense, and for a few moments she thought she'd done the wrong thing, but then tremors racked him and like a dam breaking he clung to her and she clung to him as if her life depended on it. There was only one thing missing, and that was to tell Tyr it would be all right now, but a trite response was no good to him. Only time would heal his wounds.

'You don't have to tell me anything right now,' she whispered with her mouth against his chest. 'I just want you to know I'm always here for you.'

'Just so long as you keep on hugging me.'

She thrilled to hear Tyr's voice so warm and wry. 'It's a deal.'

Removing the robe she'd thrown over her shoulders, he tossed it aside. 'Relax, Jazz. Move down in the bed so you're more comfortable. You can even steal the covers, if you like.'

'It can get bitterly cold in the desert at night,' she agreed.

She laughed softly when they both glanced at the braziers surrounding them at the same time. These had been lit as soon as the sun went down to keep the pavilion pleasantly warm.

'I know you've led a sheltered life,' Tyr murmured as he toyed with a lock of her hair.

'What are you saying?'

'Why don't we find out?'

The look in Tyr's eyes was everything she'd hoped for. And they were husband and wife, Jazz reminded herself, so nothing was forbidden. It wasn't so bad feeling small and vulnerable when you felt so safe. Safe and with every nerve ending on super-high alert. Her thigh only had to touch Tyr's to start trembling, while her shoulder quivered when it brushed his arm.

Where to look?

If she looked straight at Tyr, that was like an invitation, while staring straight ahead seemed absurdly prim. So she looked down as she made a big performance of arranging the covers over her.

'You won't need those,' Tyr assured her, pushing them back.

'But you said—'

'I know what I said. I just don't want you getting overheated.'

Her eyes widened as Tyr released her hands from their death grip on the fabric. 'You're in my bed so I can keep you warm. Remember telling me that?'

Was that really her suggestion? 'I'm not very good at this, Tyr. I mean…'

'I know what you mean, Jazz,' Tyr assured her softly. 'You've already told me you're a virgin.'

'Well, I can hardly pretend to have run rampage through all the eligible youths in Kareshi.'

Tyr's hard mouth curved in a smile as he stared down at her. 'There isn't much I don't know about you, Jazz Kareshi, or that I can't read in your eyes, and I don't want you to be frightened of me, ever.'

'I'm not frightened of you.' She gasped as Tyr's hands encircled her waist as he drew her down beside him.

'Really?' Tyr's mouth tugged up in a wicked smile as

he soothed her with an embrace that was both light and warm. His touch was so light, she could have broken away at any time, but did she want to?

'Calm down,' he whispered when her breathing quickened. 'I don't bite.' That wicked smile again. 'At least, not yet.'

She laughed. Tyr made everything so easy for her. Smiling against his lips, she closed her eyes. Breathing the same air, she kissed him. Every part of her was firing at once, while Tyr's kisses were gentle and teasing as he held her back. She was still basking in delicious sensation when he drew her nightgown over her head.

'What—?'

'You're overdressed,' he reprimanded her.

Drawing the coverlet up to her chin, she lay trembling and acutely sensitive. How could she become so responsive suddenly? Just the lightest pass of Tyr's fingers on her naked skin was enough to make her tremble with desire for him.

'What are you staring at?' she asked suspiciously when he pulled the covers back.

'You. I'm staring at you, Jazz.'

As the familiar smile carved a crease in his cheek, she turned her face away from him and closed her eyes. No one had seen her naked since she was a child in the nursery. What did Tyr think of her? How would she compare to all the other women he must have known? She didn't dare open her eyes to find out.

'Look at me, Jazz. Open your eyes and look at me,' Tyr commanded.

Cupping her face in his hands, he kissed her so gently, her heart welled with love for him.

'That's better,' he said when she searched his eyes.

'You can trust me, and you can make me stop any time you want to.'

She smiled nervously. Tyr was so much bigger than she was. How was she supposed to do that?

'You ask me to stop whenever you want,' he said, reading her mind with his usual ease. 'Anything you don't like, you tell me, and I'll stop right away.'

Was it likely there would be anything she didn't like?

No. But she had been ultra-protected all her life, and had set such strict rules for herself that she couldn't help but be nervous. She'd heard people talking about *things happening naturally*, and had concluded that was their way of getting out of having to explain to a nervous virgin that there would be pain—or, at the very least, discomfort, together with huge embarrassment. But Tyr was distracting her with irresistible kisses, and each time he caressed her she wanted more. The fact that he was in no hurry reassured her, and when he caressed her back with long, leisurely strokes, she wanted the sensation to last for ever. Perhaps that would be enough for him.

She had to stop this and trust him. She had always trusted Tyr, and while he had her suspended in an erotic net like this, she was in no mood to distract him.

She'd had no idea she was so sensitive, or so receptive to pleasure. Or that Tyr could make her shiver with excitement and anticipation, just by rasping his sharp black stubble very lightly against her neck. And when his hands found her breasts—

'Relax, Jazz,' he whispered when she dragged in a shocked and shuddering breath.

At first she was too surprised to register anything apart from the shock. They might be husband and wife, but Tyr had touched a most private part of her. What shocked her most was that it was a part that badly wanted to be touched. When he drew her nipple into his mouth and gently tugged, sensation streamed through her. The thought that no man but Tyr had ever looked upon her naked body aroused her even more. Tyr's kisses were deepening with every passing moment, and he was touching her everywhere that wanted to be touched until, far from needing lessons from him, she called upon her own, inbuilt intuition to show her how to respond. Though she did lose courage a little bit when his hand moved firmly over her belly.

'We're husband and wife, remember?' Tyr's eyes blazed into hers. 'Unless you'd like me to stop?'

'I don't want you to stop.' Though once she'd made this statement, her eyes begged him to be gentle with her.

Tyr answered this by kissing her again, his tongue plundering her mouth in a way that mimicked the act she was so afraid of.

'You're tensing up again,' he said. 'Why? You know I'd never hurt you, Jazz.'

His eyes were warm and concerned now as they stared into hers, and she hated lying to him. The ache inside her was unsustainable, but her fear of Tyr plundering her body was greater still.

'Jazz,' Tyr soothed as he smiled against her mouth.

He teased her with kisses, and then his hands began to stroke and soothe, and before she knew what was happening, the hunger for him had overtaken everything else. She held her breath when his hand travelled lower, his fingers grazing the place where she so badly needed him. The urgency to have her hunger answered was stronger than any fear she had ever known, and, arching her back in the hunt for more contact from his hand, she gave a soft moan of thanks when he found her.

And lost control instantly. Her world exploded in a

burst of light, the pleasure so extreme, she was lost in a sea of violent, buffeting waves, while she bucked frantically and shamelessly, working her body against Tyr's strong hand to prolong the incredible feeling for as long as she could.

She gasped as the storm subsided and, still recovering, could barely manage to gasp out a single word.

'You're very responsive, Princess,' Tyr murmured against her mouth.

'Are you surprised?' She smiled into his eyes and saw an answering warmth. 'So, I'm inexperienced,' she challenged with a shrug. 'I just hope you're not laughing at me, Tyr Skavanga.'

'I'm happy for you, Jazz,' he whispered. 'You've waited too long for that.'

'It feels like for ever,' she agreed. But waiting for Tyr to come home had been the longest wait of all.

'More?' he suggested.

She was about to say no, and couldn't believe it when the hunger stirred inside her again. 'Much more,' she confirmed, stretching out her body like a contented cat, against the immense, powerful length of Tyr Skavanga.

'Why don't you just lie back and let me do all the work?' he suggested.

'Why didn't I think of that?'

'Oh, I think you did,' he countered with amusement.

So why was he teasing her? She writhed and sighed with the pleasure of anticipation as a hint. Tyr took the hint. Enclosing her wrists in one giant fist, he brought her arms over her head, pinning her to the bed, and, feasting on her breasts, sucking, licking, working magic, he drew a cry of pleasure from her lips. What made it even more amazing to Jazz was the way one sensation could travel through every part of her until it gathered in pulsing desire between her legs.

Maybe she could lose control with nothing more than this?

But would that be enough for Tyr?

The answer came when she lost control and he didn't. Instead, he laughed softly as she struggled to replace the air in her lungs.

'What are you laughing at, Tyr?'

'You,' he said as if that were obvious. 'This is promising to be a long night.'

'Are you pleased?'

'Yes, of course I'm pleased.' Shifting position, he stared down at her.

She narrowed her eyes. 'And why are you smiling at me, Tyr Skavanga?'

'Because my wife amuses me.'

Jazz faked a frown. 'I think you'd better explain that remark.'

'Let's just say, you're a natural in the bedroom, and you've been hiding this talent for how long?'

'As I tried to explain, a princess of Kareshi doesn't exactly have the opportunity to express that side of herself as freely or as often as she might like.'

'Oh, so you would have expressed yourself before now, if it had been permitted?'

'Stop fishing, Viking. I'm a good girl. Always have been.'

'Then I'm glad you changed for me.'

'I'm wicked now,' she agreed happily. 'So I hope when you talk about a long night, you mean a long night of pleasure for me?'

Tyr's brow furrowed, but his mouth was still curved in a smile. 'I'm counting on it, Princess.'

Jazz was still floating high on the rippling aftermath of pleasure, and that was exactly what she needed to hear. But had she really thought there was nothing left that Tyr could do to shock her?

One more thing she was wrong about, Jazz realised as Tyr placed his big, work-calloused hands beneath her buttocks and lifted her. He positioned her to suit him with her legs spread wide across his powerful shoulders.

She felt exposed. She felt vulnerable.

She *was* exposed. She *was* vulnerable. And had to remind herself yet again that this was Tyr Skavanga and she trusted him. They were husband and wife, and nothing was forbidden to them.

Tyr used pleasure like a spell to make her forget any embarrassment she might have suffered, and to the point where she actively encouraged him when he placed a cushion beneath her hips. Kneeling in front of her, he lifted her even more as he dipped his head and worked another spell, with his mouth and with his tongue, and with his fingers as she pressed urgently against his mouth.

But shouldn't she be doing something?

'Shouldn't I…?'

'Reciprocate?' Tyr supplied, flashing his wicked smile.

Now she wished she hadn't said anything, though she guessed a pause suited him, as it only made her more frustrated than ever.

'There's no rush, Jazz,' Tyr remarked, confirming this. 'We've got all night, remember? All night to please you, Princess, so stop worrying. Instinct is all you need.'

But did she have the right sort of instinct?

The pleasure was so intense, she turned her head away, feeling embarrassed at the overwhelming power of her response. She wanted to cry out, and moan and sigh. It was taking everything she'd got just to remain silent.

'Let yourself go,' Tyr advised, his tone husky and amused. 'You'll enjoy it so much more if you do. Why deny yourself pleasure, Jazz?'

'I can't take without giving something back, that's why. And you can stop smiling,' she warned, longing to touch Tyr, to explore him and test his responses. But Tyr was too skilled for that, and made sure she lost control again before she had chance to put her plan into action.

'You're just too good at this,' she panted out.

'Are you complaining?' he murmured against her mouth.

'I just want to know when it's my turn.'

'That was your turn.'

'Oh, you're impossible,' she complained, finding she lacked even the strength to play-punch him.

'Agreed.' He dragged her close.

'Is this meant to soothe me down?' she demanded when Tyr finally lifted his head. 'Because if it is, you've failed miserably.'

'That's great news,' Tyr murmured.

Every part of them was touching as he kissed her, but she couldn't wait any longer and took the initiative, transferring her kisses from his mouth to his ear, and then his neck. And when she heard his sharp intake of breath, she moved over him and pressed him down onto the cushions. 'You're mine, Tyr Skavanga.'

'Your sex slave?' Tyr suggested. His smile broadened. 'Excellent. Feel free to use me any way you like.'

'I do like.' And she would. Tyr was magnificent. His body was beautiful. Built on an epic scale to a flawless design. Flawless, except for the scars that she traced with her fingertips—

'Don't,' Tyr warned softly as she examined the map of memories. 'Don't spoil the mood, Jazz.'

That map might take a lifetime to unravel, she accepted. Tyr repaid her restraint with a slanting smile that made heat rush through her. Now she could think of only one thing, and that was Tyr. She wanted to bring him pleasure, and, kissing her way down his heroic frame, she only stopped when she reached the waistband of his shorts. Drawing a deep, steadying breath, she hooked her thumbs beneath the elastic at the waistband and drew them down.

Daunted?

To say she was daunted by the size of him would be massively understating the case. She was shocked rigid. Along with all the other expressions of amazement she could name. She had expected Tyr to be built to scale, but…

It just wouldn't be possible.

She hadn't reckoned with the demands of a body that had been denied for too long, or her own fierce desire to bring Tyr pleasure. Closing her eyes, she gathered her courage, and, wrapping her hands around him, she felt his warmth and power and virility. It took both her hands to encompass him, as well as several seconds to get over the shock of what she was doing. Steadying herself, she concentrated on fathoming out Tyr's pleasure points and how best to please him. And when he groaned in grateful response, she dipped her head and kissed the smooth, velvety tip. But even that wasn't enough for her, so, settling to the task, she took him in her mouth and laved him with her tongue. She worked him with her hands at the same time, while Tyr showed his appreciation with groans of pleasure. This was so much better than she had imagined, and it seemed she knew exactly what to do.

'Stop.'

She stopped immediately. 'Did I do something wrong?'

Tyr gripped her shoulders as he let go of a shuddering breath. 'You did everything right, but you have to stop before I lose control completely.'

I did that?

Jazz sat back on her heels while Tyr stared up at her. His steel-grey eyes were half closed, and his lips had curved in a brooding smile as he reached up to embrace her. Leaning her head back, she closed her eyes as his hands moved slowly down her arms. This felt so good, so right. Could the fates be kind for once, and give them a second chance?

When Tyr drew her down to him, she sank into his arms with renewed certainty, and, turning her face into his chest, she inhaled deeply, knowing this was the safest place on earth to be. Cupping her chin, Tyr brought her up to face him, and when he kissed her this time she was filled with a new confidence. But though they were close, they weren't close enough. She wanted to be one with him.

There was a moment when Tyr moved over her and she tensed and he pulled back, but he helped her to relax with his hands and with his kisses until she clung to him, gasping with pleasure and with frustration too. And then he allowed just the tip to catch inside her.

'No,' she exclaimed as he pulled away.

'No?' Tyr queried, teasing her as his eyes smiled into hers.

'Don't—'

'Don't make you wait?'

'Correct,' she gasped.

Several short sharp breaths shot out of her. She clung to Tyr. She almost panicked and pulled away. *Could she do this? Would it hurt?*

Tyr's steady gaze didn't leave her face and his teasing

kisses excited her until sensation fused seamlessly with all the emotion inside her and she couldn't think or reason any more. She only knew that she had got past that last barrier to find some new, higher level of awareness.

This wasn't a barrier; this was closeness; this was unity; this was love.

'I love you,' she exclaimed impulsively as Tyr moved deeper and with more purpose.

He stretched her beyond anything she would have believed possible, but the pleasure was so intense she was lost to reason, so she didn't know if he'd heard her, or if he replied, or if he even cared.

CHAPTER SIXTEEN

IF ONE NIGHT could be said to be long enough to learn how to give and receive pleasure, then last night had been that night, Jazz reflected as she rolled over in bed, sighing with contentment. At some point Tyr had carried her from the cushions to the rug, and sometime after that he had carried her from the rug to the bed, where he'd made love to her again. It was as if they could never get enough of each other. They had a lot of time to make up for, Tyr had reminded her.

'We've only been married a few hours,' she had argued.

'But I'm talking about all those years when I was away when I could have been with you.'

'But then we would have been two very different people.'

Reaching out, she gasped with alarm. Where was Tyr? Panic-stricken, she shot up in bed and gazed around. It was still shadowy inside the pavilion with the first thin shafts of light slanting through the windows. Was last night a dream?

'You're awake, Princess.'

'Tyr!'

Crossing the pavilion in a few big strides, her Viking lover, dressed in jeans and not much more, dragged her into his embrace. 'You're shaking,' he exclaimed softly, keeping her warm in his arms as he kissed the top of her head.

'I thought you'd gone away again. I must have been half asleep. The bed was empty, and—'

'You don't get rid of me that easily.'

'Who says I want to get rid of you?' She rolled closer. 'I have plans for you.'

Laughing, Tyr kissed her. His sexy growl warmed her through, and, remembering his exhaustive attentions the night before, she reached for the buckle on his belt.

Tyr might have helped her with that belt buckle or he might have hindered. She wouldn't know; they were in such a rush. Tearing off his jeans, he threw her down on the bed and drew her beneath him. Lifting her, he nudged one powerful thigh between her legs and took her with a deliciously firm thrust. The pleasure when Tyr began to move was indescribable, and she moved with him, fiercely and rhythmically, and as fast as she could. She cried out as she dropped into the abyss and Tyr fell with her. This was the best yet. And extremely necessary, Jazz concluded contentedly as Tyr fell back and they both began to laugh. Turning his head, Tyr stared into her eyes. 'Why did we waste so much time sleeping?'

'We must be mad,' Jazz agreed wryly. 'But as I'm not in the mood for sleep right now...'

Tyr took the hint and helped her to climb on top of him. Gripping his shoulders, she settled slowly into position. 'Oh, that's so good. So good!' Her screams could probably be heard in the village, and, with Tyr holding her firmly as he guided her back and forth, she extracted the last ounce of pleasure and rode the storm.

'This can't get any better, can it?' she managed later

when they were both taking a break with their limbs lazily entwined.

'Why do you ask?' Tyr murmured without opening his eyes.

'Because I don't think I can take any more.'

'You underestimate yourself, Princess, but perhaps we should find out?'

Jazz exclaimed softly with anticipation as Tyr brought her beneath him. Lifting her legs onto his shoulders, he pressed her knees back and took her in long, lazy strokes that she could do nothing to resist or control, and within seconds she had lost control again. 'Stop—stop,' she begged him, laughing as Tyr lowered her onto her side and curled around her. 'I can't take any more.'

'You're wrong,' he insisted.

He was right, thank goodness. When Tyr moved behind her and his hand worked some sort of magic as he moved, the impossible became possible again. Arching her back, she thrust her buttocks towards him so he could see just how thoroughly she was enjoying his attentions, and how eager she was to assist.

When she quietened this time, Tyr embraced her and kissed her so tenderly, it took her a while to notice that the pavilion was filled with the most intoxicating scent. 'What is that delicious perfume?'

Tyr pulled his head back to stare down at her. 'Arabian jasmine and desert lavender.'

'Really?' She sat up, and then realised the pavilion was full of desert flowers. 'You did all this for me while I was sleeping?'

'I stopped short of bringing in the horses to trample the plants to release their scent as you suggested when we were down at the oasis.'

'You're a secret romantic?'

'No need for such a frown. I might not be in touch with my feminine side, but I do know what matters to my wife.'

Jazz laughed and nuzzled close. 'You are full of surprises.'

'I try not to disappoint.'

'Not a chance,' Jazz confirmed. 'But you didn't need to do all this for me.'

'Yes, I did. A bride should feel special, and I'm guessing you spent most of your wedding day feeling anything but.' Tyr's massive shoulders lifted in a shrug. 'I wanted to make it up to you.'

As he got out of bed, she joined him, oblivious to the fact that she was naked. 'Tyr Skavanga out at dawn picking flowers for me? I'll be able to eat out on that story for years to come.'

They were close, almost touching, and with a husky growl Tyr yanked her closer. Lifting her, he encouraged her to wrap her legs around his waist, and, dipping at the knees, he took her deep. Thrusting rhythmically as he kissed her, Tyr made her forget everything apart from the wild ride he was taking her on, and by the time he lowered her to her feet, her legs refused to support her.

'That must have been good,' he observed as he carried her to the bed. 'Perhaps you should just lie back on the bed and recover.'

He was joking. Having brought her to the edge of the bed, Tyr moved over her, and, bracing his arms either side of her on the bed, he teased her with the tip while she groaned.

'You can't do that,' she panted out as Tyr drew the smooth tip of his massively engorged erection up and down the place that needed him the most. 'Please,' she begged. 'Please. I need you now.'

'This much?'

She shuddered out a wordless reply.

'Or a little more?'

'You're not playing fair,' she complained as Tyr withdrew fully, drawing a whimper of disappointment from her throat. But he rewarded her patience—*and her impatience*—by cupping her buttocks and positioning her to his liking, *and hers*, as he very slowly took her deeply again.

'Was that worth the wait?'

Surely, he didn't expect an answer? She was incapable of speech.

Pressing her knees back, Tyr stared down as he withdrew fully again and then sank deep. The look of concentration on his face alone was enough to tip her over the edge. Her wild cries filled the pavilion, and she had barely come down from that high when they fell on each other and, bucking furiously, raced towards the next inevitable conclusion.

The best thing about it, Jazz reflected when they were quiet for a moment, was the more pleasure Tyr gave her, the more her capacity for pleasure seemed to grow. Her hunger for him was insatiable. She would never be ready for Tyr to stop.

'What?' she said as he stilled to listen.

Tyr had tensed. Her legs were still wound around his, so she could feel every part of him on high alert.

Swiftly disentangling himself, he swung off the bed and stood in silence for a moment, towering and magnificent. And then she heard it too. One of the horses was whinnying an alarm, while somewhere in the distance came the answering yelp of a coyote's call. Coyote were rare in the deserts of Kareshi, and were a protected species, but recently breeding programmes had been more successful than expected, and hunting packs could be large and vicious.

'Tyr?'

'Stay there.'

The note of command was in his voice as Tyr dressed quickly, but she wasn't about to sit around, watching him tug on his jeans and boots.

'Jazz. What do you think you're doing?'

'I'm coming with you.'

'No, you're not. You'll stay here.'

'Not a chance.'

Hectically throwing a shirt over her naked body, she hopped, skipped and jumped her way into breeches and boots, and burst out of the entrance of the pavilion in time to see Tyr running towards the stock pen. Grabbing a broom, she followed him, as lights started going on in the village.

The pack was big, the lead animals thin enough to risk human contact as they hunted for easy pickings amongst the cattle in the corral. Jabbing her broom in the air, she yelled to frighten them away. Grabbing hold of her arm, Tyr thrust her behind him, using his own body as a shield. 'Do you never listen to a word I say? I thought I told you to stay in the pavilion?'

'You don't tell me what to do,' she yelled back, wrestling free.

By this time, the lead animals, having measured their opponents, had slunk away into the scrub. And now the headman had arrived with a crowd of villagers following. Turning away, Tyr spoke to him, effectively cutting Jazz out. She was invisible again—surplus to requirements as the men discussed the next course of action. Was this the husband she adored, the man who had made such tender love to her?

'Am I allowed to ask where you're going?' she demanded as Tyr, having issued his instructions, headed back to the village without another word.

'There's no time to discuss this, Jazz. I want to get back to order the equipment we need.'

She was running to keep up with him. 'So I'm invisible when it suits you, but not in bed?'

'Jazz—there's no time for this.'

Tyr didn't even break stride. He didn't stop until they reached the village hall, where he could access the computers. She was about to follow him inside the building when he stopped her. Caging her against the door with his arms either side of her face, he brought his face close. 'You could have been killed back there.' He shot each word into her face like a bullet. 'At the very best, you could have been seriously injured. You should have stayed in the pavilion when I told you to.'

'So I'm supposed to hide under the pillows until you come back? Forget it, Tyr.' Thrusting her hair out of her eyes, she made a contemptuous sound. 'If you think I'm going to take orders, you picked the wrong wife.'

'I didn't pick you. This situation was thrust on both of us.'

Her mouth fell open on empty air as Tyr's harsh words resonated around them. Her stomach curled with shame because what he said was true, and everything they had been to each other last night was obliterated in the stinging aftermath of those few destructive words. She'd told Tyr she loved him, but now she remembered he'd never said anything in return.

'You're right about this situation being thrust upon us,' she agreed, relieved her voice sounded so steady. 'And in case you're in any doubt, I don't like this situation any more than you do. How can I, when I'm tied to a husband whose attitude towards women is stuck in the Dark Ages?'

'Not now, Jazz.'

She was ahead of him when Tyr reached the door and stood in his way. 'You will listen to me,' she insisted, thrusting her hands out to hold him off. 'I'm not the helpless female you seem to think I am. I'm your equal in every way. Either we do this together, and I mean all of it, Tyr, the good bits and the bad, or you can forget this marriage.'

A long silence followed, then Tyr pulled back. 'Wait there and calm down,' he advised.

Jazz ground her jaw, but at least she didn't say anything she might regret later. She leaned back against the door, grudgingly accepting that if she had followed Tyr inside, the emails he had to send would probably not be sent, and right now the desperately needed equipment was more of a priority than her pride.

After sending the messages he came outside. Jazz had moved from the door and was standing a few feet away. She was the first thing he looked for, her eyes the first destination he sought. She was still angry and who could blame her? Taking hold of her shoulders, he brought her in front of him. 'Understand this, Jazz—I will never allow you to endanger yourself. Understood?'

She tipped her chin up. 'And I will never allow you to face risk alone. Got that?' She stared at him, unflinching. 'And now it's time for you to tell me everything, don't you think?'

Releasing his hold, he stood back.

'Don't you dare say there's nothing to tell,' she warned as he shook his head.

'This isn't the place, Jazz.'

'Oh? Where is the place? Shall we wait until we're

sitting round the boardroom table in Skavanga?' Firming her jaw, she gave him such a look. 'There is no right place, Tyr, but there is a right time, and that time is now.'

'That piece of paper we signed? It might make us husband and wife, but it doesn't give you the right to rifle through my mind.'

'Coward.'

Jazz had always known exactly which of his buttons to press. 'I'm a killer, Jazz. And I'm very good at what I do. Is that enough for you?'

She shook her head. 'You're a soldier and a hero who was following orders,' she argued evenly. 'You never could shock me, Tyr, so don't even try that tactic with me. You don't frighten me and I'm not going anywhere. I'm staying put until you tell me everything.'

'You think I'm a hero?' he flashed. 'Is that what you think?'

'That's what I know. Sharif hasn't kept all your secrets, so I know exactly what you did.'

'Everything?' he said scathingly.

'Enough to know the man I married is a hero,' Jazz said quietly. 'Enough to know you rescued your battalion by risking your own life. And before you start trying to frighten me off with tales of how dangerous that makes you, let me ask you one simple question: Would a brother who adores me agree to our marriage if Sharif thought you were a dangerous man? Isn't it more likely that Sharif loves you as he loves me, and that he believes somehow, and even I'm not even sure how, yet, that I can help you?'

He said nothing for the longest time, and then he voiced his haunting thoughts. 'I can never forget the children's faces.'

Reaching out for him, Jazz gripped his hand.

'There are no age limits in war, Jazz. No sanitised

battlegrounds where only adults hold a gun and only bad guys do the shooting.'

'Don't you think I know that, Tyr? But you have never stopped trying to help people. You haven't given a thought to yourself. You're a creator, not a destroyer, and now it's time for you to think about rebuilding your own life, when you decide what it is you want.'

They were talking as they had years back. They were older and the topics had changed radically, but so had they, he reflected as Jazz's frank gaze pierced his heart.

'Who do you think stood at my brother's side when Sharif reclaimed the kingdom?' she went on gently. 'Who walked through the battlefield with Sharif so we could learn together what we had to do to repair the damage of our parents' rule? I didn't flinch then and I won't flinch now, from whatever you have to tell me.'

He shook his head. 'I don't have time for this. I only wish I did. I can't halt my work for selfish reasons. I can hardly keep pace with all the rebuilding in Kareshi as it is, so I certainly can't indulge myself in marriage or children.'

'You talk as if you're doing this alone,' Jazz interrupted. 'But you're not alone any longer, and I don't want you to stop your work. I want to work with you, Tyr. I want our children to know the satisfaction that comes with building and repairing. I want to mine your time and your energy, and your vision for Kareshi. I want to share you with Kareshi. Just one small step at a time,' she argued stubbornly when he obviously looked unconvinced. 'And if there's more you haven't told me, I know you will, but not now, not all at once. Wounds take time to heal and even you can't rush that process.'

'You always were stubborn,' he murmured, flashing her a glance.

'You bet. And I haven't changed,' Jazz assured him.

Taking hold of both his hands, she stood in front of him. 'Submit,' she suggested in a whisper. 'You know you're stuck with me for life.'

A few tense moments passed and then with a laugh of triumph he kissed his love, his passion, his life, his soulmate Jazz, and one kiss led to another as the flame between them raged white-hot. There might have been people around, but neither of them noticed. Passion as fierce as theirs could accept no restrictions. They remained locked in their own world until the headman passed on his way home and made some remark. 'What did he say?' he asked Jazz.

'He said a passion as fierce as ours is a blessing for the village,' Jazz explained, smiling, her lush mouth still swollen from his kisses. 'That blessing comes in the form of many children, all in the service of Kareshi.'

'We'd better get on it, then.'

Jazz faked a punch. He dodged out of the way, then, grabbing hold of Jazz's wrist, he strode back at speed towards the pavilion. He paused at the entrance. 'You were scared for me?' He wanted to hear her say it again.

She smiled into his eyes. 'You have no idea, do you, Tyr?'

'No idea about what?' He frowned down at her.

'About how much I love you, you inflexible, infuriating man. You have to accept people care about you, and I'm one of those people. So if you face a pack of wild dogs on your own, or any other danger you care to name, you'd better get used to the idea that I'm going to be right there by your side.

'What are you doing?' she demanded as he swung her into his arms.

'Shutting you up the only way I know how.'

'You can try,' she fired back at him as he carried her into the pavilion.

'That would be my absolute pleasure, Princess.'

Mine too, Jazz thought as Tyr started kissing her. Tyr was exactly what she needed—a challenge—a man she could pit herself against in every way. A man she could love, she amended as Tyr held her close and kissed her deep. Every inch of his hard, toned body was pressing into hers, and her desire for him had never been stronger.

'Now, let's get one thing straight.' Dipping his head, Tyr hit her with his uncompromising stare. 'You won't put yourself in danger again, because if something happened to you—' He stopped. He took a breath. 'My life would be over. You're everything I need, Jazz Kareshi.'

'Jazz Skavanga,' she reminded him, laughing as she wound her arms around his neck, sighing as Tyr kissed her neck.

'I love you, Jazz Skavanga, and I won't risk losing you ever again.'

'You love me?' Pulling back, she lifted her chin to stare into his eyes.

'More than life itself.'

'You love me,' she repeated, savouring the words.

Reaching for her hands, Tyr enclosed them in his. 'Will you marry me, Jazz?'

She laughed as she leaned forward to plant a kiss on his mouth. 'We're already married. Are you asking me to commit bigamy?'

'I'm not sure that's strictly possible when you're marrying the same man, but when we marry this time, I want it to be for you and me, and not because tradition demands it, or the people demand it. So, what do you say, Jazz? Will you marry me?'

Lifting Tyr's hands to her lips, she kissed them and stared into his eyes. 'Of course I will.'

Tyr's kiss was tender and cherishing, but when he pulled back he was frowning.

'What's the matter?' she said. 'Not having second thoughts, I hope?'

Tyr laughed. 'Far from it. The only downside to loving you so much is that I keep on having to make love to you.'

'Oh, no.' She pretended dismay. 'But is that permitted when we're not even married yet?'

'Let's break the rules. Unless of course you have some objection?'

'None I can think of right away. Oh, well, maybe one…'

'Which is?'

A tremor of anticipation ran through her as Tyr's gaze dropped to her lips. 'Don't think for one moment that I'm going to promise to obey you.'

'And break the habit of a lifetime?' Shaking his head in pretended dismay, Tyr smiled faintly as he glanced at the bed. 'You're such a bad girl, you've given me no alternative but to send you straight to bed.'

'Really?' She slanted a look at him. 'I was hoping you might say that.'

CHAPTER SEVENTEEN

THEIR HUNGER FOR each other remained fierce. Would they ever get enough of each other? Jazz wondered when Tyr finally swung out of bed around noon. And that was only because they'd heard helicopters overhead and knew it had to be the equipment he'd ordered.

'I'll be back soon—' He emerged from the bathing tent dressed in a muscle-defining top and snug-fitting jeans that outlined his virile form with loving attention to detail. Rolling over in bed, Jazz closed her eyes on Tyr's distracting below-the-belt architecture, which was currently putting a considerable strain on his jeans.

'Be ready for me, Jazz. I'll be hot and dusty, and in desperate need of your attention.'

'Before you go—'

'Jazz, there isn't time for this.'

'Are you sure?' She spoke quietly and intently as she stared up at him. 'The helicopter hasn't landed yet.'

Tyr was already reaching for the zipper on his jeans. 'You're shameless.'

'And you're here, sex slave, so get on with your duties.' Easing into position on the edge of the bed, she settled back and rested her legs on his shoulders. Tyr was standing up and looming over her, his leverage perfect. 'I won't keep you long,' she promised shakily as he thrust deep.

She kept her word. Tyr did too. He worked skilfully to bring her the fastest maximum relief. But it still wasn't enough. 'I need more,' she groaned when he withdrew carefully.

'Keep that thought,' Tyr advised as he secured his belt.

'Now—' She reached for him greedily.

'If you're going to disobey me, I may have to spank you,' he warned.

'And if you dare do that, I would have to send you straight to bed.'

'It's a deal, wife.' Dipping low, Tyr smiled as he dropped a short, but seductive kiss on her lips.

Lying back on the cushions, she watched Tyr stroll across the pavilion towards the entrance. His sexy swagger made her hot for him all over again. Tyr was a highly sexual being and hers to love. What was not to like when the man she married was the love of her life *and* the hottest thing on two magnificent, hard-muscled legs?

'When I've finished unloading the equipment, I'm taking you to watch the villagers fly their kestrels.'

'Only when I've worn you out, I hope?' she called back to him.

'By that time your legs won't hold you up.'

'Then you'll have to carry me to the dune to watch the kestrels flying.'

Tyr laughed. 'That's how I got into trouble the first time around,' he reminded her as he ducked his head and left the tent.

Throwing herself back on the bed, she grabbed a cushion to cuddle. It was a poor substitute for Tyr, but he often made her wait, and one thing she did know: it was always well worth it.

* * *

When Tyr came back after unloading the equipment, they made love. It was very different this time as he embraced her in the gathering shadows of early evening. He kissed her gently on the lips as he moved, and it was as if he wanted to take his time to savour every moment, as if this was a precious interlude before everyday life intruded. Being close, and staring into each other's eyes, added a special depth to their lovemaking. It wasn't just a hunt for physical satisfaction that drove them now, but a desire to be one in pleasure, in aim and in life. This was love, Jazz realised as she stared into Tyr's eyes.

'Now,' he instructed softly, holding her firmly as he skilfully tipped her over the edge.

'Those are the only instructions you're allowed to give me,' she teased him later as she snuggled contentedly against Tyr's powerful chest. 'But you can give them to me as often as you like.'

'Was that a hint?'

'If you need one,' she confirmed, moving to accommodate him.

Tyr was so big—huge. She would never get used to the way he stretched her and filled her completely, or his ability to bring her so much pleasure. He knew her body and her responses better than she knew them herself. He knew exactly what she needed and how to give it to her, as she hoped she pleased him.

'What do you think, Princess?' Tyr stopped moving briefly. 'Sinking into you is heaven. Working you is bliss. Seeing you come apart in my arms is the best thing in the world for me.'

She smiled as she used her hidden muscles to grip him tight.

'That's what I like about you,' Tyr whispered against her mouth. 'You're never at a loss for something to do.'

She laughed with him, loving the way they were so close now, and when Tyr lost control this time, he called out her name and told her he loved her.

'I can never get enough of hearing that,' she whispered when Tyr rolled onto his back.

'You shouldn't be so amazing,' he confided with a smile.

'Is sex the only reason you love me?'

Staring deep into her eyes, Tyr grew serious. 'The sex is just one wonderful part of it, of you.'

'Cue violins?' she murmured, smiling back at him.

'Must I punish you for making light of my protestations of love?'

'You can do anything you want to me when your mouth looks so sexy when you talk. In fact, just speak to me, just tell me that you love me, over and over again. I'll never get enough of hearing it.'

'You're in luck, Princess,' Tyr said as he drew her into his arms. 'You're going to be hearing me tell you that I love you quite a lot.'

The sky over the desert at dusk had turned a sultry violet tinged with gold. A big ivory moon hung low in the sky as Jazz and Tyr watched the villagers fly their kestrels. The sky was so clear, Jazz could see the blackened craters on the face of the moon, and the huge dark shadows on its cream-cheese surface. The villagers had been so thrilled to see them, they had immediately handed Tyr the best bird.

'Here, Jazz, you take him,' Tyr offered.

She smiled up into the eyes of the man she loved, thinking how Tyr had changed, but then so had she. He was relaxed now, as well as open and tender, while she was a woman in love.

Tyr handed her the gauntlet to protect her hand from the kestrel's talons, and then passed the beautiful bird over. The kestrel was quite calm as it was still wearing its intricately embroidered hood.

'It's a long time since we've done this,' Tyr observed as they admired the bird.

'Another time, another world,' Jazz agreed. Which was why she wasn't surprised by the weight of the bird on her hand, which was almost literally as light as air, thanks to its hollow bones. 'But this is the prize falcon and you're supposed to be flying this one.'

'They're bringing another bird over. And be warned, it looks as if my silver lady is around twice the size of your male.'

'But not half as determined.'

'Should I be jealous?' Tyr asked as Jazz stroked her bird's feathers.

'When my male bird wins, you can be pleased for me—even relieved that I'm prepared to accept that there might be the odd occasion when a male can prove himself superior to a female.'

Tyr laughed; then someone blew a horn to alert the bait man who was standing on a bluff almost half a mile away. His job was to throw up the meat that the birds had been trained to catch before bringing back their prize to the person flying them.

Tyr and Jazz loosed the cords on their kestrels' hoods at the same moment, and with their keen sight restored, the birds soared high into the air. Tyr and Jazz watched until the kestrels had disappeared from sight. The villagers were taking bets on which bird would return first, but as Jazz stood leaning her back into Tyr, with his arms around her waist, she sucked in a deep breath of desert air and thought, *All bets are off. I love this man, and everything else we have*

*to face, we'll face together. The only thing that matters is
that we are together, and so close in every way.*

Excited shouts went up in less than a minute. The birds
had been spotted. They travelled fast, and it was only a
matter of seconds before they returned. They could travel
at over ninety miles an hour, Jazz remembered.

'The male's back first,' Tyr noted, grimacing as he
stared up at the sky. 'Small and fast.'

'But caring too.' Jazz laughed as the male bird she
was flying hovered instead of landing on her hand, as it
should have done. It continued to wait in the sky until the
female had landed safely on Tyr's gauntlet. 'You win,'
she conceded.

'Only because your bird waited for his mate before
he came in to land,' Tyr observed as they rewarded the
kestrels with tidbits before replacing their hoods. 'They
mate for life.'

She flashed a look at him. 'This I know.' Her cheeks
warmed as her heart filled with love for Tyr. For the first
time since their marriage ceremony, she really did feel
like a young bride on the brink of a new life and a lifelong adventure with the man she loved.

'And now there's only one thing left to do,' Tyr remarked
as they watched the villagers start to pack up and leave.

'And what's that?'

'Make love to my wife.'

'I have to agree,' Jazz said softly as they joined a group
of villagers heading for home.

Linking fingers, they walked in silence, their steps in
perfect harmony until the pavilion came into sight, when
they started to walk faster. Jazz hoped that no one noticed they were practically running now. If anyone had
noticed, they were far too polite to mention it.

EPILOGUE

THEY RENEWED THEIR vows in a very different land from Kareshi. In Skavanga beneath an ice-blue sky, where the heat of their love threatened to melt the tundra, along with Tyr's three sisters, Britt, Eva and Leila, who attended this very special ceremony of dedication and renewal of their marriage vows with their husbands, Sharif, Roman and Raffa. Leila and Raffa brought their twins along, as well as their newborn baby boy, while both Britt and Eva were heavily pregnant, though even in the last months of her pregnancy Britt had gone the extra mile to work her usual magic on the party.

The ceremony was being held in the open air on the shores of the frozen lake, outside the cabin that had been in the Skavanga family since that first prospector had followed his dream and slammed his pickaxe into the icy ground. Back then there had been no facilities to speak of at the cabin, but each generation had made improvements, and now it had been transformed into a twinkling haven of warmth and welcome: a cosy nest amidst the snow, with flowers of the desert arranged around the door, and around the wedding arbour outside, beneath which Tyr and Jazz would stand.

'I'm happy to get you off my hands,' her brother teased Jazz as he kissed her warmly on both cheeks.

'No more wedding plans to make and break?' she teased him back.

Sharif's eyes were warm with amusement. 'I knew this would happen before you did, but if I'd said anything...'

'My stubbornness would have held things up even more,' Jazz suggested wryly.

'So long as you're happy, Jasmina.'

'You can see I am, Sharif.'

'Yes,' he agreed. 'I can. And as my wedding gift to both of you,' Sharif said in a louder voice so everyone could hear, 'I am happy to announce that I am going to hand over control of home affairs in Kareshi to my sister, Jasmina, and to her husband, Tyr—my dear and trusted friend, who is like a brother to me. I do this because I know you will both put the interests of our people above your own, and I hope this edict will allow Jazz to continue with the work she has already started so successfully in Kareshi.'

'Just hearing you call me Jazz is a great step forward.' Laughing, Jazz threw herself into her brother's arms and hugged him tight. 'Thank you. Thank you, Sharif. There's no limit to what we can achieve together.'

'I think this might work, don't you?' Sharif turned his dark amused stare on Tyr.

'I never had any doubt, Sharif.'

'Oh, no. You don't do that,' Jazz exclaimed as she moved to stand between them. 'I am never going to be invisible again.'

'Invisible? Jazz?' Eva exclaimed.

The two men exchanged a look over her head and laughed.

'Not a chance,' Tyr whispered as Sharif left them to join his wife, Britt. 'You are the least invisible person I know.'

'And now you're distracting me,' Jazz said, frowning

as everyone left them to go inside the cabin for the feast the Skavanga sisters had insisted on preparing between them. 'What was I complaining about?'

'Not enough sex, I think,' Tyr said, straight-faced.

Jazz could only be thankful that her brother had gone inside. There were a few things she definitely didn't want to share with him.

'And I've got something for you,' Tyr whispered.

'Later,' Jazz warned.

'No. Now,' Tyr argued. Reaching inside the pocket of his impeccably tailored suit, he brought out a ring. It was studded with the flawless, flashing blue-white diamonds of Skavanga; he showed it to Jazz.

'"For ever",' she said, having read the inscription on the inside of the band.

'"And always".' As Tyr finished off the quotation he'd had inscribed inside the ring, he placed it next to the simple platinum wedding band on Jazz's marriage finger. 'This is for you, Jasmina—Jazz—the woman I've loved for ever, and will continue to love for ever. My friend, my lover, the woman who gave me back my life.'

* * * * *

EXPECTANT PRINCESS, UNEXPECTED AFFAIR

MICHELLE CELMER

*To mothers and fathers, brothers and sisters,
family and friends. Cherish your loved ones
and keep them close. You never know
what tomorrow will bring...*

Michelle Celmer is a bestselling author of more than thirty books. When she's not writing, she likes to spend time with her husband, kids, grand-children and a menagerie of animals.

Michelle loves to hear from readers. Visit her website, www.michellecelmer.com, like her on Facebook or write her at P.O. Box 300, Clawson, MI 48017, USA.

One

June

Though she had always considered her reserved nature one of her best qualities, there were times when Princess Anne Charlotte Amalia Alexander wished she could be more like her twin sister.

She sipped her champagne and watched from across the ballroom as Louisa approached one of the guests: a tall, dark and handsome gentleman who had been eyeing Louisa all evening. She smiled, said a few words, and he kissed her proffered hand.

It was so easy for her. Men were naturally drawn to her delicate beauty and enthralled by her childlike innocence.

But Anne? Men considered her cold and critical. It was no secret that people in society, men in particular, often referred to her as *The Shrew*. Usually she didn't let that bother her. She liked to believe that they felt threatened by her strength and independence. However, that was little consolation on a night like this one. Everyone around her was dancing and drinking and socializing, while she stood by herself, alone in her principles. But with her father's failing health, was it so hard to fathom that she just didn't *feel* like celebrating?

A waiter carrying a tray of champagne passed by and she snagged a fresh glass. Her fourth for that night, which was precisely three more than she normally drank.

Her father, the king of Thomas Isle, who should at least be able to attend the charity event they were holding in his honor, was too weakened by heart disease to even make an appearance. Her mother refused to leave his side. It was up to Anne, Louisa and their brothers, Chris and Aaron, to act as hosts in the king's absence.

Getting hammered probably wasn't in her or the rest of the family's best interest. But didn't Anne always do as she was told? Wasn't she always the rational, responsible twin?

Well, almost always.

She knocked back the champagne in two swallows, deposited her empty glass on another passing tray and grabbed a fresh one. She would drink this one slower, she promised herself, but already she could feel the alcohol warming her belly and she began to get a soft, fuzzy feeling in her head. It was…nice.

She downed glass number five in one long swallow.

"You're looking lovely, Your Highness," someone said from behind her.

She turned to the voice, surprised to find Samuel Baldwin, son of the prime minister of Thomas Isle, greeting her. Sam was the sort of man a women looked at and instantly went weak in the knees. At thirty he was more cute than handsome—at least she thought so— with naturally curly, dark blond hair that never seemed to behave and deep dimples in both cheeks when he smiled. He was several inches taller than her own five foot eight, with a lean, muscular build. She had spoken to him a time or two, but nothing more than a casual hello. The gossip mill pegged him as one of the island's most eligible bachelors, and he had been groomed since birth to take over his father's position.

He bowed in greeting, and as he did, a lock of that unruly hair fell across his forehead. Anne resisted the urge to reach up and brush it back, but couldn't help wondering what it would feel like to run her fingers through it.

She would normally greet him with cool indifference, but the alcohol was doing funny things to her head because she could feel herself smiling. "How nice to see you again, Mr. Baldwin."

"Please," he said, "call me Sam."

Out of the corner of her eye Anne saw Louisa on the dance floor, her mystery man holding her scandalously close, gazing into her eyes. A pang of jealousy soured Anne's stomach. She wanted a man to hold her close and look at her as though she were the only one in the room, as if he couldn't wait to get her alone so he could ravage her. Just this once she wanted to feel…wanted. Was that really too much to ask for?

She finished her champagne in one gulp and asked, "Would you care to dance, Sam?"

She wasn't sure if his look of surprise was due to her barbaric behavior, or the actual invitation. For a dreadfully long and horrifying instant, she thought he might turn her down. Wouldn't that be ironic considering all the dance invitations she had declined over the years? So many, in fact, that men had stopped asking altogether.

Then a grin curled his mouth, his dimples a prominent dent in each cheek, and he said, "I would be honored, Your Highness."

He offered his arm and she slipped hers through it. Then he led her out onto the crowded dance floor. It had been so long since she'd danced that when he took her in his arms and began to waltz, what used to be second nature suddenly felt clumsy and awkward. Or maybe that was the champagne making her knees soft…or the spicy scent of his aftershave making her light-headed. He smelled so delicious, she wanted to bury her face in the crook of his neck and breathe him in. She tried to recall the last time she'd been this close to a man she found so sexually appealing.

Maybe a little *too* long.

"Black suits you," Sam said, and it took her several seconds to realize he was talking about her gown, a floor-length, sequined number she had purchased off the rack in Paris. She didn't know if the color suited her so much as it had suited her mood when she'd picked it out. Now she wished she had worn something brighter and more cheerful. Like Louisa in her trademark pink, who, come to think of it, looked a bit like the Good Witch of the North. Which Anne supposed would make her the Wicked Witch of the West.

"Yes," she told Sam. "All that's missing is the pointy black hat."

It was the sort of remark that might put a man off. Instead Sam laughed. A deep, throaty laugh that seemed to vibrate through her, causing delicious friction that warmed her insides. "Actually, I was thinking that it brings out your milky complexion."

"Oh, well, thank you."

A slow song began, and Anne couldn't help noticing how Louisa's mystery man drew her in even closer. A little *too* close.

"Do you know that man dancing with my sister?" she asked Sam, gesturing with her chin.

"Garrett Sutherland. He's the richest landowner on the island. I'm surprised you don't know him."

The name was definitely familiar. "I know *of* him. I've heard my brothers mention him."

"It looks as though he and your sister are quite… friendly."

"I noticed that, too."

He watched Anne watching her sister. "You look out for her?"

She nodded and looked up at him. "Someone has to. She can be very naive, and far too trusting."

He grinned, his dimples so adorable she wanted to rise up and press a kiss to each one. "Then who looks after you?"

"No one needs to. I'm entirely capable of looking out for myself."

He tightened the arm around her back, tucking her

closer to his chest, and his smile went from teasing to sizzling. "Are you sure about that, Highness?"

Was he *flirting* with her? Men never teased and flirted with her. Not unless they wanted their head handed back to them on a platter. Samuel Baldwin was a brave man. And she realized, she *liked* it. She liked the weight of his hand on her back and the way it felt when her breasts skimmed the wall of his chest. She'd never been what anyone could call a sexual woman—not that she didn't enjoy a quick, meaningless roll in the hay now and then—but being close to Sam awakened feelings in her she never knew were there. Or was it more the champagne than the man?

No. No amount of alcohol had ever given her this warm, shivery, feverish ache. This primitive longing to be taken and…possessed. To rip Sam's clothes off and put her hands all over him. She wondered what he would do if she wrapped her arms around his neck, tugged his head down and kissed him. His lips looked so soft and sensual and she was dying to know what they would feel like, how they would taste.

She wished she possessed the courage to do it, right here, right now, in front of all these people. She wished she could be more like Louisa, who was now walking arm in arm with her dance partner, out the doors and onto the patio, seemingly oblivious to the hundred or so pairs of eyes following their every move.

Maybe it was about time Louisa learned to fend for herself. For tonight at least. From this moment forward, she was on her own.

Anne turned her attention to Sam and smiled. "I'm

so pleased you could attend our benefit. Are you having a good time?"

"I am. I was sorry to hear that the king wasn't well enough to attend."

"He has to have a procedure done and adjustments made to his heart pump so he must stay in tip-top shape. Being in a large crowd could expose him to infection. His system is very vulnerable."

Her siblings all seemed to think he was going to be fine, and the heart pump he had been attached to for the past nine months was going to give his damaged heart the time it needed to heal, but Anne had a bad feeling it was a waste of time. Lately he'd begun to look so pale and he had so little energy. She worried that he was losing his will to live.

Though the rest of the family was hopeful, deep down Anne knew he was going to die and her instincts were telling her that it would be soon.

A sudden feeling of intense grief welled up inside her, and hard as she tried to push it back down, tears sprang to the corners of her eyes and a sob began to build in her throat. She never got upset, at least not when other people were around to see it, but the champagne must have compromised her emotions because she was on the verge of a meltdown and she couldn't do a single thing to stop it.

Not here, she begged. *Please not in front of all these people.*

"Anne, are you okay?" Sam was gazing down at her, his eyes so full of concern and compassion, it was almost too much.

She bit down hard on her lip and shook her head, and he seemed to know exactly what to do.

He swiftly whisked her off the dance floor, while she struggled to maintain her composure. "Where to?" he whispered, as they exited the ballroom, into a foyer full of people socializing and sipping drinks. She needed to be somewhere private, where no one would see the inevitable breakdown. A place where, when she finally pulled herself together, she could fix her makeup and return to the party as though nothing were out of the ordinary.

"My room," she managed.

"Upstairs?" he asked, and she nodded. She was biting her lip so hard now she tasted blood.

The staircase was roped off and two security officers stood guard, but as they approached one unhooked the rope to let them pass.

"Her Highness was kind enough to offer me a tour of the castle," Sam told them, which really wasn't necessary. Then she realized he'd said it not for the guards' sake, but for the guests who were watching them. She would have to remember to thank him. But the fact that he cared about her reputation, that he would be so kind as to help her avoid embarrassment, brought the tears even closer to the surface. They were halfway up to the second floor when her eyes started to leak rivers of warm tears down her cheeks, and when they reached her door and he ushered her inside, the floodgates burst.

She thought for sure he would leave her alone, but after she heard the door close Sam's arms went around her, pulling her tight against him. The idea that he cared enough to stay, when normally she felt so isolated in her grief, made her cry even harder.

Anne clung to him, sobbing her heart out against his chest, both mortified and desperately grateful that he was there.

"Let it out, Annie," he whispered, rubbing her back and stroking her hair. No one but Louisa had called her Annie, and it made her feel close to him somehow, which made no sense because she barely knew him. Still it felt as if they had shared something special. Something intimate.

As spontaneous and intense as the emotional outburst had been, it was surprisingly short-lived. As the sobs subsided, Sam handed her his handkerchief and she dabbed her eyes.

"She cries," he said, sounding amazed.

"Please don't tell anyone," she whispered against his jacket.

"They wouldn't believe me if I did."

Of course they wouldn't. She was the ice princess, *The Shrew*. She didn't have feelings. But the truth was she felt just as deeply as anyone else, she was just damned good at hiding it. But she didn't want to be the ice princess anymore. At least, not tonight. Tonight she wanted someone to know the woman underneath.

Sam cradled her face in his palms and gently tipped it up to his, wiping the last of her tears away with his thumbs. She gazed up into eyes as clear blue as the ocean, and she could swear she felt something shift deep inside her.

She wasn't sure if he made the first move, or she did, or they met halfway, but suddenly their lips were locked, and in that instant she had never wanted a man more than she wanted him.

Any man who accused Princess Anne of being cold and unfeeling had obviously never kissed her. She tasted sweet and salty, like champagne and tears, and she put her heart and soul, her entire being into it.

Though Sam wasn't quite sure who kissed whom first, he had the feeling he might have just unleashed some sort of wild animal. She clawed at his clothes, yanking his jacket off his shoulders and down his arms, tugging his bow tie loose. She fumbled with his belt, unfastened his pants, and before he could manage to catch his breath, slid her hand inside his boxers and wrapped it around him. Sam cursed under his breath, a word that under normal circumstances he would never dare utter in the presence of royalty, but he was having one hell of a tough time reconciling the princess he knew with the wild woman who was now walking backward toward her bed, unzipping her dress and letting it fall to the floor. She plucked a jewel-encrusted comb from her hair and he watched as it spilled down over her shoulders like black silk. She grinned wickedly, tempting him with eyes the color of the sky just before a storm—smoky gray and turbulent.

Though under normal circumstances he would find it juvenile and downright rude, when his mates dared Sam to ask Princess Anne, *The Shrew,* to dance, he'd had just enough champagne to take the bait. But never in a million years did he expect her to ask him first. Nor did he expect to find himself in her bedroom, Anne undressed to her black lace strapless bra and matching panties. And as she draped her long, lithe body across the mattress, summoning him closer with a crooked finger and a seductive smile, he guessed it wouldn't be long before she wore nothing at all.

"Take your clothes off," she demanded as she reached around behind her to unhook her bra. Her breasts were small and firm and he could hardly wait to get his hands on them, to taste them. He ripped his shirt off, losing a button or two in his haste, then stepped out of his pants, grabbing his wallet for later. That was when he realized the mistake he'd made and cursed again.

"What's wrong?" Anne asked.

"I don't have a condom."

"You don't?" she said, looking crestfallen.

He shook his head. It wasn't as if he came to these events expecting to shag, and even if he had, he would have anticipated taking the woman in question home, where he kept an entire box in his bedside table drawer.

"I've got it covered," Anne told him.

"You have a condom?"

"No, but I have it covered."

In other words, she was on birth control, but that wouldn't protect either of them from disease. But he knew he was clean, and it was a safe bet to assume she was, too. So why not? Besides, Anne was wearing a look that said she wouldn't be taking no for an answer.

He dropped the rest of his clothes in a pile and joined her. As she dragged him down onto the bed, ravaging his mouth with a deep, desperate kiss, rolling him onto his back and straddling him, he had the feeling this was a night he wouldn't soon forget.

They had barely gotten started and it was already the best sex he'd ever had.

Two

I've got it covered, Anne thought wryly as she dragged herself up from the bathroom floor, still weak and shaky, and propped herself against the vanity over the sink. What the bloody hell had she been thinking when she told Sam that? Had she not bothered to even consider the consequences? The repercussions of her actions?

Well, she was considering them now. And she had no one to blame but herself.

She rinsed her mouth and splashed cold water on her face and the wave of nausea began to pass. The family physician, whom she had sworn to total secrecy, had assured her that she'd feel better in her second trimester. But here she was in her fifteenth week, three weeks past that magical date, and she still felt like the walking dead.

But it was worth it, she thought, as she laid a hand over the tiny bump that had begun to form just below her navel.

It was hard to believe that at first, when she learned she was pregnant, she wasn't even sure that she wanted to keep it. Her initial plan had been to take an extended vacation somewhere remote and warm, live in exile until it was born, and then give it up for adoption. Then Chris's wife, Melissa, had given birth to their triplets and Anne cradled her tiny niece and nephews in her arms for the first time. Despite never having given much thought to having children—it had always seemed so far off in the future—in that instant she knew she wanted her baby. She wanted someone to love her unconditionally. Someone to depend on her.

She was going to have this baby and she was going to raise it herself. With support from her family, of course. Which she was sure she would get just as soon as she told them. So far only her twin sister, Louisa, knew. As for Sam, he obviously wanted nothing to do with her.

Their night together had been like a fantasy come to life. She'd heard her sister talk for years about destiny and finding one true love. And in fact, Louisa's dreams had come true at the ball—she was now married to her mystery man, Garrett Sutherland. But until Sam kissed Anne, until he made love to her so passionately, until, exhausted, they fell asleep in each other's arms, Anne hadn't truly believed in love. But now that she did, it would seem that Sam didn't share her feelings.

She had been sure that it had been as special for him as it had been for her, that they had connected on some deeply visceral level. Even when she had woken up alone and realized that at some time in the night he had slipped away without saying goodbye, she wouldn't let her hopes be dashed. She kept waiting to hear from him. For weeks she stayed close to the phone, willing it to ring, hoping to answer and hear his voice. But the call never came.

She shouldn't have been surprised, really. Sam was a politician, and everyone knew that politics and royalty did not mix well. Not if Sam wanted to be prime minister someday, and that was what she'd heard. By law, no member of the royal family was permitted to hold a position in government. Could she honestly blame him for choosing a career he had spent his entire life preparing for over her? That was why she had made the decision not to tell him about the baby. It was a complication that neither of them needed. And one she was quite sure he didn't want despite the scandal it would cause for her.

She could see the headlines now. *Princess Anne Pregnant with Secret Love Child.*

No matter how liberal the world had become in such matters, she was royalty and held to a higher standard. The stigma would follow her and, even worse, her child, for the rest of their lives. But at this point, she saw no other options.

Feeling half-human again, she decided she should get back to the dining room and try to choke down a few bites of dinner. Geoffrey, their butler, had just begun to serve the first course when her stomach lurched and she'd had to excuse herself and dash to the loo.

She gave one last furtive look in the mirror and decided that short of a total makeover, this was as good as it was going to get. She opened the door and almost collided with her brother Chris, who was leaning against the wall just outside.

Bloody hell.

His grim expression said that he had heard her retching, and he wanted to know what would cause her to be so ill.

"Let's have a talk," he said, jerking his head toward the study across the hall.

"But, supper…" she started to say, and he gave her that *look*.

"*Now,* Anne."

Since arguing would be a waste of time, she followed him. With their father in poor health, Chris was acting king, and technically the head of the family. She was duty-bound to follow his lead. And didn't she always do as she was told? Wouldn't everyone be surprised when they learned of her predicament.

She could lie and tell him that she had a flu bug, or a mild case of food poisoning, but at the rate her tummy was swelling, it wouldn't be long before it was impossible to hide anyway. But she wasn't sure if she was ready for the truth to come out just yet.

Or maybe he already knew. Had Louisa blabbed? Anne would kill her if that was the case.

Anne stepped into the study, and, shy of her mother, father and the triplets, the entire family was there!

Aaron and his wife, Liv, a botanical geneticist, sat on the couch looking worried. Louisa and her new husband, Garrett, stood across the room by the window. Louisa wore a pained expression and Garrett looked as though he wanted to be anywhere but there. Melissa, Chris's wife, stood just inside the door, looking anxious. Not five minutes ago they had all been in the dinning room eating supper.

Her first instinct was to turn and walk right back out, but Chris had already followed her in and shut the door.

What a nightmare.

"I don't suppose I have to tell you why I asked you here," he said.

Ordered was more like it. Now she was sorry she'd agreed.

"We're very concerned," Melissa said, walking over to stand beside Chris. "You haven't been yourself lately, Anne. For the last couple of months you've been pale and listless. Not to mention all the times you've dashed off to the loo."

So they didn't know. Louisa had kept her secret.

"It's obvious something is wrong," Aaron said. He normally wasn't one to butt into other people's business, so she knew he must have been genuinely concerned. Maybe waiting so long to tell everyone had been an error in judgment. She didn't honestly think that anyone really noticed the changes in her or for that matter cared about them.

"If you're ill—" Melissa began.

"I'm not ill," Anne assured her.

"An eating disorder is a disease," Chris said.

Anne turned to him, amused because Louisa had suspected the same thing at first. "Chris, if I were bulimic, I would be dashing off to the loo after supper, not before."

He didn't look as though he believed her. "I know something is wrong."

"It all depends on how you look at it, I guess."

"Look at what?" Melissa asked.

Just tell them, dummy. "I'm pregnant."

All through the room jaws dropped. Except Louisa's, of course.

"If this is some kind of joke, I'm not amused," Chris said.

"It's no joke."

"Of course!" Melissa said, as though the lightbulb had just flashed on. "I should have realized. I just never thought…"

"I would be careless enough to go out and get myself in trouble?" Anne asked.

"I…I wasn't even aware that you were seeing anyone," Aaron said.

"I'm not. It was a one-time encounter."

"Maybe this is a silly question," Chris said. "But are you sure? Have you taken a test? Seen the family physician?"

She lifted the hem of the cardigan she'd been wearing to hide the evidence and smoothed her dress down over her bump. "What do you think?"

Had his eyes not been fastened in they might have fallen out of his head. "Good God, how far along are you?"

"Fifteen weeks."

"You're *four* months pregnant and you never thought to mention it?"

"I planned to announce it when the time was right."

"When? After your water broke?" he snapped, and Melissa put a hand on his arm to calm him.

"There's no need to get snippy," Anne said.

Ironic coming from her, his look said, the princess of snip. Well, maybe she didn't want to be that way any longer. Maybe she was tired of always being on the defensive.

"This isn't like you, Anne," Chris said.

"It's not as if I went out and got knocked up on purpose, you know." Although he was right. She had been uncharacteristically irresponsible.

I've got it covered. Brilliant.

"This is going to be a nightmare when it hits the press," Melissa said. Being an illegitimate princess herself, she would certainly know. Until recently she'd lived in the U.S., unaware that she was heir to the throne of Morgan Isle.

"And what about the Gingerbread Man?" Louisa asked, speaking up for the first time. "I'm sure he'll use the opportunity to try to scare us."

The self-proclaimed Gingerbread Man was the extremely disturbed man who had been harassing the royal family for more than a year. He began by hacking their computer system and sending Anne and her siblings twisted and grisly versions of fairy tales, then he breached security on the palace grounds to leave an ominous note. Not long after, posing as housekeeping staff, he'd made it as far as the royal family's private waiting room at the hospital. Hours after he was gone, security found the chilling calling card he'd left behind. An envelope full of photographs of Anne and her siblings that the Gingerbread Man had taken in various places so they would know that he was there, watching.

He would sometimes be silent for months, yet every time they thought they had heard the last of him, he would reappear out of the blue. He sent a basket of rotten fruit for Christmas and an e-mail congratulating Chris and Melissa about the triplets before her pregnancy had even been formally announced.

His most recent stunt had been breaking into the florist the night before Aaron and Liv's wedding in March and spraying the flowers with something that had caused them to wilt just in time for the ceremony.

Anne was sure he would pull something when he learned of her pregnancy, but she refused to let him get to her. She wouldn't give him the satisfaction. "I don't care what the Gingerbread Man does," she said, lifting her chin in defiance. "Personally, I'm all for drawing him out into the open so he makes a mistake and gets caught."

"Which we have agreed not to do," Chris said sternly.

Aaron asked the next obvious question. "What about the father of the baby? Is he taking responsibility?"

"Like I said, it was a one-night thing."

Chris frowned. "He didn't offer to marry you?"

This was where it was going to get tricky. "No. Besides, he's not a royal."

"I don't give a damn who he is. He needs to take responsibility for his actions."

"Liv and Garrett aren't royals. And I'm only half-royal," Melissa added.

"It doesn't matter. He's out of the picture," Anne insisted.

"And that was his choice?" Aaron asked.

Anne bit her lip.

"Anne?" Chris asked, and when she remained silent he cursed under his breath. "He doesn't know, does he?"

"Trust me when I say, he's better off."

Melissa made a clucking noise, as though she were thoroughly disappointed in Anne.

"That is not your decision to make," Chris said. "I don't care who he is, he has a right to know he's going to have a child. To keep it from him is unconscionable."

She knew deep down that he was right. But she was feeling hurt and bitter and stubborn. If Sam didn't want her, why should he be allowed access to their child?

"Sam may be a politician, but he's a good man," Chris said.

Once again, mouths fell open in surprise, including her own. She hadn't told anyone the father's identity. Not even Louisa. "How did you—"

"Simple math. You don't honestly think Melissa and I could go through months of infertility treatments and a high-risk pregnancy without learning a thing or two about getting pregnant? Conception would have had to have occurred around the time of the charity ball. And do you really think that Sam's sneaking out in the middle of the night would go unnoticed?"

No, of course not. They were under a ridiculously tight lockdown these days. "You never said anything."

"What was I supposed to say? You're a grown woman. As long as you're discreet, who you sleep with is your business." He put both hands on her shoulders. "But now, you need to call him and set up a meeting."

"Why, so you can have a *talk* with him?"

"No. So *you* can. Because it's not only unfair to Sam, it's unfair to that baby you're carrying. He or she deserves the chance to know their father. If that's what Sam wants."

"He's right," Louisa said. "Put yourself in Sam's place."

"You should definitely tell him the truth," Aaron said.

She fiddled with the hem of her sweater, unable to meet Chris's eyes, knowing he was right. If not for Sam, then for the baby's sake. "I'm not sure what to say to him."

"Well," Melissa said. "I often find it's best to start with the truth."

Sam had just ended a call with the Secretary of State of DFID, or what the Brits called the Department for International Development, when his secretary, Grace, rang him.

"You have a visitor, sir."

A visitor? He didn't recall any appointments on the calendar for this afternoon. This was typically his time for any calls that needed to be made. Had Grace scheduled another appointment she'd forgotten to mention? Or maybe she had entered information incorrectly into the computer again.

He was sure at one time she had been an asset to his father's office, but now she was at least ten years past mandatory retirement.

"Do they have an appointment?" he asked her.

"No, sir, but—"

"Then I don't have time. I'll be happy to see them after they schedule an appointment." He hung up, wishing he could gently persuade his father to let her go, or at the very least assign her to someone else. But she had been with the office since the elder Baldwin was a young politician just starting out and he was as fiercely loyal to her as she was to him. Sam may have suspected some sort of indiscretion had it not been for the fact that she was fifteen years his father's senior, and they were both very happily married to other people.

There was a knock at his office door and Sam groaned inwardly, gathering every bit of his patience. Did Grace not understand the meaning of the word *no?* "What is it?" he snapped, probably a bit more harshly than she deserved.

The door opened, but it wasn't Grace standing there. It was Anne. *Princess* Anne, he reminded himself. Spending one night in her bed did not give him the privilege of dispensing with formalities.

"Your Highness," he said, rising from his chair and bowing properly, even though he couldn't help picturing her naked and poised atop him, her breasts firm and high, her face a mask of pleasure as she rode him until they were both blind with ecstasy. To say they'd slept together, that they'd had sex, was like calling the ocean a puddle. They had transcended every preconceived notion he'd ever had about being with a woman. It was a damned shame that they had no future.

He must have picked up the phone a dozen times to call her in the weeks following their night together, but before he could dial he'd been faced with a grim reality. No matter how he felt about her, how deeply they had connected, if he wanted to be prime minister, he simply could not have her.

He had accepted a long time ago that getting where he wanted would involve sacrifice. Yet never had it hit home so thoroughly as it did now.

"Is this a bad time?" she asked.

"No, of course not. Come in, please."

She stepped into his office and shut the door behind her. Though she was, on most occasions, coolly composed, today she seemed edgy and nervous, her eyes flitting randomly about his office. Looking everywhere, he noticed, but at him.

"I'm sorry to just barge in on you this way. But I was afraid that if I called you might refuse to see me."

"You're welcome anytime, Your Highness." He came around his desk and gestured to the settee and chair in the sitting area. "Please, have a seat. Can I get you a drink?"

"No, thank you. I'm fine." She sat primly on the edge of the settee, clutching her purse in her lap, and he took a seat in the chair. She looked thinner than when he'd last seen her, and her milky complexion had taken on a gray cast. Was she ill?

"Maybe just a glass of water?" he asked.

She shook her head, her lips folded firmly together, and he watched as her face went from gray to green before his eyes. Then her eyes went wide, and she asked in a panicked voice, "The loo?"

He pointed across the room. "Just through that—"

She was up off the settee, one hand clamped over her

mouth, dashing for the door before he could even finish his sentence. It might have been comedic had he not been so alarmed. He followed her and stood outside the door, cringing when he heard the sounds of her being ill. There was obviously something terribly wrong with her. But why come to him? They barely knew one another. On a personal level at any rate.

He heard a flush, then the sound of water running.

"Should I call someone for you?" he asked, then the door opened and Anne emerged looking pale and shaky.

"No, I'm fine. Just dreadfully embarrassed. I should have known better than to eat before I came here."

"Why don't you sit down." He reached out to help her but she waved him away.

"I can do it." She crossed the room on wobbly legs and re-staked her seat on the settee. Sam sat in the chair.

"Forgive me for being blunt, Your Highness, but are you ill?"

"Sam, we've been about as intimate as two people can be, so please call me Anne. And no, I'm not ill. Not in the way you might think."

"In what way, then?"

She took a deep breath and blew it out. "I'm pregnant."

"Pregnant?" he repeated, and she nodded. Well, he hadn't seen that coming. He'd barely been able to look at another woman without seeing Anne's face, but it would seem she'd had no trouble moving on. And what reason had he given her not to? Maybe that night hadn't been as fantastic for her as it was for him. It would explain why she had made no attempt to contact him afterward.

But if she was happy, he would be happy for her. "I hadn't heard. Congratulations."

She looked at him funny, then said, "I'm four months."

Four months? He counted back and realized that their night together had been almost exactly—

Sam's gut tightened.

"Yes, it's yours," she said.

He *really* hadn't seen *that* coming. "You're sure?"

She nodded. "There hasn't been anyone else. Not after, and not a long time before."

"I thought you said you had it covered."

"I guess nothing is one hundred percent guaranteed."

Apparently not.

"If you require a DNA test—"

"No," he said. "I trust your word." What reason did she have to lie?

They were going to have a baby. He and the princess. He was going to be a *father*.

He had always planned to have a family someday, but not until he was a bit more established in his career. And not until he met the right woman.

"You're probably wondering why I waited so long to tell you," she said.

Among other things. "Why did you?"

"I just…I didn't want to burden you with this. I didn't want you to feel…obligated. Which I realize now was totally unfair of me. And I apologize. I just want you to know that I don't expect anything from you. I'm fully prepared to raise this baby on my own. Whether or not you want to be a part of its life is your choice entirely."

What kind of man did she take him to be? "Let's get one thing perfectly clear," he told her. "This is my *child,* and I'm going to be a part of it's life."

"Of course," she said softly. "I wasn't sure. Some men—"

"I am *not* some men," he told her firmly. "I hope that won't be a problem for you or your family."

She shook her head. "No, of course not. I think it's wonderful. A child should have both its parents."

He leaned back in the chair, shaking his head. "I'm… *wow.* This is quite a surprise."

"I can relate, believe me. This was not the way I imagined starting a family."

"I suppose some sort of announcement will have to be made." He could just imagine what his friends would say. For weeks after the ball they had tried to bully him into explaining his and the princess's sudden absence from the party, but he'd refused to say a word. Now everyone would know. Not that he was embarrassed or ashamed of what he'd done. "You know that the press will be brutal."

"I know. When they learn you're the father and that we're not…together, they won't leave us alone."

If that was some sort of hint as to the future direction of their relationship, he hated to disappoint her, but he was not about to give up everything he had worked so hard for, his lifelong dream, for a one-night stand.

He cared for Anne, lusted after her even, but a marriage was absolutely out of the question.

Three

"The press will just have to get used to the idea of us being friends," Sam told her.

"I hope we can be, for the baby's sake."

"And your family? How do they feel about this?"

"So far only my siblings know. They were surprised, but very supportive. My father's health is particularly fragile right now, so we've decided to wait to tell him and my mother. I have to admit that *you're* taking this much better than I expected. I thought you would be angry."

"It was an accident. What right would I have to be angry? You didn't force me."

"Didn't I?"

He wouldn't deny that she had started it, and she had been quite...*aggressive*. But he had been a willing participant. "Anne, we share equal responsibility."

"Not all men would feel that way."

"Yes, well, I'm not all men."

There was a short period of awkward silence, so he asked, "Everything is okay? With the pregnancy, I mean. You and the baby are healthy?"

"Oh yes," she said, instinctively touching a hand to her belly. "Everything's fine. I'm right on schedule."

"Do you know the sex of the baby?"

"Not for another month, at my next ultrasound." She paused, then said, "You could go, too. If you'd like."

"I would. Are you showing yet?"

"I have a little bump. Want to see?" She surprised him by lifting up the hem of her top and showing him her bare tummy. But why would she be shy when he had seen a lot more than just her stomach?

Her tummy had indeed swelled and was quite prominent considering how thin she was. He wasn't sure what possessed him, but he asked, "Can I touch it?"

"Of course," she said, gesturing him over.

He moved to the settee beside her and she took his hand, laying it on her belly. She was warm and soft there, and the familiar scent of her skin seemed to eat up all of the breathable air. His hand was so large that his fingers spanned the top of her bump all the way down to the top edge of her panties.

Maybe this wasn't such a good idea. Knowing they couldn't be together didn't make him want her any less. And knowing that it was his baby growing inside her gave him an almost irrational desire to protect her, to claim her as his own.

And hadn't he felt the same way the night they had made love?

"Have you felt it move?"

"Flutters mostly. No actual kicks yet. But press right here," she said, pushing his fingers more firmly against her belly, until he hit something firm and unyielding. She looked up at him and smiled, her mouth inches from his own. "You feel it?"

Did he ever, and it took all of his restraint not to lean in and capture her lips. He breathed in the scent of her hair, her skin, longing to taste her again, to...*take* her. But a sexual relationship at this stage, with her all hormones and emotions, could spell disaster.

She seemed to sense what he was thinking, because color suddenly flooded her cheeks and he could see the flutter of her pulse at the base of her neck. Without realizing it, he had started to lean in, and her chin had begun to lift, like the pull of a magnet drawing them together. But thank goodness he came to his senses at the last second and turned away. He pulled his hand from her belly and rose to his feet. His heart was hammering and she'd gone from looking pale and shaky to flushed and feverish.

"This is not a good idea," he said.

"You're right," she agreed, nodding vigorously. "I wasn't thinking."

"It would be in our best interest to keep this relationship platonic. Otherwise things could get confusing."

"Very confusing."

"Which could be a challenge," he admitted. Total honesty at this point only seemed fair, as she had been forthcoming with him. "It's obvious that I'm quite attracted to you."

"There does seem to be some sort of…connection."

That was putting it mildly. It was taking every bit of restraint he could gather to stop himself from taking her, right there in his office. Pregnant or not, he wanted to strip her naked and ravish her, drive into her until she screamed with release. The way she had that night in her bedroom. He'd never been with a woman so responsive to his touch, so easy to please. He couldn't help wondering if her pregnancy had changed that. He'd often heard that it made women even more receptive to physical stimulation. And maybe it was true, because he could clearly see the firm peaks of her nipples through her clothes. Her breasts looked larger than they had been before, too. Rounder and fuller. What would she do if he took one in his mouth…?

He swallowed hard and looked away, turning toward his desk, so she might not notice how aroused he was becoming. "You mentioned an ultrasound. Do you know the time and date, so I can mark it on my calendar?"

She rattled off the information and he slid into his chair behind the safety of his desk and made himself a note.

"Maybe we could have dinner this Friday," she said, then added quickly, "A platonic dinner, of course. So we can discuss how we plan to handle things. Like the press and custody."

That would give him three days to think this through and process it all. He always preferred to have a solid and well-considered plan of action before he entered into negotiations of any kind.

However, he wasn't sure he was ready to be thrown

in the mix with her family just yet. Not that he didn't feel as though he could hold his own. He just felt these matters were private, between himself and Anne, and in no way concerned her family.

"How about we eat at my place," he said. "Seven o'clock?"

"If you don't mind your residence being swarmed with security. We're still on high alert."

He frowned. "Is the royal family still being harassed?"

"Unfortunately, yes."

All he knew of the situation was what he'd read in the papers. "So it's serious," he said.

"More than anyone realizes, I'm afraid. There have been threats of violence against the family. I should probably warn you that once we're linked together, you could become a target, as well."

He shrugged. "I'm not worried. As far as the baby goes, I'm assuming that until you've told your father, there will be no announcement to the press."

"Of course not."

"I do intend to tell my family, but they can be trusted to keep it quiet."

"Of course you should tell them. Do you think they'll be upset?"

Her look of vulnerability surprised him. He didn't think she was afraid of anything. Or cared what anyone thought of her. But hadn't he learned that night at the ball that she wasn't nearly as tough as she liked people to believe? "I think they'll be surprised, but happy," he told her.

He just hoped it was true.

* * *

Sam stopped in to see his parents that evening to break the news. When he arrived they had just finished supper and were relaxing out on the veranda with snifters of brandy, watching the sun set. Despite his father's career in politics, and his mother's touring as an operatic vocalist, they always made time for each other. After forty years they were still happily married and going strong.

That was the sort of marriage Sam had always imagined for himself. He had just never met a woman he could see himself spending the rest of his life with. Until Anne, he admitted grudgingly. How ironic that when he finally found her, he couldn't have her.

He wasn't quite sure how they would react to learning that they would be grandparents to the next prince or princess of Thomas Isle, but under the circumstances, they took it pretty well. Probably in part because they had been vying for grandchildren for some time and Sam's older brother, Adam, had yet to deliver.

"I'm sure I'm going to sound old-fashioned," his mother said, "but ideally we would like to see you married."

"Mother—"

"However," she continued. "We understand that you need to do what you feel is right."

"If I married Anne, I would be considered a royal and I would never be prime minister. That isn't a sacrifice I'm willing to make." Of course, with that in mind, he shouldn't have slept with her in the first place, should he? He suspected that was what his mother was thinking.

"You would be giving your child a name," his father pointed out.

"I don't need to be married to do that. He had my name the moment he was conceived."

"He?" his mother asked, brows raised.

"Or she."

"Will you find out?"

"I'd like to. And I think Anne would, too. She has an ultrasound in four weeks."

"Maybe I could invite her for tea," she suggested, and at Sam's wary look added, "I should be allowed to get to know the mother of my future grandchild."

She was right. And he was sure Anne would be happy to oblige her. Didn't pregnant women love to talk about their condition with other women? Especially the grandparents? "I'll mention it to her."

"You know that this is going to be complicated," his father said. "They think differently than we do."

"They?"

"Royals."

"Not so different as you might expect," Sam said. "Not Anne, anyway. She's actually quite down-to-earth."

"I've only spoken briefly with the princess," his mother said. "But she seemed lovely."

There was a "however" hanging there, and Sam knew exactly what she was thinking. What they were *both* thinking. He couldn't deny he'd thought the same thing before his night with Anne. "I know you've probably heard things about her. Unfavorable things. But she isn't at all what you would expect. She's intelligent and engaging." And fantastic in bed...

"It sounds as if you're quite taken with her," his mother not-so-subtly hinted.

He was. Probably too much for his own good. He just hoped that once Anne began to look more pregnant, and especially after the baby was born, it would be easier for him to see her only as the mother of his child and not a sexual being.

"I have every hope that Anne and I can be good friends, for the child's sake, but that is as far as it will ever go."

He knew they were disappointed. This wasn't the sort of scenario his parents had envisioned for him, and honestly neither had he. He had assumed that it would have been like it had been for them. He would meet a woman and they would date for a reasonable period of time, then marry and have a family. Sam would eventually become prime minister, and his wife would have a rewarding and lucrative career that still allowed her time to put her family first.

So much for that plan.

"As long as you're happy, we're happy," his mother said.

Sam hoped she really meant it. Even though they gave no indication that Sam was disappointing them, he couldn't help but feel that he'd let them down. That he had let *himself* down.

Even worse, was he letting his child down?

What had happened was an accident, but ultimately the person who would pay for it would be the baby. The baby would be the one relentlessly dogged by the press. And being a royal, the stigma of illegitimacy could potentially follow him or her for life. Was it fair to put the baby through that for his own selfish needs?

It was certainly something to consider.

He had just arrived home later that evening when he got a call on his cell phone from Prince Christian's assistant, with a message from the prince. It was odd enough that she would call at almost 10:00 p.m., but how had the prince gotten his private cell number? The prince's calls typically went through Sam's office line.

Silly question. As acting king, he probably had access to any phone number he wanted.

"His Royal Highness, Prince Christian, requests your presence in the royal family's private room at the Thomas Bay yacht club tomorrow at one-thirty," she said.

Oh did he? That was an odd setting for a business meeting. Unless it had nothing to do with business. "And the nature of this meeting?" he asked her.

"A private matter."

Well, so much for believing that this would stay between Sam and Anne. He should have anticipated this. Prince Christian probably considered it his obligation to watch his sister's back. That didn't mean Sam would let him intimidate or boss him around.

"Tell the prince that I would be happy to meet him at three."

There was a brief pause, as though the idea of some-one actually refusing an invitation from the prince was beyond her realm of comprehension. Finally she said, "Could you hold, please?"

"Of course."

She was off the line for several minutes, then came back on and said, "Three will be fine. The prince asks that you please keep this meeting to yourself, as it is a sensitive matter."

This suggested to Sam that Anne probably had no idea a meeting was being arranged and the prince preferred it to stay that way. He didn't doubt that the prince would try to persuade him to marry Anne. Truth be told, if Sam had a sister in a similar situation, he might do the same thing.

But this was the twenty-first century and people had children out of wedlock all the time. On occasion, even royalty. Prince Christian's wife, Princess Melissa of their sister country, Morgan Isle, was an illegitimate heir. In fact, with two illegitimate heirs, and a former king who reputedly lacked the ability or desire to keep his fly zipped, the royal family of Morgan Isle was positively brimming with scandal. By comparison the royal family of Thomas Isle were saints. Would a little scandal be so terrible?

But was it fair to the baby, who had no choice in the matter? Wasn't it a father's responsibility to protect his child?

But at what cost?

Sam slept fitfully that night and had trouble concentrating at work the next day. It was almost a relief to leave the office early, even though he doubted his meeting with the prince would be a pleasant exchange.

He arrived five minutes ahead of time, and the prince was already there, sitting in a leather armchair beside a bay of windows that overlooked the marina. He rose to greet Sam.

"Your Highness." Sam bowed his head then accepted Prince Christian's hand for a firm shake.

"I'm so glad you accepted my invitation," he said.

The Prince requests your presence sounded more like an order than an invitation. "I wasn't aware it was optional."

"I'm sorry if you were given that impression. I just thought it would be appropriate, in light of the situation, if we had a friendly chat."

Friendly? Sam doubted that.

The Prince gestured to the chair opposite him. "Please have a seat. Would you like a drink?"

A few too many glasses of champagne had gotten Sam into this mess. Had he been sober, he probably never would have approached the princess, much less danced with her. "Nothing for me, thanks."

They both sat.

"No disrespect intended, but if the *situation* you're referring to somehow involves my being the father of your sister's child, we have nothing to discuss, Your Highness."

His blunt statement seemed to surprise the prince. "Is that so?"

"It is."

"I'm afraid I disagree."

"This is between me and Anne."

"No one wishes that were the case more than I. Unfortunately, what Anne does affects our entire family. I had hoped you would do the right thing, but I understand that's not the case."

"Of course I'll do the right thing. But I'll do what *I* feel is the right thing."

"And may I ask what your idea of the right thing is?"

"As I said, that is between me and the mother of my child."

His expression darkened. He obviously didn't like that Sam wasn't falling into line. But Sam would be damned if he was going to let the prince, or any member of the royal family, walk all over him.

Prince Christian leaned forward slightly. "I won't see my sister's reputation, not to mention that of her child, decimated, because you couldn't keep out of her knickers."

What was that phrase the Americans used? It takes two to tango? "If blaming me for this situation makes you sleep better, I can live with that."

"You're being unreasonable."

"On the contrary, I'm being very reasonable. I'm considering your sister's privacy."

"This concerns more people than just you and Anne. You know that our father isn't well. A scandal like this is more than his heart could take."

So now not only was Sam decimating reputations, but he was essentially killing the king? "I'm sorry to hear that, but I'm still not talking to you."

"I could make your life unpleasant," Prince Christian said ominously. "If I feel that you're disrespecting my sister's name, I will lash out at you in any way I see fit."

So much for their *friendly* chat. He couldn't say he was surprised.

Sam shrugged. "Knock yourself out, Your Highness. I'm still not discussing my and Anne's private matters with you."

For a long moment Prince Christian just stared at him, and Sam braced himself for the fireworks. But instead of exploding with anger, the prince shook his head and laughed. "Christ, Baldwin, you've got a pair."

"I just don't respond well to threats or ultimatums."

"And I don't like giving them. But I have an obligation to look out for my family. The truth is, if it weren't for my father's fragile state, we wouldn't be having this conversation. He's in extremely poor health and it would make him very happy to see his oldest daughter married before she has a child."

He found what Prince Christian was doing utterly annoying, but in a way Sam actually felt sorry for him. "I'm truly sorry to hear that your father isn't well. I hold him in the highest regard."

"And I sympathize with your situation, Sam. I honestly do. It's common knowledge that you intend to follow in your father's footsteps and I believe you have the fortitude to pull it off. But marrying my sister would make that impossible. For what it's worth, you've built a reputation as one hell of a foreign affairs advisor. If there *were* a marriage, you would be offered a powerful and influential position within the monarchy."

After serving in, and being around, government for most of his life, the idea of taking a position with the monarchy was troubling to say the least. Not that they weren't on the same side when it came to serving the people of the country. But in Sam's eyes it had always been something of an "us against them" scenario.

Not to mention that, while he enjoyed foreign affairs, he had set his sights higher.

"Have you given any thought to how difficult it could be for your child, being illegitimate?"

"That's *all* I've been thinking about." And the more he thought about it, the more he came to realize that marrying Anne might be the wisest course of action. They may not have planned this pregnancy, but it had happened, and from now on he would have to put the welfare of his child above all else. Including his political ambitions.

"What's it like?" Sam asked. "Being a father?"

The prince smiled, his affection for his children undeniably clear. "It's exhilarating and terrifying and more rewarding than anything I've ever done. Ever *imagined*. I have these three perfect little human beings who are completely helpless and depend on me and their mother for everything they need to survive. It can be overwhelming."

"And if someone gave you a choice? Give up the throne or your children would live a life of disgrace and shame."

"No question. My children come first."

As it should be.

"You know that my wife was born out of wedlock," the prince said.

Sam nodded.

"She didn't find out that she was a royal until she was in her thirties, but it was *still* extremely difficult for her. To lay that on a child? As if life as a royal isn't tough enough already. Kids need stability, and consistency."

Things that would be much harder to give a child who

was being bounced back and forth between two parents, two households, all while being under the microscope of the press.

Sam had grown up in an ideal situation and had always hoped to provide the same for his own children. Didn't his child deserve that?

He had gone from flirting with the idea of marrying Anne to seriously considering it. And now, after talking to the prince, there seemed to be little question in his mind.

He could give it more thought, mull it around in his head for a while just to be sure, but he knew deep down the decision was already made.

He was going to marry the princess.

Four

Sam's home was not at all what Anne had expected.

She'd pictured a modern-style mansion or a seaside condo with every amenity a wealthy bachelor could want. Instead, as her driver pulled up the long gravel drive, what she got was a scene straight out of *Hansel and Gretel*.

Sam lived in a quaint cottage tucked deep in the forest and nestled under a canopy of towering pines and lazy oaks so dense only dappled sunshine dotted its sagging roof. It was quiet, and secluded, and utterly charming. Not to mention a security *nightmare*.

"Maybe we should have had dinner at the palace," she told her bodyguard, Gunter, who sat in the front seat beside her driver.

"Is no problem," he replied in a thick Russian accent. He checked his reflection in the side mirror, running a hand through his blond brush cut. Preening, she thought with a quiet smile. Physically Gunter bore a striking resemblance to Arnold Schwarzenegger in his early *Terminator* days, with a face that, Anne hated to admit, was far prettier than her own. Women swooned in his presence, never suspecting that a man so ridiculously masculine and tough lived with a cat called Toodles and a life partner named David. He had a killer fashion sense and was more intuitive than most women she knew. In fact, he had guessed that she might be pregnant before anyone in her family had even noticed. She had been in serious denial and Gunter showed up for duty with a pregnancy test.

"Is good you should know, yes?" he'd said, then he'd sat on her bed waiting while she took the test, then listened to her vent after it came back positive.

He was also ex-KGB and could snap a man's neck like a twig without breaking a sweat.

The car rolled to a stop and Gunter got out to open her door.

"I do sweep," he said, as he helped her out.

"He's the father of my child. Is that really necessary?"

Gunter just gave her one of those looks and she knew it wasn't even worth arguing. She blew out an exasperated breath for good measure and in her best annoyed tone said, *"Fine."*

The door to the cottage opened as they started up the walk and there stood Sam, looking too adorable for words, wearing dark blue slacks and a sky-blue button-up shirt with the sleeves rolled to the elbows.

He smiled, both dimples showing, and she caught herself hoping that the baby looked just like him.

Out of the corner of her eye she noticed Gunter's brows lift, almost imperceptibly, and she could swear she heard him say, *Nice,* under his breath.

Up until that instant she had only been a little nervous about seeing Sam, but suddenly her heart was going berserk in her chest and her hands were trembling.

"Hi," she said as she stepped up to the tiny, covered porch complete with a rickety rocking chair and a terra-cotta pot overflowing with yellow and purple petunias.

Sam leaned casually in the doorway, the sweet smile not budging an inch, taking in her taupe cotton skirt and yellow silk sleeveless blouse. It was the most cheerful outfit she could dredge up that still fit. Only lately had she realized just how dark and dreary her wardrobe had become over the past few years. She swore that when she got around to buying maternity clothes they would be in only bright and cheerful colors. She was turning over a new leaf so she could be someone her baby would respect and be proud of. The way she respected her own mother.

Sam's eyes traveled very unplatonically down her body then back up again, clearly liking what they saw. "You look beautiful."

"Thank you. You look nice, too." Talk about swooning. Being close to him did funny things to her head. Neurons misfired and wires crossed, creating total and utter chaos.

You're only here to talk about the baby, she reminded herself, *not to indulge your ridiculous crush.*

Beside her Gunter softly cleared his throat. Right. The sweep.

"Would you mind terribly if Gunter did a quick security check of the house?" Anne asked Sam.

It was the kind of request that might insult some people, but Sam just shrugged, gestured inside and said, "Have at it, Gunter."

Gunter pinned her with a look that said, *Don't move,* but she knew the drill.

"Wouldn't want to meet him in a dark alley," Sam said, after he disappeared inside. "Gunter. German, right?"

"On his mother's side, but he was raised in Moscow." Anne peered past him into the cottage. It was just as quaint and old-fashioned as the exterior, with older but comfortable-looking furniture and more knickknacks that even Gunter would deem appropriate for a man. And it smelled a little like…old people.

"Your house is lovely," she said. "Not at all what I expected."

"Needless to say, I'm exceedingly secure in my masculinity."

"I guess so."

He laughed. "I'm sorry but no man is that secure. The truth is, it's my grandmother's place."

Which explained the geriatric bouquet. "You live with her?"

"Only in spirit. She passed away three years ago."

"Oh, I'm so sorry."

"I'm just staying here temporarily. While my place is being worked on."

"You're remodeling?"

"You could say that, although not by choice. I've had a leak in the roof for a while, but when my bedroom and kitchen ceilings started to droop, I decided it was time to finally do something about it. But then I figured, since I would be gone anyway, it only made sense to update the kitchen while I was at it. So, three days' worth of work turned into more like three weeks." He gestured inside. "Can I give you the tour?"

"I can't, not until I get the all clear."

"Right," he said. "Just in case I have an assassin hiding under the davenport."

"I know, it's ridiculous."

His expression turned serious. "Not at all," he said, then he reached out and placed a hand over her baby bump. The gesture was so surprising, so unexpected, that her knees went weak. His eyes locked on hers, clear and intense, and his mouth was close. Too close. "Not if it keeps you and Sam Junior safe."

Hadn't they agreed that it would be prudent to keep a safe physical distance? That when they got too close they— Wait, what did he say? "Sam who?"

He grinned and gave her belly a gentle pat before he moved his hand away. "Sam Junior."

"So you think it's a boy?"

"That's the beauty of it. It works for a boy or a girl. Samuel or Samantha. Either way we call it Sam."

She folded her arms across her chest. "It would seem you have it all figured out."

He pinned his eyes on her, his gaze so intense she swore she could feel it straight through to her bones. "I'm a man who knows what he wants, Your Highness."

His eyes said he wanted her, but she knew he was

probably only teasing. But if Gunter hadn't reappeared at that very second, she might have melted into a puddle on the doorstep.

"Is all clear," Gunter said, stepping onto the porch and gesturing her in. As Sam closed the door, Anne knew that Gunter would stand on the porch, in a military stance, unmoving until it was time to leave.

"Ready for that tour?" Sam asked and she nodded. Although, honestly, there really wasn't that much to see. The front room had just enough space for a couch, glider and a rickety television stand with a TV that was probably older than her. The kitchen was small but functional, with appliances that dated back to the dark ages. But if the flame under the pot on the stove, and the hum of refrigerator, were any indication, they were both still working. The loo was also tiny, with an antique sink and commode and an antique claw-foot tub.

Next he took her into the bedrooms. The smaller of the two was being used as an office and the larger was where Sam slept. As they stood in the doorway, Anne couldn't help thinking that the last time they had been in a bedroom together they had both been out of their brains with lust for each other. It seemed like so long ago, yet she recalled every instant, every detail in Technicolor clarity.

"Sorry it's a bit of a mess," he said.

The bed was mussed and there were clothes piled over a chair in the corner. The entire house had something of a cluttered but cozy feel. And though the entire square footage was less that her sleeping chamber at the castle, she felt instantly at home there.

"I was under the impression your family had money,"

she said, feeling like a snob the instant the words were out. "I didn't mean that the way it sounded."

"That's okay," he said with a good-natured smile. "The money came from my grandfather's side. My grandmother grew up here. After her parents died, she and my grandfather would spend weekends here. After my grandfather died, she moved back permanently and stayed until she died."

"I can see why she moved back," she told him as they walked back to the kitchen. "It's really lovely."

"It's not exactly the castle."

"No, but it has loads of charm."

"And no space."

She shrugged. "It's cozy."

"And it desperately needs to be updated. Did you see that tub?"

She gazed around. "No, I wouldn't change a single thing."

He looked at her funny. "You're serious."

She smiled and nodded. She really liked it. "It's so... peaceful. The minute I walked in I felt completely at home." She could even picture herself spending time here, curled up on the couch reading a book or taking long walks through the woods. Although, until the Gingerbread Man was caught, that would never be allowed.

"I'm glad," he said, flashing her the sexy grin that made her knees go weak. "Would you like something to drink? I have soda and juice."

"Just water, please."

He got a bottle from the fridge and poured it into a

glass with a wedge of lime. As he handed it to her, their fingertips touched.

"Something smells delicious," she said.

"Chicken soup. My grandmother's recipe."

Not your typical summer food, but that was okay. "I didn't know you could cook."

He grinned and wiggled his brows. "I am a man of many talents, Your Highness."

Oh, did she know it. Although under the circumstances many of those talents were best not contemplated. "What else can you make?"

"Let's see," he said, counting off on his fingers. "I can make coffee. And toast. I can heat a pizza. Oh, and I make a mean tray of ice cubes. And did I mention the toast?"

She smiled. "So in other words, you eat out a lot?"

"Constantly. But I wanted to impress you and I figured the soup might be good since you haven't been feeling well."

It was sweet of him to consider her temperamental stomach. He was so considerate and…nice. And oh, how she wished things could be different, that they could at least try to make a go of it, try to be a family. She wanted it so much her chest ached. It was all she had been able to think about since their talk in his office the other day. He was, by definition, the man of her dreams.

But some things just weren't meant to be.

"I think maybe it was stress making me feel sick," she said. "Since I told you about the baby, I've felt much better. I'll get nauseous occasionally, but no more running to the loo. I've even gained a few pounds, which I know will make my physician happy."

"That's great." He lifted the lid off the pot of soup and gave it a stir with a wooden spoon. "The soup is ready. But would you prefer to talk first and get it out of the way? So we can relax and enjoy dinner."

"I think that would be a good idea."

He gestured to the front room. "Shall we sit on the sofa?"

She nodded and took a seat, and he sat beside her, so close that his thigh was touching hers. Was this his idea of platonic?

He had given no indication that he would be difficult, or make unreasonable demands when it came to the baby, but she still wasn't sure what to expect. Sam, in contrast, sat beside her looking completely at ease. Did the man never get his feathers ruffled? When she had fallen apart at the ball he had snapped into action and rescued her from imminent public humiliation. When she told him about the baby he had been calm and rational and even sympathetic. She had never seen, or even heard of him ever losing his temper.

She, on the other hand, always seemed to be irritated and cranky about one thing or another. She could learn a lot from Sam. Although, if he knew the truth, if he knew that this little "accident" could have easily been prevented, he might not be so understanding. She would just have to be sure that he never found out.

"Before we get started," she said, "I just want to tell you again that I appreciate how well you've taken all this. I know things could potentially get complicated at some point, with custody and financial issues, and even different parenting styles. I just want you to know that I'm going to try my best to keep things civilized. I know I don't have a reputation for being the most reasonable woman, but I'm going to try really hard."

Sam's expression was serious. "Suppose I thought of a way to make things exponentially easier on both of us. On all three of us, actually."

She couldn't imagine how, but she shrugged and said, "I'm all for easy."

"I think you should marry me."

He said it so calmly, so matter-of-factly, that the meaning of his words took several seconds to sink in. Then she was sure that she must have heard him wrong, or he was playing some cruel joke. That any second he was going to laugh and say, "Gotcha!"

"I know it's fast," he said instead. "I mean, we barely know each other. But, for the baby's sake, I really think it's the logical next move."

My God, he was *serious*. He wanted to marry her. How was that even possible when only a few days ago it supposedly hadn't been an option?

"But…you want to be prime minister."

"Yes, but that isn't what's best for the baby. I'm going to be a father. From now on, I have to put his or her best interests first."

She had a sudden, unsettling thought. "My family isn't making you do this, are they? Did they threaten you?"

"This has nothing to do with your family." He took her hand and held it between his two. "This is what I want, Annie. What I think is best for everyone. We have to at least try, for the baby's sake."

She was thrilled to the center of her being…and drowning in a churning sea of guilt. If she had just acted responsibly, if she hadn't lied about being protected, they wouldn't be in this situation. He wouldn't be forced to give up everything that he had worked so hard for.

What if it was a decision he regretted someday and he grew to resent her and the baby? But what if he didn't? What if they fell in love and lived a long and happy life together?

She folded her other hand over his two. "Sam, are you *sure* about this? Because once we're married, that's it. A divorce can only be granted with the consent of the king."

"Let's try this another way," he said, then he dropped down on one knee in front of her and produced a diamond ring from his pants pocket.

She could hardly believe that this was really happening. It was a real, honest-to-goodness proposal.

He took her hand, looked deep in her eyes. "Will you marry me, Annie?"

There was only one answer she could give him. "Of course I'll marry you, Sam."

Grinning, he slid the ring on her finger. It was fashioned from white gold with a round cut diamond deeply set and surrounded by smaller stones. Despite its shine it was clearly an antique, not to mention exquisitely beautiful.

"Oh, Sam, it's amazing."

"It was my great-grandmother's," he said.

"We must have the same size finger," she said, turning her hand to watch it sparkle. "It's a perfect fit."

"I had it sized."

"But how did you know what size to make it?"

"Princess Louisa."

"You asked my sister?"

"Is that okay?"

"Of course. I just can't believe she didn't say anything. She's horrible at keeping secrets."

"I guess she wanted our moment to be special."

"It is." She threw her arms around his neck and hugged him and he hugged her back just as hard. It felt so good to hold him, to be close to him. It felt like… coming home. And she realized, she was truly happy. The happiest she had been in a long, *long* time. Maybe ever.

It was astonishing how, out of such a complicated situation, something so fantastic could arise. Ideally, he would have slipped sentiments of love somewhere between the rationale, but she was sure that would come later. Not that she believed it would be all smooth sailing. She knew that marriages took work and this one would be no exception. But they seemed to be off to a fairly good start under the circumstances.

"I know he's not well, but if at all possible, I'd like to be there when you tell the king and queen," Sam said. "I'd like to do this by the book and have the chance to ask for your hand."

His words made her practically burst with joy, because he would be giving her father something he had always looked forward to. "We'll go to them tomorrow," she said, already excited at the prospect, because she knew that her parents would be thrilled for her. Even if Sam was a politician. And they would be so excited about the baby.

"Needless to say, we should have the wedding soon," he said. "I was thinking next week."

That was really soon, but he was right. The sooner the better. It would have to be a small ceremony, if for no other reason than her father's health. It was the reason Louisa had kept her own wedding small and intimate, despite having always dreamed of a huge, traditional affair.

Not one to like being in the spotlight, Anne would be quite content with small and simple. That didn't mean there weren't a million things to do to prepare.

Her mind was suddenly flooded with all the plans they had to make and the short amount of time they had to make them. Where would they have the ceremony and who would they invite? And would the king be well enough to walk her down the aisle? And what about a honeymoon? Where would they—

That thought brought her mind to a screeching halt.

What about the honeymoon? And even more important, the *wedding night?*

Suddenly she was ultra-aware of Sam's arms around her, his body pressed against hers. The heat of his palms on her back and the spicy scent of his aftershave.

Suddenly her heart was beating so hard and fast she was sure Sam must have felt it through her clothes and skin. And all she could think about was getting him naked again. Touching him and kissing him all over. He must have been able to read her mind, because his breath hitched and his arms tightened around her.

"So, I guess this means that we don't have to keep our relationship platonic any longer," she said.

"Funny," he said. "But I was just thinking the exact same thing."

Thank God. Because frankly, a marriage without sex would be bloody awful.

She turned her face into the crook of his neck and kissed the side of his throat, could feel the heavy thump-thump of his pulse against her lips, and knew that he was just as aroused as she was. "We could make love right now if we wanted to."

"We could," he agreed, groaning when she nipped him with her teeth. She felt as though she wanted to eat him alive. Swallow him whole. She lifted her head, and the second she did he captured her lips with his own, but instead of the slick, ravenous kiss she was expecting, *hoping* for even, his lips rubbed softly, almost sweetly over hers. He kissed her chin and her throat, working his way down.

"Take me into your bedroom," she urged, sliding her hands up to tangle in the curls at his nape, feeling so hot she could burst into flames. "Right now."

"God knows I want you," he said, brushing his lips over her collarbone. "I've wanted you since that night. It's all I've been able to think about."

"You can have me. Right now."

He trailed his way back up to her mouth and whispered against her lips, "Or we could wait until we're married."

She groaned her disappointment. She wasn't even sure she *could* wait. "I feel as though I might go out of my mind if I can't have you right now."

"All the more reason to wait," he said, sounding far

too rational. "Think of how special it would be on our wedding night."

She opened her eyes to look at him and smiled. "Isn't that supposed to be *my* line?"

He grinned. "Poke fun all you want, but you know I'm right."

Yes, he was right. Not that anything about their relationship up to this point could be called conventional. She might have worried that he just didn't want her, and was trying to let her down gently, but the tent in his pants and the color in his cheeks said he was just as aroused as she was.

"Is that really what you want?"

He took her hands from around his neck and held them, his expression earnest. "I think we should wait."

It was clear that this wasn't an easy decision for him to make, and if she pushed the issue he would probably cave and make passionate love to her all night long. She didn't really understand why this was so important to him, but it clearly was. Besides, what was a few more days?

She would respect his wishes and wait for her wedding night, she decided grudgingly. But that didn't mean she had to like it.

Five

Anne was barely home for five minutes that evening when Louisa knocked on her bedroom door. It was nearly eleven—well past Louisa and Garrett's usual bedtime. Garrett had taken over management of all the royal family's vast farmlands so their brother Aaron could go to medical school, so he rose well before sunrise every morning. Not to mention that Louisa and Garrett were still newlyweds. They were constantly holding hands and touching. Sharing secret smiles and longing glances, as though they couldn't wait to be alone.

Anne would even admit to being jealous a time or two. But soon it would be her turn.

"You're up late," Anne said, pretending she had no idea why Louisa was so eager to speak to her, keeping her hand casually behind her, so she wouldn't see the ring.

"I just wondered how your date went," Louisa said, stepping into the room and closing the door behind her.

"Technically it wasn't a date," Anne said, walking to the bed and sitting down with her hands under her thighs. "We just had things to discuss."

Louisa sat beside her. "What did you talk about?"

"The baby mostly."

"That's it?" Louisa hedged.

"Pretty much," she said, then added casually, "Oh, and he asked me to marry him."

Louisa squealed so loudly Anne was sure the entire castle heard her. "Oh my God! Congratulations! What did you say?"

She shrugged. "I told him I would think about it."

Louisa gasped in horror, looking as though she wanted to throttle her. "You didn't!"

"Of course not." She grinned and pulled her hand from under her leg, flashing Louisa the ring. "I said yes."

Louisa threw her arms around Anne and hugged her. "I am so happy for you, Annie. You and Sam are going to be perfect together."

"I really hope so," Anne said.

Louisa held her at arm's length. "You will. If you believe it, it'll happen."

She wished that were true, that it were that easy. "I just keep thinking about you and Aaron and Chris. You all found the perfect person for you—you're all so happy."

"And you will be, too."

"It just seems as though every family has at least

one person who goes through life always ruining relationships. What if I'm that person? I've always been so negative. What if I don't deserve to be happy?"

"After all we've been through with our father, don't you think we *all* deserve some happiness? Besides, nothing is predetermined. Your life is what you make of it."

"That's what I'm worried about. Up until now, I've made a mess of it. Especially my love life."

"That was just bad luck. You just happened to meet a string of jerks. But anyone who knows Sam will tell you he's a great guy. And he'll be a fantastic husband and father."

Anne didn't doubt that at all. She never would have accepted his proposal otherwise. It was herself she was worried about. For the first time in her life she had a real shot at happiness—and she was terrified that she would find a way to screw it up.

"I'm sure you're right," she told Louisa.

"Of course I am," she said, as if there was never a doubt. Her relentless optimism never ceased to amaze Anne.

After Louisa went back to her room, Anne changed into her softest pajamas and crawled into bed, but her mind was still moving a million miles an hour and she was practically bursting with excitement. Thinking that a cup of tea might soothe her nerves, she climbed out of bed and put on her robe. The halls of the castle were silent but for the muffled wail of a baby crying from Chris and Melissa's room. Five months from now Anne could look forward to the same. She *and* Sam, she reminded herself with a smile.

She expected the kitchen to be empty and was surprised, when she switched on the light, to find their butler, Geoffrey, sitting at the butcher-block table. He squinted at the sudden bright light.

"I'm sorry," Anne said. "I didn't mean to startle you."

"No need to apologize," he said. His jacket was draped over the back of his chair and his tie hung loose around his neck. In front of him sat a bottle of scotch and a half-full highball glass. "What brings you down here at this late hour, Your Highness?"

"Couldn't sleep. I thought I would make some tea."

"You should have called down," he scolded. "I'd have brought it to you."

"I didn't want to bother you."

He rose and gestured to an empty chair. "Sit. I'll make it for you."

Because this was Geoffrey's domain, and he could be a little territorial, she did as he asked. She gestured to his drink and said, "Rough day?"

"Worse than some, better than others." He put the kettle on to boil. "How about you?"

"Actually, I had a very good day."

He pulled a cup down from the cupboard and dropped a tea bag in. "Would that have something to do with a certain young man and that ring on your finger?"

"It might." She should have realized he would notice the ring. Geoffrey didn't miss a thing. He may have been getting up in years, but he was still sharp as a tack. He had been with the family since before she was born and in some ways she had come to think of him as a second father. As far as she knew he had no family of his own, no one to care for him if he ever became incapacitated. But after so many years of loyal service, he would always have a place at the castle with the royal family.

"I suppose you heard about the baby."

"I might have," he said cryptically, but knowing him, he'd probably suspected all along.

"Are you disappointed in me?"

"If you had murdered someone, I would have been disappointed in you. A child is a blessing."

"Yes, but I know you have...*traditional* values."

He poured boiling water into her cup then set it on the table in front of her. "Then I suppose you'll be surprised to learn that I was once in a similar situation."

Surprised? For a moment she was too stunned to even respond. She never knew him to have a girlfriend, much less a pregnant one. He'd never spoken of any family. "I—I had no idea."

He sat across from her. "It was many years ago. Before I came to work here."

"You have a child?"

He nodded. "His name is Richard."

"Why didn't you ever say anything?"

He shrugged, swirling the amber liquid in his glass. "It isn't something I like to talk about."

"Do you see him?"

He shook his head, looking remorseful. "Not for many years."

"What happened?"

He downed the last of his drink then poured himself another. She wondered if the alcohol was responsible for his sudden loose tongue. He looked so sad. And when had he gotten so old? It was as though the lines on his face had appeared overnight. Or maybe she just hadn't wanted to see them.

"His mother was a cook for my previous employer," he told her. "We had an affair and she became pregnant. I did the responsible thing and married her, but it didn't take long to realize that we were completely incompatible. We stayed together for two years, then finally divorced. But working together was unpleasant for both of us, so we decided it would be best if I left and found a new job. That was when I came to work here."

"When did you stop seeing your son?"

"When he was six his mother remarried. At first I was jealous, but this man was good to Richard. He treated him like his own son. A year later he was offered a position in England. I objected at first, but my ex pointed out what was obvious. I didn't have time for my son and his stepfather did. She convinced me that it would be best if I let him go."

"That must have been devastating for you."

"It was the hardest thing I've ever done. I tried to keep in touch with phone calls and letters, but we drifted apart. I think he just didn't need me any longer."

He looked so sad that tears burned the corners of Anne's eyes. She reached out and placed a hand on top of his. Learning this was such a shock. Had she never considered that he had a life that she knew nothing about? Had she believed his life hadn't really begun until he'd come to work for them? That his world was so small and insignificant? "I'm so sorry, Geoffrey."

Even his eyes looked a bit misty. "I was saddened,

but by then I had you and your siblings to chase around. Only now I fear I made a terrible mistake by letting him go."

He looked so sad it made her want to hug him. "You did what you thought was best. And that doesn't mean you can't try to contact him now. Do you have any idea where he lives? What he does for a living?"

"The last time I talked to his mother, he was serving as a Royal Marine Commando."

"Goodness! That's impressive."

"She bragged that he was some sort of computer genius. But that was more than ten years ago."

"You could at least try to look him up."

He rubbed his thumb around the rim of his glass. "What if I do, and I don't like what I find?"

She wondered why he would think a thing like that. He should at least try to find him.

Geoffrey swallowed the last of his drink and looked at his watch. "It's nearly midnight. I should turn in. And so should you, young lady."

She smiled. He hadn't called her that in years. "Yes, sir."

As he walked past her to his quarters behind the kitchen he patted her shoulder. She was struck by how his capable hands were beginning to look wrinkled and bony.

She looked down and realized she hadn't taken a single sip of her tea, and now it had gone cold.

The king had been out of the public eye for such a long period of time that Sam was genuinely stunned when he saw him the following afternoon. Though he knew the king was in ill health, never had he expected him to look so pale and fragile. Practically swimming in too-large flannel pajamas and a bulky robe—that Sam was sure had probably fit him at one time—the king looked painfully thin and small. A mere shell of the larger-than-life figure he used to be. And it was obvious that the months of sitting at his side had visibly taken their toll on Anne's mother. The queen looked utterly exhausted and beaten down. Her features, once bright and youthful, now looked drawn and tired, as though she had aged a decade in only months.

But the grief they suffered did nothing to dampen their joy when Sam announced his intention to marry Anne and asked them for her hand. Though the king may have been physically fragile, when it came to his mental faculties, he was clearly all there. "I had hoped you would do the right thing, Sam," the king told him. "For my grandchild's sake."

"Of course you'll want to have the wedding soon," the queen told Anne. "Before you're really showing."

For a moment Sam felt slighted, since they had agreed to tell her parents together, then he glanced over at Anne, saw her stunned expression, and realized that she hadn't said a word.

So much for the news being too much for the king's heart to take, Sam thought wryly. His children obviously underestimated him.

"I'm going to kill Louisa!" Anne growled, looking as though she would do just that. "Or was it Chris who snitched?"

Sam folded his arms across his chest and casually covered his mouth to hide a grin. So this was the feisty side of Anne he had heard so much about. He kind of liked it.

"No one said a word," the queen assured her. "They didn't have to. I know my daughter."

"And though I may be an invalid," the king added, shooting a meaningful look Sam's way, "I stay well-informed as to what goes on in my castle."

Things like Sam sneaking out of his daughter's bedroom in the wee hours of the morning.

The king chuckled weakly. "Don't look so chastened. I was a young man once, too, you know." He looked over at his wife and smiled. "And there was a time when I did my fair share of sneaking around."

The queen reached over and took his hand and they shared a smile. It was clear that despite all they had been through, or maybe because of it, they were still deeply in love. Sam hoped that someday it would be like that for him and Anne.

"Why didn't you say anything?" Anne asked, looking genuinely distressed.

"Sweetheart," her mother said. "You've always been one to take your time and work things through. I assumed that when you were ready for us to know, you would tell us. And if you needed my guidance, you would have asked for it."

"You're not upset?" Anne asked, looking a bit like a naughty child who feared a sound lashing for misbehaving.

"Are you happy?" the king asked her.

She looked over at Sam and smiled. "I am. Very happy."

"Then what do I have to be upset about?"

"Well, the baby—"

"Is a blessing," the queen said.

Their casual attitude toward the situation surprised Sam, but then, after all they had been through, and knowing the king was living on borrowed time, what point would there be to make a huge fuss and create hard feelings?

Sam had always respected the king, but never so much as he did now. And despite what his father believed about them thinking *differently,* they seemed to be exceptionally well grounded in reality.

"I assume that you intend to live here, at the castle," the king said.

Anne glanced nervously his way. Where they would live hadn't yet come up, but Sam knew what was expected. "Of course, Your Highness."

"And of course you will work for the royal family."

Sam nodded. "I would be honored."

"Have you thought about what colors you would like for your wedding?" the queen asked Anne.

"Yellow, I think," Anne said, and she and her mother drifted off to discuss wedding plans while Sam spoke to the king about his future position in the monarchy. He assured Sam that his talents would not be wasted, nor would they go unrewarded. Sam's inheritance guaranteed him a financially sound future, so salary wasn't an issue, but he was happy to know they valued his service. And relieved that under the circumstances, this entire situation was running as smoothly as a well-oiled machine.

So well that, were he not such a positive thinker, he might be waiting for the other shoe to fall.

* * *

The following Friday, with only the royal family, Sam's parents and a few close friends in attendance, Sam and Anne were wed in a small, private ceremony in the garden on the palace grounds. The weather couldn't have been more ideal. Sunny and clear with a temperature in the low seventies.

Louisa was the matron of honor and Sam's older brother, Adam, flew in from England to be his best man. A musician and composer, Adam couldn't have been less interested in politics, yet the artist in him understood Sam's lifelong passion, and his desire to follow in their father's footsteps.

"You're sure you want to do this?" he asked Sam just before the ceremony was about to begin. "If you're doing this to salvage the princess's reputation—"

"I'm doing this because my child deserves to have parents who are married."

"A one-night fling does not make for a lasting relationship, Sam. You barely know her. If the royal family is forcing you into this—"

"This is my choice, and mine alone."

Adam shook his head, as though Sam were a lost cause. Then he grinned and said, "My baby brother, a *duke*. Who would have thought?"

Sam appreciated his brother's concern, that after all these years Adam was still looking out for him. But Sam had already put the political chapter of his life behind him. He'd spent the last two days cleaning out his office at work since, as of that morning, he had been given the official title of duke and by law could no longer serve in government. His secretary, Grace, had tearfully said goodbye, telling him what an exceptional boss he'd been and how she would miss him. She said she was proud of him.

"I know I haven't been the most efficient secretary and I appreciate your patience with me."

Of course he felt guilty as hell for all the times he'd gotten frustrated and snapped at her or regarded her impatiently.

After he and Anne returned from their honeymoon Sam would take up his new position with the monarchy. He couldn't say he was thrilled by the prospect, but he was trying to keep an open mind and a positive attitude. At least they didn't try to force him into their agricultural business. A farmer, he was not. He didn't know the first thing about managing farmland and raising crops. Nor did he have any inclination to learn.

His new goal was to surpass his new position as foreign affairs director and when Chris officially became king, become his right hand.

The music began, and Sam looked up to see Anne and her father taking their places. She wore a crème-colored floor-length dress with layers of soft silk ruffles. But even that did little to disguise the fact that she was pregnant. Not that everyone there didn't already know. He would swear that since she had come to see him last week her tummy had nearly doubled in size. But as far as he was concerned it only made her look more ravishing.

Her hair was piled up on her head in loose curls with soft wisps trailing down to frame her face. And of course she wore a jewel-encrusted tiara.

Everyone stood to receive her, and Sam watched,

mesmerized as she walked slowly toward him, looking radiant. She seemed to glow from the inside out with happiness.

It was obvious, the way the king clung to her arm as he walked her down the short path, that it was taking every bit of strength he could muster to make the short trip. But he did it with grace and dignity.

Here we go, Sam thought, as the king linked his and Anne's hands together. It was the end of life as he once knew it. But as they spoke their vows and exchanged rings, instead of feeling cornered or trapped, he felt a deep sense of calm. He took that as a sign that he truly was doing the right thing. Maybe not just for their child, but for the two of them, as well.

Following the ceremony, drinks and hors d'oeuvres were served under a tent on the castle grounds. After a bit of mingling, Sam stood by the bar, watching his new wife. She was chatting with his brother and Adam seemed quite taken with her. Under the circumstances Sam might have expected some tension between their families, but everyone seemed to get along just fine. Almost *too* well.

Price Christian stepped up to the bar to get a drink, and told Sam, "Nice wedding."

Sam nodded. "It was."

He got his drink then turned to stand beside Sam. "I've never seen my sister so happy."

She did look happy. And Sam was glad that his family had the chance to see this side of her, the one so unlike what they had read in the press and heard about through the rumor mill. He liked to think of this Anne as *his*

Anne, the real woman inside, whom he had rescued from an existence of negativity and despair.

They had done a lot of talking this week in preparation for their wedding and she'd opened up about some of the past men in her life. The ones who had used and betrayed her. After all she had been through, it was a wonder she hadn't lost her ability to trust entirely.

She saw him watching her and flashed him a smile.

"Your sister deserves to be happy," Sam told the prince.

"I think so, too." Then he added with a wry grin, "And if you ever do hurt her, I'll have to hurt you back."

Sam was quite sure, despite the prince's smile, it was said only partly in jest. "I'll keep that in mind, Your Highness."

From across the tent a baby's cry split the quiet murmur of conversation and they both turned to see Princess Melissa wrestling with two squirming bundles.

"I guess that's my cue," the prince said. He started to walk away, then stopped and said, "By the way, since we're family now, you can drop the 'Your Highness' thing and just call me Chris."

"After all these years of addressing you formally, that might take some getting used to."

"Tell me about it," Chris said with a grin before he walked off to rescue his wife.

Sam felt a hand on his arm and turned to see Anne standing there.

She slipped her arm through his and tucked herself

close to his side and said excitedly, "Can you believe it, Sam? We're *married*."

"Strange, isn't it?"

"Do you think it's odd that I'm so happy?"

"Not at all." He leaned down to brush a kiss across her lips. "I would be worried if you weren't."

"How soon do you think we can sneak out of here? I'm guessing that we could squeeze in some alone time before we leave for our honeymoon."

He was about to say, *as soon as possible,* when an explosion pierced his ears and shook the ground beneath his feet. Startled cries from the guests followed and Anne screeched in surprise. Sam instinctively shielded her with his body and looked in the direction of the sound as a ball of fire and smoke billowed up from the north side of the castle. At first he could hardly believe what he was seeing—his first instinct was to get Anne somewhere safe as quickly as possible—but before he had an instant to act, the entire area was crawling with security.

"What the bloody hell is going on?" Anne demanded, shoving past him to see, and when she saw the flames and smoke darkening the clear blue afternoon sky, the color drained from her face.

Security was already rounding everyone up and guiding them in the opposite direction, away from the blast.

"It's him," Anne said, looking more angry than afraid, watching as acrid smoke began to blow in their direction. "The Gingerbread Man did this."

Threatening e-mails and occasional pranks were an

annoyance, but this was a serious escalation. He was obviously out of control. If it was even him. "For all we know it could be an accident," he told her.

"No," she said firmly. "It's him. And this time he's gone too far."

Six

As Anne had suspected, the explosion had been deliberate.

The device had been hidden in the undercarriage of a car that belonged to Sam's aunt and uncle. The police bomb squad still had investigating to do, but as far as they could tell, the bomb had been detonated remotely.

Four other cars had been damaged in the blast and the castle garage had taken a serious hit. Four of the five doors would need to be replaced and the facade would require repair. Thankfully, no people had been seriously hurt. He'd had the decency to do it when there weren't a lot of people close by. Or maybe that had just been dumb luck. A few maintenance people walked away with mild abrasions and first-degree burns, but it could have been so much worse.

Sam's poor aunt and uncle, whose car had been sabotaged, were beside themselves with guilt. They felt responsible, even though Anne and her siblings assured them repeatedly that they were in no way being blamed. There was only one person responsible for this.

The Gingerbread Man.

They knew this for a fact now because shortly after the explosion he'd sent an e-mail to Anne via the security office.

Sorry I couldn't make it to your wedding.
Heard it was a blast.

"This has got to stop!" she told Chris, who sat slumped in a chair in the study, nursing a scotch. The wedding guests had all been driven home in the royal fleet—since their own cars had been casualties of the explosion—and most of the family had gone up to bed. Only she, Sam and Chris stayed behind to talk. Or in her case, castigate. She was so filled with nervous energy she hadn't stopped pacing, hadn't stopped moving in hours. "Someone could have been seriously hurt. Someone could have *died!*"

"You think I don't know that?" Chris said, looking exhausted. "We're doing all that we can. What else would you have me do?"

"You know what I think we should do," she said, and his expression went dark.

"That is *not* an option."

"What's not an option?" Sam asked from his seat on the settee. He had been so understanding about this, considering his wedding day had literally gone up in smoke. But she had warned him that being with her could potentially suck him into this mess. And so it had. She shuddered to think what would have happened if the Gingerbread Man had waited until the guests were leaving to sink the plunger. She was sure Sam had considered the same possibilities.

"She wants us to try to draw him out so we can catch him," Chris said.

"Draw him out *how?*"

"I assume by using one of us as bait."

Sam turned to look at her. "You're not serious."

"Maybe I trust our security team to do their job. Besides, no one else has had a better idea. How long are we supposed to go on like this? Living like prisoners, in fear of what he'll do next. He's obviously escalating the violence."

"Obviously," Chris snapped. He rarely lost his cool, so Anne knew that he was much more upset about this than he was letting on. "And now we know what he's capable of. He's not just some twisted stalker. He made a bomb. He's more dangerous than *any* of us anticipated."

"Okay," she acknowledged. "Maybe luring him out wouldn't be such a hot idea after all."

"I think that, in light of what happened, it would be best if you two canceled your honeymoon."

"What!" she screeched, indignation roiling up in her like a volcano. "You can't be serious."

"I'm very serious."

"But you're the one who suggested we go there, because it would be safe."

She and Sam had been invited by Chris's brother-in-law, King Phillip of Morgan Isle—the sister to Thomas Isle—to use their family hunting lodge. In fact, they should have been on a boat to the other island hours ago. If things had gone as planned, they would already be celebrating their honeymoon.

"I thought it would be the safest place for you, but—"

"Louisa went to Cabo for her honeymoon and no one gave her a hard time," Anne reminded him.

"Circumstances have changed."

"Chris, he *ruined* my wedding. I refuse to let him ruin my honeymoon, too. We'll have plenty of security there. We'll be *fine*."

He still looked hesitant.

"The location was kept so hush-hush that by the time he figures out where we are, and comes up with his next diabolical plan, we'll be back to the castle."

"All right," he finally agreed. "As long as you promise not to take any unnecessary risks."

"Of course." Did he think that she was a complete dolt? She wanted the man caught and brought to justice, but not so badly that she would endanger the life of her child.

Chris looked at Sam, who nodded and said, "We won't."

Is that how it would be now? Her family looking to her husband to keep her in line?

She realized she was clenching her fists and forced herself to relax. Getting this worked up wasn't good for her or the baby. What she needed was an outlet for all this tension and stress. And she didn't have to look far to find one.

She gazed over at Sam. Her *husband*. He was still wearing his wedding clothes but he'd shed the jacket and loosened his tie. The hair that had been combed back from his face earlier now fell forward in soft curls across his forehead. He looked too adorable for words and she couldn't wait to put her hands all over him.

Her wedding day may have been decimated, but they still had their wedding night. After four months of missing his touch, and a torturous week of waiting for this very night, she was determined to make it a memorable one.

"I'm exhausted," she announced, forcing a yawn for added effect, when in reality she was so awake she was practically buzzing. "Are you ready for bed, Sam?"

He nodded and rose from the settee.

"I'll arrange to have the boat ready for your trip to Morgan Isle at 10:00 a.m.," Chris told her.

"Thank you," she said, taking Sam's hand, leading him out of the study and up the stairs to her room. Make that *their* room. Most of Sam's clothes and toiletries had been moved in earlier that morning, which had necessitated her clearing a place in her closet for him. Sharing her space again would require some getting used to. Louisa and Anne had shared a bedroom until they were thirteen and Anne could no longer stand the frilly pink bedcovers and curtains, the childish furnishings. Furnishings Louisa had still used until a few months ago.

What Anne really hoped was that when this Gingerbread Man business was behind them, she and Sam could spend time at his grandmother's cottage. Away from her family and the confines of her title. A place where she could just be herself. A place where, unlike the castle, portraits of her relatives didn't stare accusingly from every hallway. And where she could make herself a cup of tea without feeling like an intruder in the kitchen. Where she could make love to her husband and not worry that someone on the opposite side of the wall would hear her.

Privacy. That was what she wanted. A place of her own.

"I need to apologize," Sam said.

She looked over at him. "For what?"

"Until today, I really didn't take this Gingerbread Man thing very seriously. It seemed more an annoyance than a serious threat. But when that car exploded, I swear I saw my life flash before my eyes."

She squeezed his hand. "I'm sorry I dragged you into this."

He looked at her and smiled. "I'm not. I just want you to be safe."

Which he had proven. The first minute or so after the blast was a bit of a blur, but the one thing she did remember with distinct clarity was the way he had used his own body as a shield to protect her. She could say with much certainty that in a similar situation, the men who had come before him would have ignored her entirely and saved their own asses.

And now it seemed only fair to reward him for his chivalry. Right?

They reached her room—*their* room—and the instant they were inside with the door closed, she launched herself at him. He let out a startled "Oof!" as she threw her arms around his neck and crushed her lips to his.

But it didn't take him long to recover from his surprise, before his arms went around her and he leaned in, took control of the kiss. In that single joining of their mouths, the tangling of their tongues, they seemed to unleash months of pent-up sexual frustration. She curled her fingers through his hair and sucked on his tongue, wishing she could crawl inside his skin, anything to be *closer* to him.

When they came up for air they were both breathing hard and he was wearing a slightly confused expression. "I thought you were exhausted."

"What was I supposed to say? Let's go upstairs so you can shag me silly?"

A slow smile curled his lips. "Is that what I get to do?"

"If you want to," she said, already knowing by the look in his eyes the answer was yes. She pulled the pins from her hair, shaking it loose and letting it spill down over her shoulders. His eyes raked over her and she could swear she actually felt his gaze caressing her skin.

"Unless you'd rather just go to sleep," she teased.

To answer her, he wrapped an arm around her waist, tugged her against him and kissed her. And kissed her.

And *kissed* her.

A part of her wanted to drag him to the bed, rip off his clothes, impale herself on his body and ride him to ecstasy. The other part wanted to take her time, draw out the anticipation and make this last.

She broke the kiss and backed out of his arms, wearing a come-and-get-me smile as she unzipped her dress and pulled it over her head. All she wore underneath was a beige lace bra and matching panties.

"Take it all off," he ordered, transfixed as she unhooked her bra and dropped it on the floor.

"They're bigger," she said, cupping her breasts in her palms.

"I don't care what size they are, as long as they're attached to you."

How was it that he always knew the exact right thing to say?

She gave each one a gentle squeeze, careful to avoid her nipples. They had been especially sensitive since the second month of her pregnancy. Sometimes just the brush of her pajama top made them hard and tingly, almost to the point of pain.

"The panties, too," he demanded.

She slid them down, anticipating the slow smile that curled his mouth when he realized what she was hiding—or more to the point *wasn't* hiding—underneath.

"I think I just died and went to heaven," he said.

"It was Louisa's idea," she told him, touching her fingers to the smooth skin from the recent Brazilian wax that her sister had *insisted* would drive Sam wild. If the look on his face was any indication, she was right.

"Louisa, huh?" He shook his head. "She just doesn't seem the type."

No kidding. For someone who had clung to her virginity until her engagement several months ago, Louisa seemed to know an awful lot about sex. "She said it enhances sensation."

"I guess we'll have to test that theory."

She was counting on it. She backed toward the bed and Sam watched as she pulled back the covers and draped herself across the mattress, letting her legs casually fall open. Giving him a view of the full package.

He started to walk toward her but she shook her head and said, "Uh-uh," and he stopped in his tracks. She gestured to his clothes. "Your turn to undress. Take it all off."

If there were a land speed record for disrobing, he probably broke it. And he had the most beautiful body she had ever seen. Long and lean and perfect. Simply looking at him made her feel all hot and fidgety and anxious.

"Lie down," he ordered.

She scooted over and lay back against the pillows. Sam crawled in and settled down beside her. She was so ready for him she ached, but she didn't want to rush this. She wanted to savor every second. Sam seemed content just lying there looking at her, lightly caressing the tops of her breasts, the column of her throat.

"You are so beautiful," he said, his eyes already shiny and heavy-lidded with arousal. He cupped her breasts, testing their weight in his hand, then he leaned over and licked the dark crest of one. She knew her nipples were sensitive, she just hadn't realized *how* sensitive until he nipped one with his teeth. Her body jerked violently, as though he were holding a live wire to her skin, and a strangled moan ripped from her throat.

He lifted his head, looking equal parts alarmed and intrigued. "What just happened?"

"I don't know," she said, her voice unsteady with shock and arousal. "I've never felt anything like that."

"Was it bad?"

"Not exactly. It felt…*electric*." Pleasure and pain all wrapped up in one.

"Should I stop?"

She shook her head. "Do it again."

"You're sure?"

She bit her lip and nodded. He lowered his head to try again and she grabbed his shoulders, bracing herself. But nothing could have prepared her for the assault of sensation as he sucked her nipple into his mouth. There was a tremendous, almost unbearably intense throb between her thighs, as if her breasts had somehow been hardwired directly to her womb. A moan rolled up from deep in her chest and her nails dug into his flesh. Then he did the same to the opposite side and she nearly vaulted off the bed, so far gone that she was on another planet.

Sam released her nipple and gazed down at her, looking fascinated, like a child who had just been handed a new toy. "Wow."

No kidding. This was completely crazy. He'd barely touched her and already she was hovering on the verge of an orgasm. Her body was so alive that if he so much as looked at her cross-eyed, she was going to lose it.

"If you do that again, I'll come," she warned him.

"Seriously?"

She nodded.

He looked like he wanted to, if for no other reason than to see if she really would. He even started to lean forward, then seemed to change his mind at the last second. Instead he pushed himself up, pressing her thighs apart and kneeling between them.

She thought he would enter her right away, but he leaned forward instead and licked her. Whether it was the bare skin enhancing things, or her fragile sexual state making it especially erotic, she couldn't really say. And didn't really care. All she knew was that it felt so out-of-this-world fantastic she actually forgot to breathe.

"I've been fantasizing about being with you since that night in your room," he said, pressing a kiss to her swollen belly. "I haven't been able to even look at another woman. I've only wanted you."

She threaded her fingers through his hair as he kissed and nibbled his way up her body, driving her mad. She was sure that was exactly what he intended. When he finally lowered himself on top of her, she was half out of her mind from wanting him and desperate for release.

He eased into her, one slow, steady, *deep* thrust, and a burst of electricity started deep in her core and zinged outward until only the boundaries of her skin kept it from jumping from her body to his.

His eyes locked on hers as he pulled back, then he rocked into her again, only this time she arched her hips up to meet him halfway and there were no words to describe the shocking pleasure, the sensations building inside her. It robbed her ability to think, to reason. All she could do was feel.

Every thrust drove her higher, closer to nirvana, then Sam clamped his mouth over her breast and her body finally let go. Pleasure flooded her senses in a violent rush, sinking in like a wild animal, feral and out of control.

Through a haze she heard Sam moan, heard him

say her name, felt his breath hot on her neck as his body locked and shuddered. In that instant nothing else mattered. It was just the two of them, just her and Sam against the world. Two souls twining and fusing in an irreversible bond.

She knew without a doubt that she loved him. And not just because he'd given her the best orgasm of her life. They were soul mates. She had known it the minute he'd taken her in his arms on the dance floor the night of the charity ball.

But she couldn't tell him. Not yet. The time just didn't feel right.

Sam started kissing her neck, nibbling her ears, whispering how delicious she tasted and she felt herself being dragged back under, into that deep well of desire. And before she even had a chance to catch her breath, he was making love to her all over again.

Seven

Considering it was owned by royalty, the hunting lodge on Morgan Isle was just about as stripped down and bare bones as it could be. It was a log cabin shell with a small kitchen, great room, two bathrooms—one on each floor—and four small, sparsely furnished bedrooms. Two upstairs, two down. And of course there were the obligatory stuffed dead animals all over the place.

There was no television or radio. No phone. Sam even insisted that he and Anne surrender their cell phones to Gunter, and made it clear that shy of a catastrophic disaster or urgent family matter, they were not to be disturbed. He didn't want a single thing to distract them from his primary goal. Get Anne naked and keep her that way for the next six days. And she seemed to have the same thing in mind. When he'd commented on her conspicuous lack of luggage—she'd brought only one small bag—she'd shrugged and said, "It's our honeymoon. What do I need clothes for?"

It was nice to know they were on the same page, since last night had been, by far, the hottest sex of his entire life. He'd been fantasizing about being with her for months, but the scenarios he'd created in his mind had paled in comparison to the real thing. And though he enjoyed getting off as much as the next man, nothing could have been more satisfying than watching Anne writhe and shudder in ecstasy. He'd made her come six times—*six times*—which under normal circumstances should have earned him some sort of accolade. But the truth was, he'd barely had to work at it.

He'd been with women who were difficult to please. But with Anne it didn't make a difference what position they happened to be in—if he was on top or she was, or if he took her pressed up against the shower wall, which he'd done twice. All he had to do was play with a nipple—a suckle or a pinch—and she went off like a rocket.

They probably could have gone for seven, but by then she was exhausted and clenching her legs together, begging him to let her sleep. And he'd figured it was only fair to let her reserve some of her strength for the actual honeymoon.

It was a cool day, so while she took a shower, Sam changed into jeans and a sweater and built a fire in the stone fireplace in the great room. He checked the cupboards and refrigerator and found they were stocked with enough food to last a month.

He was just putting on a kettle for tea when Anne appeared at the top of the stairs, her hair wet and twisted up, held in place with a clip, wearing a black silk robe. Sam couldn't help wondering if she wore anything underneath.

"I know this is a hunting lodge," she said. "But do there have to be so many *dead* things mounted on the walls?"

"Personally, I've never understood the appeal in killing defenseless animals," he told her, watching as she walked down the stairs. When she got the kitchen where he stood, she stopped, looked him up and down and smiled.

"What?" he asked.

"I've never seen you dressed so casually."

"It happens every now and then."

"I like it." She crossed the room to him and rose up to kiss him on the cheek.

She smelled clean and girly and looked delicious enough to eat. He was tempted to scoop her up and carry her off to bed that very instant, or even better, make love to her right there in the kitchen. The butcher-block table looked just the right height for fooling around, although it was pretty rough and scarred from many years of use. He didn't want her getting splinters in her behind. Besides, they had all week. It had been a hectic few days and it would be nice to just relax for a while. Maybe even take a nap. Anne had slept like the dead last night but Sam had tossed and turned, worrying about this Gingerbread Man business.

If something had gone wrong with that bomb, if they had hit a pothole and it had detonated too soon, his uncle and aunt—two of the sweetest people he knew—could have been blown to kingdom come. He agreed with

Anne that something needed to be done, but also saw Chris's point, and he was right, it wasn't worth putting someone's life at risk.

He and Chris would have to have a serious talk when Sam and Anne returned to Thomas Isle. Maybe it was time they considered a new course of action.

"Is everything okay?" Anne asked, her brow wrinkled.

"Of course. Why do you ask?"

"You sort of drifted off there for a second."

He smiled and kissed her forehead. "Just thinking about what a lucky man I am."

She wrapped her arms around his waist and snuggled against him. "I feel lucky, too."

"I was making tea. Would you like a cup?"

"I'd love one. Can I help?"

"You could find some honey. I think I saw it in the cupboard above the coffee maker."

She rooted around in the cupboard while he took two cups and a box of tea bags out.

Suddenly she gasped and stepped back, clutching her belly. "Oh my God!"

Thinking she'd hurt herself, or something was wrong with the baby, he was instantly at her side. "What's the matter? What can I do?"

She looked down at her stomach. "I think I just felt the baby kick."

"You did?"

She nodded excitedly. "When I was pressed up against the cupboard. I've felt flutters before, almost like butterflies in my stomach, but this was different. Like a poke." she said, demonstrating with her index finger on his stomach. "But from the inside. If you press down maybe you can feel it, too."

She unbelted her robe and pulled it open and—*bloody hell*—was naked underneath. She took his hand and pressed his palm firmly over her belly.

"I don't feel anything," he said.

"Shh, just wait a minute." She leaned into him, resting her head against his shoulder.

Looking down, he realized he must have gotten a little carried away last night. She had a few faint love-bites on her breasts. He was willing to bet that he'd find some on her neck as well, and maybe one or two on her inner thighs.

Maybe it was wrong, but with her pressed up against him, smelling so sexy, her skin soft and warm, her breath hot on his neck, he was getting a hard-on. And he definitely wasn't feeling the baby kick. Maybe it was too soon.

He started to move away but she held his hand firmly in place. "Just wait."

He was convinced he *wouldn't* feel anything, and when he actually did—a soft little bump-bump against his palm—he was so startled he almost pulled his hand away.

Her eyes darted up to his. "Did you feel it?"

He laughed in amazement. "I did."

She smiled. "That's our baby, Sam."

He felt it again. Another bump-bump, as if the little guy—or girl—was in there saying, *Hey, here I am.*

He'd heard that for men, feeling their baby move for the first time often made the experience more real, which he'd always thought was total bollocks. It felt bloody well real to him the moment she broke the news. But now, after experiencing it, he suddenly realized what they meant. That was *his* baby. No longer just a concept, but something he could feel.

He kept his hand there, hoping it would happen again, but after several minutes more Anne said, "He must be asleep again."

Sam smothered his disappointment and reluctantly pulled his hand away. The kettle had begun to boil, so Anne belted her robe and turned the burner off.

"Why don't we have our tea by the fire?" she suggested.

While he fixed it, she pilfered a fluffy down comforter from one of the beds and spread it out on the floor. He carried their cups over and set them on the hearth.

Anne let her hair down and flopped onto her back, the sides of her robe slipping apart over her belly. Instead of readjusting it, she tugged the belt loose and let the whole thing fall open. He certainly couldn't accuse her of being modest. Even that first night, during the ball, she hadn't been shy about taking it all off. And he could never get tired of looking at her body.

He sat cross-legged facing her, thinking that if the baby started to kick again he would be right there to feel it.

She closed her eyes and sighed contentedly. "The heat from the fire feels nice."

But a little too warm for the sweater he was wearing, so he pulled it up over his head and dropped it on the floor beside him. Anne was looking up at him, smiling.

"What?"

"You have a beautiful body. I like looking at it."

"The feeling is mutual."

"Does it bother you that I'm getting fat?"

He rolled his eyes. "You are *not* getting fat."

"You know what I mean," she said. "My belly is going to get huge."

"And it will look beautiful that way," he assured her, pressing a kiss just above her navel.

"You know, I already found a stretch mark. By the time I give birth I could be covered in them."

He examined her stomach but didn't see anything but smooth, soft skin. "I don't see any stretch marks."

"It's there."

"Where?"

She reached down, feeling around the lowest part of her belly. "Right here...see?"

He leaned in to get a closer look and saw what was, at best, a microscopic imperfection that may or may not have been an actual stretch mark. "It's tiny."

"Yes, but it will probably get bigger, until it's huge."

He seriously doubted that, but her concern surprised him a little. She'd never struck him as the type to be hung up on body image. She seemed so comfortable in her own skin. "You could be covered with them and I wouldn't think you were any less beautiful." He stroked the offending area. Her skin was warm and rosy from the heat coming off the fire. "In fact, I happen to think it's sexy."

She pushed herself up on her elbows. "And I think you're full of bunk."

"I mean it. If I found it off-putting, would I do this?"

He leaned down and kissed the spot, just a soft brush of his lips, and heard her inhale sharply.

When he lifted his head she had that heavy-lidded sleepy look that she got when she was turned on. And seeing her that way gave him an instant erection.

"See," he said.

"I think there might be another one," she said.

"Another stretch mark?"

She nodded solemnly.

"Really?" He manufactured concern. "Where?"

"This one is lower."

"How low?"

"Oh, a couple of inches, maybe."

He knew for a fact that there wasn't one *there,* but he stifled a smile. "I didn't see it."

She put a hand on the back of his head and gently pushed it down. "I think you should look closer."

Enjoying the game, he leaned in and pretended a thorough inspection, close enough that he was sure she could feel the whisper of his breath on her skin. He wasn't sure what the Brazilian wax was doing for her, but he sure was enjoying it.

After a minute or so he shrugged and said. "Sorry, I just don't see it."

He tried to straighten up and she not-so-gently shoved his head back down.

"Look *again.*"

He smiled to himself. "Wait…oh yes, I see it now. Right here." He pressed a kiss right at the apex of her puffy lips, paused, then swept his tongue between them.

Anne moaned and curled her fingers in his hair.

For a brief moment he considered torturing her a bit longer, but the sweet taste of her, her tantalizing scent drew him in like a bee to a flower. Unfortunately his jeans didn't have a lot of give, and he was so hard that a few more minutes of bending over like this was going to do mortal damage. He stretched out beside her in the opposite direction, relieving the pressure, and in a millisecond Anne was tugging at his belt. She worked with impressive speed and in seconds had his erection out of his pants…and into her mouth. It felt so damned fantastic, he might have swallowed his tongue if wasn't already buried in her.

Her mouth was so hot and wet and soft, and the damp ribbons of her hair brushing his stomach and thighs was unbelievably erotic. But when she reached into his jeans and cupped him…well, everything after that was a bit of a blur. A jumble of wet heat and intense pleasure, moans and whimpers that at times he wasn't sure were from him or from her. Or both. Too soon he felt his control slipping, but he never came first. It was against his personal code of conduct. He considered it selfish and impolite. Fortunately, he knew exactly what to do.

When he'd reached the point of no return, he slid a hand up to her breasts, took her nipple between his fingers and squeezed. She moaned, and her body started to quake, which sent him right over the edge with her. He would have cursed in blissful agony if his mouth hadn't been otherwise occupied. Afterward, she collapsed beside him and they lay side by side on the blanket, still facing opposite directions, breathing hard. He felt limp, as though every last bit of energy had been leeched from his body, and the heat from the fire was making him drowsy. Maybe now would be a good time for that nap.

His eyes drifted closed, but he felt Anne sit up beside him.

She gave him a shove. "Hey, wake up."

"I'm tired," he mumbled.

"But I'm not finished with you."

"I can't function. I need rest."

That didn't seem to deter her, because a second later he felt her tugging his jeans down and pulling them off. Now he was exhausted and *naked*. Did she really think that was going to help?

He opened one eye and peered up at her. She flashed him a wicked smile and, starting at his ankles, began kissing and licking her way up his body, and despite his fatigue, he was getting hard again. Apparently she wasn't taking no for an answer this time. And it looked as though that nap would have to wait.

If the perfect honeymoon included staying perpetually naked, eating hastily prepared meals on the floor by the fire and making love on a whim, Sam considered it safe to deem the first three days of their honeymoon a success. In fact, he would be a bit sorry when they had to return to real life.

He lay limp on the blanket in front of the fire, listening to the sound of the shower running overhead. He knew he should probably get up and throw something together for breakfast, as he'd promised Anne he would—the woman had a ravenous appetite lately—but he was so comfortable and relaxed he simply couldn't make himself move. Maybe food could wait, and instead he would pull her back down with him and make love to her one more time first. In the past three days he had mapped and memorized every inch of her, each curve and crevice. There wasn't a place on her body he hadn't caressed and kissed. In fact, it was quite possible that he knew her body better than his own.

What continued to astonish him was that, discounting those four months apart, technically, they had known each other the sum total of less than two weeks. Yet he had never felt so comfortable with a woman. With *anyone,* actually. It was as if they had known one another all their lives. He'd dated his share of women but he had never come close to finding one he could imagine spending the rest of his life with. One who was everything he had ever imagined a wife should be. He was beginning to wonder if he might have found his soul mate. And all because a few intoxicated mates had dared him to ask her to dance.

It was funny how fate worked.

A firm knock on the front door startled him. Sam cursed and pulled himself to his feet, grabbing a throw from the back of the davenport and wrapping it around his waist. As he crossed the room, the words *this better be important* sat on the tip of his tongue, ready to assault whoever was standing on the other side of the door.

The cool air rushing in didn't chill him even close to as much as the look on Gunter's face did. He didn't look upset, exactly. Gunter didn't show emotion. But there was something in his eyes that told Sam this wasn't going to be good news.

"Is urgent call from Prince Christian," Gunter said,

holding out Sam's cell phone. Sam's heart lodged somewhere south of his diaphragm.

"Thank you," he said, taking the phone. Gunter nodded and backed out the door, shutting it behind him. Deep down Sam knew, even before he heard Chris's solemn tone, what the prince was going to say.

"I'm afraid I have some bad news. The king passed away last night."

Sam cursed silently. "Chris, I'm so sorry."

"We'll need you and Anne back at the castle as soon as possible. I'm sure she'll want to see him one last time. Before…"

"Of course."

"Gunter will take you to an airfield not far from the lodge and a chopper will be waiting there. I've already arranged for your things to be brought back separately."

Chris certainly was on top of the situation, and Sam suspected that seeing to all the details was the only thing holding him together.

"Do you want me to tell her, or would you rather do it?" Chris asked.

"I'll tell her."

"Tell me what?" Anne asked.

Sam turned to find Anne standing behind him, wearing her robe, her hair still damp. He hadn't even heard her come down the stairs.

"We'll see you soon," Chris said and disconnected.

"Who was that?" Anne asked as he snapped the phone closed.

"Chris."

"What did he want?" she asked, though her expression said she already suspected.

"I'm afraid he had bad news."

She took a deep breath. "My father?"

He nodded.

"He's gone, isn't he?"

He took her in his arms and held her. "I'm so sorry."

She pressed her cheek against his chest and he could feel that it was already damp. "I'm not ready for this."

"I know." Even if they were ill, and suffering, was anyone ever ready to lose a parent?

Eight

Everyone was surprised to learn that it wasn't a heart attack. The king had just gone to sleep, and sometime in the night his heart had simply stopped beating. According to the physician, he hadn't suffered or felt a thing.

The only solace Anne could take was that he was finally at peace. The last few years had been so hard, and he'd put up one hell of a fight, but he had made peace with the fact that it was his time. Even if his family wasn't ready, he had been.

Chris and Aaron were somber and, like typical men, kept their feelings to themselves. Louisa cried constantly the first day, then miraculously seemed to pull herself together. The worst part was watching her mother cope, knowing that she must have been falling to pieces on the inside, but forcing herself to be strong for her children.

Anne was simply heartbroken. Her father would never know her children, and they would never see firsthand what a wonderful father, and grandfather, what a wonderful *man* he was. It just didn't seem fair that someone with so much to live for should be taken far too soon.

When she checked her e-mail the day of the funeral, reading condolences from friends and relatives, she found one from the Gingerbread Man, too. It said simply, *Boo Hoo*.

Anne had been so furious that she actually picked her laptop up and hurled it at the wall.

Those first few days after the service, she walked around in a fog, functioning on autopilot during the day and falling apart at night in the privacy of their bedroom, crying herself to sleep in Sam's arms while he stroked her hair and murmured soothing words. He was truly a godsend, taking care of her while dealing with the stresses of a new job.

But as the days passed it started to get easier. She began to focus not on her loss, but her new marriage and the baby who seemed to grow exponentially every day. Gradually everyone seemed to get back to their lives. Within a few weeks she and Sam had fallen into a comfortable routine. Before she knew it the day arrived when it was time for her ultrasound.

She drank what felt like *gallons* of water, and by the time they got to the royal family's private wing at the hospital she was in misery. Thank goodness the specialist was in the room and ready for them. When she lay back and exposed her belly he looked a little surprised.

"You're quite large for twenty-one weeks."

"Is that bad?" Sam asked, looking worried.

"Every woman carries differently," the doctor said as he squeezed cold goo on her belly, and used the wand thingy he was holding to spread it around. Images appeared on the screen immediately.

"Hmm." He nodded, his brow furrowed. "That would explain it."

Anne's heart instantly skipped a beat. She simply couldn't handle any more bad news.

"Is something wrong?" Sam asked.

"Not at all. So far everything looks great. I'll have to take a few measurements, but development seems to be just where it should be. For both of them."

At first Anne was confused, thinking he meant her and the baby, then the meaning of his words sank in and she was dumbstruck.

"Are you saying that there are two babies?" Sam asked. "We're having twins?"

The doctor pointed to the screen. "This is baby A, and over here is baby B."

"But there was only one heartbeat," Anne said.

"It's not uncommon for the hearts to beat in unison, making it difficult to differentiate between them. I'm sure your doctor explained that because you're a twin it was more likely you would have twins."

"Of course, but…"

"I guess that explains why you're so big already," Sam said, sounding surprisingly calm about this. In fact, while she was stunned, he looked as though he couldn't be happier.

"Would you like to know the sex of the babies?"

the doctor asked. She and Sam said "yes" in unison, then laughed because they were obviously very much in agreement.

"We'll see if we can get them to cooperate," he said, trying different angles. Then he pointed to the screen. "See there. This is baby A. There's the left leg, and the right, and see that protrusion in between?"

"A boy!" Sam said, beaming.

Baby B didn't want to cooperate, so he had Anne turn on her side, so the babies would shift position. "There we go!" the doctor finally said, pointing out both legs again, and there was no little protrusion this time.

"A girl," Anne said excitedly, squeezing Sam's hand. "One of each!"

The doctor took the measurements he needed and announced that everything looked wonderful. Her children were healthy, Sam was beaming with pride, and Anne could say with certainty that it was one of the happiest days of her life. After all that had happened lately, she figured they deserved it.

When the doctor was finished Anne dashed to the loo to empty her bladder before it burst. When she met Sam in the waiting room, he had an odd look on his face.

What if the idea of having twins had finally sunk in and he'd realized it was more than he bargained for? What if he was overwhelmed by the responsibility?

"What's wrong, Sam?"

"The doctor and I had an interesting discussion while you were gone."

"What kind of discussion? Is something wrong with the babies?"

"I voiced some concerns about you being on birth

control when you conceived. I was afraid it might cause complications or defects."

Anne's breath hitched. "What did he say?"

"He checked your chart."

Oh God. Anne's heart sank so hard and fast it left a hollow feeling in her chest. "Sam—"

"I want the truth, Anne. That night, when you said you had it covered, did you mean it, or did you lie to me?"

It felt as though the entire room had flipped on its axis and she had to grab the wall to keep from pitching over. "I can explain—"

"Did. You. *Lie*." He was angry. Not just angry, but seething mad. This man who had never so much as raised his voice looked as though he wanted to throttle her.

She had to force the words past the lump of fear blocking her throat. "Yes, but—"

The door opened and Gunter stuck his head in to tell them the car was ready.

"Sam," she said, but he silenced her with a sharp look and said, "When we get home."

The ride back to the castle was excruciating. Sam sat silently beside her, but she could feel his anger. It seemed to fill the car, until it became difficult to breathe. Or maybe that was her guilty conscience.

There had to be a way to fix this. To make him understand.

When they got back they went straight to their room and Sam closed the door firmly behind him. Then he turned to her and in a voice teeming with bitterness said, "I should have known."

"Sam…" She tried to touch his arm but he jerked it away.

"I was raised on the principle that royals are never to be trusted, that they always have an agenda. I knew it that night, and still I ignored my instincts."

It crushed her that he would ever think of her that way. Yet she couldn't deny she slept with him knowing they were unprotected. "It's not what you think. I didn't have any agenda. I wasn't trying to trap you."

"So, you just wanted sex."

He made it sound so sleazy. He had been there, too, he knew damn well how deeply they had connected. He had wanted her, too. "I wanted you, Sam, and I honestly didn't think I would get pregnant. The timing was completely off."

"So what you're saying is, with no regard to anyone but yourself and your own selfish needs, you took a chance. You didn't even have the decency to stop and consider the repercussions of your actions, and how it might affect me."

When he said it that way, it *was* pretty awful.

"I'm sorry," she said in a whisper, because suddenly she couldn't seem to draw in a full breath, as though his animosity was leeching all the oxygen from the air.

"You're *sorry*," he said, spitting out a rueful laugh. "You stole *everything* from me and all you can say is you're sorry?"

"I made a mistake. I know. But I love you, Sam."

"You love me?" he said, astonished. "Playing Russian roulette with my future? Lying to me? You call that *love?* I think there's only one person here that you give a damn about, Your Highness, and that's you."

He couldn't be more wrong. She hated herself right now. For not having the guts to tell him the truth right away. "Sam, I just wanted—"

"You wanted to screw me," he said. "And I guess you succeeded because as far as I can see, I am thoroughly screwed."

He yanked the door open and stormed out, slamming it behind him.

Anne's heart was pounding and she was trembling so hard her legs wouldn't hold her upright. She slid down the wall to the floor, her legs finally folding under her like a marionette whose strings had been cut.

Sam was right. Everything he said about her was true, and he had every right to be furious with her. But was he mad enough to leave her? To demand a divorce?

Maybe after he had some time to cool down and think things through, he would remember how happy he'd been and how good they were together.

And what if he didn't? What then?

The worst part was that she had no one to blame for this mess but herself. And the happiest day in her life had just turned into her worst nightmare.

Anne didn't know where Sam went, but she learned from Gunter that he took his own car and left without a bodyguard. Which, considering the Gingerbread Man's escalating violence, probably wasn't the smartest idea, but she was in no position to be telling him what to do.

He had arranged to take the afternoon off for the ultrasound, so she knew he probably wasn't at the office. He could be anywhere. And even if she did know where he went, there was nothing she could do about it. She needed to give him space, time to think things through.

She wasn't the least bit hungry, but with two babies growing inside her, she knew skipping meals wasn't an option. But since she didn't feel like facing her family—and any questions—she asked Geoffrey to bring her dinner to her room. She was so beside herself she couldn't choke more than a few bites down.

To kill time while she waited for Sam, she started a list of all the baby things they were going to have to get. They would need two of everything. And they were going to have to think about names. It still amazed her that she was having twins, and she realized her family didn't even know yet. But that was the kind of news she and Sam should announce together.

A little later Louisa knocked on her door and Anne called for her to come in.

"I'm not disturbing you, am I?" Louisa asked, peeking her head in and looking around for Sam.

"I'm alone."

She stepped inside. "Oh, where's Sam?"

If she told Louisa they'd had a fight, she would have to tell her why, and she was too ashamed to admit how badly she had screwed things up.

"He had a thing with his parents," she said, keeping it vague. "I was supposed to go, but I wasn't feeling well."

Louisa frowned. "Are you all right?"

"Fine, just normal pregnancy stuff."

She flopped down on the bed beside her. "Is that why you didn't come down for dinner?"

"I had Geoffrey bring me a tray."

"Mother ate with us again."

"That's good," Anne said. For months now, since their father became so ill, he and their mother shared dinner in their suite. And right after the funeral she continued to eat alone, until they all finally talked her into coming back down to the dining room.

"She told Chris that she thinks he and Melissa and the triplets should move into the master suite. Since he is king now. And there's five of them and just one of her."

"What did he say?"

"At first he said no, but she insisted, so he said he would think about it. Maybe she just has too many memories there."

"She shouldn't rush into anything. It hasn't even been a month. She needs to give herself time to grieve."

"I agree, but try telling her that. And people wonder where we got our stubborn streak."

One of the babies rolled and Anne placed a hand on her belly.

"Kicking?" Louisa asked, putting a hand beside Anne's. She loved feeling the baby move.

"More like rolling."

"I wish I were pregnant, too," she said, looking sad.

"It'll happen. It's only been a few months. Sometimes it takes a while." And sometimes it worked on the first shot, whether she wanted it to or not.

"Well, it's certainly not for a lack of trying. Last night alone—"

"Please," Anne interrupted. "Spare me the gory details. I believe you."

Louisa grinned. "I'm pushing thirty. If I'm going to have six kids, I have to get the ball rolling. Besides, don't you think it would be fun if we were pregnant together?"

"We still could be. I've got nineteen weeks to go." Although maybe less, because the doctor said it wasn't uncommon for twins to come as much as four weeks early. That meant she and Sam could be parents in only *fifteen* weeks.

"Well, if not this time then the next," Louisa said with a shrug. But Anne didn't tell her there wouldn't be a next time. She hadn't even been sure she wanted *one* child. Two kids, especially since she was having one of each gender, was going to be her limit.

She wanted so badly to tell Louisa about the ultrasound. It was right there on the tip of her tongue, dying to come out, but she restrained herself. She and Sam should tell everyone together and she didn't think it was fair to deprive him of that. And she didn't want to give him yet another reason to be mad at her.

After Louisa left—probably to work on making that baby with Garrett—Anne picked up a novel she'd been meaning to start. Even though it was written by one of her favorite authors, she just couldn't concentrate. Her mind kept wandering and her eyes drifting to the clock on the bedside table.

It was going on eleven. Where could he be?

At midnight she finally changed into her pajamas and crawled into bed, but she couldn't sleep. It was after one when Sam finally opened the bedroom door and stepped inside.

Her heart stalled, then picked up double-time.

He went to the closet to change, the light cutting a path though the darkness. Then the light went out and she heard him in the bathroom. The shower turned on and she lay in the darkness listening and waiting. Finally the bathroom door opened, the light went out and he walked to the bed. She could smell the scent of soap and shampoo as he climbed in beside her.

For a long moment she lay silent, afraid to make a sound, afraid that he was still angry. She waited to see if he made the first move, but after several minutes he hadn't said a word. Maybe he thought she was asleep.

She rolled on her side facing him and asked, "Can we talk about this?"

"There's nothing to talk about."

"Sam…" She laid a hand on his arm but he shrugged it away. "Please."

"Nothing you could say or do will erase what you did to me."

His words cut deep and she realized he wasn't even close to being ready to forgive her. "I understand. So long as you know that when you're ready to talk, I'll be here."

He sat up suddenly and switched on the light, blinding her for a second. When her eyes adjusted she saw that he looked tired, and angry and…betrayed. "You don't get it. I know what you did, and why you did it, and nothing you can say will ever change it. You stole my life from me. It's done. I'm not just going to get over it."

Her heart sank. He didn't even want to try to forgive

her? To understand her side of it? He was just going to give up?

She had grown to love Sam, but obviously for him, she was as easily discarded as a used tissue. "So what are you saying? That it's over?"

"We both know that isn't an option. Like you said, once we're married, that's it. Royals don't do divorce."

Her relief was all encompassing. And it must have shown because he added hastily, "Don't think for a second that I'm doing this for you. I'm staying married to you for my children. That's it."

Yes, but as long as he was still there, still a part of her life, he would eventually have to forgive her. He couldn't stay mad forever.

"I didn't tell anyone our news yet," she said. "About the twins. I thought we should announce it together."

"You needn't have bothered waiting. I already told my parents. Tell your family whenever and whatever you want. It really doesn't matter to me."

His words cut so deep, she wouldn't have been surprised to find blood on her pajamas.

With that he switched off the light and lay back down, turning his back to her. A clear indication that the conversation was now over. Though her stubborn, argumentative side wanted to push, she forced herself to let it go. She just needed to give him time. Eventually he would remember how happy they'd been, how good they were together.

Sam may have never said he loved her, but she knew he did. She could feel it. And people didn't fall out of love instantly. The fact that he was feeling so angry and betrayed was a sure sign that he cared deeply for her. Otherwise it wouldn't matter what she had done to him.

It simply had to work out. Because the alternative was not an option.

Nine

How had Sam gotten himself into this mess?

He sat at his desk, in his new office—which he couldn't deny was far larger and more lavish than even his father's, with a secretary on the other side of the door who had already proven herself more than competent—contemplating the disaster that was now his life.

Their marriage was supposed to be perfect. And it had been. They had been happy. Right up until the instant he learned that it was all a lie.

People had always accused him of being too laid-back and easygoing. Too trusting, especially for a politician. But he had always considered it one of his strengths. Now it would seem that everyone had been right, and his ignorance had finally come back to bite him in the ass.

However, that wasn't a mistake he intended to make again.

All he'd ever wanted was a marriage like his parents had. He wanted a partner and a soul mate. He wasn't naive enough to believe there wouldn't be occasional disagreements or spats. That he could live with. But what Anne had done to him was unforgivable. And not just the part when she lied about the birth control. She'd had a chance to redeem herself and tell him the truth when she came to tell him about the baby. Instead she had lied to him again. And she kept lying.

Now he was trapped in a marriage with a wife he could never trust. Never love, even if he'd wanted to. And he had been close. So close that the thought of his gullibility sickened him.

At least something good had come out of this miserable union. Three things actually. His son and his daughter. He would never consider a child anything but a blessing—no matter the circumstances of its conception—and he would never hold them responsible for their mother's deception.

The third good thing was his job with the royal family. He'd always been a people person, and in his new position as foreign ambassador, communication was the main thrust of his position. He actually looked forward to going to work every morning. Even before it meant getting away from his wife. So of course the last thing he wanted to do was put that position in jeopardy. And despite what Anne had done to him, he didn't doubt her family would take her side. Sam could easily find himself working out of an office the size of a closet pushing papers. Or even worse, they might delegate him to work in their agricultural department, possibly picking weeds in the fields, so he figured it was in his best interest not to let anyone know that he and Anne were, for all intents and purposes, estranged.

But it wasn't easy to play the doting newlywed husband when he was so filled with resentment. And though he hadn't yet discussed it with Anne, he was quite sure she would agree to the charade. She owed him that at least.

It had taken him hours to finally fall asleep last night, and when he woke this morning he almost reached for her, the way he usually did. Making love in the mornings had become a part of their regular routine.

Then he remembered what she had done and rolled out of bed instead.

He didn't doubt that he would miss the sex. When it came to sexual compatibility, they were off the charts. But he couldn't abide by having sex with a woman whom he no longer respected. One he didn't even like.

She had still been sleeping, or pretending to, when he left for work. He usually ate breakfast with the family, but he'd had no appetite this morning. Now it was barely eight-thirty and he'd already been in the office forty-five minutes. But it was better than being at home. With her.

At nine Chris knocked on his door. "I hear congratulations are in order."

Sam must have looked confused, because Chris added, "Twins?"

"Oh, right!" Of course, Anne must have told them this morning.

Chris laughed. "Don't tell me you forgot."

"No, I just…" He shook his head. "Busy morning. And I didn't sleep well last night."

"As the parent of triplets, I can tell you it's not quite as daunting as it sounds. Not yet anyway. Get back to me when they're teenagers."

"It was definitely a surprise, but we're both thrilled." At least, she had seemed thrilled. Until the walls caved in on them.

"And like Anne said, you get one of each, so you don't have to go through this again."

A wise decision in light of the situation. Not that he'd have wanted more than that anyway. Two was a nice tidy number. It seemed to suit his parents fairly well. Although he was sure his mother would have liked a little girl to spoil. He was sure a granddaughter would be the next best thing. And he was happy to be able to give her that.

"Of course," Chris added, "I understand some women enjoy being pregnant. Melissa was carrying three, so it wasn't the easiest of pregnancies. But Anne seems to be doing well."

Sam wasn't sure how Anne felt about being pregnant. Other than a few halfhearted gripes about stretch marks and occasional complaints about heartburn, if she had reservations, he didn't hear about them. Even when she was getting sick she didn't grumble about it. Truth be told, she was fairly low maintenance for a princess. "I imagine it will get uncomfortable closer to her due date. Her only concern at this point seems to be stretch marks."

"That was a big issue for Melissa, too. But it's kind

of an inevitability with multiples, I think. Mel has a list of plastic surgeons she's considering already."

"I guess that means you're stopping at three?"

"Neither of us wants to take another spin on the fertility roller coaster."

It struck Sam as ironic that Chris and Melissa had worked so hard to have a child, while Sam and Anne, who weren't even trying, hit the jackpot the first time. Maybe she had been thinking the same thing that night. Not that it was an excuse to put his future on the line without his knowledge. If she had been honest and said that she wasn't taking birth control, but the timing was off and she most likely wasn't fertile, he might have said what the hell and slept with her anyway. But that would have been *his* choice. She had deprived him of that.

Chris's cell phone rang, and when he looked at the display said, "It's Garrett."

He answered, and not ten seconds into the conversation Sam could see by his expression that something was wrong.

He listened, nodding solemnly, then asked, "Were there any injuries?"

Sam sat a little straighter is his chair. Had there been another incident?

"How bad?" Chris asked. He listened for another minute, his expression increasingly grim, then said, "I'll be right over."

He shut his phone and told Sam, "I have to get to the east field greenhouse facility."

Sam knew that was the heart of the royal family's vast organic farming business. When an unidentifiable blight infected the crops there last year, it put the economic fate of the entire island in jeopardy.

"Did something happen there?" he asked.

"Yeah, it just blew up."

It was a bomb identical to the one detonated at Anne and Sam's wedding, activated remotely from God only knew where, and was hidden in the men's loo. The force actually shot a commode through the roof and it had come crashing down on a car parked in the lot several hundred feet away. Thankfully an *empty* car. But half a dozen people were injured in the blast, two of them with third-degree burns, and one with shrapnel to his eye that could possibly cost him his sight. The greenhouse itself had sustained hundreds of thousands of pounds' worth of damage.

A busload of school children had been scheduled to tour the facility only an hour later and Anne shuddered to think what would have happened if he'd detonated the bomb then. That alone was cause for great relief as the family gathered in the study after dinner the following night to discuss the investigation. The only other bright spot in this tragic situation was that this time the Gingerbread Man had made a crucial error. He'd allowed himself to be caught on surveillance. And not just the top of his head this time. This was a straight-on, up-close-and-personal view of his face.

He'd entered the facility the previous day posing as a repairman. He had the proper credentials so no one seemed to think twice about letting him in. He wore a cap, and kept his head down so that the brim covered his face. It was sheer dumb luck that, on his way out, someone carrying a large piece of equipment bumped into him in the hallway, hitting his cap and knocking it off his head. For a split second he jerked his head up and just happened to be standing under a surveillance camera. If they had planned it, it couldn't have been more eloquent.

"He's not the monster I expected," Louisa said, looking at the still shot of his face that had been taken from the tape. It had already been distributed to the authorities and would run on the national news. Someone would recognize him, meaning it was only a matter of time before he was identified and apprehended.

"He looks…intense," Liv said, taking the photo from Louisa to study it. "It's his eyes, I think. There's an intelligence there."

"If he's so intelligent," Aaron quipped, "why did he make a mistake?"

"Intelligent or not, it was inevitable that he would eventually screw up," Chris said, taking the photo, giving it another quick look, then setting it on the bar before he walked over to sit next to their mother on the settee. "This nightmare is almost over."

"This would have pleased your father," she said with a sad smile. "It's about time we had some good news. We should have a toast, to celebrate. Don't you think?"

"I'm all for a little celebrating," Aaron said.

"I'm sure we could scrounge up a bottle or two of champagne," Chris said, ringing Geoffrey.

"Champagne please, Geoffrey," their mother said, when he stepped into the room.

Geoffrey nodded and said, "Of course, Your Highness."

"Water for me," Anne told him.

"Me, too," Melissa added as he walked to the bar.

"I thought you stopped nursing," Louisa said.

"I did. But champagne makes me groggy and I have to be up for a 2:00 a.m. feeding."

That would be her and Sam in a few months, Anne thought, and she could only hope their situation had improved by then. And as much as she wanted the Gingerbread Man caught, it was difficult to feel like celebrating.

All evening Sam had acted as if nothing was out of the ordinary, but she knew that was for her family's sake. They had agreed that it would be best if they kept up the ruse of being happily married newlyweds. The kind who no longer had sex. Or *spoke*. At least she would be spared the humiliation of having to admit that barely a month after their wedding they were already having issues.

There was a sudden crash behind the bar and everyone turned simultaneously to look.

"My apologies," Geoffrey said, leaning down to clean up the glass he'd dropped. Anne was standing close by so she walked around to help him, picking up some of the larger pieces. She noticed, as he swept the smaller shards into a dustpan, that his hands were shaking, and when he stood, his face looked pale.

She took his hand. It was ice cold. "Are you okay?"

"Arthritis," he said apologetically, gently extracting it from her grasp.

She helped him pour the champagne and when everyone had a glass they toasted to the new lead in the investigation.

"I have an excellent idea," their mother said. "You kids should play poker. It is Friday."

Everyone exchanged a look. Friday used to be poker night, but since the king's death they hadn't played.

"We could do that," Chris said.

"I'm in," Aaron piped in, then he turned to Sam. "Do you play?"

"Not since college, but I'm pretty sure I remember how."

Like sharks smelling fresh blood in the water, Chris and Aaron grinned.

"Count me in, too," Garrett said.

"I think I'll head down to the lab instead," Liv said.

"You don't play poker?" Sam asked her.

"We don't let her," Aaron said, shooting her a grin. "She cheats."

Liv gave him a playful shove, her cheeks turning a bright shade of pink. "I do not!"

"She counts cards," Aaron said.

"Not on purpose," she told Sam. "It's just that when it comes to numbers I have a photographic memory."

"How about you, Anne?" Chris asked. "You up for a game?"

Though Anne normally played, she figured it might be a better idea to give Sam some space. Maybe relaxing with her brothers, not to mention a few drinks, would make him forget how angry he was with her. "I don't think so."

"Why don't you help me get the triplets ready for bed," Melissa suggested. "For practice. After that, having two babies will feel easy."

"I'd love to."

"I'll help, too!" Louisa said excitedly.

"I thought we could watch a movie," their mother said.

"Of course," Louisa said with a bright smile, though Anne guessed that deep down she preferred to help Melissa.

Everyone went their separate ways and Anne followed Melissa to the nursery.

"Have you decided if you're taking the master suite?" Anne asked her.

"I don't know. It just seems like it should belong to the queen."

"Have you forgotten that you *are* the queen?" When Chris became king, Melissa automatically became queen, and their mother was given the title of Queen Mother. Which was technically more of a lateral move than a demotion.

"It's just really hard to fathom," Melissa said. "Three years ago I didn't even know I was a royal. But I can't deny it would be nice to have all the space."

Instead of going into the nursery, Melissa walked past it to her and Chris's bedroom and opened the door.

Anne stopped, confused. "I thought…"

"The nanny put them to bed already. I wanted to talk to you, and I didn't want to say anything in front of everyone else." She gestured Anne inside.

Anne got a sinking feeling in her chest. Was she so transparent that Melissa had figured out something was wrong? Or had she heard Anne and Sam fighting the other night?

They sat on the sofa by the window and Anne held

her breath. If Melissa did ask about Sam, what would Anne say? She didn't want to lie, but she had promised Sam, for the sake of his job, not to tell anyone.

"I wanted to talk to you about something. About Louisa."

Anne felt a mix of relief and confusion. "Louisa? What did she do?"

"Oh, she didn't do anything. It's just…something happened." She stopped and sighed.

"What happened?"

"Chris and I are going to be making an announcement, and I'm afraid she's going to be upset. I talked to your mother, but she suggested I talk to you. You know Louisa better than anyone. I thought maybe you could think of a way that we could…soften the blow."

"What could you possibly have to say that would make her so up—" She gasped when she realized there really was only one thing. "Oh my God! Melissa, are you *pregnant?*"

She bit her lip and nodded. "I took a test today."

"Already?" She laughed. The triplets were barely four months old.

"This obviously wasn't planned. I was all ready to schedule my tummy tuck. After the fertility hell we went through, and the in vitro, I didn't think I could even get pregnant naturally. Not to mention that you're not supposed to be able to get pregnant while you're nursing. As far as I can tell, it had the opposite effect on me. If we had known it was even a possibility we would have been a lot more careful."

"How far along are you?"

"Probably four or five weeks."

"So your children will be almost exactly a year apart."

"Don't remind me," she groaned.

"Six babies born within a year." Anne shook her head in disbelief. "We're going to have to build another wing onto the castle."

"Which is why I'm worried about Louisa. She's so desperate to get pregnant. Have you looked at Garrett lately? The poor guy is exhausted."

"Yeah, but he's always smiling."

"Still, she's so…fragile. I'm afraid this might put her over the edge."

That was a common misconception. But Louisa was a lot tougher that she let people think. "First off, Louisa is not that fragile. And second, if the tables were turned, you know she wouldn't hesitate to announce her news to the entire world. Even if that meant hurting someone's feelings."

Melissa nodded. "You've got a point."

"Louisa has never been a patient person. When she wants something, she doesn't like to wait for it. But she and Garrett have only been trying for a couple of months. It can take time. She's going to have to accept that."

"So you really think I shouldn't worry?"

"I do. And if she does get upset, she'll get over it."

"Thank you," she said, taking Anne's hand and giving it a squeeze.

They talked about Anne's pregnancy for a while, and she pretended that everything was okay. That she wasn't miserable and scared. It had only been two days, but what if Sam really couldn't forgive her? Could she stay with a man who resented her so? Would she even want to?

When he came to bed that night she was already under the covers but wide-awake. He didn't say a word. He just crawled in beside her, facing away. She wasn't sure how relaxing the game had been, but she could tell from the whiff of alcohol that he'd been drinking. Still, he didn't even kiss her good-night. On top of that, she had a case of heartburn that wouldn't quit and her back was aching. She slept in fits and starts, and finally crawled out of bed around six-thirty and wandered down to the kitchen for a glass of milk.

She was surprised to find Chris there, still in his pajamas, drinking coffee and reading the paper.

"You're up early," she said, pouring herself a glass of milk.

"It was my morning for the 4:00 a.m. feeding," he said, setting the paper aside. "Then I couldn't get back to sleep. I'll be very happy when the triplets are sleeping through the night."

"Isn't that what you have nannies for?"

"Only to assist. Mel and I agreed that if we were going to have children, we wouldn't rely on the hired help to do all the dirty work."

"Excuse me, Your Highness."

They both turned to see Geoffrey standing in the doorway to his residence behind the kitchen. He looked terrible. His hair was mussed, his eyes red and puffy, as though he hadn't slept a wink all night. Though she had never once seen him emerge in anything but his uniform, he was wearing a velour robe over flannel pajamas. The idea that maybe he really was sick made her heart sink. Chris looked concerned, as well.

"I was hoping to have a word with you," Geoffrey said.

"Of course, Geoffrey, what is it?"

He walked over to where they stood. He had a sheet of paper clutched in his hand. The surveillance photo of the Gingerbread Man, she realized. He set it down on the countertop.

"I need to speak with security, about this photo."

"You recognize him?" Anne asked.

Geoffery nodded. "I do."

"Who is he?" Chris asked.

"This man," he said, in an unsteady voice, "is my son."

Ten

His name was Richard Corrigan.

The entire family was shocked and saddened at learning he was Geoffrey's son, but at least now they had a good idea what had started this whole thing.

According to Richard's mother, whom Geoffrey contacted immediately, he had always deeply resented the royal family. Especially the children, whom he felt his father had chosen over him. But his bitterness didn't manifest into violence until recently.

He was Special Forces in the military and highly decorated, until an assignment gone terribly wrong in Afghanistan, where he saw many of his fellow soldiers brutally slain, left him suffering from PTSD. Rather than giving him the counseling he needed, he was discharged from the service instead. Apparently he snapped, and started to blame the royal family for his troubles.

The reference to the nursery rhymes, Geoffrey suspected, dated back to when Richard was small and he would read to him. He admitted that deep down he suspected it might be his son months ago, but he hadn't wanted to believe it. He thought it might be his own guilty conscience playing tricks on him. Only when he saw the photo could he no longer deny the truth.

In his guilt and grief Geoffrey tried to quit, but no one would accept his resignation. He was a part of the family and families stuck together. Chris assured him that when Richard was apprehended, he would see to it personally that he got the psychiatric help he needed.

Unfortunately, after a month, and a worldwide bulletin calling for his capture, he hadn't been arrested. There had been dozens of reported sightings and tips called in, but none of them panned out.

Anne couldn't help thinking that their champagne celebration had been hasty and they may have jinxed themselves irrevocably. And though she wanted to believe that he would be caught before he detonated another bomb and hurt more people, her life in general was in such a shamble, she couldn't help but expect the worst.

It had been a long and miserable month since their fight, but Sam still hadn't come around. It wasn't even that he was bitter or unkind. At least to that she had defenses. What she couldn't bear, what was slowly eating away at her, was the indifference. The silence. They only spoke when it was necessary, and even then she usually got one-word answers from him. He often worked late, or went out for drinks with his friends. He kept up the ruse of their happy marriage in front of her family, for which she was infinitely grateful, but otherwise, he ignored her.

She didn't understand how he could go from being so sweet and attentive to acting as though she didn't exist. Was it really so easy for him to shut her out, to flip his emotions on and off like a light switch?

In a month he hadn't so much as kissed her, and though she had tried a few time to initiate sex, she was met with icy indifference. She suspected that given the choice, he would opt to not share a bed with her any longer. What was the point when he had drawn a very distinct and bold invisible line down the center of their mattress? But it was her experience that men could only go so long without sex before they explored alternative options, and she couldn't help worrying that it was only a matter of time before he came home smelling of another woman's perfume.

For that reason alone, and despite the indignity of his perpetual cold shoulder, she continued to try to seduce him. She waited until nights when she knew he was in a particularly good mood, when his defenses might be down. She kept thinking that if they made love, reminded him how good it used to be, it would make him want to forgive her.

She kept telling herself that if she was persistent, eventually he would give in, and if she kept him sexually satisfied, he wouldn't think about straying. Even if he couldn't love her, at least he would be faithful.

Then she began to wonder if he was refusing her advances not because of their fight, but because he was completely turned off by her body. Maybe, with her huge belly and expanding hips, she disgusted him to the point that he couldn't stand to even touch her. Maybe their fight had been a convenient excuse to act on feelings he'd been having as far back as their honeymoon.

With the seed planted, the idea began to fester, until she became convinced Sam was disgusted by her body. Until the sight of her own reflection in the mirror disturbed and humiliated her. She stopped undressing in front of him and began showering with the lights off so she wouldn't have to look at herself.

She had never been one of those women with body issues. She had always been comfortable in her own skin, and didn't particularly care what anyone thought. Being in the public eye, Anne found that people didn't hesitate to voice their very critical opinions. Now it consumed her thoughts. She dressed in baggy clothes and oversize sweaters to hide the grotesque curves.

She had herself so convinced that she was hideous that she gave up on trying to seduce Sam. She threw in the towel and resigned herself to the inevitable. Eventually he was going to find someone else to satisfy him sexually. They were going to be one of *those* couples. The kind who kept up the ruse of their marriage for appearances, even when rumors of infidelity became common knowledge. In public people would stare and whisper behind her back. Sam's friends would be polite to her face and snicker when she was out of earshot.

"Poor Princess Anne," they would say. "Too naive to realize she's been played the fool."

The possibility was like the final hit to the spike that he had slowly been driving through her heart.

Anne had been going to bed earlier and earlier lately, so when Sam came home late from work one evening, he wasn't surprised to hear that at nine, she had already gone upstairs.

After a quick bite in the kitchen, and a short conversation with Chris about the conference call they had both stayed late for, Sam headed upstairs. He expected Anne to be asleep already, but the bed was empty. He walked into the closet to change out of his suit and heard the shower running. The bathroom door was open a crack, and he had to fight the urge to peek inside, to get a glimpse of her.

Despite everything that had happened, he was still sexually attracted to Anne, still desired her with an intensity that sometimes had him taking cold showers to control his urges and waking in the middle of the night in a cold sweat.

Lying beside her every night, not touching her, was a special kind of torture. It had taken more strength than he thought he possessed to keep turning down her overtures. But he didn't feel it was fair to make love to her, to give her hope that things might change, when he knew that wasn't true.

He knew he was making her miserable, and despite what she probably believed, that wasn't his intention. Since they were stuck with each other, he had hoped they would reach an understanding, find some middle ground where they could coexist peacefully. But his life was anything but peaceful.

It had been almost two weeks since she'd initiated sex; she'd even gone so far as to stop undressing in front of him, which he'd thought would be a relief. Instead, the longer he went without seeing her, or touching her, he wanted her that much more. But giving in, making love to her, would just do more damage.

He walked closer to the bathroom door, thinking he would just accidentally bump it with his elbow while he hung up his suit jacket. But when he did, he still couldn't see a thing. The room was black as pitch.

What would possess her to shower with all the lights off?

Puzzled, he walked into the bedroom to drop his watch and phone on the bedside table. Then he remembered that he had to be to work early for another conference call and set the alarm on his phone for six-thirty. He walked back into the closet, tugging his shirt off, and saw that Anne was out of the shower and drying off with her back to him. Seeing her naked again made him hard instantly. She dropped the towel and turned his way, shrieking when she saw him standing there.

At first he thought he'd only startled her, until she reached down and clawed at the ground for the towel she'd just dropped. She fumbled to untwist it, holding it up to cover herself, a look of sheer horror on her face.

She acted as if he were a rapist or molester. The fact that he had seen her frequently, and intimately, naked made her reaction more than a little peculiar. He was so surprised his first instinct was to ask, "What the hell is the matter with you?"

His harsh tone made her flinch. "I…I'm sorry. I didn't know you were here."

What did she think she was doing? Punishing him by not letting him see her undressed? Torturing him? Well, he had news for her. It was torture no matter what she did. Dressed, undressed, he still wanted her.

She fumbled with the towel, trying to cover as much of herself as possible, and something inside him snapped. What right did she have to deprive him of anything? Damn it, she *owed* him.

He reached out, fisted the towel and yanked it away from her. She tried desperately to shield his view with her hands, looking around for something to cover herself, deep red splotches blooming across her cheeks.

She was embarrassed, he realized. Not just embarrassed, but mortified. "Anne, what is the matter with you?"

"I'm fat," she said in a wobbly voice, tears gathering in the corners of her eyes. "My body is disgusting."

Suddenly it all made sense. The reason she didn't undress in front of him. And why she showered with the lights off. She was ashamed of her body. A woman who, six weeks ago, had no issue walking around naked, flaunting herself to him.

If she were anyone else, he might have suspected it was an act, to make him feel guilty for ignoring her. But she'd had weeks to pull that sort of stunt. This was real.

He had finally done it. He had broken her. He'd taken a woman who was sharp and feisty and full of life and he had shattered her spirit. He'd made her hate herself and he hated *himself* for it.

And he could no longer live with himself if he didn't fix it.

When Sam came toward her he looked so furious that, for a terrifying second, she thought he was going to hit her. She even put her hands up to shield herself. But instead he swooped her up in his arms, which, despite her added tonnage, he did effortlessly. Only then, with her hip pressed against his pelvis, did she realize that he was erect.

Was that what it took to arouse him? Exposing and humiliating her?

He carried her into the bedroom and dropped her on the bed, right on top of the covers. She tried to pull the duvet up over herself and he yanked it back into place. Then he started unfastening his pants.

"Wh-what are you doing?" she asked, and cursed herself for sounding so fragile and weak. So afraid. She was tougher than this.

"What does it look like I'm doing?"

"I—I don't want to."

"You've obviously got some warped version of reality and I feel obligated to set you straight." He shoved his pants down and kicked them away. "Not touching you has been the *worst* kind of torture. But I restrained myself. I thought it wasn't fair to lead you on, to make you think that anything was going to change. But I can see now that I've only made things worse."

She was afraid to say a word. To even open her mouth. He got on the bed and lowered himself over her, his familiar weight pressing her into the mattress. It felt so good, she could have cried.

"This changes nothing," he said firmly. "Not about our relationship, or the way I feel about you. You understand that?"

She understood it, even if she couldn't accept it. But she missed him so badly, she didn't care what happened after tonight. She just wanted to touch him, to feel him inside her. There was a huge lump in her throat, and she feared that if she tried to talk she would start to cry, so she nodded instead.

"You are a beautiful woman, Anne. I'm sorry if my actions made you think otherwise." He lowered his head and kissed her. Hard. He centered himself between her legs and drove into her, deep and rough, again and again, almost as if he were trying to punish her. But it was so wonderful, such a relief to know he still wanted her, tears leaked from the corners of her eyes. Almost instantly her body began to shudder with release and Sam wasn't far behind her. She didn't want it to be over so fast, she wanted to be close to him, then she realized, he wasn't finished. She barely had a chance to catch her breath before he began thrusting into her again, still hard. He lasted longer this time, making her come twice before he let himself climax. And after what couldn't have been more than a moment or two of rest, he was ready to go again. It was almost as if his body was making up for lost time and refused to rest until it had its fill of her, and her own body accepted him eagerly.

They eventually fell asleep in a sweaty tangle. Then sometime in the middle of the night she woke to feel his hand between her legs, stroking her. She moaned and pulled him to her, and they made love again.

Eleven

When Anne woke the next morning Sam was already up, and she could hear the shower running. She lay there waiting for him. She had never been so physically satisfied, and was feeling a troubling combination of joy and dread.

Never had sex been as passionate as last night. But what now? Would he go back to ignoring her? Would they only connect at night between the sheets of their bed? And could she live with that? Was it even worth it?

She heard the shower stop, then the bathroom door opened. She heard him moving around in the closet. He came out a few minutes later, a towel riding low on his hips, his hair damp and curly. She held her breath, waiting to see what he would do. If he would talk to her, or move through his morning routine without a word, the way he had been for weeks.

He walked over to his side of the bed, sat on the edge of the mattress. He sat there for thirty seconds or so, not saying a word, then finally turned to face her. "I'm tired of holding on to my anger. It's exhausting and it's not doing either one of us any good."

She braced herself for the disclaimer that she knew would follow. And it did.

"However," he added firmly, "that doesn't change the fact that I'm here—I'm in this marriage—for our children." He caught her gaze. "We're clear on that?"

"Yes." For now maybe. But eventually he would come around. She knew he would. He simply had to. They had taken a huge step last night. Whether he wanted to admit it or not. Before the fight he'd been so close to falling in love. They could get there again. She would just have to be patient.

"That said, there's no reason why we shouldn't try to make the best of it."

"I have been," she reminded him.

"I know. And I've been selfish. But things will be different this time. I promise."

She wanted to believe him. She *had* to.

One of the babies rolled and started kicking her, and she automatically put a hand to her belly.

"Kicking?" he asked.

"Want to feel? You haven't in a long time." Not since the fight.

"I feel them every night. As soon as you go to sleep, they're all over the place. It amazes me that you can sleep through it."

She'd had no idea that he did that, that he felt his children moving inside her while she slept. That had to mean something, right?

He rolled onto his side next to her and laid a hand on her belly.

"We still have to talk about names," she said, watching her skin undulate with kicks and punches. "I was hoping we could use James. For my father."

"We could do that," he said, stroking her belly lower, and maybe it was wrong, but she was starting to get turned-on. "I was thinking Victoria, after my grandmother."

"I like that name," she said, closing her eyes, savoring the sensation of his hands on her skin. Then he slipped his hand between her legs, stroking her. It felt so good a moan worked its way up and past her lips.

"Wet already?" he asked, filling her with his fingers, and she gasped, arching to take them deeper. "I could make you come right now," he said, flicking her nipple with his tongue, causing that deep tug of pleasure in her womb. He could, but she hoped he wouldn't. She wanted to make this last, just in case for some reason, it might be the last time. She wanted to savor every second.

She tugged his towel open and his erection sprang up, so she leaned over and took him into her mouth. Sam groaned and tangled his fingers through her hair, letting his head fall back against the pillow. She knew exactly what to do to set him off, too. The perfect rhythm, the sensitive spot just below his testicles that she knew made him crazy. But when she could feel him getting close, his body tensing, he stopped her. He pushed her onto her back instead and climbed over her. He took her legs and hooked them, one over each of his shoulders, then he thrust inside her. Morning sex was usually slow and tranquil, but this was different. This was hot and sexy and…wild. In no time she was shuddering with release, but he didn't let himself have pleasure, wouldn't give in until she'd climaxed a second time. Would he be so concerned with her pleasure if he didn't care about her? Didn't *love* her?

She could drive herself crazy questioning his motives, so instead she cleared her mind, closed her eyes and just let herself feel.

Afterward Sam collapsed beside her, his chest heaving with the effort to catch his breath. "Bloody hell… that was…fantastic."

She lay on her back beside him, limp, her body buzzing with afterglow. "You probably noticed that my stomach is starting to get in the way."

"I did." He looked over at her and grinned. "Maybe next time we'll have to try it on our hands and knees."

She was going to suggest they try it right now, but then he looked at the time on his phone and cursed.

"You've made me late."

"Don't blame me. You started it."

"Yes, but if you weren't so irresistible, I wouldn't have been tempted."

Two days ago he wouldn't touch her, now she was irresistible? This was just too odd. But she wasn't about to complain. She felt as though she finally had her husband back. The emotional switch had been flipped back on. Now if she could only manage to keep it on, or even *find* the damned switch in the first place, everyone could be happy.

"I have to get ready," he said, pressing a kiss to her forehead before he rolled out of bed.

She listened to the sounds of him getting ready for work, as she had dozens of times before.

Like magic, Sam was back to his old self. He talked to her, teased her and spent time with her. And the sex? Good Lord, it had never been so fantastic. Or frequent. It was as though, despite how many times they made love, he simply couldn't get enough of her. It was a much needed salve to her ego, and at the same time, confused the hell out of her.

He had been quite clear in saying that he was only there for the children, yet he treated their relationship, their marriage, like the real thing. He had done a complete one-eighty, as if the weeks of misery had never happened. Or maybe it had been a terrible nightmare that she had finally woken up from. Whatever the reason, he was back to being the sweet, patient man she had married.

It was all she had ever hoped for, so she should be blissfully happy. Hell, she should be jumping with joy. Instead she was a nervous wreck, walking on eggshells. She was terrified that if she let her guard down she might say or do the wrong thing, and he would fall off the deep end again. Shut her out of his life.

She began to feel there was something wrong with her. Why couldn't she just relax and let herself be happy?

Maybe she really was the family screwup. Maybe she was destined to live her life in perpetual dysfunction. Or was it just that she was afraid the happier she let herself feel, the more it would hurt when the other shoe finally dropped?

Since their wedding, Anne had only seen Sam's parents a couple of times. And that was before their fight. Every time he had gone there since, he had some excuse why he couldn't take her. Although most times he didn't even bother to tell her he was going. She would find out later. It was almost as if he was sheltering them from her, maybe so they wouldn't get attached, and it made her feel terrible. She didn't want them to think that she was avoiding them, or even worse, didn't like them. She wanted a good relationship with her in-laws.

Finally, when they asked her and Sam to dinner one evening in late November, either he had run out of excuses, or he actually wanted her there, because he accepted. But then she found she was nervous. What had he told them about their marriage?

"Do they know?" Anne asked him as they were getting ready to leave, after she had obsessed for an hour about what to wear, trying on a dozen different outfits before she settled on a simple slip dress.

"Know what?" Sam asked.

"About us. How things have been." She hated mentioning it, reminding him—as if he would ever forget.

"I never said anything about it to them," he told her, holding her coat so she could slip it on. "As far as they know, everything is fine. And as far as I'm concerned, everything is."

She wished she could be so confident.

It had begun snowing that morning, the first of the

season, and by the time she and Sam got to his parents' house, a Tudor-style mansion, several inches had fallen, making the roads a bit treacherous.

The first thing his mother did, after they shed their boots and coats and gloves, was take Anne upstairs to show her the nursery and playroom they had already begun to set up for the twins.

"It's beautiful!" Anne told her, running her hand along the rail of one of the cribs. There were two. One with boy bedding and one for a girl. The walls were painted a gender-neutral shade of green, and there were shelves overflowing with toys and books. Many, she told Anne, used to be Sam's and Adam's.

"I haven't even started setting up the nursery," Anne told her. "Once Chris and Melissa move into the master suite, we'll be taking their old room, since the current nursery is right beside it."

"I hope you don't mind that we have a nursery," his mother said.

"Of course not."

"We know that as new parents it will be nice to occasionally have some time to yourselves. We would love to have the twins spend the night here every now and then. But we don't want to overstep our bounds."

"They're your grandchildren. Of course they can stay here."

She looked relieved. "I'm so glad. We weren't sure how you felt."

Because Anne was so absent from their lives. Her mother-in-law didn't say it, but Anne knew that was what she was thinking. And what could Anne say? *"It's not my fault. Your son has been keeping me from you."*

Then she would have to admit they had been having problems, and her mother-in-law would want to know why. Anne would be too humiliated to tell her what she had done to their son. The way she had lied to Sam. They would probably draw the same conclusion he had. They would think she was spoiled and selfish. That she had trapped him.

From now on, she would make an effort to spend more time with her in-laws. She would ask her mother-in-law to tea, or maybe they could go shopping in Paris or Milan. And she could invite them both to dinner at the castle.

"I'm sorry I don't make it over more," Anne said guiltily. "I feel I haven't been a very good daughter-in-law."

"Oh, Anne," she said, touching her arm. "Please, there's no need to apologize. Sam has explained how complicated it is for you with security and such. He said that you and your family are practically prisoners in the castle."

That was true, but it wasn't the reason for her absence. Sam had flat-out lied to his parents, and she couldn't help but think bitterly that dishonesty seemed to be okay if it suited his own needs, but if she wasn't completely candid all the time, it was wrong somehow. Talk about a double-edged sword and she was getting really tired of falling on it.

"I'll be so relieved when the man harassing you is caught," her mother-in-law said. "They should lock him up and throw away the key."

It was odd, but since they learned he was Geoffrey's son, and that he was emotionally disturbed, the profound hatred and resentment she felt before had fizzled out. Instead she felt deeply sorry for him. Not that she didn't want to see him locked up, but only so he could get the help he needed. She could only imagine the horrors he'd experienced in the military. Then to be refused help. It was unconscionable.

"He's a disturbed man who needs psychiatric help," Anne said. "Everyone will be relieved when he's caught."

Sam's father appeared in the doorway. "I thought I would find you two in here. Supper is ready."

She was probably being paranoid, but all through dinner Anne had the feeling that something was up. Sam's parents seemed…anxious. They picked at their food, a traditional English stew that was so delicious Anne actually had seconds. After dessert, they moved to the living room for brandy, or in Anne's case, mineral water. After they were all served, and the maid out of the room, Sam asked his parents, "So, are we going to talk about whatever it is that's bothering the two of you?"

Apparently Anne hadn't been the only one who noticed something was off.

"There is something we need to tell you," his father said, and his wife took his hand.

Anne had a feeling it wasn't going to be good news, and Sam must have shared her impression, because he frowned and asked, "What's wrong?"

"I went for my annual physical a few weeks ago and the doctor discovered that I have an enlarged prostate. They did some tests and they've come back positive for cancer. However," he added swiftly, "I'm in the early stages and he says it's one of the less aggressive types."

"He's not even recommending surgery," his mother said. "He thinks that with a round of radiation your father will be as good as new."

She could feel Sam's relief all but leaking from his pores as he sagged into the sofa beside her. "That's great. It could be much worse, right?"

"*Much* worse."

Sam looked from one parent to the other. "But there's something else, isn't there?"

They exchanged a look, then his father said. "I've decided that, for the sake of my health, it's time that I retire."

"Retire? But you love being prime minister. What will you do?"

"Relax, for a change. The truth is I've grown weary of politics. The long hours and constant conflict. I'm tired of it. I'm stepping down, and until my term ends six months from now, the deputy prime minister will take my place."

The change in Sam's stature was subtle, but Anne felt it right away, and she knew exactly what he was thinking. If it weren't for his marriage, for *her,* Sam would be running to take his father's place. And he would get it, because out of anyone else who might choose to run, he would be the most qualified. He would be prime minister, just as he had always wanted.

But now that was never going to happen. And it was all her fault.

Maybe she imagined it, but she swore she could feel

that emotional switch snap off. And all she could think was, *Oh God, here we go again.*

"I suppose he'll run for your seat after that," Sam said.

"I'm sure he will," his father said, and Anne knew just what Sam was thinking. He had declared more than once that the deputy was a moron.

"I know this will be difficult for you, son," his father said, avoiding Anne's gaze.

"I'm fine," Sam told him, forcing a smile. Another lie. "You shouldn't even be worrying about how his will affect me. All that matters right now is your health. If you're happy, I'm happy for you."

He sounded sincere, but Anne knew better, and in the back of her mind she heard the distinct clunk of that pesky other shoe dropping.

Since the weather was getting progressively worse, they left his parents' house a short time later. Only when they were in the car and on their way back to the castle did Sam let down his guard, and she saw how truly upset he was.

"The deputy is a wanker," he said.

But he was handsome and congenial, and people had been elected on far less.

"Sam," she started to say, but he held up a hand to hush her.

"Please, don't. Not now."

She knew this was going to happen. That it was inevitable. She'd felt it in her bones. Unfortunately, that didn't make the reality of the situation any easier to accept. Although in a very strange way, it was a relief to finally have it over with.

She leaned back against the seat and looked out into the night, watching as fat snowflakes drifted past the car window. She tried to tell herself that this was just a small blip, and in a day or two, everything would be okay.

She told herself that, because the alternative was unimaginable. If he shut her out again, how long would it take this time to drag him back out of his shell?

And this time, did she even want to try?

Twelve

He knew it was selfish and unfair, but Sam couldn't even look at Anne.

The idea of never following in his father's footsteps had been upsetting, but easier to stomach when the prospect seemed so far in the future. Now here it was staring him right in the face. He was forced once again to rehash everything he'd lost. Everything he wanted and would never have. And he blamed her.

On top of that his father had cancer. Sam could only hope he was being honest about the prognosis, and not sugarcoating the truth so Sam wouldn't worry.

With the inclement weather it took twice the normal time to get home. And he used the term "home" loosely, because right now he felt as if he were in limbo. One foot in and one out of his marriage. His life. He needed some time to himself, to work things through and regroup. If there was any possible way he could justify not staying at the castle for a day or two, he would be gone. The construction on his town house had been completed months ago, so he could stay there. But then there was the problem of her family. If he wasn't careful, he would find himself miserable *and* unemployed. At least with a job he enjoyed, he had someplace to escape to.

Otherwise, he was trapped.

Anne was quiet while they got ready for bed, but when they climbed under the covers, she reached for him. Though he felt like a bastard for it, he shrugged away from her. She was only trying to comfort him, trying to be a good wife, but he couldn't let her in. Not yet. The wound was still too fresh.

It'll be better tomorrow, he assured himself. But the next morning, after a long night of tossing and turning, he only felt worse. Anne tried to talk to him, but he shook his head and told her, "I'm not ready," hating himself for the hurt look she didn't bother trying to hide. He wasn't being fair—there had to come a time when he forgave her and moved on—but he couldn't help the way he felt. The bitterness and resentment. He kept telling himself, tomorrow it will better. But it wasn't. Every day that passed he pulled deeper inside his shell.

Only days ago he had been close to forgiving her—to putting it all behind them. Now he felt as though he would be angry with her indefinitely.

It was killing Anne to see Sam so unhappy.

She had hoped that by now he would have come around, but since his father's announcement two weeks ago they had been in a steady free fall. She had tried to be patient and sympathetic. She tried to give him space to work things through. And still he kept telling her that he needed time. She just wasn't sure if she had any left to give.

He was miserable, and she was miserable, and though she loved him, she simply didn't have the strength to fight anymore. Not when it was a one-sided battle. And forcing him to stay with her, when he clearly didn't want to be there, wasn't right. It wasn't fair to him, or her, or even the babies.

She wasn't a quitter, and she had tried damned hard to make it work, but this was a losing battle. She could no longer take his Jekyll and Hyde mood swings. And even if he did come around again, how could she be sure that the next time things got hard, he wouldn't do this again? And again. She couldn't live like this anymore, always on her guard. Waiting for the next disaster.

It was clear that the only way they would ever be happy again was if they were apart. For good.

Making that final decision had been hard, but at the same time a huge burden had been lifted. She felt…free. The really tough part was going to Chris and admitting that, after only a few months, her marriage was over.

"I had the feeling something was wrong," he told her. "But I had hoped you would work it out."

"We tried," she said. Or at least, *she* had. But this whole mess was her fault in the first place, so it didn't seem fair to blame only him. "It just isn't going to work. We're miserable."

"So what you're saying is, you want permission to divorce."

"I understand the position I'm putting the family in and I'm sorry."

He sighed. "A little scandal won't kill us."

"So you'll allow it?"

"If there's one thing we've learned, it's that life is short. You deserve to be happy, not chained to a marriage that isn't working. I can't deny that I'm very fond of Sam. He's done one hell of a job as ambassador."

"But after the divorce, he'll be able to go back to politics. Right?"

"He'll be stripped of his title, so yes, he can hold any office he wants."

Well, she could give him that at least. And telling Chris made it feel so much more...*final*. She had to fight not to give in to her grief, reach deep inside herself to find the old Anne. *The Shrew*. The Anne who didn't need anyone, or care what anyone thought of her. And still, somewhere deep down, she couldn't help but cling to the slender hope that when faced with the real prospect of their marriage ending, Sam would suddenly comprehend everything he was giving up. Maybe he would even realize that he loved her.

She waited until that evening to approach him. He had just come home from work and was in their room changing for dinner. She walked in and shut the door behind her.

"We need to talk," she said.

Without even glancing her way he said, "Now isn't a good time."

"Then I'll talk and you can just listen."

He turned to her, looking pained, and she almost felt

sorry for him. He was miserable and he was doing it to himself. "I'm not ready. I need time."

"Well, I can't do this anymore," she said.

"Do what?"

"This. *Us*. We're both unhappy. I think it would be best…" The words caught in her throat. *Come on, Anne, hold it together.* She squared her shoulders. "I think it would best for everyone if we called it quits."

He narrowed his eyes at her, as though he thought it might be a trick. After a pause he asked, "Is this the part where I have a change of heart and realize I can't live without you?"

Apparently not. She swallowed back the sorrow rising up from deep inside her. This was it. It was really the end. Her marriage was over. "No. This is the part where I ask you to leave, and tell you I want a divorce."

He just stood there, like he was waiting for the punch line. When it didn't come he said, "You're serious."

She nodded.

"So that's it? Just like that, it's over?"

She shrugged, tried to pretend she wasn't coming apart on the inside. "Just like that."

"You're just giving up?"

"It takes two people to make a marriage work, Sam. You gave up a long time ago. And I can't fight for this anymore."

He didn't deny it, because he knew she was right.

"I've already talked to my attorney and he's drawing up the divorce papers immediately."

"You said before that once we're married, that's it."

"I talked to Chris and he's going to allow it. And he assured me that the second it's legal you will be stripped of your title. That should give you plenty of time to set up a campaign and run for prime minister. You'll have everything you've ever wanted."

He still looked hesitant. Honestly, she thought he'd have been packing by now.

"Why are you doing this?" he asked. "Why now?"

"Because I can't live like this anymore. I may have made a terrible mistake, Sam, but I can't pay for it for the rest of my life. I deserve to be happy. To be married to someone who loves me, not a man who tolerates me for the sake of our children."

"I married you for their sake."

Yes, he had, and shame on her for forgetting that. "There's no benefit to their parents being married if everyone is miserable. We'll share custody, and they will grow up knowing both their parents love them very much, even if they don't live in the same household. They'll live perfectly happy lives, like millions of other kids whose parents are divorced."

"And my ambassadorship?"

"Chris is arranging for a replacement as we speak. You are free to pursue a job you actually like. Effective immediately."

"I did like my job," he said.

"But now you can have the one you want."

He was quiet for a long time, as though he was working it through. Processing it. She started to feel the faintest glimmer of hope. Maybe he was beginning to realize what he was about to lose.

But then he nodded and said, "It probably is for the best." Driving the proverbial stake through her heart.

If he loved her, even a little bit, he would want to fight for her.

"I'd like you gone tonight," she said, struggling to maintain her composure. To keep her voice even, her expression cold.

She was *The Shrew,* she reminded herself. She didn't let people hurt her.

"If that's what you want," he said.

No, she wanted to shout. She wanted *him,* the way he had been right after their wedding. The man who had been so sweet and caring when she lost her father. Her *partner.*

She wanted him to love her. But that was never going to happen.

"It's what I want. I'll go so you can pack."

"You're sure about this?"

"I've never been so sure of anything in my life. I just…" She swallowed hard. "I just don't love you anymore."

"It was never about love."

Not for him maybe, but it had been for her. And saying she didn't love him now was a lie.

But this was one lie she was sure he could live with.

Sam was relieved.

He was out of a job, a signature away from divorce, and wouldn't live in the same house as his twin infants. And he was happy about it.

At least, that's what he had been telling himself. Over and over. And he was sure, in time, he might actually start believing it.

He moved back into his town house, with its shiny new kitchen and sagless ceilings. Exactly where he had wanted to be. Only to realize that it didn't much feel like home anymore.

It would just take time to adjust, he kept telling himself. He could get on with his life now. He could follow in his father's footsteps and run for the prime minister's seat. Even though the mere idea of an arduous campaign exhausted him. He hadn't even thought about whom he would hire to run it, much less a platform to run on.

But he had made the right decision, leaving Anne—of course, he hadn't left so much as been kicked out.

And if he was so sure then why, after three days of moping, hadn't he told his parents? It was only a matter of time before the story made it to the press. He couldn't abide by them reading in the newspaper that their son had failed at being a husband.

And that was how he felt. Like a complete failure.

But he couldn't put it off any longer.

"What a nice surprise!" his father said, when Sam popped in unannounced. But as he shrugged out of his coat and handed it to the maid, his father frowned. "Have you been sick?"

"What makes you ask that?"

"Well, it's Wednesday. You're not at work. And forgive me for saying so, but you look terrible."

He must have been a sight with tousled hair and several days' worth of beard stubble. Not to mention his wrinkled clothes. He hadn't unpacked yet and had been living out of a suitcase and boxes. "No, I'm not sick. But I do need to talk to you about something."

"How about a drink?" his father offered.

Figuring he would need the liquid courage, Sam said, "Make it a double."

While he poured, Sam asked, "Is Mom around?"

"She had some luncheon to attend." He shrugged. "One of her charities, I think. I lose track."

He had hoped to tell them both together, but since he was already here... Besides, it might be easier talking to his father first.

He handed Sam his drink. "Shall we sit in the den?"

"Sure." He followed his father down the hall, thinking how, in all the years they had lived there, not much had changed. But Sam had. And he would be the first to admit he was very fond of the familiar. He was a creature of habit, so change made him...edgy. And right now, his entire life felt turned upside down.

When they were seated in the den, Sam on the sofa and his father in his favorite chair, he asked, "So, what's up?"

Sam sat on the edge of the cushion, elbows resting on his knees, swirling the scotch in his glass. "I thought you should know that I moved out of the castle last week. Anne and I are getting a divorce."

"I'm sorry to hear that, Sam. You two seemed so happy."

They were. For a while. Until things got so complicated.

"Can I ask what happened?"

Sam considered telling him the truth. About the night of the twins' conception and the fact that Anne had lied about birth control. Then continued to lie even after they were married. But he realized that really had nothing to do with this.

So, she had made a mistake. Yes, he'd been angry, and he'd felt betrayed. And he'd struggled so damned hard to hold on to to it, to…punish her. When he finally let go, let himself forgive her, it had been a relief.

This was different. This wasn't about what she had done, although at first it had been easier to blame her than to admit what was really bothering him. Because that was the way he liked things. Easy.

But really, he'd only made things more complicated.

"I screwed up," he told his father, taking a long swallow of his drink, but the path of fire it scored in his throat didn't come close to the burning ache in his heart. "I screwed up and I don't know how to fix it. If it even is fixable."

"Do you love her?"

It surprised him how quickly the answer surfaced. "Yeah. I do."

"Have you told her that?"

No. In fact, he'd told her specifically that he *didn't* love her. That he never would. That he was only in it for the kids. "It wasn't supposed to be about love. That wasn't part of the plan."

His father laughed. "In my experience, son, things rarely go as planned. Especially when it comes to love."

Yes, but if it wasn't about love, then it would be easy. No messy emotions to get in the way and complicate things. It was when he started falling in love with her that everything got so confusing.

He downed the last of his drink and set the empty glass on the coffee table. "It shouldn't be this complicated."

"What?"

"Relationships. Marriage. It shouldn't be this hard."

"If it were easy, don't you think it would get... boring?"

"Is it too much to want what you and Mom have?"

"And what do we have?"

"The perfect marriage. You never fought or had problems. It was so *easy* for you. It just...worked."

"Sam, our marriage is *far* from perfect."

"Okay, I know you two have had your little spats, but—"

"Infidelity? Do you consider that a little spat?"

At first he thought his father was kidding, and when he saw that he was, in fact, *very* serious, Sam's jaw dropped. "You cheated on Mom?"

He shook his head solemnly. "Never. I've never once been unfaithful to your mother. Not that I didn't have the opportunity. But I loved her too much. Too much for my own good."

"If you didn't—" The meaning of his father's words suddenly sank in and they almost knocked him backward. "Are you saying that *Mom* was unfaithful to *you?*"

"You remember how much she toured, all the attention she got. Not to mention that she's an incredibly beautiful woman."

Sam could hardly believe what he was hearing. *"When?"*

"You were eight."

"I—I'm *stunned*. I had no idea."

"And we never meant for you to find out. Now I'm beginning to think that sheltering you from the realities of our relationship was a mistake. Marriages take work, son. They're complicated and messy."

"What did you do when you found out?"

"I was devastated. And I seriously considered leaving. I went so far as to pack my bags, but she begged me to forgive her, to give her a second chance. We decided together that we would go to counseling and try to save our marriage. She even took a year off from touring, to prove to me that she was serious. That our relationship came first."

"I remember that," Sam said. "I remember her being home all the time. I just never stopped to think why, I guess."

"Why would you? You were a little boy. And always so happy. So bright and cheerful. We didn't want our problems to reflect negatively on you. Or Adam. Although I think he suspected."

"How could you ever trust her again?"

"It wasn't easy. Especially after she went back to touring. We had a few very rough years. But I think our marriage is better for it. If we could survive that, we can survive almost anything."

Sam felt as if his entire world had been flipped on its axis. His parents' perfect marriage hadn't been perfect at all. He had been holding himself, his own marriage, to such a ridiculously high standard that the instant they hit a snag, he'd felt like a failure, that he wasn't measuring up. He had expected Anne to conform to some cardboard cut-out version of his perfect mother, never knowing that person didn't even exist.

He pinched the bridge of his nose. "I. Am. A *wanker.*"

His dad grinned. "You can't learn if you don't make mistakes."

"Well, I've made a monumental one. All of the troubles Anne and I have been having revolve around one thing, my desire to run for the prime minister's seat. And I've been so damned busy focusing on what I can't have, instead of what I do have, I've completely overlooked the fact that I don't want to be prime minister anymore."

When his father announced his retirement, it had been the perfect excuse to push Anne away. So he wouldn't have to admit that he was falling in love with her.

"Are you disappointed?" he asked his father.

He looked puzzled. "Why would I be disappointed?"

"Well, I always planned to follow in your footsteps."

"Sam, you have to walk your own path, make your own footprint. You have to do what makes *you* happy."

"I'm happy as an ambassador. And I'm damned good at it. Or at least, I *was.*"

"They fired you?"

He shrugged. "Anne, the job, it was a package deal." And he had blown it.

His entire life Sam had known exactly what he wanted, and he had never been afraid of anything. But now he wasn't just afraid. He was terrified. Terrified that it was too late.

"Do you want her back?" his father asked.

"More than anything. But I'm not so sure she'll give me another chance. Or if I even deserve one."

"Can I give you a bit of advice?"

Sam nodded.

"The most precious things in life are the ones you have to fight for. So ask yourself, is she worth fighting for?"

He didn't even have to think about it. "Yes, she is."

"So what are you going to do?"

There was only one thing he could do. "I guess I'm going to fight."

Thirteen

Sam headed back to his town house to shower and change before he went to see Anne, only to be met at the front door and served with an envelope containing the divorce papers.

He didn't bother to open it, since he had no intention of signing them. But it was clear, when he got to the castle, that she wasn't going to make this reconciliation easy for him.

"I'm sorry, sir," the guard posted at the gate said, when Sam pulled up. "I can't let you in."

"It's very important," Sam told him, but the man didn't budge. "Come on, you *know* me."

When he was part of the family, the guard's expression said. "I do apologize, sir. But I have strict orders not to let you in."

He said he would fight for her, and that was what he

planned to do, even to the detriment of his pride. "Can you just call up and tell her I'm here?"

"Sir—"

"Please, just do me this favor. Call her and tell her that I *need* to see her."

He hesitated, then stepped back into his booth and picked up the phone. Sam breathed a sigh of relief. If Anne knew he was out here waiting, that he needed to talk to her, surely she would let him in.

The guard spoke into the phone, nodded a few times, then hung up. Sam waited for him to reach for the lever that would open the gate and wave him past. Instead, he stepped back out of the booth and over to Sam's car window. "If you require an audience with the princess, it was suggested that you contact her personal assistant or the palace social secretary."

Now she was being ridiculous. They were still *married* for God's sake. And had she forgotten that she was pregnant with *his* children?

He pulled out his cell phone and dialed her private number. It rang three times, then went to voice mail. He tried her cell phone next. This time it went straight to voice mail. He listened to the generic message, and after the tone said, "Anne, this is ridiculous. Pick up the phone."

He disconnected, then immediately dialed again. Again, he got her voice mail. Either she was rejecting his calls, or the phone was off, but he knew that she always kept her phone on, so he was guessing it was the latter.

He texted her a message: CALL ME!!!!!!

He waited, but after a moment she hadn't replied, and his phone wasn't ringing.

"Sir," the guard said firmly. "I'm going to have to ask you to leave."

"Hold on."

He tried Louisa's phone with no luck, then Melissa's, then as a last-ditch effort, he called Chris's office line, but his secretary fed him some garbage about His Highness being out of the office.

He was being stonewalled.

He texted her again: I'm not giving up. I'm going to fight for you.

"Mr. Baldwin." A second, more threatening-looking guard with a holstered sidearm appeared at his window. "I'm going to have to insist that you leave right now."

Sam could insist that he was staying, and demand to see Anne, but it would most likely land him in jail. He could try to sneak onto the grounds, but with Richard Corrigan still at large, Sam would no doubt be shot on sight.

"All right, I'm going," he grumbled.

She'd completely shut him out. And hadn't he done the exact same thing to her? Hadn't he shut her out emotionally?

He couldn't help thinking that he was getting a taste of his own medicine. That didn't mean he had any intention of giving up.

She had told him she was tired of being the only one fighting to save their marriage. Well, if it was a fight she wanted, that was what she was about to get.

"Sam again?" Louisa asked, when Anne's cell rang for the *bazillionth* time that morning. They were in

Louisa's room, on the Internet, registering for baby things in preparation for Anne's shower in January.

"Who else?" Anne grabbed it and rejected the call. He had been calling and texting and e-mailing incessantly. "I'm going to have to change my bloody number. And my e-mail address."

Louisa bit her lip.

"What?" Anne said.

She pasted on an innocent look and said, "I didn't say a word."

"No, but you want to. I can tell."

Louisa had seen Sam leave with his suitcases that night a week ago—although it felt more like a month—and Anne had finally broken down and told her everything that happened.

"It's just that he's very…persistent," Louisa said gently. "Maybe you should talk to him."

According to his numerous texts—which Anne had grudgingly read but refused to answer—and all the messages he had left on her phone, he loved her, and he wanted to fight to make their marriage work. But she didn't have any fight left in her.

"I have nothing left to say to him."

"You're having his babies, Annie. You can't ignore him forever."

She didn't plan to. She would talk to him eventually, but not until she felt it was safe. Not until she woke in the morning without that sick, empty feeling in her heart, until she could go more than five minutes without seeing his face or hearing his voice in her head. Not until she could face him and not long to throw herself into his arms and hold him.

She needed time to get over him.

Her phone buzzed as a text came through.

I'm not giving up. I love you.

Apparently he'd forgotten that this wasn't about love. Besides, he didn't really love her. He just didn't like losing. But this time he wouldn't charm his way back into her heart. Not when she knew he would only break it again.

"You know I love you, Annie, and I'm always on your side…" Louisa began.

"But?"

"Don't you think you're being just a little…unfair?"

"Unfair? Was Sam being fair when he ignored me for weeks?"

"So you're getting revenge? Giving him a taste of his own medicine?"

"No! That's not what I meant."

"Just call him. Tell him it's over."

"I did tell him. The night I kicked him out."

"Well, apparently the message didn't get through, and until you level with him, he's going to keep thinking there's hope. I don't have to tell you what that's like."

She hated that Louisa's words made so much sense.

Her phone started ringing again. Louisa picked it up and handed it to her. "Talk to him. If not for yourself, then do it for me."

She hesitated, then took the phone and Louisa walked out, leaving her alone. She took a deep breath, terrified that when she heard his voice, she was going to melt.

You are *The Shrew,* she reminded herself. A cold-hearted bitch who doesn't need anyone.

Now, if she could just make herself believe it.

* * *

Anne had ignored so many of his calls that when she finally did answer, he forgot what he was going to say. But that wasn't a problem, because she didn't give him a chance to say a word.

"I only accepted your call to ask you to please stop bothering me. I don't want to talk to you."

"Then I'll do the talking and you can listen."

"Sam—"

"I am so sorry for the way I treated you. I love you, Annie."

"It's not supposed to be about love," she said, throwing his words back in his face. Not that he blamed her.

"I know, but I fell in love with you anyway. And it scared the hell out of me."

"Why?"

"I thought that loving you would be too hard. Turns out, loving you was the easy part. The hard part was pushing you away."

"I can't be with someone who flakes out on me every time things get hard. Every time I make a mistake."

"I know my track record up until now hasn't been great, and I'm sorry, but if you give me another chance, I swear it will be different this time."

"That's what you said the last time."

"This time I mean it."

"I want to believe you. I truly do. But I just can't take the chance. The way things were, I just…I can't do that again."

"Annie—"

"It's over, Sam. Please don't call me again."

The line went dead, and Sam stared dumbfounded at the phone.

She was turning him down?

And why shouldn't she? Why should she believe a word he said? Had he just assumed, after the way he had treated her, that he could simply pour his heart out and she would beg him to come home?

A part of him wanted to be angry. He wanted to believe that she was only doing this to be stubborn. To get revenge. But that wasn't Anne's style. She'd loved him, and she had done everything she could to try to make their marriage work. She stuck by him, even when he was treating her like a pariah. And what thanks had she gotten? Absolutely none. He hadn't been the least bit grateful. He hadn't even *tried* to make it work.

The truth was, he didn't deserve her. And maybe they would both be better off if he just let her go.

Anne's feet were swollen and sore and her back ached something special, so the last place she wanted to be was standing out in the freezing cold in front of a crowd of doctors, nurses and television media. But Melissa was in the throes of twenty-four-hour morning sickness, so Chris asked Anne to accompany him to the ground-breaking ceremony for the new pediatric cancer center at the hospital.

They stood on the platform, in the brisk wind, waiting for the hospital administrator to finish his spiel. She kept her hands tucked in her coat pockets, probably looking to everyone like she was just trying to stay warm, when in fact, she clutched her cell phone in her right hand, waiting to feel the buzz alerting her to an incoming call or text message. But as it had been the past two weeks, it remained stubbornly silent.

There had to be something wrong with her. For days Sam had called nonstop and all she had wanted was for him to leave her alone, but now that he had, she longed to hear his voice.

She kept thinking about what he'd said the last time they talked, wondering if he actually meant it this time. He'd told her that he loved her and she was starting to believe him. But she was still too afraid to accept it, to face the possibility that he might just hurt her all over again.

But if he called, if *he* made the first move…again. Why would he when she had asked him to leave her alone? But if he loved her, would he really give up that easily? And was she forgetting all the texts and phone calls that she had refused to answer?

She shivered and hunched her shoulders against a sudden burst of icy wind.

"Whose brilliant idea was it to do this in December?" she grumbled under her breath.

"It's almost over," Chris assured her softly. "Just hang in there."

She glanced over at him, irritable and cold, and wanting to do something really childish, like stick her tongue out at him. She did a swift double take when she noticed a tiny red spot on the lapel of his coat. Had that been there earlier? At first she figured it was some sort of stain, or a stray fleck of lint. Then it moved.

What the—?

She was sure her eyes were playing tricks on her, then the spot moved again, from his lapel to the left side of his chest. It was a light, she realized, like a laser pointer—

It hit her then, what it could be, and her heart clenched. She knew there was no time to alert Gunter, who stood behind her. She had to do something. Now.

Time screeched to a halt, then picked up in slow motion, the seconds ticking by like hours as she yanked her hands free from her pockets and reached up, shoving Chris as hard as she could. She saw his stunned expression the same instant she felt her arm jerked back painfully, and felt herself being pulled over. She braced for the pain of the hard platform as she landed, but instead she landed on a person. Gunter, she realized. He rolled her over to her side away from the crowd and shielded her with his enormous body. Then someone shouted for a medic and her heart froze. Had she been too late? Had Chris been hit?

She tried to push up on her elbow, to see him, and Gunter ordered, "Stay down!"

She lay there helpless, imagining her brother bleeding to death only a few inches away. Her ears began to ring, all but drowning out the frightened screams of the people fleeing the area.

Then everything went black.

Sam sat slumped on the couch in his town house, nursing a scotch and brooding. Or sulking. Or a combination of the two.

His cell had been ringing almost constantly for two hours, but none of the calls were from Anne and he didn't feel like talking to anyone. Not when he was perfectly content to sit here alone and contemplate the fact that he'd had everything a man could hope for and he had callously thrown it away.

The divorce papers lay on the coffee table in front of him, still unsigned. He just couldn't seem to make himself pick up a pen. He didn't want a divorce. Didn't want to lose Anne.

But she wanted to lose him and hadn't he put her through enough grief? Didn't he owe it to her to set her free? Even though the idea of her falling in love with someone else and some other man raising his children made him physically ill. But he knew Anne well enough to realize that refusing a divorce wouldn't stop her from getting on with her life. She was so stubborn, it would probably make her that much more determined to forget him.

He sat up and grabbed the document. He hadn't read it, but his lawyer assured him it was pretty cut-and-dry. They would both leave the marriage with exactly what they had brought to it. It would almost be as if it had never happened.

He flipped to the page that was flagged for him to sign. He could *do* this. He grabbed the pen off the table, took a deep breath, raised the pen to the paper…and his damned phone started ringing again.

"Bloody hell!" He snatched the phone up off the table, flipped it open and barked, "What do you want?"

"Sam?" his brother, Adam, asked, clearly taken aback.

"Yes, it's me. It's my phone you called."

"Where have you been? We've been trying to reach you for an hour."

"I'm home. And the fact that I haven't answered should tell you that I don't feel like talking to anyone."

"I thought you would have been at the hospital by now."

"Why would I be at the hospital?" Did his brother think he was so depressed that he would be suicidal?

"You haven't heard the news?"

"What news?"

"There was a shooting. The king and Anne were outside the hospital for some ceremony and there was an assassination attempt."

Oh Jesus. He grabbed the remote and switched the television on. "Is Chris okay?"

"It was confirmed he wasn't hit. Anne shoved him out of the way at the last minute. She saved his life. But, Sam…"

Adam's words faded into the background as the banner announcing a "breaking story" flashed across the screen, and he saw the headline, *Assassination Attempt. Princess Anne Rushed to Hospital.* The remote slipped from his fingers and clattered to the floor and his heart slammed the wall of his chest so hard he couldn't draw in a full breath.

This was not happening.

He listened numbly as the newscaster relayed the events of the shooting. Then they ran a clip of the shooting taken by one of the television cameras in the crowd. Sam watched in disbelief as one minute Anne and Chris were just standing there listening to the hospital administrator, then Anne glanced up at her brother, and suddenly shoved him hard. Gunter was on her immediately, taking her down and out of the shooter's line of sight, then the camera's view was blocked by the podium. Sam couldn't tell if she'd been hit and when it cut back to the newscaster, she said there was still no word on the extent of the princess's injuries, only that she had been unconscious.

He didn't hear anything after that. What must have been a rush of adrenaline propelled him up off the couch. Only when he was on his feet and heading for the door, grabbing his keys and coat on the way out, did he realize he was still holding his phone and Adam was shouting his name.

"I'll call you back," he said, and disconnected. He needed to get to the hospital now.

This was *his* fault. He should have been there with her, standing by her side on that platform. And he would never forgive himself if she and the babies weren't okay.

Fourteen

If a person had to be shot at, what better place than right outside of a hospital?

Anne sat in bed, in the royal family's private wing, wearing one of those irritating, backless gowns that left her behind exposed. And she had no idea why she required a bare ass when all she had were a few minor bumps and bruises from Gunter pulling her down. They had admitted her only because she'd passed out, which embarrassed her terribly, and, even though she'd landed on Gunter, they worried the fall may have hurt the babies. And though everything was fine, they still insisted she should stay overnight for observation.

It was worth it to know that Chris was safe.

The police told her that if she hadn't pushed Chris aside, he would almost assuredly be dead.

Had she acted an instant later, he would have taken a

bullet to the chest, and if she'd reacted a second sooner, the bullet probably would have hit her head instead. Either Chris would be dead, or she would. The idea still gave her cold chills.

The best part was that the police had *finally* arrested Richard Corrigan. Apparently being on the run, and in hiding, had gotten to him. He hadn't even tried to get away this time. The plan had been to kill Chris and then himself, but the police got to him before he could carry out the second half.

Finally, this terrible nightmare, the harassment and threats, were over. They were free again.

As soon as the doctor would allow visitors, her family had flooded the room, needing to see with their own eyes that she was all right. Even though the doctor assured them she was doing exceptionally well for someone who was just shot at and pregnant with twins to boot.

Chris chastised her for putting her and the twins' lives in jeopardy for him, then he hugged her fiercely. She could swear she even saw the sheen of tears in his eyes.

She wanted to call Sam. The last thing she wanted was for him to see it on the news and think the worst, but her phone had gone missing in all the chaos. Everyone had been trying to reach him. Her family, and Gunter, and even the police, but apparently he wasn't answering his phone.

"I'm sure as soon as he hears he'll be here," her mother assured her. She had been sitting on the edge of the bed holding Anne's hand since they let the family in. Louisa was on the opposite side and both her brothers stood near the foot of the bed. There was nothing like a near-death experience to bring a family closer.

Everyone but Sam.

Maybe Sam had heard about the shooting but she had driven him so far away he just didn't care anymore.

She immediately shook the thought away, writing it off as utterly ridiculous. Even if he didn't care about her anymore, he still loved his children.

Gunter stepped into the room about fifteen minutes later and Anne looked to him hopefully, but he shook his head. "We send car, but he was not home."

"So where the heck *is* he?"

"He'll come," Louisa assured her.

"Could he have gone out of town?" Melissa asked, stepping up beside Chris.

"Or to his parents' house?" Liv suggested.

"We already tried there," Anne said.

As she was combing her mind, trying to imagine where else he could possibly be, the door flew open and Sam was there.

His eyes darted to the bed, and when he saw her sitting there, she could actually see him go weak with relief. She didn't have to ask her family to give them privacy. They were barely out the door before Sam had crossed the room and was holding her. The feel of his body, his familiar scent, nearly brought her to tears. How could she have even thought that letting go of him was a good thing?

"On the news all they said was that you might have been shot." He squeezed her, burying his face in her hair. "I didn't know if you were alive or dead. If I would ever see you again. Then I got here and the stupid people downstairs wouldn't tell me anything."

"Well, I'm not dead," she said, and he held her even tighter.

"You're okay? The babies are okay?"

"We're fine. I'm only in here because I passed out."

"I thought I lost you. For good this time." He cupped her face in his hands and kissed her. Firmly and prickly. Then he pulled away and she realized why. It had been so long since he'd shaved, he'd surpassed stubble and now had a full-fledged beard. His hair was shaggy, too, and in need of a trim. And she was guessing, by the dark smudges under his eyes, that he'd been sleeping as poorly as she had. And to top the look off, under his cashmere coat he wore a T-shirt and cartoon-emblazoned cotton pants.

He looked terrible. And wonderful.

"Nice pants," she said.

He looked down at himself and laughed, as though he'd just realized he'd left the house in his pajamas. And because she could, she reached up and touched his dimple.

"Suffice it to say I left in a hurry." He took her hand in his and kissed it. "Annie, I have been such an ass—"

She put a finger over his lips to shush him. "We *both* acted really stupid. But we're smarter now."

"Definitely." He kissed her fingers, her wrist. "I didn't sign the divorce papers. And I'm not going to. I flat-out refuse. I plan to spend the rest of my life with you."

"Good, because I didn't sign them, either. After you move back to the castle, we'll build a big fire in the study and watch them burn."

His eyes locked on hers. "And then we'll make love all night."

She sighed. That sounded wonderful.

He smiled, touched her face. "I am so proud of you."

"For what?"

"For *what?*" He laughed. "What do you think? You saved your brother's life. You're a hero."

"I wasn't trying to be. Everything happened so fast. I saw the laser sight on his coat and I just pushed him."

His brow furrowed. "I should have been there for you."

"But you're here now."

"I'm not leaving you again, Annie. I love you so much."

"I love you, too, Sam.

"I've said it before, but things will be different this time. I know, because *I'm* different."

"Me, too. There's nothing like a near-death experience to set your priorities straight."

He kissed her again, then said, "Scoot over."

He dropped his coat on the floor and crawled into bed beside her, drawing her close to his side. She had never felt more content, more happy in her life. And it was nice to know that she wasn't the family screwup after all. She could finally just relax and be happy.

"I have a confession to make," he said. "About the night of the charity ball. My friends dared me to ask you to dance. And I was tipsy enough to take the bait."

"And here I just thought you were exceedingly brave," she teased.

"You're not angry?"

"I think it's sort of funny, actually. Considering you got a whole lot more than just a dance."

"But you know what? I'm glad you lied to me that night. If it wasn't for the babies, I never would have had the guts to take a chance on myself." He kissed the tip of her nose. "On us. Because we're supposed to be together."

"I think I figured that out a long time ago."

He grinned. "You're clearly smarter than I am."

"I have a confession, too," she said. "And it's a little… well, *racy,* I guess."

One brow peaked with curiosity. "I'm all ears."

She slipped her hand under his shirt, laid it on his warm stomach. "I've always wondered what it would be like to fool around in a hospital bed."

His smile was a wicked one. "You don't say."

"But until now," she said, sliding her hand upward, to his chest. "I've never had the chance to test it out."

He must have had his hand right by the bed controls, because suddenly the head of the bed was sliding down. "I have an idea, Princess."

"Oh yeah? What's that?"

He lowered his head and kissed her, whispering against her lips, "Let's fool around and find out."

Epilogue

June

The babies were finally asleep.

Anne blew a silent kiss to her slumbering angels, made sure the baby monitor was on, then gathered the skirt of her gown and crept quietly from the nursery.

"I'll be back to check on them later," she told their nanny, Daria.

"Have a good time, Your Highness."

A glance up at the clock said she was already an hour late, but motherhood was her number one priority these days. Still, she didn't want to make him wait *too* long.

She stopped in her room to check her makeup one last time, then rushed down to the ballroom. In honor of her father, they were holding their second annual charity ball. And she could see, as she descended the stairs, that the turnout was even more impressive than last year.

Standing just inside the ballroom, chatting with Chris and Melissa, was Melissa's family, the royals of Morgan Isle. King Phillip and Queen Hannah, Prince Ethan and his wife, Lizzy, and the Duke, Charles Mead, and his wife, Victoria.

Several feet away Louisa and Princess Sophia stood, both pregnant and just beginning to show, comparing baby bumps while their husbands wore amused grins.

But the one person she wanted to see, who was supposedly waiting for her, was nowhere in sight.

Anne nabbed a glass of champagne from a passing waiter—the babies would be getting pumped milk tonight—sipped deeply and scanned the crowd.

"You're looking lovely, Your Highness," someone said from behind her.

The sound of his voice warmed her from the inside out.

She turned to face him. "A pleasure to see you again, Mr. Baldwin."

He bowed in greeting, and as he did a lock of that unruly blond hair fell across his forehead. "Please, call me Sam."

"Would you care to dance, Sam?"

He grinned, his dimples winking. The fire in his eyes still burned bright after a year. "I thought you'd never ask."

He took her hand and led her out to the dance floor, pulling her into his arms and holding her close. She pressed her cheek to his, breathed in the scent of his cologne.

"I'm the envy of every man in the room," he whispered.

She didn't know about that, but no one called her *The Shrew* any longer. That woman had ceased to exist the moment she met this amazing man. He brought out the best in her.

He nuzzled her cheek. "I'm the luckiest man here. And the happiest."

"How soon do you suppose we could sneak upstairs and do some real celebrating?" she asked and he cast her a sizzling smile. It was, after all, their one-year anniversary. And though there had been hard times and sad times, they had so much to celebrate. So much to be thankful for. Two healthy and gorgeous children, a family who loved and supported them.

And better yet, they had each other.

* * * * *

ROYAL HOLIDAY BABY

LEANNE BANKS

Leanne Banks is a *New York Times* bestselling author with over sixty books to her credit. A book lover and romance fan from even before she learned to read, Leanne has always treasured the way that books allow us to go to new places and experience the lives of wonderful characters. Always ready for a trip to the beach, Leanne lives in Virginia with her family and her Pomeranian muse.

Chapter One

Tina adjusted her mask and breathed a sigh of relief. The masquerade party was in full swing with the house band slipping into a hip-hop number. For the next two hours, she could be anyone she wanted to be. In her case, that would be anyone other than the older sister of Her Highness Fredericka Anna Catherine of the small kingdom of Chantaine.

Thank God her college friend, Keely, had invited her to Dallas to celebrate her daughter's christening and catch up. Tina couldn't bear any more of the pitying glances she received when people talked about her beautiful younger sister's marriage to a wealthy Parisian film director. It was all so glamorous, so exciting, and while she was happy for her sister, she was sick of everyone asking when she was getting married. After all, she was older than Ericka and the event had stirred up her brother's suggestion that Tina should marry someone who could aid in Chantaine's political interests.

But she wasn't going to think about that tonight. Tonight

the only person who knew her true identity was dancing with her husband at the other end of the room. Keely caught her glance and waved.

Tina waved in return, glad to see her friend enjoying a night out with her hubby.

"Wanna dance?" a man said.

She glanced up, surprised at the invitation. "Oh, no, thank you very much. I'm enjoying watching right now."

"Maybe a drink would help you loosen up," he suggested.

A little pushy, she thought and gave him a once-over. He stood about an inch shorter than her in heels. She didn't like his slicked-back hair or his voice. It was whiny sounding.

Tina had always had a weakness for a sexy voice, though she'd kept that to herself. She shook her head. "No, thank you. Excuse me, I see a friend," she fibbed and moved away.

She accepted a crab cake appetizer from one waiter. Another offered her a glass of champagne. Seconds later, Keely appeared by her side. "How's it going? Are you sure you don't want me to introduce you around?"

"Absolutely not," Tina said. "I'm ecstatically anonymous."

"If you're sure," she said in the warm friendly twang that had welcomed Tina since they first became roommates in college. "I guess it's nice not to have to put on your princess face."

Tina felt a twinge of guilt. She knew her position carried both benefits and responsibilities and she'd tried to never shirk from her duties, but lately it had felt overwhelming. "Just a little break," she said. "I'll be headed back to Chantaine day after tomorrow. I can't tell you how much I've appreciated having this time with you."

"We've loved having you," Keely said. "Are you sure you can't stay a little longer?"

Tina shook her head. "No. Remember, the wedding takes place in two months."

Keely shot her a look of sympathy. "Duty calls. You're always giving up what you want for others, Tina. One of these days you're going to rebel and shock everyone."

Tina laughed. "Not likely. Someone's got to toe the line in Chantaine and it looks like it's going to be me." Uncomfortable with the discussion, she pointed to the dance floor. "As you would say, time's a wasting. Enjoy your time with your husband."

Keely gave a mocking dip of her head. "Yes, your highness, but there's no reason you can't kick up your heels yourself. If a gorgeous guy asks you to dance, promise me you'll do it," she whispered.

"I don't know," Tina said, thinking of the man who'd approached her earlier.

"Promise," Keely said.

"Oh, okay," Tina relented, because she knew there wasn't much of a possibility for such a thing happening. "But he has to be gorgeous."

"Agreed," Keely said and left to drag her husband out on the dance floor.

Tina took a step back and observed the crowd. She enjoyed the novelty of being the observer rather than the observed. To her left, she heard a group of men discussing the fate of the Dallas Cowboys. To her right, she noticed a man seductively feeding his date an appetizer. Feeling a strange stab of envy at the romance oozing from them, she immediately looked away.

When had a man wanted her just because she was a woman, just because she was herself, instead of wanting her because she was Princess Valentina Catherine Marie of Chantaine? Try never, she thought and immediately felt frustrated with herself. She led an amazing life. Why had she been so dissatisfied lately?

"Let me take you on the dance floor," the man who'd approached her earlier said. "I can show you a good time."

Be careful what you wish for, she told herself, but this was not the guy of her dreams. She sighed. "No, again," she said firmly. "But thank you."

His hand on her arm took her off guard. "No need to be so shy. We could have some fun."

"No, thank you," she said, pulling back her arm and frowning when he didn't release her. She didn't want to make a scene, but this man was making things difficult. In other circumstances, her security detail would handle this, but tonight she'd successfully ditched them. She hadn't done that since college.

"I'm really not interested—"

"Excuse me," she heard another man say. A deeper, sexier male voice slid down her spine like the smoothest cognac in the history of the world.

She glanced up and saw a tall, broad-shouldered man with black hair wearing a black Stetson, a black mask and a tux. "I believe you promised this dance to me," he said, his blue eyes searing into hers through the slits of the mask.

Tina's heart tripped over itself. She met his gaze and felt an instant inexplicable trust and attraction. She gave it a second thought, then dismissed it. "Yes, I did," she said and accepted the hand he offered.

"Well, I guess," the whiny-voiced man began.

The lone ranger, however, led her onto the dance floor and guided her into a slow dance to a romantic song. "It looked like he was causing you trouble."

"I suppose so," she said, hyper-aware of his strong chest and clean, musky scent.

"Should I not have interrupted?" he asked.

"No," she said then corrected herself. "I mean yes." She swallowed a groan.

His hard mouth lifted into a slight grin. "Which is it? Yes or no?"

"Both," she said, stiffening her spine. "He was causing me trouble, but I should have handled it."

He spun her around then drew her back against him. "Now you don't have to."

She couldn't help smiling. "So I don't."

Tina danced through another song with the mysterious stranger, then the band took a break and he lifted her hand to his lips. "Maybe later," he said and moved away. The crowd closed behind him like the Red Sea.

Tina looked around for him but couldn't see him.

Keely appeared in front of her. "I'm sorry, sweetie, but the babysitter called and Caitlyn won't stop crying. Brent and I are going home."

"I'll go with you," Tina said.

"Absolutely not," Keely said with a firm shake of her head. "This is your last chance to have fun for a while. We've already asked a friend to look after you."

Tina cringed. "That's not necessary."

"It's either that or your security," Keely said. "There's no need for you to leave now."

Tina thought of the handsome man who'd danced with her earlier. Why not? "Okay. But I'll probably get to your house in less than an hour."

"Don't rush. Remember, you've got Ericka's wedding coming toward you like a freight train."

The very thought exhausted her. "Okay, you've convinced me."

"Hey," Keely said. "The crab cakes are great."

Tina laughed and gave Keely a hug. "Go home and comfort your baby."

"Yeah, yeah," Keely said then pulled back. "Call me if you need me."

As Tina watched her friend walk away, she felt a combination of exhilaration and terror. She was officially all alone at a party. Except for Keely's mysterious friend.

Zachary Logan watched the brown-haired beauty accept a glass of champagne from the tray the waiter offered her. She also accepted a crab cake.

He smiled to himself. He liked a woman with an appetite. His good friends Keely and Brent McCorkle had asked him to look after Tina Devereaux. The only thing he knew about the woman was that she was Keely's guest from out of town. He owed Brent a favor so he would do what his good friend asked despite the fact that he had been counting the seconds until he could escape this party.

Zach had been cajoled into attending this party by both friends and relatives. It had been two years since his Jenny and their baby had died, and he'd gone into seclusion at his ranch outside of Fort Worth. The pain of his loss still stabbed at him, the memories gutting him like a fish.

For the first time, the gaiety of the social gathering lifted his spirits, and Tina flat-out made him smile. Full-figured, with good manners and an accent he couldn't quite place, she looked at him with a feminine curiosity that grabbed at him and drew him.

She took a sip of bubbly, then licked her lips and he felt an odd twist in his stomach. With the mask covering much of her face, it was easy to focus on her full, puffy mouth, the color of a deep rose. Soft and sensual looking. He rubbed his thumb over his own mouth, feeling a slight buzz.

He shook his head at himself. Where had that thought come from? Noticing how she tapped her toe to the music, he took the hint and walked toward her.

"Another dance?" he suggested, extending his hand.

Her green eyes lit up. "That would be nice," she said and looked around for a place to put her glass. He took it from her and nodded toward a waiter who came to collect it, then led her onto the dance floor.

She shimmied to a dance club tune, laughing throughout the song as if she were getting away with something. Her attitude was contagious and he caught himself smiling more than he had in months. The song blurred into another and another until a slow tune began and he pulled her into his arms.

"I just realized I don't even know your name," she said. "I'm Tina."

"Zach," he said. "Zach Logan."

"I would have never expected it, but this is the most fun I've had in—" She paused, a surprised look coming over her face. "Forever," she confessed.

He chuckled. "Maybe you're like me. Maybe you need to get out more."

"Oh, I get out," she said. "Just not like this. I hate to see it end, but I need to leave before the big reveal."

"What do you mean?" he asked.

"I need to leave before everyone takes their masks off at the end of the evening."

"Why? Do you want your identity to remain secret?"

She shot him a cautious glance and shrugged. "Something like that." The music stopped and she started to pull away. "I should go. Thank you, Zach Logan."

He couldn't let her leave on her own. He'd promised Keely and Brent he would make sure she got home safely. "Let me take you," he said. "Can't have a beautiful woman like you leaving by herself. And I know a place close by that serves the best ice cream floats if you're interested."

She looked tempted. "I shouldn't," she said, her voice oozing reluctance.

"Why?" he challenged, not eager for the evening to end either. He would go back to his apartment, full of memories that reminded him of how much he'd lost. "It's just ice cream with a local boy."

"Boy," she echoed in breathless disbelief, giving him a once-over.

"Okay," he amended. "It's just ice cream."

"Well, you did rescue me from that creep," she said, caught in indecision. She squished her eyes together for a half beat then opened them. "I really shouldn't get into a car with a man I've just met."

"I can get you a cab," he said.

"Thank you," she said, disappointment leaking through her tone. He escorted her to the door of the private club and waited with her while the valet waved a car forward.

He opened the door and just before she stepped inside, she glanced over her shoulder. "I could still meet you for that ice cream float if I knew the address."

"Calahan's Diner on 54th and Poplar," he said to the driver and her. "See you soon."

Forty-five minutes later after Tina removed her mask, she sat across from the rugged man with the magnetic eyes. "I can't remember the last time I had one of these," he said as he drained the last drop.

Her gaze slid down his hard jaw, taking in the slide of his Adam's apple, then lower to his broad shoulders. Watching him drink the float was the most seductive experience she'd had in a long time.

Tina wondered if that was just plain pathetic as she took another sip of her own float. She liked the way his bedroom eyes crinkled at the corners. The fact that he was knocking back an ice cream float made him seem a little less dangerous than if he'd been swilling whiskey. She supposed that if she were ever going to do something wild and impetuous with a man, he might be a good choice. Not that she ever would.

"You never mentioned where you live," he said.

"Out of the country, right now," she said. "But I attended college at Rice."

"Is that where you met Keely?" he asked.

Tina blinked, digesting his comment and what it meant. She felt a rush of self-consciousness. "You were the one Keely asked to look after me."

He nodded and his lips tilted into a half smile. "My pleasure."

She resisted the urge to fan her heated face. "This is a little embarrassing. I didn't know you were assigned to look after me. I shouldn't keep you any longer—"

His smile fell. "No," he said. "When I said it was my pleasure, I meant it. I haven't been out in awhile. Being with you has—" He broke off and shrugged those broad muscular shoulders. "It's been great. I haven't felt this good in a long, long time."

His eyes darkened with emotion, and she felt a visceral tightening in her stomach.

"I don't want it to end," he said.

His words echoed her own feelings. She sucked in a quick breath, determined to clear her head. She had responsibilities. Her duty was most important. Always. "I don't either, but it must end." She closed her eyes for a quick moment, trying to stiffen her resolve. Opening her eyes again, she shot him a smile that she knew was weary. "Grown-ups have to be grown-ups."

He nodded, giving a slight chuckle as he slid his gaze over her from head to waist, heating her from head to toe. "Damn shame, isn't it?"

"Yes," she said, wishing she were a little less responsible, wishing she could be impetuous and follow her heart…or hormones….

"I'll get the check, then get you a cab," he said.

Moments later, she sat in the back of a cab driving her toward Keely's house. Damn chivalry, she thought and gave a dark laugh at herself. It would have been so much easier if he'd taken advantage of her. Oozing his sexy Texan charm, it would have been sooo easy. Instead, he'd given her a choice, which meant she'd had to take the chaste high road when she'd wanted to be a bad girl. Just once. She'd always been the good daughter. At the moment, that halo she wore felt way too tight.

The taxi stopped at a red light. When it turned green, the vehicle sputtered and stalled. Great, she thought. She was accustomed to riding in perfectly maintained limousines. Riding in a taxi was an adventure. Under a torrential downpour, she looked outside her window and hoped the cab would start.

The driver cranked the engine again. And again. And again. To no avail.

Darn it, she didn't even have an umbrella with her. Her staff usually provided that. Tina sighed. Perhaps she should call her security. Heavens, she hated the idea. There would be a fuss from the head of security and her brother and maybe even her father.

She waited several more moments, her cell phone ready in her hand. An SUV pulled alongside the cab. A moment later, a knock sounded at her window, startling her. Frightened, she stared into the rain, reluctant to open her door.

"Tina," a male voice said. "Open up."

Recognizing the voice of Zachary Logan, she opened the door. "Zach," she said.

His Stetson dripping with raindrops, he swung an umbrella toward her. "Need a ride?"

"To where?"

His gaze gave a dark flicker. "Wherever you want. I can take you to Keely's or I can take you to my place in town."

Tina stared into his eyes and felt as if she were balanced on a precipice. She could be sensible or cautious or for once, give into her passions. She saw a ravenous need in Zach's gaze that called to something inside her. She'd been taught to ignore her needs. But somehow, the tug she felt toward Zach was stronger than anything she'd ever felt before.

Tina rose from the cab with all the grace she'd been taught since she could walk and accepted his hand. "Your place," she whispered.

Chapter Two

Tina stepped across the threshold of Zach's apartment, her heart hammering in her chest. When Zach flicked on the light behind her, she stared into the spare, generically furnished living space and felt her stomach dip with reticence. What was she doing?

"Let me get you something to drink," he said, walking past her and removing his hat. "Sorry I don't have much to offer. I spend most of my time working when I stay here instead of at my ranch."

She followed after him and watched as he stared into a near-empty refrigerator. "Juice, water." He craned his neck. "Beer and chardonnay."

"Water's fine," she said, licking her lips.

"Sure you don't want wine?" he asked, looking over his shoulder.

"Maybe just one glass," she said. "Besides ranching, what kind of business do you have?"

Zach grabbed a beer, then opened the bottle of wine and poured the golden liquid into a glass. "My brother and I own some companies together—information-sharing systems and upgrading equipment for mid-size companies. We also offer consultation for trading futures and trade them ourselves."

"Sounds busy," she said and accepted the glass of wine. "What do you do?"

"I work in public and international relations," she said, not wanting him to ask any further questions. She took a quick sip and stared into his gaze, feeling her stomach dance with nerves.

He skimmed his gaze over her, then took a long drink of beer. "Listen, if you'd like me to take you to Keely's—"

"No," she said, quickly, breathlessly. "Unless you want me to go."

"No," he said just as quickly, but his voice was rougher with a sensual edge to it that affected her on a visceral level.

She took another sip of wine and willed herself to be more brazen. She took two steps forward then stopped. "I'm not accustomed to making the first move," she whispered.

He raised his eyebrows and nodded, taking another long drink of beer. "Maybe I can help with that," he said and closed the space between them.

Inhaling deeply, she caught the scent of him, soap, cologne and just a hint of musk. He smelled male, good, seductive. He slid his hand over hers and tugged her toward the kitchen counter where he propped his can of beer.

His hand felt strong and warm around hers. Taking her wine glass from her hand, he took a quick sip, then also set the glass on the counter. He dipped his fingers into the wine and rubbed them over her lips.

She blinked at the raw seductive move, but had no desire to object.

"I think I need another taste of that wine," he said and

lowered his mouth to hers. His mouth was firm and sensual. He slid his tongue over her lips and she felt his hunger vibrate inside her. When he pulled her against him, his hard-muscled frame made something inside shudder and relax at the same time.

She wasn't dealing with a college boy here.

She remembered her first time as heavy kisses, awkward fumbling, a rushed penetration followed by a stab of pain. Afterward, she'd wondered *Why bother?*

Tina knew she was experiencing the opposite side of the spectrum. Zachary was a man, and he clearly knew what he was doing. He knew what he wanted and at this moment, she knew that he was what she wanted. From the time she'd been born, Tina had been bred for duty and responsibility. Her position was more important than her desires or personal needs. She was always to behave responsibly. If things went wrong, then she was supposed to fix them. She would always need to remain on guard.

For the first time in a long time, if not forever, she let down her guard. She had the bone-deep sense that Zach was the most responsible man she'd ever met. For now, his responsibility meant taking care of his needs and her own, and she felt a delicious anticipation that he could achieve both tasks. She sighed with a combination of relief and excitement and clung to his strong frame.

Giving herself into his sensual care, she drew his tongue into her mouth, savoring his taste. He quickly inhaled in surprise or approval, or both, and rocked her pelvis against his hardness.

A thrill raced through her and she pressed her breasts against his chest. He gave a low growl. "Are you sure you—"

"Yes," she whispered desperately against his lips and slid her hands upward, knocking his hat from his head.

Within seconds, he had pushed off her coat and unzipped her dress. Tina felt a draft of cool air when her dress pooled at her feet, but his warm hands replaced the fabric, quickly distracting her. She tugged at his jacket and tie then fumbled as she unbuttoned his shirt.

It seemed like both forever and no time at all before she felt his naked warm skin against hers. The sensation of her breasts against his chest made her nipples tight with need. Heat and desperation grew inside her. When had she wanted like this? When had she allowed herself to want like this?

Her brain shorted out as he dipped his head, taking one of her nipples into his mouth. Tina gasped in pleasure.

He swore under his breath. "You're so sexy. Don't know how long I can wait."

"Don't," she urged, sliding her fingers through his hair. "Don't wait."

Taking her by surprise, he pulled her into his arms and carried her out of the kitchen down a hallway. In a darkened room, he set her down on a bed and pulled back. During those few seconds, she felt cold without him.

"Zach?"

"Right here," he said, returning, leaning over her as he opened a foil packet and protected himself. "I don't trust myself much longer."

He slid his hand through her hair and down her face to cup her jaw. "I never thought I'd feel this—" He broke off and shook his head. He trailed his hand down over her breasts and lower, over her abdomen and between her legs where she was hot and moist. "Perfection," he muttered. "All woman."

Toying with her, he took her mouth in a French kiss. The desperation and need tightened inside her so she could hardly stand it. Unable to bear another second, she slid her hand down to where he was hard and big and all male. She stroked down his shaft and he gave a hiss of arousal.

"That's it," he said and pushed her thighs apart. One breath later, he plunged inside her, stretching her, filling her.

He swore. "You feel so good," he said and began to pump. She moved in counterpoint to his sexual invasion, craving every millimeter of him.

She felt the first flush of a climax soar through her. She was so close, so very close, but then he plunged one last time crying out, and sank on top of her.

His weight was heavy, but somehow sweet. His breath flowed over her and she was left with a strange feeling of satisfaction despite the fact that she hadn't gone over the top.

He struggled up to rest on his elbows, looking deep in her gaze, his eyes still dark with sex. "You didn't come," he said.

Surprised, a little self-conscious, she dropped her jaw. "It's not a big deal. Not—"

"I can fix that," he said and lowered his mouth to hers again.

Tina awakened to darkness and a man's heavy leg trapping her lower body. A clock on the bed stand displayed the time as 3:47 a.m. She wasn't sure what had awakened her—perhaps the unfamiliar sensation of sharing a bed with a man who gave satisfaction a completely new and wonderful meaning. Guilt and responsibility that had developed before she exited her mother's womb. Or just the fact that her left leg was falling asleep.

Alarm rushed through her. *What on earth had she done? What on earth was she doing?* Her security detail would be descending on her any minute. She was surprised they hadn't shown up already.

Oh, that wouldn't do, she thought, cringing at the image of Rolfe, her head security man, bursting through the door. *She* had never caused a scandal. *She* was the dependable one. Her brother Stefan, the crown prince, was the one with a temper. Her younger sister was the beautiful, impetuous one with the whole family breathing a sigh of relief that she was settling down. Her other younger siblings were involved with their own lives and personal dramas. Getting them to help with royal duties was like pulling teeth from a wild boar.

Tina was the go-to princess. Someone had to be. She should leave before Zach was dragged into the craziness of her life. Her heart twisted with regret as she studied the hard planes of his face, his dark eyelashes and his dark hair, mussed by her fingertips.

He'd given her a sliver of an out-of-time, out-of-body experience. Thank goodness for these few hours, she thought. She'd never felt more like a woman. Sadness twisted through her as realization sank through. She might never feel like this again.

Sunlight seeped through the blinds of Zach's condominium window. He didn't open his eyes, feeling a bone-deep relaxation and satisfaction that prevented him from any muscle movement. His muscles were relaxed, his mind blessedly blank. For a full moment.

Then flashes of the night before skittered across his brain. His eyes still closed, he saw a woman with sexy, plump lips and inviting eyes and a body that made him hard. Again.

He opened his eyes. *Tina.* He glanced around the bed and inhaled, smelling the scent of her. *Where had she gone?*

"Tina," he called, lifting up on his elbow.

Silence answered him.

"Damn," he muttered and raked his hand through his hair. He shouldn't have brought her here, he thought. She was Keely and Brent's friend. He was supposed to see her safely back to their place.

But she'd been so soft and sexy and irresistible. And now she'd run out on him.

Not until he'd taken her over the edge, he reminded himself. Several times. For both of them. He couldn't remember a wilder night. Not even with his wife.

His gut squeezed at the thought. His dead wife and his dead baby. For a little while, Tina had given him something else to think about. His elbow scraped against something. Metal, he thought, scooping up a small chain. He studied it for a moment, noting the catch had broken. He remembered the way the silver bracelet had played over her skin when she'd caressed him with her hands and mouth.

He closed his eyes, his sense of pleasure and ease evaporating quickly. His little break from pain was over, and his time of torture and self-recrimination had returned.

Twelve hours later, Tina sat in her brother's parlor waiting for his to-do list. He usually delivered it via e-mail, but Tina suspected that since she'd ditched her cell phone for that one night at the masquerade party, he didn't trust electronic communication. Or perhaps he just didn't trust her.

Her brother's assistant had already bowed in greeting a few moments ago. Standing, he waved his hand to the door to Stefan's office. "His Royal Highness will see you now," he said.

Tina could have pushed to eliminate the wait, but after rushed good-byes to her friend Keely, and her transatlantic flight to Chantaine, she was grateful for a moment to catch her breath. "Thank you, Pete," she said and entered her brother's office.

Her brother stood, even though his royal position made it unnecessary, and rounded his large, antique desk. He opened his arms to give her a quick hug. "Welcome home," he said.

"Why is it that we seem to get hit with an onslaught of royal duties every time you leave the country?"

She smiled. "It's the same amount of duties as always. No one picks up the slack."

"I've noticed that," he said with a frown. "Both Bridget and Phillipa have finished their education. They should take on more."

"Good luck with that," she said. "They both have more excuses than there are grains of sand on Senesia Beach," she said, referring to the most popular beach of their island kingdom. "I take it you tried giving them assignments."

"They ignore me," he said, his expression incredulous. "Turn off their cell phones, lose e-mails. If they were staff, they would have been fired ten times over."

Tina laughed. "Tough to fire your sisters."

He shook his head and his mouth drew into a frown. "I'm considering other measures. You've told me again and again about your American friends who believe in earning their way. I can put a limit on their charge cards."

"Ouch," Tina said. "There will be lots of screaming. You may try negotiating first."

"I'm thinking of putting you in charge of them. They need to be trained."

Tina shook her head. "No way. Even Mother didn't train me. A longtime advisor taught me everything. You can bring her out of retirement for the job," she said. *If she doesn't quit.*

Stefan wrinkled his brow. "Something has to be done. With Ericka's upcoming wedding, you'll be busier than ever. I'm focused on plans for the economy and facilitating our diplomatic relationships with countries that can boost our GDP."

"What do the advisers say?

"They recommend that I take a wife. I have no time for courting with my schedule."

"You could always just accept one assigned by the advisers. That's what you wanted me to do," she said, unable to resist the dig. Both her father and brother had urged her to accept an arranged marriage to a man twice her age because he was an Italian count.

"You could have done worse," he said.

"What about Princess Margherita from Italy?" she retorted.

He cringed. "I couldn't bear her laugh for a night let alone for the rest of my life."

"But think of your country, your duty," she began, echoing the same words he'd used with her.

"Enough," he said sharply, lifting his hand.

Tina could tell by the flicker of the tiny muscle in his jaw that she'd pushed a little too far for his comfort. Stefan struggled with his temper, especially when he felt as if things were out of his control.

"The purpose of this meeting is not to discuss your marital prospects or mine," he said. "The purpose is to discuss where you disappeared to for over eight hours last night. Rolfe said he couldn't reach you by cell and that your hostess refused to name your whereabouts when asked."

Tina felt a twist of irritation. "Rolfe is a tattletale."

"He was doing his job," Stefan said. "You know better than this. You must always remain available via your cell. You must always have protection."

"How many times have I been unavailable?" she demanded.

"None to my memory, but that's not the point."

"For that matter, how many times has Ericka been unavailable?"

"Do you really want to be compared to someone who spent

two stints in rehab? Thank God, she's clean now. And who would have thought she would bring a French movie director into the family?" he marveled. "But we count on you to be mature and dependable. You understand your obligations and duties."

"Maybe too much," she whispered to herself, glancing toward the window, feeling more trapped than she'd ever felt in her life. She rubbed her bare wrist, wondering where she'd left her favorite bracelet. She would search through her luggage again for it.

"Valentina," Stefan said in his ruler voice. "Where were you?"

In the past, she would have felt intimidated or at the least, guilty for causing trouble. For some reason, this time she didn't. This time she felt impatient with Stefan's demands.

"I was out," she said, meeting his gaze dead-on.

The muscle in his jaw began to tick again. "These next three months, the eyes of the world will be watching our country in anticipation of Fredericka's wedding. I need you to act with utmost maturity and responsiveness. Ericka will be under enormous pressure now that she's placed in the spotlight. Of all our family, Ericka will trust you."

Tina shook her head. "I can't promise miracles. She needed rehab."

"But even you talked her into that," Stefan said. "I need you to be supportive of her. Keep her together."

"I told you I can't perform miracles."

"Just be your best self," he said. "That's more than almost everyone else on their best day."

She couldn't hold back a semi-smile. "Flattery," she said. "You must be desperate, your highness."

Chapter Three

Zach paced the dentist's office as he waited for his longtime housekeeper to get her broken tooth fixed. Hildie was no wimp. She'd been known to face down two intruders at once with only a frying pan as her weapon. She'd even confronted a brown bear that came a little too close to the house.

Under usual circumstances, Hildie would drive herself to the doctor if she were sick. Hildie had helped deliver babies. She wasn't squeamish at all. Dentists, however, were her waterloo. She'd procrastinated going to the dentist and now the poor woman winced every time she breathed.

Zach had insisted she go in and Hildie agreed only if he would take her and wait for her. They never knew which sedation the dentist would use. It was all determined by Hildie's anxiety level, which today, hovered at one hundred on a scale of one to ten.

Bored, Zach sank onto one of the chairs and checked his BlackBerry. His brother wanted him to cover for him in

Dallas while he took a scuba diving trip. No problem. Zach was always around. It wasn't as if anything exciting was going on in his life, and he preferred it that way. Particularly in his personal life.

He couldn't deny, at least to himself, though, that ever since that night with Tina, he'd almost asked his friends how to get in touch with her. Every time he was tempted, however, he remembered the tragic ending of his marriage.

No. He wasn't ready to have a woman in his life. He didn't know if he would ever be ready. Restlessness nicked at his nerve endings and he rolled his neck to release some tension. Desperate to distract himself, he picked up the trashy gossip rag on the table and skimmed the front page.

The theme of the day seemed to be babies. He felt his gut clench at the memory of the loss of his own child, but shook the paper and kept reading. Senator's love child living in an igloo in Alaska. Movie stars adopt three more children. Dog helps deliver baby. Pregnant Princess? Who's your daddy?

He almost tossed it back onto the cheap table holding the rest of women's magazines. But as he flipped through the pages in disgust, an image of something he'd seen before flashed before him. A young curvy woman with brown hair. In the photo, she wore a hat and a loose-fitting dress. Her belly was amplified in a photo insert.

Zach frowned at the photo and quickly read the article. *Princess Valentina of Chantaine has stood by the side of her fragile sister bride nonstop during the huge wedding that drew the focus of the entire world. Tina has always been the good girl in the royal family, but maybe she isn't so perfect after all. Has Tina gained a little weight? Strange that her weight gain isn't all over...just in her belly. Insiders report Princess Tina fought nausea throughout the wedding festivities. If the princess is pregnant, where is the baby daddy?*

Or did she give up on her prospects and enlist the services of a sperm bank? Time will tell.

Princess, Zach thought. What the— *Princess Tina.* She hadn't mentioned being a princess. What kind of job had she said she had? Something in international relations.

He gave a cynical laugh. Cute, he thought. Real cute. He wondered how in hell Keely was friends with a princess.

Glancing at the slight baby bump, he felt a tight knot form in his chest. She couldn't be pregnant, he thought. He'd used protection. He mentally flipped through the night they'd spent together. Every time they'd made love. And they'd made love a lot. Had there been one time when he'd forgotten or been too eager to feel her close around him or—

He had a vivid memory of feeling her wet velvet with no barrier.

"Damn," he muttered, pulling off his hat. Was she pregnant? If so, that baby could be his.

Panic ripped through him. His heart raced, skipping and sinking. A horrible dread tugged at him, sinking to his gut and lower, dragging him down. He swore at himself ten times over. What had he been thinking?

He hadn't been thinking. He'd been feeling. That was the problem. Feeling always caused problems.

Sucking in a long breath, he stared at her photo and that damned baby bump insert. He would find out if she was pregnant and he would find out if the baby was his. He clenched his fist in determination. It wouldn't take him long.

For once, Tina's sister came through for her. It was a huge switch. Although Ericka was happily busy and traveling hither and yon with her new husband, she said Tina could stay at her new home just outside of Paris. Close enough to the city, but far enough from the congestion, the new home was perfect for the respite Tina needed.

Tina had escaped just as her brother began to insist she was due for an examination from the royal doctors. Before her plane landed in Paris, rumors in the gossip rags had exploded. She'd only been away for twenty-four hours and her voice mail box was full. She didn't even want to look at her e-mail.

She knew her brother was going to freak out, and her security man, Rolfe, was watching her every move. Thank goodness she and her sister had worked out a plan for this very situation. An older woman, Genieve, brought fresh vegetables most every morning and brought pastry treats for the staff. She usually left from the back entrance of the house around noon. Except today. Today Genieve would stay until 4:00 p.m. and watch television with one of the favorite staff members in a room upstairs while Tina dressed in dark clothes with a dark scarf covering her head and drove the woman's car to a small, out-of-the-way museum with beautiful gardens.

There, Tina could think about her and her baby's future. There, she could make plans.

Tina told Rolfe she planned to take a nap and didn't want to be disturbed. As soon as he left her hallway, she took the back stairs to the back entrance and got into the ancient vehicle and escaped.

The July heat was oppressive, but the temperature inside the small museum was cool. She noticed only a few tourists, but an abundance of caution made her keep her head covered. Glancing outside, she saw no one in the gardens and walked outside to a stone bench beside a small pond. Despite the shade from the tree, the heat forced her to pull off her scarf.

She closed her eyes, craving peace and quiet for her mind and soul. She didn't need panic in this situation. She needed to remain calm. Since everyone else was going to be emotionally jumping out of windows.

Tina could see the headlines now. *Unwed Pregnant Princess.* She, the one everyone counted on to be scandal-free. She laughed softly to herself, although she still struggled with a twinge of hysteria. Was she prepared to be a single mother? It didn't matter. That's what she would be. She stroked her abdomen, feeling protective of the baby growing there.

Tina had always put her loyalty to her position first, but there was no doubt in her mind what was most important to her now. Her child. Her pregnancy might be unexpected, unplanned and her situation not exactly optimal, but that didn't change the fact that Tina would make her child her priority.

That solid knowledge released a tension from inside her. She took a deep breath and gave into the temptation to build a perfect little world for her and her baby in her mind. The two of them could live here in France, near her sister. She would lead a simple life raising her child, serving as a patron for her favorite charities and making rare appearances in Chantaine.

Her sisters would pitch in and take over her assignments. *That was pure fantasy,* she thought. And her brother would marry a woman who would keep him out of her hair. *More fantasy.*

She inhaled again, lingering over the idyllic image in her mind.

Something fell beside her on the bench. *A chain?* She opened her eyes and glanced beside her, immediately spotting the bracelet she'd thought she'd lost.

"Been missing that?" a deep male voice that had haunted her dreams said to her.

She glanced behind her, directly into the hard blue gaze of Zachary Logan. Her heart stopped in her chest. Her breath froze in her lungs.

"The baby's mine, isn't it?"

* * *

Zach didn't like her color. She'd gone past the pale stage and she looked gray. He handed her his bottle of water. "Here, you look like you need this."

She stared at him without blinking, seemingly without breathing for another long moment. "Tina," he said and squeezed her shoulder. "Drink some water."

At his touch, she finally took a breath and looked away. "I didn't think I would ever see you again," she said. "How did you find me?"

"A combination of Keely and a private investigator. I've had a guy watching your sister's house for every person who came and went. I tried calling your assistant, but she blew me off."

She looked up at him in alarm. "Did you tell her you and I had—"

"No, but I was tempted," he said, reining in his frustration from the last several days. "When were you going to tell me about the baby?"

Tina blinked. "I—I wasn't," she said with a shrug.

Shock rushed through him. "You what?" he nearly shouted.

Tina glanced around in alarm. "Please keep your voice down. I don't want to draw attention. I came here to think."

Zach's stomach turned. "Are you saying you're not keeping the baby?"

She looked at him in confusion. "What do you mean? Give the baby up for adoption—"

"No, I meant," he said and stopped, his throat closing over his words. "I meant end the pregnancy."

Shock widened her eyes. "Absolutely not."

Some small something inside him eased and he took a quick breath. "That still doesn't explain why you weren't going to tell me."

She gave a sigh of frustration. "It was a one-night stand. It didn't seem fair to drag you into it."

"It's my child too," he said in a deadly firm voice.

"Yes, but it's not just about the baby," she said and lifted her hands. "Dealing with who I am, who my family is, what's expected of me and my family. Not many men can handle that. You don't really even know me. It's not as if we're in love. Being involved with the baby and me would turn your life upside down."

"You don't think it already has?"

Her lips parted in surprise, as if she had truly believed he wouldn't be interested in his own child. "I'm sorry," she said softly. "I shouldn't have rushed to the assumption that you would only view this as a burden."

"There's a difference between burden and responsibility," he said.

She nodded. "That's very true. I'm just not accustomed to dealing with men who know how to distinguish the two."

"Maybe you've been hanging around the wrong men," he said.

Her lips lifted in amusement. "Maybe so."

"Do you know what your plans are?" he asked. "Are you going to live in your country?"

Tina looked down at her hands folded in her lap and shook her head. "My brother is going to freak out. He might have expected something like this from my younger sister, but never me. I know he's in a difficult situation, but I just wish I could go away for a while. I need to get my head on straight about all this and doing that in Chantaine is going to be very, very difficult, if not impossible."

"I have the perfect place if you need to think. My ranch," he said.

She blinked at the recommendation. "Your ranch?" she echoed as if that possibility was last on her list.

"Sure," he said with a shrug. "It's no palace, but most people who visit like it. It's quiet. You would be able to think. Plus," he said, "it would give you an opportunity to get to know the father of your child better."

She met his gaze and a glimmer of the night they'd shared seemed to pass through her eyes. Licking her lips, she glanced away. Zach felt a surprising bolt of sexual awareness stab at him. *Where the hell had that come from?*

"What do you say?" he asked.

"I don't know," she said. "I hadn't even considered this until this moment. I can't make an instant decision."

"Why not?" he asked. "You have a passport. You're an adult. You can do whatever you think is best for you and your child."

At that moment, a group of men with cameras and microphones burst into the garden. "Princess Valentina, tell us the truth. Are you pregnant?"

"Oh, no." Tina stood and backed away.

Zach automatically stepped in front of her. "Leave her alone," he said.

"Who are you?" the short, portly reporter continued. "You're not her regular bodyguard. Are you her lover?" he asked. "The father of her child?"

Cameras snapped and the reporter pressed against him. "Leave us alone. Get out of here."

The reporter continued to push against Zach, irritating him with his persistence. "You sound American. What's your name?"

"None of your damn business," Zach said. "Step aside. You're bothering Tina."

The reporter pushed past Zach and began to crowd Tina. "Tina," the reporter echoed. "Who is this man? How far along are you? Are you getting married?"

Zach pushed his way between the reporter and Tina. "Last warning. Step aside."

The reporter ignored him and Zach knocked him to the ground. He picked up Tina and carried her out of the garden.

Tina gawked at Zach. "What are you doing?"

"Getting you the hell away from those wackos," he said, heedless of the stares he drew as he hauled her through the small museum.

"Where are we going?" she asked as he tucked her into a rental car and got into the driver's seat. He started the engine and put the car into gear.

He glanced at her. "Where do you want to go?"

Her heart dipped at his expression. Her heart, in fact, hadn't beat regularly since she'd looked up to see him in the museum courtyard.

"Do you want to go back to your sister's house?" he asked.

Her stomach twisted. "Not really. My bodyguard will insist that I talk to my brother. He may even push me into going back to Chantaine."

Zach made a U-turn. "Okay, that's out. We could go to my hotel."

"So public," she said. "If you think the paparazzi was bad here…"

He shrugged. "Okay. How about my ranch?"

She gulped, taking in the way his large hand shifted gears. "That would require a flight. That could take some time."

Zach shifted gears and accelerated. He met her gaze. "Not necessarily. I can have a jet ready in an hour."

Surprise raced through her. "That would be expensive," she said, aware of the cost of private transatlantic flights because she usually flew first-class to save the royal family some change.

"I can handle it," he said with a shrug of his powerful shoulders. "I usually fly first-class for the legroom, but the jet's always at my disposal. But are you sure about this?"

Tina felt another forbidden thrill. Her brother would wring her neck. Her sisters would curse her for leaving them to deal with her brother. She bit the inside of her lip and nodded. "I'm sure."

Chapter Four

Half a day later, Tina awakened to the sensation of Zach's jet landing on a runway. Rousing herself from her slumber, she squinted out the window to see the flat landscape surrounding the Dallas Fort Worth International Airport.

She glanced across the aisle at Zach. He was looking outside the window on his side of the jet. His long lean legs extended before him, his dark hair was mussed. She wondered if he had slept half as much as she had.

She realized again that she had committed to going to his ranch. He was a man she knew intimately. In most ways, however, she barely knew him at all, and he barely knew her.

A knot of nerves formed in her throat. What in the world had she done? Tina took a deep breath. *Give yourself a break. You didn't have a lot of choices.*

Zach turned to look at her. "We're here. I can get a helicopter. Otherwise it's an hour and a half drive to my ranch."

"There's no need for a helicopter," she said. "I've slept most of the flight. A car will be fine."

"You're sure?" he asked.

She nodded, smiling. "I'm sure."

His gaze did things to her. She looked away to gather her things. He ushered her out of the plane and down the steps to the tarmac.

Two armed officers immediately approached them. "Mr. Logan, we need to question you about the kidnapping of Valentina Devereaux."

Zach blinked. "Excuse me?" he said.

"Oh, no," Tina whispered. "This is either my brother or my security guard. Or both." Refusing to be a victim, refusing to allow Zach to be a victim, she went into Princess-mode. "Pardon me, officer, but there's obviously been a misunderstanding. Mr. Logan graciously allowed me to be a passenger on his jet. I was being pursued by the paparazzi and he provided me with a safe escape."

The uniformed men exchanged glances. "His Majesty, Stefan Devereaux, insists you were taken against your will."

"His Majesty is mistaken," she said, lifting her chin. "I am here and this is where I wish to be."

"Give me a minute," one of the officers said.

The two men exchanged an extensive whispered conversation, then turned toward her. One pulled out a cell phone. "Clear it with His Majesty. I don't want a diplomatic incident on my head," the man said with a southern drawl.

"Clear it," she echoed, unable to keep the indignation from her voice. "I'm an adult. I don't have to clear this with any—"

"Tina, make the call or I'll be here all night," Zach said.

Giving a heavy sigh, she took the officer's phone, stabbed out her brother's personal cell number and waited. One ring. Two rings. *He damn well better pick up,* she thought.

"Stefan," the male voice finally announced. Two seconds later, he swore. "What the hell are you doing, Valentina?"

"I'm visiting Texas by my own free will," she said. "I sent both you and Rolfe a text message explaining my plans."

"The paparazzi said you were carried out of a museum by a madman," Stefan said.

"He was protecting me," she said.

"Humph," Stefan said, disbelief oozing through his voice. "Who is this Zachary Logan?"

She paused a half beat, then decided to break the news. "He's the father of my baby."

Silence followed. "So it's true," Stefan said, his voice turning hard. "Tina, how could you?"

She bit her lip at the disapproval in his voice. "The usual way," she said.

Stefan let out a litany of oaths.

She narrowed her eyes and interjected. "I'm putting you on speaker phone for the armed officers so there won't be a need for Zachary Logan to be detained."

The litany abruptly stopped.

"So, Stefan, we now agree that there has been a terrible misunderstanding and I have not been kidnapped. Correct?"

"Correct," he said in a clipped voice.

"And just for the benefit of the kind officers, please state your name," she said.

"Tina," he said, with a warning note in his voice.

"You're the one who pushed the kidnapping charges," she said.

Stefan cleared his throat. "Stefan Edward Henri Jacques the fifth."

"Thank you, Stefan," she said and he hung up. "Good luck," she whispered, thinking of her sweet, but spoiled sisters.

Zach glanced down at her. "Ready to go?"

"You have no idea," she said.

He slid his hand behind her back and steered her toward the private terminal. "I've heard of overprotective older brothers, but—"

"He's terrified of losing me. My sisters are useless." She felt a stab of guilt. "By choice. They would be terrific if they would think about anyone but themselves."

"Isn't that true of half the world?" he drawled.

"Yes," she said, smiling. "I guess it is. I apologize about the near-arrest."

"Something tells me that won't be the last excitement I see as a result of having you around," he said.

Tina winced. "I warned you."

"Yeah," he said. "You did. Let's get out of here."

Zach ushered her into the same SUV he'd driven all those months ago when he'd taken her to his apartment. She inhaled the scent, feeling a flood of sensual memories skitter through her.

She sank into the leather seat, feeling safe and for the first time in months, not judged. Closing her eyes, she tried to make sense of her most recent, most impulsive decision of her life.

"I don't have any clothes," she said.

"No problem," he said. "You can sleep in one of my T-shirts and go shopping tomorrow or the next day."

"Your T-shirt," she echoed, finding the prospect incredibly sensual and forbidden.

"Yeah," he said. "Unless her highness requires silk."

She paused a half-beat and decided to push back a little. She suspected she'd been way too easy for him. That put her at a disadvantage. "Silk? I can skip a night."

He gave a low laugh that rippled along her nerve endings.

"Tell me something I don't know," he said. "You skipped every stitch of clothing the night you spent with me."

"I'm surprised you remember," she said. "It was just one night—"

He whipped his head around to meet her gaze. "I remember everything about that night, Tina. Everything."

Just as Zach had said, ninety minutes later, he pulled down a long driveway lined with scrubby landscape. "Is this it?" she asked, preparing herself for a log cabin.

He nodded and she noticed the dirt and scrub were replaced by green grass and trees. "Is this your family home, or did you acquire it?"

"It's been in my family for generations. Some of the staff live in the original homeplace. I had a new home built about six years ago," he said.

A large white building with a wraparound front porch sat amidst tall trees and flowering shrubs. The waning sunlight glistened on the leaves. "It's beautiful," she said.

He glanced at her. "You sound surprised."

"I didn't know what to expect. A ranch can mean different things to different people."

"Ah, so you were expecting something more primitive. I hope you're not disappointed," he joked.

"Not at all," she said, looking forward to a shower.

"If I know Hildie, she'll have a meal waiting for us when we walk in the door," he said.

"Hildie?"

"Cook and housekeeper. She's been working at the ranch since before my parents passed away," he said.

"It's nice to have that continuity. We have a few staff members and advisers who have been around a long time."

"Are you worried about getting homesick? This is a lot different than Chantaine."

"I'm counting on that," she said with a sigh. More than anything, Tina craved an opportunity to hear herself think.

Zach pulled the SUV to a stop, then got out and stepped to the passenger door to open her door. He extended his hand and she took it, remembering the sensation of his calloused palms on various places of her body. Leading her up the steps, he opened the door and she stepped into a terra cotta tiled double-story foyer that featured a double staircase. A copper and crystal chandelier hung from the ceiling.

The foyer was warm and welcoming without being pretentious. She felt a sliver of tension ease from inside her. She took a short breath and inhaled the scent of a mouthwatering meal.

"Zach, is that you?" a woman called. Seconds later, a tall, sturdy woman with iron gray hair and a stern face entered the foyer. Her mouth softened slightly, but she still didn't quite smile. "There you are. The phone's been ringing off the hook. Some kook named Rolfe got all snippy with me, accusing you of kidnapping. I finally just hung up on the man."

Tina cringed. She generally tried to avoid creating drama, but this time she hadn't seen any other way around it.

"Yeah, well, I think we took care of that," Zach said, shooting Tina a sideways glance. "This is Valentina Devereaux, Hildie." He cleared his throat. "Princess Valentina Devereaux."

Hildie's eyes widened in surprise. "Princess?" she echoed. "You didn't really kidnap a princess, did you?" She glanced at Tina. "I mean, I know it's been awhile since you've been on a date, but—"

"Hildie," Zach interjected. "Tina is pregnant with my child."

Hildie's jaw dropped. "When in tarnation did that happen?"

Tina felt her cheeks heat at Hildie's suspicious expression. "It wasn't planned, Miss—?"

"Just Hildie. Everybody calls me Hildie. And what do I call you? Your majesty? Your highlyness."

"Tina would be fine," she said.

"Humph," Hildie said and lifted an eyebrow at Zach. "You said you were bringing a guest, not a princess. She may not like beef stew."

"I'm sure it's wonderful," Tina rushed to say. "I'll try not to be any trouble. I'm just looking forward to the quiet."

"Well, we've got a lot of that around here. Come on in. Dinner's waiting," Hildie said and walked down the hall.

"Oh, dear," Tina said. "I believe I've already upset her."

"Don't worry," Zach said, putting his hand on her lower back and guiding her farther into the house. "Hildie may look like she's just taken a bite out of a green apple, but she's got a heart of gold."

Hildie served the hearty meal in the kitchen nook instead of the formal dining room. Zach was pleased to see Tina eat a healthy portion of the stew and corn bread, although he didn't eat as much as usual. Although he'd been determined to bring Tina home, now that she was here, he was on edge. The ranch had become his cave, the place where he could hide and grieve. He hadn't brought a woman to the ranch since his wife had died.

Hildie refilled the water glasses. "So when's the wedding?"

Tina choked on a bite of her corn bread. "Oh no," she said, taking a long drink of water. "No wedding. Zach and I barely know each other."

"Well, you know each other well enough to get preg—"

"Hildie," Zach interjected. "Tina just arrived here. She just made the decision to come to the ranch yesterday. Let her settle in."

"Humph," Hildie said. "It don't make sense to me."

Hildie left the room and Tina leaned toward him. "Is she always this opinionated?"

He nodded. "And she doesn't hold back. Don't worry. She'll adjust. If she gets too pushy, just tell her to back off."

Tina bit her lip. "I can't fathom telling that woman to back off."

"Pretend she's your brother," he said.

Her lips lifted in a smile and he felt something in his gut twist. The sensation took him by surprise. "If you're done, I'll show you around the house."

"Thank you. That would be nice," she said and followed him to her feet as he rose.

Zach led her through the den, formal areas and his office area downstairs, then took her upstairs. Proud of the home he'd designed and helped build several years ago, he couldn't help wondering what Tina thought of it. She paused at the collection of family photographs in the upstairs hallway. "Is this your mother and father?" she asked. "And these other children? I think I remember you mentioning a brother."

He nodded. "Yeah, those are my parents, and my brother and sister," he said, pointing to another photograph. He felt a twinge of regret. His relationship with his brother and sister had suffered after the death of his wife. He'd shut everyone out.

Surprised at the onslaught of emotions he was experiencing, he cleared his throat. "Your room is down the hall," he said and walked toward the largest of the guest rooms. His former wife had chosen the colors for this room. Shades of green and blue-green provided a soothing haven. His own blood pressure always seemed to drop a few notches when he stepped into this room.

"Oh, it's lovely," Tina said. "I love the colors."

"Good," he said with a nod. "There's a connecting bath

with plenty of towels. I'll bring a couple of shirts for you. The remote for the TV should be on the nightstand. Anything else you need that you can think of?"

"Toothbrush and toothpaste," she said.

"I'll tell Hildie to bring you some. Anything else?" he asked, feeling his heart tug at the vulnerable expression on her face. Giving into an urge, he extended his hand to her arm and gently squeezed. "You're safe here," he said. "I'll make sure of it."

She took a deep breath and appeared to stiffen her spine. "Thank you. I'm afraid of how much I'm imposing."

"You're the mother of my child," he said firmly. "This is no imposition. You've been taking care of everyone else. It's damn time someone looked after you."

She blinked. "I have royal doctors and assistants. I didn't mean to give you the impression that I have to do everything on my own because I don't."

"Maybe," he said. "But it's pretty clear your family doesn't put your health or your need to take a break first. Now that you're pregnant, that needs to change. I can make sure that will happen."

"What about the paparazzi? They always show up," she said, her eyes darkening with fear.

"I have electric fences and gates. I don't usually have to close those gates, but I can and I will. Plus there's Hildie. She took on a brown bear one time. The bear turned tail and ran."

Tina stared at him for a long moment, then laughed. "Oh, my goodness, I can easily visualize that."

The sound of her laughter eased something inside him. He smiled. "I'm not stretching the truth. The only thing that scares Hildie is the dentist. I had to take her to fix a broken tooth. That's how I found out you were pregnant."

Tina lifted her hand to her throat. "At the dentist's office?"

"I was in the waiting room killing time. I saw your photo in one of those gossip sheets."

She winced. "The bump article," she said. "I received an anonymous tip from someone that the article was going to be published and left Chantaine just before the story hit. I was hoping to avoid the first wave from the media while I figured out how to handle everything."

"France wasn't far enough," he said.

"Nowhere is far enough," she said woefully. "I'm afraid you don't know what you've gotten yourself into by bringing me to your home."

"I've been through worse," he said, his own personal tragedy never far from his mind.

She widened her eyes. "With the media?"

He shrugged. "With life," he said. "Don't worry about me. The media is the least of my concern. Get some rest. If you need anything, let Hildie or me know. I'll let her take you into town so you can get what you need tomorrow."

She still looked vulnerable. His hands ached to pull her against him, but he resisted the urge. She wasn't exactly the same woman who had gone to bed with him months ago. Back then, he hadn't known she was a princess. Back then, she hadn't wanted him to know. She'd wanted one anonymous night just as he had. Now, everything was different. In a way, they were strangers more now than ever before.

She licked her lips and a flash of that dark night of need snapped through him. "Thank you for taking me away. For bringing me here."

Zach gave into the urge to stroke her hair and cup her head. "I know you're still wound tighter than a spring, but you're safe here. Soon enough, you'll realize you can relax.

And no thanks are necessary. I wouldn't have it any other way. 'Night Tina."

She took a deep breath that seemed to tremble out of her when she exhaled. "Good night, Zach."

Chapter Five

When Tina awakened the next morning, the sun slithered through the curtains covering the windows. She heard a vague vibrating sound, but couldn't quite place it. Glancing at one side of the bed then the other, she squinted at the clock on the nightstand. 10:30 a.m.

Embarrassment rolled through her. Oh, my Lord. She'd slept for twelve hours. Everyone would think she was the clichéd princess, accustomed to rising late, when that couldn't be further from the truth. The soft buzzing sound continued and she finally placed the noise. Her cell phone. Blinking, she pushed her hair from her face and slid out of bed. Where had she put the darn thing?

Following the sound, she finally found it beneath her discarded clothes from the night before. At the moment, she wore one of Zach's T-shirts and the well-worn cotton felt delicious against her skin. She pulled out her cell phone and surveyed the recent calls. Her brother, her sister in Paris, her next youngest sister, her assistant, her brother, her brother, and her sister in Paris.

Sighing, she mentally formed a strategy for each call and pushed speed dial for her brother.

"How long are you planning on staying there?" her brother demanded as he picked up the phone.

"I'm not going to have a long discussion. As I told you before, I'm here in Texas of my own free will. Not sure when I'll return. I'm figuring things out."

"Figuring things out?" her brother echoed. "And how are we supposed to deal with this? I'm shocked at your lack of consideration."

"Consider it belated rebellion," she said. "I'll be in touch when I can give you more information."

"But Tina, how are we to explain this to the press?"

"I don't really care," she said. "You have professionals on staff to take care of this. Let them do their job."

"And what about your appearances?"

"Either cancel them or let my sisters step up. Take care, sweetie," she said and disconnected the call.

She called her sister in Paris to reassure her that she hadn't been abducted. Ericka was shocked that Tina was pregnant out of wedlock, but recovered enough to offer Tina any and every assistance.

"How could you do this to me? I've only been out of college for two years and just when I'm enjoying life in Florence, Stefan insists I move back to Chantaine?" her younger sister, Bridget, said when Tina called.

"That's two more years than I had," Tina said, more blunt than she'd ever been with her younger sister.

"But this is a terrible scandal," Bridget said. "There will be questions every which way I turn. How will I answer them?"

"That's what the palace PR is for. They will help you,"

Tina said, feeling the urge to return to bed and pull the covers over her head.

"But Tina, how could you do this? Everyone was counting on you to be the normal one," her sister huffed.

Tina sighed. "Maybe that's why it happened. I just couldn't be normal and dutiful anymore. I'm sorry. I—" Her voice broke and she swallowed over the lump in her throat. "You'll do fine. Maybe better than me," she said. "Love you. Bye for now."

She disconnected the call and turned off the phone. She couldn't bear hearing the disappointment in her family's voices one more minute. Her eyes burned with unshed tears and she tried to hold them back, but they seemed to well up from her belly to her tight chest and tighter throat. A sob escaped and then another. Tears streamed down her cheeks. She couldn't remember the last time she'd cried like this. When her mother had died? When her father had passed away?

A sharp rap sounded on the bedroom door, startling her. She sniffed and swiped at her wet cheeks.

"Hildie here. I have breakfast for you," the housekeeper said and opened the door.

Horrified, Tina groped for something to cover herself. In her world, staff never entered without receiving confirmation from her.

Hildie bustled around the room. "I don't often get a chance to deliver breakfast in bed, but since you're here I do. Lord knows, Zachary never sleeps past dawn," she said with more than a twinge of disapproval as she placed the tray on a table. "It's a good thing you rested well, being pregnant and all. I read that it takes a day to adjust to each time zone change, so you've got a few days to go. And according to what Zachary said, they've been running you like a mule during harvest. A woman with child needs her rest. I hope some of this will suit you. Scrambled eggs, bacon, pancakes, grits, fruit and toast."

Hildie finally glanced at Tina. The woman narrowed her gaze as she studied her then caught sight of the phone in Tina's hand. "You've been crying. Has someone been bothering you?"

Tina sniffled but shook her head. "Not bothering. I had to return a few calls."

"To who?" Hildie asked crossing her arms over her chest.

"Just a few members of my family," Tina said, wondering why she felt the need to answer questions from staff.

"Humph," Hildie said. "Well, if they're upsetting you, it just won't do. Zachary won't allow it."

Taken off guard by the woman's suggestion that Zachary would somehow be able to control or even influence her family, she shook her head. "Excuse me? Zachary won't allow it? My family doesn't operate by everyone else's rules."

"Neither does Zachary Logan," Hildie said flatly. "But I imagine since he got you out of France in no time flat, you got a taste of what he's capable of. If not, you'll see soon enough. Go ahead and eat. Zachary tells me you need to go to the store. It takes about a half hour to drive to town and I suspect you'll tire quickly."

"I'm really not that fragile," Tina insisted, moving to the table where Hildie had placed her breakfast.

"Uh-huh," Hildie said. "That's what a lot of moms-to-be say. Then all of a sudden they're passing out or crying because they haven't had enough rest."

Offended, Tina lifted her chin. "I wasn't crying because I hadn't had enough—"

"With all due respect, Miss Highlyness," Hildie interjected. "Please eat your breakfast. We're wasting daylight."

Thirty minutes later, Tina joined Hildie in a black Ford

truck. Tina was clean, but her face was stripped clean of cosmetics except for lip gloss and a little powder. Her hair was still damp as Hildie barreled down the road.

Tina gripped the door with one hand and the edge of her seat with the other. "Are we in a hurry?" she asked.

Hildie shrugged and turned the country radio station to a higher decibel. "Not really. I just don't like to waste time getting where I want to go."

Tina swallowed over a knot of panic in her throat. "How far to the store?"

Hildie waved her hand and guided the steering wheel with her knee. "Not long," she said and cackled. "You can be sure I'll get there in no time."

If we don't meet our maker first, she thought and continued her death grip. Hildie gave a running commentary on the history of the area and talked about her niece, Eve, apparently her pride and joy.

When Hildie pulled into a parking lot and screeched to a stop, Tina breathed a sigh of relief.

"Here we are," Hildie said and winked at her. "They have a maternity department here."

Tina walked into the store and felt as if she'd stepped into a foreign country. The truth was that her assistant often shopped for her. Tina rarely visited retail stores. She was too busy.

She felt Hildie studying her. "What's wrong?" she asked. "Don't they have what you want?"

"They seem to have everything. I just don't know where to start. I'm overwhelmed," she said.

Hildie laughed. "Okay, let's start with the basics, then. Underwear," she said and led her to the intimates department.

Tina chose several pairs of stretchy panties and a couple bras.

"You'll get bigger there, too," Hildie warned.

Feeling self-conscious, Tina shrugged. "I'll deal with that later. I'd like to get a couple of skirts and a few tops."

"The maternity department is over—"

"I'm not quite ready for that," Tina said. "I'll just buy a size larger than usual."

"If you're sure," Hildie said.

"I'm not that big yet," Tina whispered. "I'm not that far along in my pregnancy. I'm not ready for everyone to know—"

"Your Highlyness, if Zach noticed your baby bump in that newspaper, then everyone knows," Hildie said dryly.

"Everyone doesn't know at first sight, though. I could just use a little breathing room," Tina said.

Hildie studied her for a long moment. "I can understand that. Let's find you a nice little skirt or two."

Less than fifteen minutes later, they left the store with toiletries, underwear, two skirts, three tops and a dress.

"You won't be able to hide it much longer, dear," Hildie said.

Tina's stomach knotted. "I know. I'm just buying a little time."

"Are you ashamed?" Hildie asked.

"Well, you have to admit it's not the optimal situation," Tina said, gazing out the window as they whizzed past the barren landscape.

"Are you ashamed of Zach?"

Tina whipped her head around to look at Hildie. "No. I'm embarrassed because I should have been more careful, more responsible. It's not as if I were a teenager."

"From what Zachary told me, you were busy being an adult when you were a teenager. No time for impulsiveness or getting into trouble."

"That still doesn't excuse—"

"Pardon me, Your Highlyness, but nobody's perfect. Even

princesses aren't perfect. You're just lucky Zachary was the man who got carried away with you. He's a good man," she said. "And it's time he got past…" Hildie's voice trailed off and she sighed.

"Got past what?" Tina asked.

Hildie frowned. "It's not my place to say."

Tina blinked, shocked that Hildie would consider any subject outside propriety. After all, Zach's housekeeper had freely given her opinions on underwear, pregnancy and marriage. What subject could possibly be so forbidden with Zach?

Glancing at Hildie's implacable expression, she felt a strange sense of forboding. What did she really know about Zachary Logan? Had she made a mistake by coming here?

For the next two days, Tina didn't see Zach. Although she appreciated the opportunity for extra rest and quiet time, she felt frustrated about the lack of opportunity to get to know him better. After all, wasn't that part of the reason she'd come to his ranch?

Donning tennis shoes her sister had included in a package she'd sent her, along with a loose pair of jeans and blouse, she decided to go for a walk. The heat and humidity were already intense, even at nine thirty. Tina wished she'd risen early but knew she was still adjusting to the change in time zones. Pregnancy exacerbated her jet lag, but she felt herself getting stronger.

Spotting a barn with a fenced pasture and a couple of horses, she walked toward it. When she was a teenager, Tina had loved horseback riding. Unfortunately she'd had little time for it once she'd left for college.

She walked into the cool barn and peeked into the stalls. Two quarter horses roomed next to each other, then a gorgeous palomino and black gelding. She wandered toward the pasture and saw a tall, slim, dark-haired woman talking to a colt. The young horse's ears twitched.

Curious, Tina continued to watch in silence.

The woman must have felt her presence, however, because she turned to look at her. "Hello, I'm working with Samson right now. There's no other riding."

Surprised and impressed at the woman's assertiveness, Tina shook her head. "I wasn't planning to ride," she said. "I'm a guest of Mr. Logan's and I was just taking a walk. Pardon me, I didn't mean to intrude."

The woman nodded. "No problem. You can watch if you like. This colt of Zach's is a little ornery, so I'm working with him."

Tina watched as the woman led the colt in a series of walking and stopping around the corral. Constantly cooing, she put a saddle on the colt. He gave a half-beat of a pause then allowed her to lead him again around the corral.

She gave the young horse an apple and praised him effusively then returned him to his stall, which was waiting with fresh oats and water.

Finally, she turned to Tina. "I'm Eve, Hildie's niece," she said.

Tina nodded and extended her hand. "I'm Tina. Hildie has talked about you. She's so proud of you," she said.

Eve nodded, giving a self-conscious smile as she shook Tina's hand. "Hildie's wonderful, but she's a little over the top sometimes."

"In your case, it's over the top in a good way," Tina said.

"Ah," Eve said. "You've obviously spent enough time with her to understand her."

"It didn't take long. She definitely speaks her mind," Tina said.

Eve laughed. "That's an understatement. How do you know Zach?"

"Mutual friends," she said. "I met him several months ago. I could have sworn Hildie told me that you worked for an international hotel chain as a regional manager."

"That's right," Eve said. "This is my fun time. My day off. I used to do more training and Zach made me promise that I would always come back in case he had any problems. Samson here is a problem."

"How did he wrangle that agreement out of you?"

"Paid for all my education that wasn't covered by scholarships," she said then shrugged. "But I don't mind. I really do enjoy my time with horses. They're lots more fun than corporate meetings." She glanced over her back at the stalls. "I should have asked after I finished with Samson. Do you ride? Would you like to ride today? Candy's a nice ride—"

"No, that's okay," Tina said. "I ride, but it's been a while…."

"She's not riding," Zach said from the other end of the barn.

Her heart jumping in her chest, Tina whipped her head around to stare at him. He wore jeans, a T-shirt, a hat, a pair of boots and a frown.

"I wasn't planning on riding," Tina said defensively. "I was just exploring."

"Just don't get into trouble," he said.

Tina frowned. "What kind of trouble? I'm just walking around *your* ranch. I can't stay cooped up in the house forever."

"I guess not," he said as he moved toward her. "Hildie told me you went for a walk."

"Why doesn't that surprise me?" Tina murmured.

"And a good morning to you," Eve said. "Samson's making progress."

Zach nodded. "Good to know," he said. "I hope he hasn't been too much of a pain in the butt."

"No more than his owner," Eve said.

Zach shot her a withering glance. "Anyone ever tell you that you look like your aunt?"

"Bite me," Eve said and turned her back to him.

"How's the job going?" he asked.

"It's going," she said. "I don't love it. I don't hate it."

"Just haven't found what you're looking for," he said.

"It pays well," she said over her shoulder. "That's good enough for me. And, hey, don't be so hard on your visitor. She's polite, which is more than you can say about yourself." She stomped out of the barn.

Feeling Zach's gaze on her, Tina wondered about the relationship between Zach and Eve. Antagonistic, yet vaguely caring.

"Don't even think about riding a horse," he said.

"I didn't," she said. "In more than a fictional sense," she added, seeing a flash of alarm on his face. "When I walked into the barn, I remembered how much I enjoyed riding. How much I missed it, but now isn't the time to—"

"Exactly," he said in a crisp tone. "Now is not the time to start this particular hobby again. It's too dangerous for you and the baby."

She saw a darkness deepen in his eyes and wondered where that originated. She thought about what Hildie had said to her. She thought about how much she didn't know about him.

Lifting her chin, she narrowed her eyes at him. "Part of the reason I came here was because you and I should get to know each other because you're the father of my child. We need to start that process. I'm not going to be here forever."

"You're not," he said, lifting a dark brow. "Is there somewhere you'd rather be?" he asked.

The south of France, a small town in Italy, a Greek island. Somewhere she could rest, somewhere she wouldn't have to answer to her brother, somewhere she could plan her and her baby's future. Somewhere she could disappear for a while. At the moment, Zach's ranch was perfect. That would change as soon as the paparazzi showed up.

"I haven't had time to make plans," she said. "I need to figure out what's best for my child and for me."

"Is it not best for your child to have access to his or her father?" he challenged.

"In most circumstances, that would be best," she conceded. "But the longer I stay here, the more I realize I don't know that much about you."

He lifted his lips in a dangerous grin. "Are you afraid I'm a bad influence?"

Her heart fluttered at the bad boy expression on his face, but she refused to give in to his charm. "As you Americans would say, the jury is out. I need to know more. You haven't been around much." She couldn't resist a wicked urge to goad. "Do I frighten you?"

Flames lit his eyes and he held her gaze as he moved closer to her. "Frighten?" he echoed in a low, deliberate voice.

She felt a twist of fear wrench through her, but she refused to give in to it. She gave the shrug that had been bred into her through generations of royals. "What else should I think?"

Stepping closer, close enough to lower his mouth to hers, he continued to hold her gaze as he gave a husky laugh. "I was giving you some space," he said. "If you're sure you're ready to take me on, I'm here, Princess."

Her stomach dipped at the sensual attraction echoing from him to her and back again. She cleared her throat. "Perhaps after you're finished for the day," she suggested.

"Dinner," he said. "I'll have Hildie fix something for us. We can have dinner in my suite so we won't be interrupted."

Her heart fluttered. "I'm not sure that would be a good

idea," she said, feeling a strong urge to back track, but trying to hold firm.

"Do you need a chaperone?" he challenged.

She stifled her protests. "Of course not," she said. "I'll see you tonight."

Chapter Six

Zach sat across from Tina in what she assumed was the outer room of his bedroom suite. Although the door was closed, she couldn't help feeling curious about what his bedroom looked like. She wondered if she could learn more about him by seeing more of his most personal space.

This room appeared to offer a combination of business and pleasure. They sat at a small dark wood table by one of the large bay windows. The view featured rolling hills of land that stretched as far as the eye could see. It occurred to Tina, that in a way, Zach could survey his kingdom from this window every day.

On the other side of the room sat a large desk with a flat-screen monitor, computer and other electronic equipment. In the center of the room, a plush brown leather sofa sat across from a flat wide-screen TV mounted on the wall.

"Missing the palace?" Zach asked as he stabbed a bite of steak.

"Not really," she said.

He lifted an eyebrow in doubt. "You sure about that? I wondered if this place might seem a little rustic in comparison."

"Well, it's not full of French antiques and the floors aren't marble, but it's far from rustic. You need to remember that I lived in Texas while I went to college. My first two years, I stayed in a dormitory. Not exactly the lap of luxury."

"True enough," he said.

"Plus, I've traveled all over the world and have stayed in places without air conditioning or with limited heat and water." She frowned. "I'm not a total sissy."

He paused, surprise glinting in his eyes, then he gave a low laugh. "Okay," he conceded. "No sissies in this room."

Mollified, she relaxed slightly and picked at her food. "I have enjoyed the quiet," she said. "And the lack of paparazzi has been wonderful, although I'm sure that won't last when they find out where I am."

"They already know," he said. "I've closed the gates and put a couple of men with rifles at the edge of my property."

"Really? I had no idea."

"No need for you to know. You're recovering and—" He shrugged. "Gestating. Those Europeans back off when they've got a rifle pointed in their direction."

"I'm not really that fragile," she protested.

"Hey, you just said it was great to get a break from the paparazzi."

"True," she said and took a bite. The steak was delicious, but her appetite had been iffy lately. She took a sip of water to wash the bite down and studied the hard planes of Zach's face. There was so much she didn't know about him.

"Well, I suppose this is a good time for us to get to know each other better. Although, you could do an internet search on me and find out quite a bit," she added wryly.

"Yeah, age, education, pedigree. Gossip about potential marriage partners."

"Trust me, that was only gossip. Only speculation. At one time, my brother was hoping I would accept a proposal from—" She broke off, remembering she should keep that information private, at least for the time being.

"From who?" he prompted.

"State business," she said. "My brother would consider it confidential."

"And you?" he asked. "What would you consider it?"

"Horrifying," she said. "Impossible."

He chuckled and lifted his beer to his lips. "I can see why it didn't work out."

"Well, enough about me. What about you? Any former loves in your past?"

A shadow crossed over Zach's face, and his expression immediately closed. "I don't discuss that part of my past. You want to know about my sister and brother, my business, my ranch, I'll tell you everything you want to know."

"But—" she said. "You just asked about mine."

"I wanted to know if there is anyone else in the picture with you. I can tell you I'm not seeing anyone. That's all you need to know."

Frustrated, stymied, she stared at him. "How am I to know what kind of father you would be?"

"I can ask the same question. How do I know what kind of mother you would be?" he countered.

"Well, that's different," she said, flustered by how he'd turned the tables on her. "You know I'd already begun to make plans to take care of the baby, to raise the child on my own."

"Without letting the child know about the father," he said, a bit of steel slipping into his voice.

"Yes, but I already explained why. It was a one-night stand. It didn't seem fair to hold you responsible."

"Well, there's where you're wrong. I never back down from my responsibilities."

"I can see how you would feel that way," she conceded. "But what I really want to know is your attitude toward children. What are your thoughts about raising them?"

"Children are to be nurtured and protected. I don't believe in raising a hand against a child. There are other ways to teach them, if that's what you're asking. I will be involved with this child," he said. "You can count on it. And if you really want to know what I think about raising a child, I think the parents should do it together," he said, his gaze meeting hers dead-on. "As husband and wife."

Tina's stomach clenched. "Of course, that doesn't apply to us," she said.

He took a slow swallow from his beer and she couldn't help watching his throat work. The sight was surprisingly sensual. Her thoughts caught her off guard.

"Yet," he said and set down his glass.

Shock raced through her and she couldn't keep her eyes from rounding. "Oh, no. You can't be serious," she said. "You don't really think you and I should—" She shook her head.

"Get married," he finished for her and she marveled at how easily the words slid off his tongue. He didn't appear the least bit troubled by the prospect.

"We don't even know each other," she said, desperation growing inside her. "We don't even know if we like each other."

"We can take some time to find out," he said. "You're early in your pregnancy."

Alarm buttons went off inside her brain and Tina stood. "I'm sorry, but I hope I haven't misled you into believing I have any intention of marrying you. I agree that it's a good idea for us to know each other, but—" She shook her head, her throat closing at the very thought.

He stood and reached for her hand. "Stop panicking. We don't do shotgun weddings around her anymore. Well, not often," he amended with a rough chuckle. "I'm not going to force you to do anything. But don't you think our baby deserves to know that we explored the option of marriage? Years from now, when our child asks why we're not married, and he or she will. You can count on it. Don't you want to know, in your heart of hearts that you have tried to give your child everything they could want? Including an on-site father?"

Her heart still frozen in her chest, she bit her lip.

"Breathe," he said.

She forced herself to do as he said. She shook her head and closed her eyes. "Since I found out I was pregnant, I always pictured myself as a single mother, handling this by myself," she whispered.

"Paint a different picture," he said.

She opened her eyes and looked into his.

"One with me in it," he said. "Because whether we get married or not, you're not doing this alone."

The next morning, Zach rose early and drove his jeep out to a fence that needed to be repaired. He stripped down to his T-shirt and got down to work with the sun blazing down on him.

The menial work usually soothed him, but today he couldn't help thinking about Tina. He wondered if he had scared her away. He wondered if she would still be there when he arrived home today.

Couldn't worry about that, he told himself as he strung new wire to fix the fence. He hadn't been deceptive, he'd been real. She would have to choose her course based on what he'd told her and her own thoughts.

He couldn't blame her hesitance. After all, she was a princess. He would never have bedded her if he'd known. That said, she'd bedded him knowing he was a rancher/businessman. What did that say about her?

He liked that she wasn't prejudiced. Despite his pride, he liked that she was determined to vet him. He wished she wasn't so determined *not* to marry him. *That* struck at his pride. What did she find so offensive about him?

He worked nonstop until lunch and finally glanced at his watch. Pulling a bottle of water from his backpack in the car, he noticed a car coming toward him. He squinted his eyes, trying to recognize the driver.

At first, he thought it was Hildie as he identified her car. The car screeched to a stop in front of him and a brunette exited the vehicle with a basket. He immediately identified Tina.

"What are you doing here?" he asked as she walked toward him.

"Bringing lunch," she said. "Hildie told me you're awful about taking a break."

"Hildie's a tattletale," Zach said with a scowl.

"But she tells the truth," Tina said, looking around. "Is there any shade around here?"

"The car is the best bet," he said. "Did you have the AC on during your drive?"

Tina laughed. "In this heat? Of course."

"Good," he said. "Part of surviving our Texas heat is relying on air-conditioning. Don't try to tough it out."

She glanced at his sweat-stained T-shirt. "Looks like you toughed it out. Hope you want a sandwich."

"I'm in," he said, surprised and pleased that she'd found

her way to him. He walked to the car and got inside. "How did you find me?"

"Hildie gave me directions and I have a GPS," she said. "It's an amazing tool. My sister sent me a box with some of my clothes, laptop and other stuff. I'd recently bought a GPS."

"I'm impressed," he said. "I wouldn't have thought a princess would have driven on dirt roads to deliver a sandwich."

She gave him a withering glance. "You clearly need to revise your ideas of what a princess does and doesn't do."

He accepted the sandwich she gave him and took a bite. "Touché," he said after he swallowed.

She took a sip of her water and studied his face. "What made you fix the fence? That task is pretty low on the totem pole."

He shrugged. "I have a ranch manager and I sometimes do the menial stuff to free him up to stay on top of other tasks. I also often have to go into Dallas for our other companies, so I can't commit to ranch duty all the time."

"You sound like a busy man," she said.

"I'm lucky to have several successful businesses," he said with a shrug of his powerful shoulders that distracted her.

She shook her head. "I don't know how you do everything," she said.

"You do what you need to do to get the job done," he said and remembered what he'd learned about how much of the load Tina had carried for the rest of her family. "Maybe you do know what that's about."

Seeing the light of recognition in her eyes, he felt his gut lift a little. "I'm just about finished here. If you like I can take you for a tour of the ranch when I'm done."

"I'd like a tour of your kingdom," she said with a smile that flashed a dimple at him.

He couldn't help grinning in return. "Kingdom?" he echoed. "That's a pretty term for a few acres of scrub and brush."

She shot him a look of disbelief. "You're doing that thing Americans do so well," she said. "Understate. Play humble."

"No play," he retorted. "I'm humble."

She gave a low, not-quite-ladylike chuckle that got under his skin. "And I'm a runway model."

"You could be. With your body," he said.

Her eyes widened in astonishment. He liked that he'd taken her by surprise.

"You are full of—" She took a breath and her lips twitched. "Flattery."

"Not really," he said. "Meet me back at the house."

"I'd rather watch you finish the job," she said.

He felt a forbidden thrill at the idea that the princess wanted to watch him flex his muscles. He wanted to flex a lot more with her. "Go right ahead," he said and stepped out of the car.

Deciding to give her a show worth watching, he stripped off his shirt and finished the repair job. Fifteen more minutes and he was done. He sucked down the rest of his bottle of water.

Strolling to the driver's side of her car, he tapped on the window. "Did I do an okay job?" he asked.

She pressed the button to lower the window and shot him a look of grudging appreciation. "You should leave your shirt on," she said. "It protects you from the sun."

"Are you saying you don't like my body?"

She gave a huff of impatience. "You're insufferable and not at all humble."

Zach chuckled. "You still want to see the ranch?" he asked.

"Yes. I'll meet you at the house," she said and the window slid upward. Seconds later, she spun away, leaving him in her dust. Her speed made him a little nervous, though he wouldn't tell her that. Winning over a princess wasn't going to be the easiest job he'd undertaken, but he was determined.

Zach grabbed a quick shower after he returned to the house and Tina took the apples and bottles of water Hildie offered. Zach descended the stairs with damp hair and wearing fresh clothes.

Her heart stuttered at the sight of him so strong, carrying his muscular frame with confident ease. He was so different than every other man she'd ever had in her life. He wasn't at all intimidated by her position, but he also seemed to respect her as a person. He was protective, but he hadn't forced her into anything. True, he'd pretty much told her he wanted them to get married, and she'd nearly lost her dinner afterward.

The truth was he still hadn't tried to force her. He'd just stated his case and let the truth sit between them. Terrifying, but in many ways, valid. Too valid.

This was a big decision. Damn. Since she'd met Zach, *everything* had been a big decision. She bit the inside of her lip, a technique she'd developed as a child to cover her nerves.

"Okay, your highness, you ready to see my little plot of land?" he asked, his eyes full of sexy humor.

She smiled. "Your kingdom," she corrected.

He chuckled and she allowed him to lead her out the door to his SUV. He ushered her into the car, started it and turned on the AC. "West first. We call it the devil's land. It's the worst," he said. "Nothing grows here," he said as he turned onto a dirt road.

She looked out the window and couldn't deny what he'd said. "Well, it does look a bit dry. No irrigation possibilities, I suppose?"

"Might as well pour water into Death Valley," he said.

She couldn't quite swallow a chuckle. "I love it that you're not trying to sell me. It's so rare."

"What do you mean?" he asked.

"I mean, everywhere I go people always show me the best stuff first and try to hide the bad. This is hideous."

Zach pulled to a stop and put his car into Park. Propping his jaw against his hand, he stared into the distance. "Yeah, in a way. In a way, if you can get through the barren desert, maybe you can make it through anything."

She searched his hard face and saw a dozen emotions. Loss, grief, resolve, strength. She wondered where it all came from and she suspected it wasn't from the scrubby landscape in front of them.

"Do you come here often?" she asked.

"Probably every few months or so," he said. "This kind of place strips you down to the basics. There's nowhere to hide. That's the bad thing. The good thing is maybe you don't need to hide."

She took a moment to absorb his words. What a concept. No need to hide? She tried to remember when she hadn't felt like she needed to hide. When had she felt like she could be herself? Safe?

She felt a whoosh of tense air exhale from her lungs.

"I heard that," he murmured.

She sucked in a quick breath.

"Relax. That's what this place is for. It's base line."

She took a deep breath. "When did you first come here and feel this way?"

He paused a halfbeat. "I was sixteen. Torn between playing football in high school and helping with the ranch. Tough year."

She knew without him saying which he had chosen. "You gave up football."

He glanced at her. "How'd you know?"

She shrugged. "Just an instinct." She met his gaze. "You and I have more in common that most people might think."

"In what way?" he asked.

"You chose family, duty, heritage. So did I," she said.

"Not entirely," he said. "When you needed to make a change, you did. That's courageous."

She bit the inside of her lip. "Maybe," she said. "Maybe just necessary."

"It's still courageous," he said. "You went against the grain. Against what was expected of you. Don't underestimate yourself, Tina. I don't. No one else should either."

Feeling a rush of pleasure surge through her, she stared into his eyes and felt herself sinking with each breath. Her gaze slipped to his mouth and she felt a tingling sensation on her lips. It felt like a thousand years ago that he'd kissed her, yet she remembered it as if it had happened yesterday.

Confused by her strange combination of feelings, she struggled with the dipping sensation in her stomach. She took a quick breath to clear her head and smiled. "I love it that we started here. What's next?"

"It gets greener," he said, putting the truck in gear and turning around.

He drove past the swimming hole where he learned how to swim, then past a field of bluebonnets, then past his parents', his grandparents', and his great grandparents' graves. She wanted to get out, but he shook off her suggestion to linger. They passed fields and fields of cattle, then he came to another stop, this one overlooked rolling green hills. Looking at the beautiful vista, she felt something inside her ease. "Nice," she murmured.

"Yeah, it does the same thing to me," Zach said.

She studied his face and saw the same peace she felt inside

her. "You're in love with your kingdom," she said, unable to keep a smile from her face.

He did a double take and lifted a dark eyebrow. "In love with my kingdom? That's a first," he said.

"You are," she insisted. "You're as devoted as my brother is, except not as arrogant, thank goodness."

He shook his head. "I wouldn't call myself in love. Maybe committed. Maybe I need to be committed," he muttered under his breath.

"Here's the important question. On your worst day, would you want to be doing anything other than taking care of your ranch?"

He searched her face. "Where did you come up with that?"

"Someone in a very poor village in Africa once told me that on her worst day she wouldn't want to be doing anything else. It was so wise. So magical. I've always wanted to find something that made me feel so strongly."

"So being a princess didn't do it for you?" he asked.

She hesitated, swamped by guilt. "No, it didn't. I don't want to be ungrateful—"

"You're not," he said, covering her hand with his. "You're just being honest. I like that," he said, his gaze wrapping around her heart and squeezing. "I like that a lot."

Chapter Seven

The next morning when Tina awakened, she found a note from Zach under her door. *Eat an early dinner. I'm taking you to town for a meeting at 6:00 p.m.—Zach*

The abrupt language jarred her after the tour of the ranch they'd shared yesterday. He clearly hadn't learned the proper way of addressing royals, she thought wryly recalling all the invitations to her that had read, *The honor of your attendance would be greatly appreciated...* Oh, well, maybe that was part of the reason he appealed to her. Nothing fake or flowery about him. He put his motives flat out in front of her.

After giving her sister Bridget some tips for her upcoming appearances via e-mail, Tina sat in the swing on the front porch, contemplating her and her baby's future with no lightning bolts of decision.

Hildie must have known about the appointment because she called Tina in for early dinner. "Do you know what this meeting is about?"

Hildie glanced at her in surprise. "Meeting?" she echoed. "Zach's taking you into town for an appointment with Dr. McAllister. Dr. McAllister's the best ob-gyn doctor in the area." Hildie shook her head. "We just wish she would have moved to town sooner."

Tina frowned, feeling more than a ripple of indignation. "Are you telling me that Zach plans to choose my doctor? If the royal doctors aren't going to deliver the baby, then I think I should be the one—"

"—It's just a checkup," Zach said from behind her. "Don't most pregnant women visit the doctor by the fourth month?"

"Yes, but the doctor usually just confirms the pregnancy and gives prenatal vitamins. I've been taking prenatal vitamins since I realized I was pregnant. I didn't want the information to be leaked. Unfortunately not everyone at a medical office is discreet."

"That's why I pulled a few strings and arranged an after-hours appointment," Zach said from the doorway. "Are you done?"

Glancing down at her half-eaten meal, she suddenly lost her appetite. "Yes, I am."

"Okay. Let's go."

"Don't you want anything to eat?" she asked.

He shook his head. "I'm not hungry."

Me either, she thought, and picked up her plate as she rose.

"I can get that," Hildie said, taking the plate from her hands. "Are you sure you don't want me to save something for you? Didn't you like it?"

"It was delicious as always, but I'm full, thank you," Tina said.

"Alrighty," Hildie said. "If you change your mind after your appointment, I'll have something waiting for you."

Moments later, Zach helped her into his SUV. She felt a mixture of relief and anticipation. She'd wanted to visit a doctor, but the thought of dealing with leaks had made her hesitant, so she'd researched the most healthy approach toward pregnancy and strictly taken her vitamins.

"What do you know about this doctor?" she asked after they'd driven several miles and the silence stretched between them.

"She's experienced with routine and high-risk pregnancies and deliveries. She's new to the area and we're lucky to get her. We had to recruit her," he said.

"Who is we?" she asked.

"The community," he said.

She frowned in confusion. "But who is the community?" she asked. "How does that work? Do all of you get together and put together a special fund?"

"Something like that," he said. "Some of us get together and pool funds for the good of the community."

"Hmm," she said and nodded. "The haves help the have-nots."

"The haves help the haves *and* the have-nots," he corrected. "The whole community."

She studied him for a long moment. "Bet you were on the steering committee for this," she said. "I wonder why."

"Don't," he said and clenched his jaw.

They were silent for the rest of the drive, leaving her to wonder what was going on inside Zachary. He pulled in front of a medical office, and her thoughts turned to her baby. She automatically pressed her hand against her abdomen.

"You ready?" he asked as he cut the engine.

She nodded. "Yes, I am."

He helped her out of the car and they entered the office. Zach knocked on the receptionist's window.

Silence followed.

"Are you sure someone is here?" she asked.

He nodded, but rapped again.

Seconds later, a door whipped open and a tall woman dressed in a white coat with short hair appeared in the doorway. "Looking for me, Mr. Logan? I don't usually take appointments this late, but you made me curious." The woman glanced in Tina's direction. "I'm Dr. McAllister."

"I'm Valentina…"

Dr. McAllister wrinkled her brow. "A lot of names and they're not southern. I'll take a wild guess. Royal and pregnant?"

A rush of self-consciousness rose from her feet up to her cheeks. "Yes. As a matter of fact, I am," she murmured.

"No need for embarrassment. Pregnancy in all its forms, planned or a big surprise, is my business. I'm here to make everything go as smooth as silk. You're safe with me," Dr. McAllister said.

Tina felt her shoulders relax and a soothing sensation seep through her. "I would appreciate it."

Dr. McAllister shrugged. "I wouldn't have it any other way. Come back for the examination." She glanced at Zach. "I'll call you to come back if necessary. Otherwise, feel free to pace the waiting room."

With a quietly reassuring nurse by her side, Dr. McAllister conducted the examination. The nurse took a vial of blood to double-check Tina's iron. The doctor set her stethoscope over Tina's abdomen and Tina heard the baby's heartbeat. The sound filled her with wonder.

"I'll do this for Zachary even though he's a pain in the butt," the doctor said. "Marie, could you please bring in Mr. Logan?"

"This will be cold," Dr. McAllister said and squirted goop on Tina's abdomen.

Tina twitched at the sensation. The doctor pressed a device over her abdomen.

"Look at the screen," the doctor said.

Tina stared at the monitor and saw a miniature combination of tiny arms and limbs with a large head and a beating heart. "It looks like an alien."

"Is it healthy?" Zach asked, walking into the room.

Hearing his voice, Tina swung her head to look at him. He looked so tense. His jaw and his fists were clenched.

"Looks very healthy so far," Dr. McAllister said. "Sex? I can't guarantee, but if I were a betting woman, I would say this is a girl. We'll know more with the next ultrasound."

A thrill raced through Tina. Even though she'd known she was pregnant and had been as healthy as possible, the fact that she was carrying a baby hadn't felt real until now. The realization took her breath away. "Wow. A baby," she whispered. "She's a real little person."

"A healthy baby," Zach said.

She met his gaze and he took her hand. Watching him stare at their baby on the screen, Tina had the bone-deep feeling that nothing between them would ever be the same.

After repeated assurances from Dr. McAllister that both Tina and the baby were healthy, Tina and Zach left the office. He helped her into the truck and they both sat silently for a long moment.

"That ultrasound was amazing," she said. "Amazing."

He nodded and his lips lifted a notch. "Yeah, it was." He studied her for a moment. "Would you like to get some ice cream?"

"That sounds wonderful," she said and remembered when they'd gotten a float after the masquerade party. She glanced around the empty parking lot then looked back at him. "I'm impressed. No paparazzi in sight."

"Like I said, I pulled some strings," he said and started

the car. "Dr. McAllister will be discreet, but you won't be able to hide the pregnancy soon."

"I know," she said, feeling the weight of her position settle on her again. "I'm just hoping to buy a little more time so I can figure out my plans and how to announce them."

"Heard any more from your brother or sisters?" he asked.

"Angry text and voice mail messages. I haven't picked up because I don't want their upset cluttering my mind. I feel as if my staying at your ranch is a rare opportunity I need to pursue to the fullest. I can't do that if I'm feeling guilty about how my family is handling my absence."

"Good choice," he said. "You need to put your well-being and the baby's health first. If they can't understand that, it's their problem. And if you'd like me to answer for you—"

"No, no," she said, unable to fight a combination of pleasure and humor at his defense of her. "Have you always been this protective about women who were important to you?"

"You're carrying my child," he said. "How else could I be?"

She felt a sharp twinge of disappointment. "Oh," she said. "So, if I weren't pregnant, you would be more detached."

He tossed a sideways glance at her full of heat and passion. "I've never acted detached toward you, Princess. Not from the first time we met."

Her heart leapt at the sensual growl in his voice. She still couldn't figure him out. She still had so many questions and she wasn't sure how to get her answers. Tina knew, however, that she wanted to know much more about Zach.

"Favorite ice cream?" she asked impulsively.

"Vanilla," he said.

"Oh, that's so—"

"Boring," he said for her and his lips lifted in a secret grin. "Bet yours is chocolate."

"Times three," she said. "Favorite color?"

"Blue, like cornflowers or the ocean," he said.

"But you're landlocked," she pointed out.

"Doesn't mean I don't like to visit," he said. "What about you?"

"Blue, too. It makes me feel peaceful. Favorite dessert?"

"Apple pie," he said. "Yours is chocolate something."

"Mousse," she said. "Chocolate mousse. But there've been times when I was visiting a third world country on the behalf of Chantaine and I was extremely grateful for Nutella."

He chuckled. "I bet you were."

"What do you think about girls playing football?" she asked.

"Not mine," he said.

"What if she could run like a jaguar, kick a ball into next month?"

"Not my daughter," he said implacably.

"Because football's not ladylike?" she asked.

"Because I don't want her hurt," he said. "She can pick a noncontact sport. If I had a son, I would warn him off professional sports too. Injuries can cut your career plans in a second."

"Hmm. That's still a bit sexist," she said.

He pulled into the parking lot of the ice cream parlor. "Are you telling me you would be okay with your little girl growing up and playing pro football?"

"No," she said.

He nodded. "No need for argument."

"But I wouldn't want my little boy playing football either," she said. "It's a primitive sport."

He grinned and slid his finger over her mouth. "Good thing we're starting out with a girl."

After the doctor's appointment, Tina felt closer to Zach. She felt a tie with him that she hadn't felt before. It made her think of him when she awakened in the morning, in the afternoon and at night before she went to sleep.

She'd felt such a connection to him. When she'd confessed her dissatisfaction with her duties as a royal representative, his lack of condemnation had made something inside her ease. She'd felt almost hopeful that perhaps she could find something that filled her heart in the future.

But Zach was nowhere in sight. He was like a ghost. After two days, she wondered if she'd imagined her time with him.

After the third day, she awakened, stepped from her bed to look out the window, wishing she could see him, but somehow knowing she wouldn't. Tina looked out onto the rolling hills and felt a mixture of emotions. Longing, desperation, hope…

Not wanting to dwell on any of these feelings, she hit the shower and got dressed. She was determined to beat Hildie before she brought breakfast. Pounding down the steps, she found Hildie on the phone.

"You don't say," Hildie said and silence followed.

"That's terrible," Hildie continued and shook her head. "We'll do something, Hannah. We sure won't leave the Gordons hungry."

A moment later, Hildie hung up the phone and sighed. "Those Gordons. It couldn't happen at a worse time."

"What's wrong?" Tina asked.

"The Gordons, our neighbors," Hildie said. "Their house burned down. One of the barns burned down too."

"That's horrible," she said. "Do they have children? How large is their family?"

"Six including Sheree's mother. Sheree's the wife. Bob Gordon, her husband, is a rancher. They have three kids." Hildie shook her head. "And another on the way. I think Sheree is due any moment."

"No family in the area?" Tina asked.

"None with enough room to take them in."

"Then they should come here," Tina insisted.

Hildie gawked at her. "Oh, Miss—" She broke off. "Your highlyness—"

"Please don't call me that," Tina said, cringing. "This makes perfect sense. The Gordons need a place to sleep. There's plenty of room here," she said, extending out her arms.

Hildie looked hesitant. "Zachary Logan is generous, but he has always wanted his privacy. He insists on it," she said.

"I can't believe he would withhold shelter from someone in such need," Tina said.

Hildie shook her head again. "I can't make that call. You'll have to talk to Zach."

Tina was surprised by Hildie's reluctance. Hildie was usually vocal with her opinions and how she thought everything should be.

"I'll do that," Tina said, "but we should get guest rooms ready."

Hildie blinked. "Alrighty," she said. "But I'm telling you that you better talk to Zach or there's going to be big trouble."

"As you wish. But if I can't reach him by cell, I'll need to use the car," Tina said, because she'd learned that cell service wasn't always reliable at the far reaches of the ranch.

Hildie winced. "I'm not sure that's a good idea."

"I need the car, please," she insisted, using her best royal voice.

Hildie frowned. "Alrighty," she said. "But I'm going on record as claiming no responsibility."

Tina gave a quick nod. "Thank you very much. I'll take the keys."

After failed attempts at reaching Zach by cell, Tina asked

where Zach was and drove in the direction of the south pasture, but she couldn't find him. She drove down several dirt roads and finally came upon several men outside a barn. She pulled alongside the barn and got out of the car.

"Hello. How are you? Is Zach here?" she asked.

The men looked at her as if she were an alien. "Zach?"

"Yes," she said. "Zachary Logan. I need to speak with him."

One of the men rested his hand on a rake and stared at her. "Who are you?"

She felt a frisson of uneasiness, but didn't give in to it. "I'm Valentina Devereaux."

The one who'd asked her name stepped forward and dipped his head. "I'm Ray and I'm sorry, but Zach left here about an hour ago. I think he was going to the next field, east," he said. "But I can't be sure."

Tina sighed. "Thank you very much, sir. If you should see him, please tell him to contact me."

"We'll do that, ma'am," Ray said and tipped his hat.

Tina climbed into the car and headed east. She came upon another barn where one man stood outside. Stopping her car, she stepped out of her car. "Hello. How are you?" she asked. "I'm looking for Zachary Logan. Have you seen him?"

The man shook his head. "I'm looking for him too. He's supposed to stop by here sometime today. You want to leave a message?"

Impatient with trying to track Zachary down, Tina returned to the car to grab a piece of paper and a pen. "Yes, I do. I'm Tina," she said. "And you are?"

"Fred," he said.

"Lovely to meet you, Fred," she said and scribbled a note to Zachary. "Could you please give this to Zachary? Please tell him to call me if he has any questions," she said, handing him the piece of paper.

"I can do that," Fred said, dipping his head. "If you need anything you can give me a call," he said and gave her a business card. "Cell phone number is on the bottom, although as you probably know, the service around here is a little sketchy."

"Exactly," she said, pocketing Fred's card. "Thank you very much."

"My pleasure," Fred said and Tina got into the car with an invigorated sense of purpose. Surely Hildie was mistaken that Zach would have a problem giving the Gordons a place to stay. Zach would want to help his neighbors.

Tired and achy from a long day outside filling in for one of his managers, all Zach wanted was a hot shower, a hot meal and a quiet evening. He stepped inside the mudroom to ditch his boots. His mind flitted to Tina as it often did lately. He wasn't quite sure how to handle the woman. How to keep her at the ranch without her getting under his skin.

A loud shriek caught him off guard. "What the—" He strode down the hallway to sounds coming from the den. Turning a corner, he quickly took in the sight of his very pregnant neighbor, Sheree Gordon, sitting on the couch, an elementary-school age boy sitting in *Zach's* chair working the remote to his large flat-screen TV and Tina sitting on the floor with two small children.

Hildie walked into the den. "Supper's ready. Everyone wash up and—" She caught sight of Zach and immediately stopped.

Tina glanced up at Hildie, then looked at Zach. Rising to her feet with the two little children still clinging to her hands, she met his gaze. "Well, there you are, stranger. I tried to call you several times on your cell today."

Zach pulled his phone from his pocket and noticed his

message sign was on. "I was out of range for most of the day."

"That's what I heard, so I drove out to find you. No luck, so I left a message with a man named Fred," she said.

"Yeah, I didn't get to him today," he said.

"Oops," Tina said.

Sheree stood and eased the children away from Tina. "Yes, I know you're having fun with your new friend, but it's time to wash your hands for dinner." She looked at Zach. "I can't tell you how much we appreciate your letting us stay here with you for a few days. You and Tina are too generous for words."

Stay here? he thought and blinked. *Here in my house?*

"I mean, I'm due in a couple of weeks and my mother is recovering from knee surgery. The fire totally wiped us out." Sheree's eyes filled with tears. "Bob and I will never be able to repay you for helping us."

Zach had heard about the fire at the Gordon ranch and he'd planned to help in some way—maybe help put the family up in a hotel for a few nights, provide a few meals and some clothes. But not this.

The youngest child, a toddler who was a girl, gave a high-pitched shriek that lit his nerve endings like a stream of fire-crackers on the Fourth of July.

Sheree winced. "Sorry, she's at the screaming stage, and being in a different place make it worse. Come on, Amy and Doug. Matthew, turn off the TV. Time to get ready for dinner."

"Mooooom," the older boy complained.

"Now," Sheree said firmly and Matt rose from the chair.

After his new guests left the room, Zach met Tina's gaze. "In the future, if you're going to invite people to stay here, I'd appreciate it if you would let me know."

"I tried, but you weren't accessible," Tina said.

"You could have waited until I got home just now," he said.

"No, I couldn't. This family has been through a devastating experience. Someone had to act quickly."

"Where did you put all of them?" he asked.

"Oh, that was easy. I put Sheree and Bob in the guest room at the front of the house, Matt in the upstairs den on the foldout sofa. We're putting Sheree's mom in the downstairs library so she won't have to take the stairs. And the two little ones will go in the room next to mine. It's such a lovely little room with the seat at the bay window and built-in shelves. I was surprised to find it completely empty," she said, confusion wrinkling her brow. "I asked Hildie about it, but the phone rang and we got busy."

Zach's gut twisted into a knot. That room had been for his baby. His baby who had died. A flash of anger rushed through him. What right did Tina have to invade that room? He'd donated the furniture to a charitable organization, but every time he went into that room, he felt the loss well up inside him again, fresh and painful.

Clenching his jaw, he swallowed over a knot in the back of his throat. "Don't do this again," he told her. "Not without talking with me first."

She searched his face. "You're angry. Why?" she asked. "This is only for a short time. Is your privacy so important that you can't—"

He lifted his hand. "Enough. I don't want to discuss it anymore."

"But how can I understand—"

"You understand to talk to me first. That's all you need to understand."

Clearly not satisfied, Tina frowned then sighed. "Well, I suppose I should also tell you that we're holding a community barbecue here tomorrow night so that neighbors can come and donate replacement clothing, furniture and household goods for the Gordons."

Zach dipped his head in disbelief. "Tomorrow night?"

She nodded. "Through my diplomatic experiences in disaster areas, I've learned that one really must move on this kind of thing right away. People forget and needs are left unmet."

Hearing her use the word diplomatic made something inside him click. "This is a princess thing, isn't it?"

She shot him a wary look. "Princess thing?"

He nodded. "Now I get it. This is the kind of thing you used to do in your country, except maybe on a grander scale. If this is going to be your M.O., then you and I are definitely going to need to have a talk. It will have to wait until later, though, since we have *guests*."

Tina stared at Zachary Logan's broad back as he walked away. She felt a deep sinking sensation inside her as she realized she had imposed upon Zach and clearly offended him.

He appeared weary and frustrated, and now she'd caused a situation where he couldn't be at ease even in his own home. Guilt suffused her. Hildie had warned her, but Tina had brushed the woman's concerns aside.

She had followed her natural instincts when she'd heard about the Gordons' tragedy. Plus, taking care of the Gordons had allowed her to take her attention off of her confusing feelings for Zach.

Hearing the approaching stampede of the Gordon children, Tina had no time to dwell on her regret. She helped Hildie serve the meal and feed the children. Afterward, Sheree offered to help clean up, but Hildie and Tina insisted the woman go rest.

"The poor woman has been through enough during the

last twenty-four hours," Tina murmured as she helped remove the dishes from the table.

"So true," Hildie said, then only the sound of clattering dishes filled the kitchen.

"You were right," Tina said in a low voice, full of misery. "Zach is angry. He was very upset that I invited the Gordons without discussing it with him first. I should have considered his feelings. I just assumed he would want to help—"

"Now, don't you be getting the wrong idea. There's no man more generous than Zachary Logan. He's always one to help out when someone needs it. He helped fund my niece's college education. The man is extremely generous," Hildie said then sighed. "But everyone has their soft spots. This home is Zachary's cave. Having this place has gotten him through some rough times."

"What rough times?" Tina asked. "I know the deaths of his parents must have been difficult, but I sense there's something more. But he won't discuss it with me. Tell me, please."

Hildie shook her head. "It's not my place."

So frustrated she could scream, Tina tamped down her feelings and finished helping Hildie in silence. All the while, her mind was going a mile a minute. This was ridiculous. How were she and Zach ever going to be able to communicate effectively if she didn't know what had caused him so much pain? She had to find out. She formulated a plan. The day after tomorrow, she was going into Dallas and she was going to get some answers.

"I'm going to heat up a plate for Zach and take it upstairs," Hildie said.

"I'll do it," Tina offered.

Hildie shot her a skeptical glance. "Are you sure that's a good idea? He's probably as cranky as a bear with a sore paw."

"Since I caused the injury, I should make amends," Tina

said, stiffening her back. She knew full well that Zach would likely give her the cold shoulder.

After heating the full plate of food, she grabbed two ice cold beers from the refrigerator and climbed the stairs to his suite. Gently tapping on his door, she stood and waited. No answer. She tapped again, this time more loudly.

The door swung slightly open and Zachary stood there wearing a towel slung around his hips and, she supposed, nothing else. His hair looked ebony from the wetness. His eyelashes surrounded his blue eyes in spikes of black and water droplets dotted his wide shoulders and muscular pecs. Her gaze drifted downward to the fine hair that arrowed down his flat abdomen.

All male, all man, she thought, her stomach dipping to her feet as she remembered that night they'd shared together. It had been months ago, she reminded herself. And everything was different now.

"Is that for me?" he asked, pointing to the plate she held.

She nodded. "Yes, yes, it is."

"Bring it in and I'll put on some clothes," he said and she followed him inside his suite. Domain, she corrected herself. Definitely his domain, she thought as she couldn't resist the urge to shoot a searching glance past the open door into his bedroom. Huge bed, she noticed. Sheepskin rugs surrounding the edge of the bed. Bedside table with a lamp and a couple of books. She wondered what he was reading. Was it for pleasure or business? Since she'd come to the ranch, Zach had seemed all business. She'd seen another side of him. Had that been a complete anomaly?

Wearing a half-unbuttoned shirt and a pair of jeans, he reentered his office/living room. "Thanks for the food. I'm assuming both beers are for me since you're not drinking?"

he said more than asked with a wry suggestion of a grin. "You thought I might need more than one?"

He popped the top on the first bottle and waved toward the sofa for her to sit. Taking a seat opposite her, he placed the plate on the table beside him.

Surprised at his lack of hostility, she lifted her shoulders in confusion. "You seemed tired and I don't think I helped matters. I apologize for taking matters into my own hands."

"I imagine it's what you've always done," he said and dug into his meal.

She opened her mouth to protest then changed her mind. "Within certain parameters," she said. "There were always the opinions of advisers and my brother."

"Bet that drove you crazy. Always having to answer to someone. Would have driven me crazy," he said and took a long swallow from his beer. "My middle name isn't Grinch or Scrooge just because I like a little notice when my house is gonna be turned into a temporary hotel."

Tina felt another twist of regret. "I know that. Again, I apologize. It's not as if this is my home. It's yours."

He met her gaze for a long moment that made her heart skip over itself. "We'll see," he said. "I talked with Bob, Sheree's husband, then I talked with Doyle, a friend of mine in Dallas. Doyle's into everything and he happens to have a large mobile home the Gordons can use until their house is rebuilt. Should be ready in two days."

Tina dropped her jaw in surprise. "Two days? My goodness, that's fast. How in the world did you—"

He rubbed his jaw. "You give me a couple minutes to think and a shower, and I'm good."

"Thank you. I'm sure the whole family will be thrilled."

"I don't know about Matthew. He looked like he was getting attached to my chair and my remote."

She laughed in agreement then silence descended between

them. "Is there anything else I can get for you?" she asked, rising.

He rose to his feet too and shook his head. "No, I'm hitting the sack. You should do the same. Tomorrow's gonna be a long one."

She walked to the door and turned around, startled to find him mere inches from her.

He lifted his hand to her chin. "I mean what I say. Part of the reason you came here was to rest."

She nodded, determined to ignore the way her heart was pounding in her chest. "Yes, I've done that."

He paused a half-beat. "So you don't need any more rest now?"

She glanced. "Too much rest is boring," she said. "Tell me you don't agree. That is," she added meaningfully, "if you've ever actually rested more than a few hours."

"Yeah, I get you. I had appendicitis and that recovery drove me crazy. But I'm not pregnant and you are," he said, stroking her jaw again. "Don't overdo it."

"I thought I wasn't going to have to take orders since I'm away from my country," she said with a sigh.

"I won't be giving you the same kind of orders your brother does," he said. "You can count on that."

Chapter Eight

"And why wasn't I invited?" Daniel Logan asked as Zach flipped burgers on the large gas grill.

Zach glanced up from the grill, surprised to see his brother. "Hey, what are you doing here?" he asked, since Daniel lived in Dallas.

"I was out this way because I'm looking into buying some land—"

Zach stared in amazement at his younger brother. "You? Land? You swore you'd never do any kind of ranching again."

"Yeah, well, we'll see," Daniel said evasively, glancing around at the crowd. "What's going on here?"

"It's a cookout," Zach said in a dry tone. "Can't you tell? Or have you forgotten since you only eat inside restaurants these days?"

Daniel shot him a sideways glance. "What's the deal? You barely ever invite me out here. Now you're throwing a big neighborhood party."

"It's not really a party. It's a charity thing, and I didn't throw it," Zach said, glancing across the large backyard at Tina fluttering from one person to the next, charming each of them. "It got thrown on me."

"What do you—" Daniel broke off as he gazed in the same direction as Zach. "A woman," he said in amazement. "You mentioned something a few weeks ago on the phone about a complication, but you didn't say it was a woman. When did you meet her? Does she live in town or out here? I can't remember seeing her before."

"If you can shut off your diarrhea of the mouth for just a moment, I'll explain," Zach said, although explaining Tina wasn't the easiest thing in the world. "Tina and I met a few months ago and got along—" He cleared his throat. "Pretty well."

Daniel gave a low laugh. "How well?"

"Well enough that she's pregnant," Zach said.

Daniel did a double take first at Zach, then at Tina. "Damn. I couldn't tell at first from how the dress fit her, but, yeah." He turned back to Zach. "What are you gonna do?"

Zach sighed, moving the cooked burgers onto the buns. "She's staying at the ranch. That's a first step."

"First?" Daniel said. "Sounds like you two skipped a few along the way. You gonna marry her?"

"I'm working on it," he said. "She's not from Texas."

"Where's she from?" Daniel asked.

"Chantaine."

"Where the hell is that?"

"It's a small principality in the Mediterranean," he said and decided to drop the rest of the bomb. "Tina's a princess."

Daniel gawked at him then swore. "A princess?" His brother shook his head and looked in Tina's direction, giving a hearty laugh. "Thank God."

Zach frowned. "What do you mean thank God?"

Daniel's face turned serious. "I mean you've been stuck in a rut since Jenny and the baby…" He lifted his hand when Zach opened his mouth. "You asked, so let me finish. You had every right to mourn. Every right. But you've become a crabby hermit. I have a feeling this woman is going to turn your world upside down."

Zach took a long look at Tina and felt his gut twist and turn. She laughed and the sound felt like honey sliding through him. When he'd arrived home last night to a full house of overnight visitors, he'd been damn sure that he and Tina would never be compatible. His privacy and solitude were too important to him.

Her energy and determination, her heart, however, did something to him. She inspired him to want to help too. To maybe do something he didn't usually do, such as flip burgers for the multitudes so they could donate what they could to help the Gordons.

On top of that, his physical attraction to her hadn't waned one bit. In fact, it had gotten worse. Tonight, he'd seen other men smiling and flirting with her and he suddenly found himself making a fist or clenching his jaw. One of his men had asked if he could take her out to dinner because he hadn't known she belonged to Zach.

The truth was she didn't belong to Zach and that bothered the hell out of him.

Hours later, after a couple of Zach's workers hustled out the last guests, Zach watched Tina sink onto a bench and walked toward her. Handing her a cold bottle of water, he noticed the signs of weariness and felt a twist of concern. "You pushed a little too hard and too long tonight, didn't you?"

She accepted the bottle of water and took a long swallow. "Not really. I think it was just that last hour when the news that I was a princess seemed to run through the crowd like wildfire." She shook her head. "I really didn't want the focus taken off of the Gordons' plight."

Zach couldn't resist a low chuckle. "You can't really blame them. We don't get a lot of royalty around here. That's why I made the announcement that the party was over and sent a few of my men to help people move along."

She shot him a sheepish look. "I guess I couldn't stay incognito forever."

He sat down beside her. "No. The paparazzi have been trying to get past my gate since you first got here. Folks around here are usually busy enough that they don't pay a lot of attention to the gossip rags, but finding out you were here tonight, everyone was curious. The good news is they'll eventually calm down."

"How do you know they will?" she asked.

"After the initial fascination wears off, they'll be a lot more interested in what kind of person you are instead of whether you have a title or not."

"If I stay," she said in a soft voice.

His gut twisted at her words. "Yeah. How do you like it so far?"

He saw several different emotions cross her face. "I'm still finding my way. As much as I needed the rest when I arrived, I know I'll have to do something. I would go out of my mind with boredom if I did nothing all day long."

Although Zach would prefer that Tina do nothing all day long so he could be assured that she and the baby were safe, he understood her dilemma. "I can understand that. I would feel the same way. Maybe you could take a little time to figure out exactly what you would like to do. You have choices here."

She gave a long exhale. "Choices. You have no idea what the possibility of making my own choices does to me."

"You're right," he said. "I don't because I've been making my choices for a long time. I think it's high time you get to follow your heart. You've got a good one," he said.

She met his gaze and her skin looked so soft in the moonlight that he couldn't resist touching her cheek. "You think so?" she said.

"Yeah, I do," he said and gave in to an instinct that had been building inside him since he'd first set eyes on her again. He lowered his head and covered her lips with his mouth.

Hearing her soft intake of breath, he paused but didn't move away. "It's still there, isn't it?" he asked against her lips.

"What?" she whispered, her lips still parted.

"Whatever was between us that night at the masquerade party," he said. "Whatever made me want you and made you want me."

He deepened the kiss, sliding his tongue inside her lips. She welcomed him, drawing him deeper, moving closer to him. Her breasts brushed his chest.

He felt like she'd hit a trip wire. An explosion of need ripped through him. He slid one of his hands down to the back of her waist, urging her body against his. A growl of desire rumbled from his throat.

She must have felt the same fire because she slid her fingers up behind his neck and matched him stroke for stroke in the passionate kiss.

"You should be in my bed," he said, his entire body twisting with need for her.

He felt more than heard her soft intake of breath. "I'm not sure that's a good idea."

He brushed his fingers lightly over one of her breasts where her nipple stood in turgid arousal. "Your body seems to think it's a very good idea."

She pulled back and stared into his eyes, seeming to try

to search his soul. "I'm not a teenager. Despite the fact that I appeared to jump into bed with you without a second thought, that's not my nature."

"I wasn't suggesting that it was," he said. "But you can't deny there's something between us. And it's more than this baby."

She tore her gaze from his and took a deep breath. "Perhaps," she said then opened her eyes. "But not tonight."

Two days later, the Gordons moved into their temporary home and Tina put together a plan for getting her questions answered. As always, first thing in the morning, she flipped through her text messages, shaking her head. "What a nasty temper," she muttered of her brother. "He needs a wife." Then she thought better of it. What woman in her right mind would put up with her brother? "A pet," she thought. "He needs a pet." She texted him the suggestion, then called her friend Keely McCorkle in Dallas. "I'm in town," she said. "May I take you and Caitlyn for lunch or pop in for a visit?"

Keely squealed. "Of course. When did you get here? Why didn't you tell me you were coming? Why aren't you staying with me?"

Tina laughed, feeling a surge of relief at the sound of her friend's voice. She also, however, knew Keely would have even more questions once she saw Tina. "We can talk about that at lunch. Where would you like to meet?"

"Oh, come to my place. I don't want to share you. If we go out in public, they'll be all over you," Keely said.

Thank goodness. "Are you sure I can't bring something?"

"Yes," Keely said. "Yourself. Now hurry up and get here."

Tina smiled. Now all she had to do was talk Hildie into letting her borrow her car.

After her shower, she ate every bite on the plate Hildie gave her even though she feared she would pop. "Hildie, I have a favor to ask you."

Hildie glanced over her shoulder and beamed at Tina's empty plate. "Good job. Now you're starting to eat like a mother-to-be should. How can I help you?"

"If I may, I need to borrow something from you please," Tina said.

Hildie gazed at her expectantly. "What?"

"I have a longtime friend in Dallas. Her name is Keely McCorkle."

"The name's familiar," Hildie said, squinting her eyes thoughtfully. "Brent," she said. "Brent McCorkle. Great guy. Brent and Zach have been friends for a long time."

Tina nodded with a smile. "Yes. I'd like to go into town to visit Keely."

"Shouldn't be a problem. Just give Zachary a call and—"

Tina shook her head. "I want to go today. I want to drive myself."

Hildie stared at her in disbelief. "Oh, hell, no."

Tina met Hildie's gaze without flinching. "I suppose I could rent a car," she said.

Hildie's left eye twitched.

"Or I could…what do you Americans call it? Thumb?"

"Omigod, you wouldn't," Hildie said.

Tina leaned toward Hildie and used her best confidential royal tone. "I *really* want to visit Keely today. And I *really* don't want to be supervised by Zachary."

"Mm, mm, mm," Hildie said with a frown as she sighed. "I'll drive you," Hildie said. "But we have to be back before Zachary returns or he *will* fire me."

An hour later as Hildie drove into the circular drive in front of the McCorkles' home, Tina turned to the woman who had muttered in disapproval for the entire drive. "Are you sure you won't join us?" Tina asked. "I'm certain Keely would love to meet you."

Hildie shook her head. "No. You two go ahead. The sooner you finish your visit, the sooner we can get back to the ranch. Just remember, we must leave by three o'clock."

"Three o'clock," Tina said. "Thank you so very much, Hildie. You have no idea how much this means to me."

Hildie nodded, but muttered under her breath.

Tina closed the passenger door of the car and walked to the front porch. She barely lifted her hand to knock before the door flung open and Keely greeted her with a squeal.

"What a treat!" Keely said, immediately wrapping her arms around Tina. "I still can't believe you were even *thinking* of coming to Texas without telling me first so we could plan a visit. Come on in," she said, taking Tina's hand. "The baby's sleeping, so we have time to gab. Are you hungry? I ordered takeout from that café you enjoyed so much the last time you were here. So tell me what you're doing here," Keely demanded as she pushed Tina into a chair in the kitchen nook lit by skylights. The table was filled with croissant sandwiches, salads and pastries.

"This looks beautiful. You did too much. As for my visit, it's complicated. I'll tell you the story, but I want to hear how you and Brent and Caitlyn are doing first," Tina said, still not exactly sure how to break the news to her best friend in the world. She was relieved Keely hadn't noticed her pregnancy. Tina had deliberately chosen a flowy silk top over white slacks to hide her bump.

Keely beamed. "Caitlyn is perfect. She's sitting up, trying to scoot and crawl. Once she's mobile, I won't get anything done but watch her."

"And Brent?" Tina asked.

"He works too hard, but I hope I can talk him into taking

a break in the fall." She poured iced tea into two tall glasses. "Now tell me about you. I read about Ericka's wedding. It looked like everything turned out beautifully. I know that was due to you. Is she doing okay?"

"She's doing great. She seems very happy. I visited her right before I came to the States," she said.

Keely frowned. "It's usually all over the news when you arrive, but I don't recall seeing anything. Although I confess I just got back from visiting my mother in Aspen."

"That's great. Did you take Caitlyn with you?"

"Of course," Keely said. "I would have never heard the end of it if I hadn't."

It occurred to Tina, for the first time, that her child wouldn't have the gift of grandparents. The twist of sadness caught her by surprise.

Keely covered her hand, her brow wrinkled in concern. "Hey, are you okay? You seem a little on edge."

Tina took a deep breath. No time like the present. "The last time I was here, I met your friend Zachary Logan."

Keely nodded. "That's right. We asked him to look after you and then you didn't show up until the next morning. Brent and I were both going to clobber him for not keeping track of you, but we haven't seen him since the masquerade party."

"Well," Tina said, clearing her throat. "He actually did keep track of me. We spent the night together."

Keely's eyes rounded. "Oh." She turned silent, a rarity for Keely. "You and Zachary," she said, shaking her head. "You're so responsible and he's so…well, still in mourning after all these years."

Tina's stomach knotted. "Mourning? Over his parents?"

"I'm sure he was sad when they passed, but no—" Keely shook her head and broke off. "He just can't seem to get over his wife and baby. I can't totally blame him…."

Tina heard nothing after *wife and baby*. "Wife?" she echoed.

Keely met her gaze and nodded. "I guess you don't know. There's no reason you should unless you'd gotten to know Zachary better. He lost his wife, Jenny, and their unborn child due to complications from her pregnancy. He totally shut himself off after it happened. We had to call in favors to get him to attend the masquerade. He always has an excuse. Brent told me he wouldn't even confide in his brother and sister."

Shell-shocked, Tina tried to absorb the information. So this was what neither Zachary nor Hildie would discuss. This was why Zachary had been so upset when she'd invited the Gordon family to stay at his home. This was why he was so determined to do the right thing for the baby. Tina realized that in some ways, by getting pregnant, she was Zach's worst nightmare.

"Tina," Keely said, patting her hand. "You've turned white as a sheet. Tell me what's going on."

Tina met Keely's gaze. "I'm pregnant with Zachary's baby."

Chapter Nine

As the afternoon thunderstorm turned into a torrential downpour, Zachary stomped into the mudroom. He could tell this wasn't going to be a short rain, so he decided to take an early break and return to work later in the afternoon.

Stepping out of his boots, he walked into the hallway listening for sounds of Hildie or Tina. He heard nothing but the tick tock of the old grandfather clock in the front room.

He strode into the kitchen and poured himself a glass of water. Glancing around for a note, again he found none. He did, however, spot Hildie's cell phone on the kitchen counter.

Uneasiness prickled along the back of his neck. "Hildie," he called. "Tina." He climbed the stairs and lightly knocked on the guest room door. Silence followed and he pushed the door open, searching for her. He caught the faintest whiff of her French perfume, but nothing more.

Where were they? he wondered. Hildie wouldn't take Tina

out without letting him know. Hildie knew Zach was trying to keep a clamp on the paparazzi. He rushed downstairs and glanced outside. Hildie's car was gone.

His heart began to pound in his chest. Had there been an emergency? If so, why hadn't they called him? He knew the cell coverage on the ranch was sketchy, but Hildie would have at least left a message. He checked his cell phone and saw messages, but none from his housekeeper. None from Tina.

He wondered if Tina had decided to leave. Had he pushed too hard last night? She'd responded to him. She'd wanted him, but she was holding back. For the sake of their child, she had to stay here with him. The possibility of Tina and their child on the other side of the world made him sweat. How could he keep them safe if they weren't here with him?

Not that he'd been able to keep Jenny and the baby safe, his conscience stabbed at him. Even though the doctor had told him that it wasn't his fault, Zach had never forgiven himself. He punched the speed dial number for Tina's cell phone and counted the rings until he received the automated voice mail response.

He swore. *Where was she?*

"I'm fired," Hildie said, her white knuckled fingers wrapped around the steering wheel as she and Tina sat stuck in a sea of never-ending traffic. Rain pelted down as the windshield wipers furiously moved from one side to the other.

"That's ridiculous," Tina said. "You won't get fired. All you did was drive a guest of the ranch to visit a friend in town and got stuck in traffic. Zachary can't fire you for that."

"You're not just a guest," Hildie said, shooting a glance at Tina's growing abdomen. "You're carrying his child. Zachary takes that seriously. He would guard you and the baby with his life. He's still suffering—" Hildie broke off and shook her head.

"I know," Tina said. "My friend Keely told me all about it. It's actually the reason I went to visit her."

Hildie stared at her in shock. "You came to town so you could snoop about Zachary's past?"

"It wasn't snooping," Tina said, feeling her indignation shoot up to heat her cheeks. "He knew everything about me, yet neither you nor he would answer my questions. I sensed there was something, but never this." Tina felt another dip of nausea in her stomach when she thought of what Zachary had been through. His loss had been devastating.

Hildie was silent for a long moment as she inched the car forward. Then she sighed. "Well, maybe it's better that you know. Now you'll understand why he acts the way he does. That doesn't change the fact that Zachary Logan is going to fire me. If it weren't bad enough that I drove you into town without telling him, I forgot my cell phone. He'll be worrying himself sick when he gets in and nobody's at home."

"If he were that worried, he would call me, wouldn't he?" Tina asked as she pulled her cell phone from her purse. She'd put it on silent as soon as she'd sent a text to her brother this morning, preferring to ignore another rant. Glancing at it, she saw three calls from Zach's phone. "Oh, no," she murmured.

Hildie shot a quick glance at her. "What do you mean *oh, no?*"

"Nothing I can't handle. I'll go ahead and give Zach a call just in case he's within range," Tina said, dialing his number.

The phone rang half a ring before she heard his voice. "Tina," he said.

The sound of the rough growl of his voice grabbed at her.

"Yes, it's me. I thought I should give you a call since we're stuck in traffic."

"We? Does this mean you're with Hildie?"

"Yes, I tried to talk her into letting me borrow her car, but she was insistent that she take me where I needed to go."

"And where was that?" he asked with an edge to his voice.

"Just to visit Keely." A vehicle rammed into the back of Hildie's car, jerking Tina from the impact. "Oh!"

Hildie started swearing.

"Tina, what the hell—" Zach began.

The vehicle rammed them again. "Oh, what's the bloody fool thinking?" Tina demanded, momentarily forgetting her decorum as she braced her hands against the dash.

"Tina," Zach repeated. "What is going on?"

"We had—you Americans call it a fender bender," she said, her heart still racing. "Lord, I hope he's done," she said to Hildie, whose face had turned white. "Are you okay, Hildie?"

"I'm fine," the older woman said, putting the car in Park. "Where are the cops when you need them? Damn lunatic. I'll teach him a lesson he won't forget."

Tina watched in shock as Hildie got out of the car and marched to the pickup truck behind them. The housekeeper immediately began pointing at her car and appeared to be giving the driver a complete verbal thrashing. "You weren't stretching the truth when you said Hildie had fought off a bear, were you?"

"Tina, are you okay?" Zach asked. "Is Hildie okay?"

"I'm fine. Hildie's fine, but I feel sorry for the man who ran into us."

An hour later, Zach pulled his SUV into the body shop where Hildie's car had been towed. His gaze flew to Tina and even though she'd assured him that she was fine, he felt a sliver of relief as she appeared to hover over Hildie, who sat on a bench outside the body shop. The rain had stopped over a half hour ago, and the hot Texas sun had dried everything in sight.

Tina glanced up and gave him a royal wave. Hildie covered her eyes. Zach wasn't sure what to do about Hildie. He gave and demanded complete loyalty from his employees, and Hildie had stepped over the line. She knew he didn't want Tina setting foot outside the ranch without his knowledge since he was still trying to protect Tina from the paparazzi.

He got out of his car and Hildie immediately approached him with regret written on her face. "I know. There's no excuse."

"Oh, this is ridiculous," Tina said. "Hildie's convinced you're going to fire her. I know you wouldn't do a thing like that. All she did was drive me to visit a friend."

Feeling like a bubbling cauldron of emotions, Zach ground his teeth. "Hildie, Tina," he said as he opened the front and back passenger side doors. "Get in the car. I'll be back as soon as I talk with the body shop manager."

Zach took care of business with the body shop and returned to the car. "I'm taking both of you to a doctor to make sure you're okay."

"That's unnecessary," Tina said.

"I'm fine," Hildie said.

"Not optional," Zach said. "Injuries sometimes show up later. It's better to know sooner rather than later."

"It was no more than a jerky ride at an amusement park," Tina protested.

"Which is one more thing you should avoid during pregnancy," he said, feeling his temper build. "I can't believe the two of you did this without telling me."

"I'm sorry," Hildie said. "There's no excuse."

"It's not as if Hildie took me out for a tour of bars or skydiving. She just took me to see Keely. I asked if I could borrow her car."

"Oh, my God," he said, envisioning Tina in Dallas traffic. "Don't even think about it. You don't have enough experience."

"I have a driver's license. I have experience. I've driven in the jungle, for Pete's sake," she said.

"But not on the right hand side of the road," he said.

"When Hildie refused, I told her I would just have to rent a car."

Zach bit back an oath. "Have you forgotten that you're trying to avoid the paparazzi? How do you plan to do that if you're renting cars and lunching in Dallas?"

"Keely had takeout," Tina said. "Tell the truth. If Hildie or I had told you we planned to visit Keely today, what would you have said?"

"I would have suggested that you wait until I could take you," he said. "Maybe sometime next week."

"Exactly," Tina said. "You have a very busy schedule and you can't be expected to be at my beck and call. I also cannot be expected to stay at home all day every day."

Even though he knew Tina was right, his gut told him different. His gut told him to keep her locked in his house. Safe from the paparazzi. Safe from an accident. Safe, period.

He was beginning to realize that he couldn't control this woman. His best bet was maintaining influence. His goal was marriage. "We can talk about this later," he said. "Right now, I'm taking you to the doctor."

Several moments of blessed silence later, he pulled in front of the doctor's office and helped both Tina and Hildie out of the car. Tina held back while Hildie walked toward the office. She stepped in front of Zach and lifted her chin, her eyes blazing in defiance. "I think you should know that if you fire Hildie, I'll leave the ranch."

He stared at her in astonishment. The woman was determined to drive him crazy. He swallowed a dozen oaths then slowly nodded. "Fine. Hildie stays as long as you stay."

Tina's jaw dropped at how quickly he'd turned her threat into his favor, but she cleared her throat and quickly collected her composure, the way any good princess would. "I didn't mean it exactly that way."

"Are you saying you're willing for Hildie to be fired?" he asked.

"Of course not," Tina said. "But I won't be manipulated into staying at your ranch against my will."

"Are you staying against your will now?" he asked.

She hesitated a half-breath. "No, but I don't know how I'll feel. How you'll feel. I can't promise to stay at your ranch forever."

He nodded. "How about a year?" he countered.

She blinked. "A year?"

"You stay a year in exchange for Hildie's unlimited employment," he bargained, buying time. More than anything, time was what he needed.

Biting her lip, Tina looked away.

Zach had noticed that she knew how to control how she revealed emotion, so he could tell she was conflicted. "A year isn't that long. It will give you time to have the baby and for you and I to know each other."

She glanced up and searched his eyes. He wondered what she was looking for. "Six months. That will be a month after the baby is due. That's all I'll promise."

Zach felt a rush of triumph. He'd just bought himself half a year.

* * *

It didn't take long for Tina to suspect that she'd been duped. She'd been so eager to protect Hildie that she hadn't considered that Zach would use her stance against her. After the doctor cleared both her and the baby and Hildie, they returned to the ranch.

"Tell Hildie she won't be fired. I can't bear her cowering. It's so out of character," she said to Zach just before they entered the house.

His lips twitched. "I told her when the doctor was seeing you."

"Oh," she said and met his gaze, thinking about all she'd learned about him today. She'd just given herself a six-month sentence with the most desirable, yet impossible, man alive. She wondered how she would survive it.

"I'm tired. Baby and I need some sleep," she said and stepped through the doorway. Two steps later, she felt Zach's hand clasp hers.

"After you have something to eat and drink," he said.

"I'm not really hungry," she said.

"Then Hildie can just fix you a sandwich," he said.

"Hildie is more worn out than I am," she said. "If you insist, I'll fix my own."

He swore under his breath. "Damn, you're a handful. I will fix your sandwich. Turkey or ham?"

"Are you sure you know how?" she countered, unable to resist the opportunity to jab at him.

His eyes lit with a combination of sensuality and irritation. "Yeah, I know how to make a sandwich. Does your highly-ness prefer mustard or mayonnaise? Pickles or naked?"

The word naked caught her off guard and a flash of his gorgeous, naked muscular body ricocheted through her brain. She blinked to push it away. "Dill pickles and I'd love sparkling water if you have some," she said, trying, but not at all succeeding in pretending he was just a member of staff. With the heat he generated inside her, she was going to have to find some way of coping with him.

For the next two days, Zachary left her alone. Tina wasn't sure if she liked that or not. She was torn between taking the time to figure out what she should do after her six months with Zach and being bored out of her mind. She wasn't accustomed to so much *rest*. Heaven help her, she began to understand the concept of being bored to death.

Of course, negotiating a field trip with Hildie was out of the question. Zach's housekeeper had been unfailingly polite since the accident but refused to chat about anything more than the weather.

Late at night after she'd had nearly zero conversation with a human being throughout the day, she decided to take a bath and listen to music and perhaps talk to her sister Fredericka, who was in England at the moment.

Making sure the bathwater was the perfect temperature, she sank into the tub and sipped a glass of sparkling water and pretended it was champagne. She turned on the music of a French rock band and closed her eyes.

Tina toyed with the spigot with her toes, noting that she could use a pedicure. When she'd lived at the palace, a mani-pedi had been a weekly ritual she'd regarded as a waste of time. Her schedule had been packed with appearances. Now, her schedule was one big yawn.

Sighing, she glanced down at her wet, slowly burgeoning belly and smiled. "Will your eyes be blue or green?" she whispered. "Are you a girl or a boy? I'll love you either way," she promised. "Your father will love you either way, too."

Taking a deep breath, she leaned back against the pillow to support her head and focused on the pleasure of the bath instead of the turmoil of her life.

Minutes or seconds later, the door to her bath opened and Zachary stepped inside, his body rigid with alarm. "Tina," he said then made a face. "Why didn't you answer the door?"

Automatically trying to cover herself, she lifted one hand to her breast and one hand much lower after she pulled an earphone loose. "What are you doing? Haven't you heard of knocking?"

"I did, but you didn't answer," he said, his gaze traveling over her body from head to toe and back again. "You didn't answer, so I thought I'd better check on you in case you drowned."

Feeling her nipples grow tighter from the cool air and his stare, she frowned at him. "I didn't drown, so you can leave."

He didn't move fast enough for her, so she picked up her wet rag and tossed it at him. He caught it, of course. "Out! Get out. You don't speak to me for days then you wait until I'm naked and enjoying a bath."

The water dripped onto his shirt. "Are you saying you feel neglected?"

Furious beyond any concern for her nudity, she stood in the tub and screamed. "Get out."

The next morning when she awakened, she found a note pushed under her door. "Oh, goody. Another trip to the obstetrician," she muttered as she picked it up. Despite her crabby mood, she opened the note instead of ripping it into a thousand pieces.

Dinner out tonight. 6:30 pm. Wear a dress.—Zach

Oh, that silver-tongued devil, she thought. How could she possibly resist such charm and seduction? She considered refusing. For at least two whole minutes. Then she realized she had nothing else to do. Dinner with Zachary. She had ten hours to choose her dress.

* * *

Zach wore a white shirt and a pair of black slacks. It was strange as hell, but he felt a little nervous about taking Tina to dinner. Despite the fact that they'd shared a bed way too many nights ago and despite the fact that she'd been staying in his home for weeks now, she was still a princess. More important, she was the mother of his child and he needed to win her over.

Considering the fact that his heart was closed to any chance of romance and love, he was facing a tough proposition. Glancing down, he hoped the bouquet of flowers would help.

He heard her first foot on the top step and glanced upward. Her legs were bare, creamy and curvy. She wore a turquoise flowing dress that hinted at her curves and pregnancy, but didn't give all her secrets away. Her hair fell like a silk curtain to her shoulders and her eyes held curiosity.

Curiosity was better than the fury he'd seen last night when she'd stood naked screaming at him. The visual of her wet, nude body would be stamped on his mind forever. It had taken two cold showers before he'd been able to pull his libido under control.

She kept reminding him that despite his missing heart, his sexual desire was alive and kicking. As she came to a stop beside him, he resisted the urge to ditch their dinner and persuade her to spend the night with him in his bed.

"You look good," he said in a voice that sounded rough to his own ears.

"Thank you," she said, her eyelids dropping to cover her eyes for a second. "So do you."

He felt a kick of arousal. She glanced up at him again and took the flowers he held in his hand. "Lovely flowers," she said softly and kissed his cheek. "Thank you."

Zach's gaze dipped to the creamy cleft of her cleavage and

he clenched his jaw. Every move she made reminded him of what he was missing by not having her in his bed. This entire evening was going to be one big pain in his groin.

Chapter Ten

The candlelight at their table for two flickered over Zachary's tanned complexion, reflecting against his white teeth and shirt. He seemed a little lighter tonight. He smiled more and laughed more. The low, husky sound was both contagious and seductive.

Except for the two of them, the small restaurant was deserted. "You still haven't told me how you managed to close down this place for this night just for you and me," she said. "That sounds like something only a king could do."

He lifted his eyebrows, but held her gaze. "I'm no king. This place is usually closed on this night of the week. I just called in a favor."

She narrowed her eyes at him, but not in an unfriendly way. "You seem to have quite a few favors you can call in."

Zach shrugged his shoulders, drawing her attention to his strength again, not that it had ever left her mind. "One hand washes the other. One good turn deserves another," he said.

"Hmm," she said. "Is this a form of the Texas mafia?"

Zach laughed and the sound rippled through her. Underneath the surface of their light romantic evening, Tina was always aware of what she'd just learned about Zach. The pain and loss he'd suffered. The fact that he'd brought in a new obstetrician after his wife and baby had died. The way he'd protected her since the first moment they'd met. Yet, he had also made her feel like a woman instead of a royal title.

Every once in a while, he showed flashes of himself beneath the hard, tough surface. She wondered what it would take to get all the way in. She wondered if it was possible. She wondered if she could do it. Did she even want to?

"You may deny it, but in your way, you're a king of your own country with plenty of diplomatic connections. Or favors, as you call them," she said.

"I'm just a rancher and a businessman," he said.

She chuckled and gave the same response he'd given her a few times. "Uh-huh. And I'm Little Bo Peep."

"Give me a break. How can I impress a princess?"

Charmed, despite all her reservations and she had quite a few, she smiled. "You did that a long time ago," she said softly.

His eyes turned serious and he reached across the table to take her hand. "Is that true or are you giving the proper princess response?"

She rolled her eyes. "I haven't been proper with you since the first time I met you."

He rubbed her fingers sensually. "I always thought I was damn lucky that night even when I had no clue you were a princess."

Torn between seduction and a need for reassurance, she lowered her gaze to their entwined hands. "What was so great about me? It's not as if I'm beauty queen material—" She broke off when his fingers covered her lips. The sensation made her heart skip over itself. The intensity in his gaze squeezed her chest so tight she could barely breathe.

He shook his head and pulled his fingers away from her mouth. "You're the strangest combination of a woman I've ever met. Mysterious, voluptuous, too sexy for your own good and mine too. And sweet. Irresistible as hell."

His response was so honest and baffled that she had to believe him. He made her feel powerful and vulnerable at the same time.

The nearly invisible waiter appeared beside their table at that moment. She tried to pull back her hand, but he wouldn't let her.

"Yes," he said to the waiter.

The waiter cleared his throat. "Dessert if you wish," he said nodding to both of them. "Chocolate mousse or apple pie à la mode."

Zach looked at her. "Ladies' choice."

"Easy," she said. "Chocolate mousse, but I'd like to share."

Zach lifted his mouth in a half-grin. "Good idea."

Within moments, the waiter returned with the mousse and two spoons. Zach put one aside. "We only need one. Should I try it first to make sure there's nothing wrong with it? Didn't the royals used to do that? Have some poor schmuck taste the food in case it was poisoned?"

She rolled her eyes at him and took the spoon. "I'm sure it's fine, especially since you called in a favor." She dipped the spoon into the mousse and lifted it to her mouth, sliding it onto her tongue. Closing her eyes, she moaned. "Now, that is good. Almost as good as my favorite restaurant in Paris."

She finally opened her eyes and met his gaze, which was filled with heat and sensual determination.

"You know, that comment could make a man want to make you forget about Paris," he said.

Her heart skittered again. "That could be a pretty big challenge. Paris is an amazing city." She dipped the spoon into the mousse and lifted it to his mouth.

He reached out and wrapped his hand around hers as she guided it to his lips. His tongue slipped out to scoop up the mousse. She watched his strong throat work down the silky confection.

"Give me a chance and see what happens," he said.

After dinner, he led her to the SUV. Before he helped her inside, however, he pushed her back against his car and lowered his head. Her stomach felt as if she were riding a jerky ride in an amusement park.

He pressed his mouth against hers and she welcomed the plush sensation and forbidden taste of his lips. He was better than the chocolate mousse they'd shared. More tempting, more…everything…

She clung to him, craving more of him. Could she possibly find the man he'd become before his loss?

"Let's go home," he muttered against her mouth. "We can figure it out there."

Plunged into a sensual, Zachary-ruled daze, she nodded. "Yes, I think that's a good idea."

Zach helped her into his car and drove back to the ranch. The drive was silent, giving her plenty of opportunity to come to her senses, but for some reason, her rational side had decided to play hooky as Keely had described to Tina years ago.

Zach pulled his SUV inside the garage and cut the engine. He looked at her and her heartbeat immediately picked up. Lowering his head, he pressed his mouth against hers again. "Come to my room."

She sucked in a quick, sharp breath, but her mind remained muddy and seduced. "Are you sure this is—"

"I'm sure," he said, cutting through her uncertainty. "Are you?"

"Ohh," she said, resting her forehead against his, searching for sanity.

"Ohh isn't good enough. I need a *yes*."

He wasn't going to let her abdicate her responsibility or her response. She couldn't help but admire him for that. He was making her play fair for the both of them.

"Yes," she managed. "Yes, I want to be with you."

One second passed and he led her upstairs. He swept her away so quickly, she wasn't sure if her feet touched the stairs. She barely took two more breaths and she felt herself falling onto his bed, staring up at him.

"That was fast," she whispered.

"Think of it as three months of foreplay," he said, unbuttoning his shirt and unzipping his pants.

She watched him in wonder, his gleaming, broad bare chest and flat abdomen. She felt the wicked urge to press her cheek against his strong belly. He stole the opportunity from her as he followed her down and stripped off her clothes between kisses.

She felt the heat inside her build to an unbearable height as she arched beneath him, straining to feel every inch of his strong, naked body against her.

Taking her mouth in a French kiss, he slid his hand down her shoulder then lower to her swollen breast. As he stroked her, she felt a corresponding tug in her nether regions.

He pushed his thigh between her legs as a prelude to his possession, and something inside her ripped loose. Need, primitive and consuming, suddenly roared through her like a forest fire.

Unable to remain still, she pressed and rolled her body

against his. He let out a low visceral moan that vibrated through their mouths.

"Careful," he muttered, slipping one of his hands over her hip. "I'm trying to keep it slow."

She didn't want it slow. She wanted it fast and furious and now. Her head was a cloud of sexual need. "Now," she whispered.

He made another low sound, one of agonizing frustration. The controlled power in his moan gave her a tiny bit of mental satisfaction. He slipped one of his hands down between her thighs and stroked her where she was wet and swollen for him.

When she didn't think she could bear the anticipation one second longer, he pushed her legs apart and thrust inside her. Staring into his eyes, she realized she'd never felt so fully possessed by a man in her life. The connection she felt went so much deeper than sex. She also realized that she wanted to possess him in the same way.

Moving in an age-old rhythm, he thrust and she arched. Her climax took her by surprise. One heartbeat later, he stiffened as his release rippled through him, echoing throughout her.

The sound of their breaths mingled in the air, the same as their bodies. He covered her with his strength, bearing his weight on his forearms to protect her. He took a few more breaths and rolled to her side.

Her heart still pounding, she turned her head to look at him, wondering if he was feeling half as much as she was. Wondering if it was more than physical for him.

The back of his opposite forearm covered his face, shielding his expression from her, and an odd vulnerability made her stomach dip.

Biting the inside of her lip, she scooted her hand over to

his and slid her fingers through his. His arm immediately dropped and he met her gaze as he rolled to his side again.

"You okay?" he asked, lifting his fingers to touch her hair. The tenderness in the gesture gave her hope.

She nodded.

He stroked her hair and she closed her eyes, her emotions pulling her in a dozen different directions. Although she was physically satisfied, her heart felt heavy. She felt shockingly vulnerable.

Taking a deep breath, she felt as if she needed to get herself back together, to cover up her emotional nakedness. She opened her eyes, but didn't look at him. "I should probably go," she said and started to get up.

Zach squeezed her hand. "No," he said in a dark, urgent voice. "Stay."

Tina did stay in Zach's bedroom, sleeping every night with him for the next two weeks. Every night she hoped for some kind of breakthrough and saw signs of it in the little things. His arm curling around her body and pulling her against him before they fell asleep. His laughter when she was too sleepy to open her eyes early in the morning. The way he stroked her hair every night and brushed a secret kiss on the top of her head.

She hoped it meant that he was beginning to feel something for her, because heaven help her, she was feeling something for Zach she'd never dreamed.

"Picnic," she told him through sleep-heavy eyes as he was getting ready to leave one morning.

"Picnic?" he echoed.

She nodded, struggling to open her droopy eyes. "I want you to take me for a picnic to your favorite place."

He paused a half-beat. "Okay. Next week."

"Today or tomorrow," she corrected.

"I have things scheduled," he said.

"Schedule me," she said, lifting up on her forearms.

He met her gaze and his lips lifted in a crooked half-grin. "Is that a royal decree?"

"Would that help?" she asked.

He chuckled. "Not necessary. Tomorrow. My workers will mock me for taking so much time out in the middle of the day."

"And you'll tell them I'm worth it," she said, brushing her hair from her face.

He stepped to the side of the bed and slid his fingers through the back of her hair and gave her a hard kiss. "Damn, you make me want to climb back in bed with you. Have a good day and stay out of trouble."

During the day when Zach was gone, Tina feared she would be bored out of her mind. That day, she approached Hildie, begging for a distraction. "Please let me help. I need to do something, or I'll go crazy."

"You need to rest," Hildie said. "You're pregnant and—"

"Oh, rubbish," Tina said, irritated. "Pregnant women have been productive for ages. I can't just sit here like a hen on an egg."

Hildie twisted her mouth as if she were trying not to smile. "Maybe you should order some books on child rearing."

"Maybe I should take skydiving lessons," Tina countered.

Hildie twitched but lifted her chin. "I won't fall for your threats again. I learned my lesson the first time when you nearly got me fired."

"Oh, you wouldn't have been fired," Tina said. "And I took care of it in case Zach lost his mind and did something impulsive."

Hildie froze. "Took care of what?"

Tina realized she'd slipped and shrugged. "It was nothing. Heavens, can you please give me something to do? I need to feel productive."

"You could always muck out a stall," Hildie's niece Eve said dryly as she cruised into the kitchen.

Tina tossed the young woman an amused grin. "You almost tempt me. How are the darlings?" she asked, speaking of Zach's horses.

"Good," she said. "The colt still needs a little extra work, but that's going to be tough to do with me gone most of the time. The price of corporate success," she said and made a face as she pushed a glass into the door of the refrigerator to get some water.

"Are you saying you wish you could be doing something different?" Tina asked.

"Of course not," Hildie said. "Eve works for a big company that pays her a big salary with nice benefits."

Eve lifted an eyebrow at Tina. "Of course. What Hildie said."

"I would think there would be lots of ranchers who would need your kind of expertise," Tina ventured.

Eve shrugged. "Probably, but matching my current pay would be nearly impossible."

Tina tucked that fact into her mind for future contemplation. After all, since she was gestating, she had plenty of time to think.

"We have the charity drive for the children's wing at the hospital coming up in a few weeks, though, so that will keep all of us busy. We do a little carnival for children and donate the money we make to the hospital," Eve said, taking a long drink from her glass.

"Charity drive?" Tina echoed.

Hildie scowled at Eve. "You need to be careful what you say in front of her."

Tina frowned. "Why? I'm not a child." She narrowed her eyes. "Has Zachary told you to shield me from what's going on in the community? If so, he and I will definitely have a discussion."

"He didn't use the word shield," Hildie said.

Tina began to stew. "I'll just bet he didn't. And did he threaten your job? Because if he did, Zachary and I made a deal about your job. As long as I stay at the ranch until one month after the baby is born, he can't fire you. Period. Not that he would have in the first place," she added.

Hildie blinked at her. "You made a deal for me?"

"Of course I did," Tina said. "I practically forced you to drive me to Dallas."

Hildie met her gaze and her eyes grew shiny with unshed tears. "I don't know what to say. Zachary has always been good to me, but you don't know me that well and you stood up for me anyway."

Tina was flattered. Hildie wasn't one to give faint praise. "It was nothing," she said. "Now can someone fill me in on the details of this charity event? After all, charity events are my specialty."

Eve exchanged a look with Hildie. "Can you imagine how much people would pay to have lunch with a princess?"

"Children?" Hildie asked.

Eve shook her head. "Adults. Think about it. You're digging weeds next to your neighbor's fence and casually mention, 'I had lunch with a princess last weekend.'"

Hildie grimaced. "Zachary will kill us."

"Maybe," Eve said. "But he can't fire you."

Excitement raced through Tina. Now, she had a project, a purpose.

The following day, however, she had a totally different

purpose. As Zachary drove his truck to the spot for the picnic, she experimented with how she would ask him the questions that had been burning inside her. It was long past time for them to discuss some very important issues, and she hoped with every inch of her that he would be both receptive and responsive. If she'd believed in crossed fingers and toes, she would be doing both.

Zachary pulled to a stop next to a weeping willow tree and a small pond. There was a small stand of grass and some bluebonnets stubbornly showing their gorgeous blossoms on the edge of the idyllic mound.

"It's beautiful," she said.

He nodded. "I stole away to this place when I was a kid as much as I could in the summertime."

"I can see why. Shade, water and grass. What more could a young boy want?"

"A swing," he said. "I would swing on that tree and go flying into the pond. Sometimes all three of us, my brother, sister and I, would play hooky on a hot day and come here."

"Good times," she said, watching his eyes light with happy memories. "Maybe they can come back sometime soon."

His happiness seemed to fade. "Maybe," he said and grabbed the picnic basket and blanket. "Let's eat."

Zach spread out the blanket and Tina unloaded the picnic basket, quelling her nerves about how he might respond to her. Hildie had prepared delicious club sandwiches, fruit and cookies for their mini feast.

"Hildie's an excellent cook," Tina said.

Zach nodded as he ate his sandwich. "She's worked for my family for a long time."

"You don't know how lucky you are. At the palace, each person receives one assignment." She shot him a dry smile. "Except for the royals. We do everything."

"Do you still like taking a break?" he asked. "I want you to feel like you can take a break."

"I can only do that for a while before I get, well, bored. I need to feel productive," she said.

He set down his sandwich. "Does that mean you want to return to your country?" he asked.

His stark expression took her off guard. "No," she said quickly. "As much as I love my country and people, I think it's time for some of my other family members to contribute. In the meantime, though, I need to be productive wherever I am. Here," she said, meeting his gaze.

He nodded thoughtfully. "I can understand that. We'll just need to coordinate it with avoiding the paparazzi. I don't want you to have to deal with that hassle."

"You've been quite successful," she said. "Perhaps the palace could take lessons from you."

He chuckled. "Amazing what a couple of cowboys with shotguns can do."

She nodded, her mind still heavy with the subject that continuously hovered in her mind. "There is something I've wanted to ask you about."

"Ask," he said and took another bite of his sandwich.

She took a sip of water to dampen her suddenly dry mouth then took a calming breath. "I know you were married and that you lost your wife and baby. I'm so sorry for all you've suffered. I'm so sorry for your loss."

His face closed up and his eyes turned hard. "I don't discuss that," he said. "With anyone."

Chapter Eleven

Disappointed by Zach's abrupt response, Tina stared into his closed gaze. She had hoped that their physical intimacy had mirrored a growing emotional intimacy. "I just want you to feel like you can talk with me about it. After all, I'm having your child and—"

Zach shook his head. "I'm not going to talk about it. If you want to push the conversation, we may as well leave. But I had something else I wanted to discuss with you and I think both of us would like that subject much better," he said.

She could tell by the set of his jaw that she wasn't going to get anywhere talking about his wife and child. The knowledge frustrated her, but she didn't want to ruin their afternoon. That didn't stop her from hoping he would open up to her some other time.

"Okay," she relented. "What did you want to discuss?"

His gaze relaxed slightly. "In a little bit. Let's enjoy the lunch, first."

"That was a tease," she said, her curiosity piqued.

"How do you like it here?" he asked.

"It's taking some getting used to," she said. "The isolation can be both good and bad. It's nice going out and not feeling like I'm being watched by everyone and my photograph isn't being taken every other second. I still find it amazing that you've been able to keep the paparazzi away."

"I'm not obligated to allow anyone to see you," he pointed out. "My job is to protect you. As far as the palace PR is concerned, they can take a royal leap."

She chuckled, imagining the response of the advisers and her brother. She couldn't deny, however, how refreshing it was to have someone so protective of her. Although the palace security force had always been quite protective, they were sworn to protect the monarchy. Zach wasn't sworn to protect anyone. He just did it.

"Do you think this is a good place to raise a child?" he asked.

She nodded slowly. "Yes, for the most part. As much as I have felt suffocated by my duties during the last several years, I would, however, like my child to be familiar with my country and family. I think the sense of history from both the mother and father is important."

"So you would want to visit Chantaine?" he said.

"I'm still figuring it out, but yes, I think so. If my brother allows it," she added.

"Allows it?" he echoed in displeasure. "How in hell could he disallow it? You're a princess. What could he do to you?"

"He's the ruling monarch. He could strip me of my title if he wanted," she said. "Stefan is very angry and although I know he loves and respects me, he doesn't understand my actions. He doesn't understand how I could turn my back on my duties."

"What about your own choices? Your own life?" he asked.

She smiled. "You sound like an American. Lots of choices. Not as many when you're born into royalty."

"Are you afraid of having your title taken away?"

"I'm not so concerned about the title, but the idea of losing all connection with my family hurts me," she said. "But I have to focus on my child's future. As grateful as I am for all the opportunities I've had, I don't want my child growing up in an environment where obligation is primary. I hope my child will learn to appreciate the rewards of service and I'll do what I can to make that happen. But I do want my child to have more choices."

He leaned toward her and took her hands in his. "You don't need to be afraid. I would always take care of you whether you have a title or not."

The expression of dedication on his face turned her heart to butter. "Thank you. That means a lot. When I realized I was pregnant, though, I knew the person I most needed to rely on was myself."

He shook his head. "But you know you don't need to do this alone."

"I know," she said.

"That's part of what I wanted to discuss with you," he said. "We've touched on the subject before, but I think it's time to take the next step." He reached into his pocket and pulled out a jeweler's box.

Tina gaped at Zach as a sense of unreality fell over her. He opened the jeweler's box to reveal a beautiful diamond ring.

"I'll always be true to you. I'll always take care of you and our child. Through thick and thin, bad and good, I know how to stick with it. I can't think of any greater gift you and

I can give our child than to be married, to be husband and wife. Marry me, Tina."

Her heart stopped, along with her breath. "You mentioned this before, but…" She stared at the diamond ring and searched his face. Tina had received proposals before. Two, in fact, but she'd known beyond a shadow of a doubt that she couldn't accept them. The very idea of binding herself to either of those men forever had made her physically ill.

Zach, however, was a totally different man. Her feelings for him were totally different. She slept with him every night and she was carrying his child.

"I don't know what to say," she said. "I didn't expect this. Not today."

"You're growing," he said and slid his hand over her belly. "Our baby is growing. You and I know we want each other and we want what's right for our child. Marriages have been built on much more shaky ground than that. It's the right thing to do."

His last sentence turned Tina cold inside. She'd spent her life doing what she was told because *it was the right thing to do.* The first time she hadn't done the right thing, she'd experienced passion beyond her imagination. She's also gotten pregnant. If anything, she was more determined than ever not to make such a huge decision simply because it was the right thing to do.

She shook her head. "I can't," she finally managed.

Zach looked at her in surprise. "Why?"

She sighed. "There's got to be more. I need for us to be—" She broke off, feeling self-conscious and vulnerable.

"Be what?" he demanded. "We're lovers. We're committed."

"We may be lovers," she said. "But we're not in love."

He pulled back and a cynical expression crossed his face.

"Even though you're a princess, I never would have tagged you as a woman who believed in fairy tales."

She frowned at him. "Who says love is a fairy tale? There are plenty of people who find love," she said. "Look at Keely and Brent."

"That's rare," he said. "And just because they feel in love now, doesn't mean it will last."

"You sound so jaded," she said. "I wouldn't have expected that of you."

"It's not jaded. It's just practical," he said. "If you base decisions on emotion, you'll end up in a big mess."

"If that's true, then what about that first night we shared together? Do you consider that we're in a big mess?"

"I wouldn't call it a big mess, but it's not optimal."

She frowned, studying him, trying to figure out where his attitude originated. "Is this about your own marriage? Was your relationship a disappointment? Or did you love her so much you can't love again?"

His eyes turned cold again. "I told you I don't discuss my marriage with anyone. We may as well go back to the house."

Her stomach twisting in knots, Tina refused to let him see how upset she was. "I agree," she said.

Zach went into Dallas to work the next day. He needed a break from the princess in his ranch. He successfully plunged himself into work until his brother took him out to a bar.

The loud strains of a country rock band played in the background as Zach drank his second Jack and Coke.

Daniel clicked his double shot of bourbon against Zach's glass. "To success," he said. "All our businesses are doing great."

"Yeah," Zach said. "To success. Thanks for staying on top of the in-town biz. I owe you."

"I'll let you pay me back over time. How are things with the princess?"

"She's okay," Zach said. He took another swig of his drink. "Just making things difficult. I asked her to marry me."

Daniel swiveled on his bar stool and stared at Zach. "And?"

"You know she's pregnant. It's the right thing," Zach said.

"I guess she said no," Daniel said.

"Pretty much," Zach said. "She wants to rehash everything that happened with Jenny and the baby."

Daniel cringed. "Oh. That would suck."

"You're telling me," Zach said and took another long swallow from his drink. "Why isn't a proposal, a ring and a commitment forever enough?"

"Women," Daniel said, shaking his head. "I'll never really understand them. Like I'm trying to take care of—" He broke off abruptly as if he'd thought better of stating his thoughts aloud.

"Take care of what?" Zach asked.

Daniel shook his head. "Nothing that's gonna make any difference."

"Sounds like a woman," Zach said.

Daniel looked at him and grinned. "Could be right."

"Does this have anything to do with the property you're thinking about buying that's close to mine?"

"Don't ask. Don't tell," Daniel said.

"Whoa," Zach said, his mind working double time. "I'm trying to think what could possibly draw you back to Logan County." He paused, searching his memory. "The only thing that comes to mind is Chloe Martin. She has a kid. Not sure what's going on with her husband…"

Daniel's face turned dark. "Like I said, don't ask. Don't tell."

"Is her husband alive?" Zach asked

"No," Daniel said. "Next subject."

Understanding how much pain a woman could cause a man, Zach cut his brother some slack and changed the subject as he'd requested. "I like that singer Trace Adkins. Do you?"

"Yeah," Daniel said. "I think the man has suffered."

"Most of us have," Zach said.

A blonde stepped between them at the bar and smiled at both of them. "How ya doin', boys? Wanna buy me a drink?"

Zach briefly thought of another time in his life when he was free and could hit the sheets with a woman for a night of mindless satisfaction. Even though the woman bared the tops of her breasts and smiled with sensual invitation, he felt nothing.

"Sorry. I could buy you a drink, but that's where it would end," he said.

"Me too," Daniel said.

The woman gave a wry smile. "Thanks for being honest. I hope I find someone like you."

Zach watched her walk away as did Daniel.

"We are in a bad, bad way," Daniel said.

"Yeah," Zach said. "It's just plain sad."

"So how you gonna work it out with the princess?" Daniel asked.

"No idea," Zach said. "Maybe another Jack and Coke will tell me."

Daniel laughed. "Good luck with that."

Zach took a taxi to his Dallas apartment and stripped out of his clothes, then sank onto his bed alone. His brain was swimming. His arms were reaching for Tina.

She'd filled his nights and dreams, making him forget his pain with her body and warmth. Tonight he instinctively reached for her, but she wasn't there. She'd become more than a warm body to him. She'd warmed his cold soul and heart. But he still couldn't let her in. Letting her in could destroy him. How could he possibly remain strong if he let down his guard to her?

His gut twisted and he felt more empty than ever. Swearing to himself, he wondered how he could keep her without becoming vulnerable....

Tina stayed awake until well past midnight. Zach didn't return, she noticed. She slept in the guest bed because she couldn't imagine returning to his bed. She didn't know if he would want her. She didn't know if she could give herself as freely as she had in the past.

She resented Zach's reluctance to discuss his loss with her. At the same time, she understood it. Sometimes loss was private, but she also knew that keeping silent could cause wounds to fester. When her father had died, she was given instructions from palace PR how to properly discuss her grief. The same with her mother, who had died years before.

Be strong, she'd been told. And Tina had done her best, but now, years later, she wanted and needed a more authentic relationship, one where they didn't hide important things from each other.

For the next several weeks, Zach spent most of his time working in Dallas. He called Tina every day to check on her, but their conversations felt stilted. Although she'd focused on helping with the children's hospital charity event, Tina couldn't help feeling cranky about the wide gulf that separated them. He might as well be in Timbuktu.

After finishing another conversation with Zach, Tina returned to the kitchen to continue counting the receipts from the charity event with Hildie and her niece.

Several moments passed while she concentrated on the pile in front of her.

"You're quiet," Eve said. "Anything wrong?"

Tina sighed. "Nothing more than usual," she muttered.

Eve widened her eyes. "Then what's the usual? The lunch with a princess event was a huge hit. We made a lot of money."

She shrugged. "It's not the charity event. It's the useless conversation I have every day with Zachary. Same question, same answer. Done in two minutes. Even after my latest ultrasound showed I'm carrying a girl, he didn't seem to have much to say. If he's going to spend all his time in Dallas, it makes me wonder why I'm staying here."

"Zachary has always divided his time between the ranch and the businesses in Dallas," Hildie said. "It's not unusual for him to be gone a month at a time if business is going well. I was surprised he managed to stay here as long as he did when you first arrived. He's usually in town at least one day every two weeks. Often more."

Tina nodded, but she wasn't at all sure Zachary's motivation didn't stem from their argument the day before he left. "The timing for this trip seems a bit coincidental."

"How's that?" Eve asked, stretching a rubber band around her receipts and setting them aside.

"We had a discussion the day before he went to Dallas. It didn't go well," Tina said.

Hildie refilled each of their cups with hot tea. "I can't imagine what kind of discussion would bother Zachary that much. Unless it concerned Jenny and the baby."

Tina couldn't quite conceal a small grimace.

"Oh, no, you didn't," Hildie said.

"I think it's important that we're open about this," Tina said. "He clearly has strong feelings about the fact that I'm pregnant. I mean, he doesn't love me, but he asked me to marry him and—"

Eve's jaw dropped. "He asked you to marry him? Why didn't you tell us you two were engaged?"

"Because we're not," Tina said. "I turned him down."

Both women stared at her in shock.

"You turned down a proposal from Zachary Logan? The father of your child?" Hildie asked.

"He doesn't love me," Tina said.

Hildie snorted. "That would change. With the right people, love will grow."

"No wonder he's camping out in Dallas," Eve said.

"You act as if this is all my fault," Tina said. "All I wanted was for Zach to share a little about his relationship with his wife with me. Just a few words."

"Easier to rip out his spleen," Eve said.

"Or his liver," Hildie added.

Frustrated by the accusatory looks from the women, Tina met their gazes one at a time. "His proposal included the words. *It's the right thing to do.*"

"Well, it is," Hildie said.

Eve paused. "Yeah, but I can see your point. If you're looking for hearts and flowers, it was missing in a big way."

"If you're looking for hearts and flowers from Zachary Logan, then you're looking in the wrong place. Zachary is more solid than all that. He's the kind of man who will stay true."

"I wasn't wanting hearts and flowers. I wanted to know that he wasn't marrying me just because I was pregnant." She folded her hands together. "I wanted this proposal to be different. I've received proposals from other men where our marriage would have been a kind of barter. A trade of my title and position for something they could offer my country.

With Zach, I just wanted to believe love between us was really possible."

"I can't blame you for that," Eve said.

Hildie's mouth was set in a frown for a long, silent moment. "Well, if you're serious about this love thing, then you better realize it's gotta go both ways. Maybe you could do a little more on your end, if you get my drift, your highlyness."

Chapter Twelve

That night, Tina tossed and turned. The suggestion that she should extend herself more to Zach irritated her. After all, she was here on his ranch in Texas instead of Paris, Italy or even her own country. That should mean something.

Besides, after their picnic disaster and Zachary's subsequent disappearance, he should come to her. He was the one who'd been unreasonable. And for goodness sake, she was a Devereaux. A Devereaux didn't go chasing after ranchers.

For one flicker of a moment, she thought how horrible that last thought would sound if she said it aloud. Tina groaned. She sounded just like a princess. Oh, heaven help her and everyone who encountered her in her current mood.

She would do something, she told herself. She didn't know what, and she didn't know how, but she would do something. Tomorrow, she resolved. It was after 2:00 a.m. and she and the baby needed their rest.

Dragging herself out of bed the next morning, she stayed

in her room while she sipped a cup of tea and wished it were coffee. Her head felt as if it were full of mud. She stared out her window at the changing colors of the landscape of Zach's ranch. Although the temperatures were still warm, the vivid greens of summer were beginning to fade with the changing of the season.

Feeling a kick from the baby, she smiled and put her hand over her belly. She had always been protective of her family and people in need, but she'd never felt such a consuming urge to shield anyone as she did her baby.

A tap on the door interrupted her thoughts. "Yes?" she called.

"It's Hildie," the housekeeper said and opened the door. "What can I fix you for breakfast?"

"I'm not very hungry. I can toast myself an English muffin," she said.

Hildie lifted her eyebrows in disapproval. "The baby may want more than that to eat."

"The baby's fine," Tina said. "She's doing her morning kickboxing. Would you like to feel her?"

Hildie looked hesitant, then quickly moved toward her. She extended her hand and Tina drew it against her abdomen. The baby gave several quick kicks and Hildie's eyes widened. "She's a little pistol, isn't she?"

Tina nodded and laughed. "My thoughts exactly."

Hildie sat gingerly on the chair beside Tina, her hand still resting on Tina's belly. Longing darkened her gaze. "I planned on having children, but when my husband died after six years of marriage—" She shook her head.

"And you never met another man who interested you enough to give him a chance?" Tina asked.

Hildie shook her head and lifted her lips in a sad smile. "Chet was my one and only. I was a lucky woman to have him every day that I had him. I just wish I still had a piece of him by having a child, but it wasn't meant to be." She removed her hand from Tina's abdomen. "Feels like she quieted down a little now."

"I never dreamed how amazing it would feel to have a baby growing inside me," Tina said. "Yes, there are definitely some discomforts, but it really is a miracle. Speaking of miracles, I have been thinking about what you said to me last night. At first, I was offended, but I've decided you may be right. Perhaps I should make an overture toward Zachary."

"I'm glad to hear that," Hildie said with a firm nod. "Shows you're a good, strong woman."

"Thank you," Tina said. "In order to make my overture, however, I'm going to need your assistance."

Hildie immediately looked doubtful. "My assistance?" she echoed and immediately shook her head. "If you think I'm going to take you anywhere without notifying Zachary, then you're wrong. Princess or no, you got me in big trouble last time. Zachary made it perfectly clear that—"

Tina lifted her hand. "I want to surprise Zachary at his Dallas apartment. I'd like to take him a meal. We can prepare the meal tomorrow and you can drive me to his apartment where I will surprise him when he arrives home from work. Now tell me," Tina said, putting her hand over Hildie's. "What could possibly go wrong with that plan?"

After Hildie showed Tina her secret recipe for Zachary's favorite pot roast with onions, potatoes and carrots, Hildie and Tina made a few quick stops along the way to Zachary's apartment so that she would arrive about an hour before Zachary was expected to leave the office.

Tina adjusted the shades on the windows and rearranged the small bouquet of flowers as she waited for him. She felt a crazy combination of emotions as she fluttered around the apartment where she and Zach had shared that first passionate night together.

She wondered how he would feel about her unexpected visit. A home-cooked meal would push aside some of his reservations she hoped, and glanced at the clock again. Hildie had given her precise instructions for reheating the roast. According to the time, she could begin the process in eight minutes.

Too edgy to relax, she poured herself a glass of water and walked through the small apartment again. Although the living space appeared comfortable, it was so generic-looking that she wondered how Zach could possibly stand to spend so much time here without adding just a few of his own belongings to make it feel more welcoming.

"It's been a rough week for both of us," Daniel said. "Let's go out for a steak."

"I don't know," Zach said. He'd been wrestling with memories and regrets all day. "I thought I would just grab a burger and watch some mindless TV tonight."

Daniel made a face. "That's what you do every night. C'mon. We can go to Hooligan's Bar and drown our sorrows together."

"We just acquired a new company for nearly nothing. What do you need to drown your sorrows about?" Zach asked.

Daniel scowled. "I don't wanna talk about it. Just like you don't wanna talk about it."

"I don't know if this is a good idea. That place can get wild on Friday nights."

"Stop arguing and come on. It's not like you have any other plans," Daniel said.

Tina put the pot roast on at precisely the time Hildie had instructed, added the dinner rolls to the oven, then put salad into bowls. Although she had rarely set a table, she knew how. Glancing at the clock, she sat at the small dinette table and wished she had brought something to read or her laptop.

Instead, she checked her text messages and voice mails. Her sisters were finally starting to settle into performing their official duties, although they often complained to Tina.

During the last few months, Tina had shared tips on making their tasks easier, but she truly believed that dividing the assignments was what made the job less of a beast.

Her brother, however, was still the same beast he'd always been. He'd gone through a threatening stage with Tina. Then he'd turned silent, refusing to speak to her. As much as Tina loved her brother, his silence had been far easier to bear.

She wished he would find a woman, or at least a mistress. Surely that would ease some of his…frustration.

The timer went off, signaling that dinner was ready. Tina glanced at the clock and frowned. No sign of Zach. He must be staying a little late, she decided, and turned off the oven. Hopefully, he would be home soon.

Minutes turned into hours and Tina didn't know what to do. This was supposed to be a surprise, so she didn't want to call him. She considered calling Hildie but didn't want to drag the housekeeper into the situation any further. Hildie had been a nervous wreck during the entire drive from the ranch.

Sighing, she decided to wait. She turned on the television. Knowing Zachary, there was a perfect explanation. And it wasn't as if he'd known she would be here. She just hoped she didn't ruin the roast before he arrived.

Hours later, Tina awakened to the sound of the door opening and footsteps. She rose from her cramped position on the sofa in front of the television. She wasn't sure when she'd fallen asleep.

"Zach?"

Zach came to a dead stop in the hallway just outside the den. "Tina?" he asked, rubbing his face as if he couldn't believe his eyes.

Relief shot through her and she walked toward him. She noticed his hair and clothes looked disheveled. "Yes, I was hoping to surprise—" She broke off as she caught a whiff of his breath then something else that immediately made her stomach knot with suspicion. "Where have you been?"

Zach raked his hand through his mussed hair. "Daniel insisted on taking me out to dinner. He said I needed to get out. How long have you been here? Why didn't you tell me you were coming?"

She noticed his words were just slightly slurred and frowned. She'd been waiting here like the good little wife while he'd been out drinking. "You smell like liquor," she said, darts of fury poking through her like spikes.

"Yeah, I had a few too many. I took a taxi home," he said. "I'm sorry I wasn't here when—"

"You also smell like cheap perfume," she said, identifying the other odor he was *wearing*.

Zach lifted his hand. "That's not my fault. Daniel was flirting with these two women and they kept trying to get me to dance. One of the women was really pushy and sat down on my lap. The only way I could get her away was by leaving."

Tina was so upset she could hardly breathe. "*Sitting on your lap*," she said, barely swallowing the urge to shriek. "Is this what you've been doing every night? No wonder you haven't returned to the ranch. You've been too busy having all your *fun*."

"No," he said, but she couldn't stand to hear any more excuses. She felt like a total fool for waiting for him while he'd been out drinking and letting pushy women sit on his lap.

"I need to go," she said more to herself than him. She couldn't stand one more minute in his presence. "A cab," she said, walking to the sofa to grab her purse. "I'll get a cab."

"Wait," he said, wrapping his hand around her arm. "Don't leave. Please."

Delaying the urge to shake his hand away from her, she took a small breath. That was all she could manage. "Why?" she demanded. "If you had decided to surprise me with my favorite dinner and I had come home smelling of liquor and another man's cologne, what would you do?"

He clenched his jaw. "After I killed the guy?" he asked.

She rolled her eyes and tugged at her arm. "Let me go. This was a huge mistake. I shouldn't have done this. If this is who you really are, then I've made more than one mistake," she said, her voice breaking.

"It's not," he insisted and stood in front of the door, blocking her way. "This isn't who I really am. You know that. You've been around me."

"But tonight—"

Pain sliced through his eyes before he closed them. "Tonight is—" He gave a rough groan as if the words were being wrenched from deep inside him. "This is the date Jenny and the baby died."

Zachary stared into Tina's eyes and immediately regretted his words.

Sympathy darkened her green gaze and he swore. "I'm so—"

"Damn it, don't feel sorry for me."

She blinked then her brow furrowed. "What am I supposed to say? Too bad. Chin up. Or you must have done something horrible for such a horrible thing to happen to you. Or why didn't you prevent it? Because, after all, you have the power to prevent all tragedy. Correct?"

This time he was taken aback by what she'd said. Due to

the excessive quantity of whiskey he'd consumed, his mind wasn't moving as fast as usual. Somehow she'd hit on every one of his worst fears. *Bad things happen to bad people. He should have done more to prevent...*

"Go take a shower," she said. "You'll feel better."

He hesitated, still holding her in his sights, afraid she might vanish in a puff of air. She could be a hallucination. "You'll stay?" he asked.

She nodded. "For now."

"You won't leave without telling me first," he said. "And the deal is I have to be cognizant. Because after I take a shower and fall into bed, I won't be conscious for a while."

Her lips twitched. "I agree to the deal," she said. "Now go take a shower."

He pushed away from the door but stopped before he passed her. "Sure you don't want to join me?"

Her eyes rounded in surprise. "In the shower?"

"And in bed," he said, wanting to feel her soft body against his. She could make him forget for a while. She already had.

She chuckled. "Go."

Walking to the bathroom, he shucked his clothes and turned on the shower. If he were smart, he would give himself a cold shower as punishment for indulging in his secret pity party tonight, but at the moment, he couldn't summon his masochistic demons. They were usually close by. With gallows humor, he wondered if Tina had scared them away.

Washing the evening from his skin with soap, he allowed the hot water to slide over him. After an extra moment of the soothing sensation, he climbed out of the tub and dried himself off. Still blinking against the bright light of the bathroom, he brushed his teeth, wrapped the towel around his waist and headed for his bed.

His mind was still muddled and seeing Tina reminded

him of everything he'd been missing since he'd left the ranch. Even half-lit he knew that he wouldn't be in his finest sexual form tonight.

Dropping the towel on the rug beside his bed, he climbed into bed and sighed.

"There's water on your nightstand if you get thirsty," Tina said from the open doorway, the light spilling around her in a backlight that resembled a halo.

Zach wondered again if she was some kind of apparition. Glancing at the nightstand, he saw a cup of water. He took a quick gulp. "Thanks. G'night," he said and surrendered to his weariness.

Crossing her arms over her belly, Tina was full of emotions as she stared into the darkened room. She had traded her crazy life at the palace for an uncertain future with a man chasing his own demons. He was, however, the father of her child and he'd granted her a glimpse of his humanity for just a few moments tonight.

That authenticity was what she'd been craving, what she felt she needed as much as water, as oxygen. Vacillating about what she should do now, she heard Zach snore softly. She shrugged and went to get her nightgown from her overnight bag. In for a penny. In for a euro.

The next morning, Zach awakened as the sun skimmed over his closed eyelids. His senses came to life slowly. He squinted then quickly closed his eyes against the light. His head throbbed unforgivingly and his throat was so dry he felt as if a troop of soldiers had stomped through it.

He groaned and rolled away from the sun, his hand encountering softness. Stretching his fingertips, he felt silky hair. He skimmed his fingers lower and felt skin that reminded him of velvet. Lower, he felt a silky strip of fabric.

"Good morning," Tina whispered, and her voice brought him into full awareness. She was in bed with him. He'd dreamed of this too many times to name.

He forced his eyes open to make sure he wasn't dreaming. His head still hammering, he took in the sight of her with her hair tousled over her green eyes, her cheeks flushed with sleep, her gown dipping low to reveal her lush cleavage.

"Morning," he said. "I can think of ten things I'd like to do to you right now, but the jackhammer in my head isn't going to let me, damn it," he muttered.

She gave a low laugh and pulled him against her for a sweet hug that was over way too quickly. He felt her roll away from him.

Wait, he wanted to say, but that damned hammer prevented him.

"Let me get you an aspirin," she said. "Go ahead and take a sip of water. I'll fix you some toast."

His stomach rolled at the prospect. "I don't want anything to eat."

"Just a bite or two," she said. "Trust me."

He leaned his head back and took some mind-clearing breaths. This was bad. Very bad. He didn't want Tina seeing him like this. He should have sent her home last night.

He heard her moving around but couldn't summon the strength to roar at her to tell her to leave. He felt like a frog paralyzed in preparation for dissection for a high school Biology lab.

"Here. Take this," she said, nudging him gently.

Shifting upward, he accepted the aspirin and water. He took a few bites of the toast and more sips of water.

"This sucks," he muttered. "I've been thinking about you every damn night and every damn morning. Now, I feel like something the cat dragged in."

She bit her lip as if she were trying to keep from laughing. "Rest. You'll feel better later."

Resisting sleep for at least three moments, he couldn't resist the call...of the pillow.

It must have been centuries later when Zach awakened to the smell of coffee. Climbing up from the depths of sleep, he struggled to open his eyes. He inhaled the scent, drawing it deep inside him, craving the jump-start of caffeine.

Rolling out of bed, he walked toward the smell of it, rubbing his eyes. His gaze traveled, then landed on Tina.

She stared at him in response, her gaze briefly lowered to his groin then rising upward. He glanced down, noting his nakedness.

"I hope there's a cup left of that coffee or I'm going to have to go out for some," he said.

Tina quickly poured a cup, brought it to him and pushed it into his hand, her gaze focused firmly on his face.

He took a long drink followed by another, then another. His head began to clear and he met her gaze. "Wanna go back to bed?"

Chapter Thirteen

Tina felt as if she should throw a dish towel over him. Oh, no, that wouldn't be big enough, she thought. A towel, she thought. Or a blanket.

"How about some more toast?" she countered.

Zach sighed and sucked down the rest of his cup of coffee. He held the empty cup out for her and she quickly refilled it.

She cleared her throat, determined not to look below his well-muscled chest. "Would you like a robe?"

He sipped his coffee and sighed again. "Give me a minute," he said and turned around, treating her to a view of his gorgeous backside as he returned to his bedroom. A moment later, he returned wearing a pair of jeans and an unbuttoned shirt.

He sat down at the dinette table and watched her through hooded eyes. "Toast sounds good," he said.

She served him four slices, then scrambled eggs. Cooking

wasn't Tina's forte, but she could manage a few things. She pushed two more slices of toast in front of him and watched him quickly consume them.

Still gazing at her, he raked his hand through his hair. "I don't remember as much as I should about last night," he said. "But I do remember you being here when I got back from dinner."

"Late, late dinner," she couldn't resist adding.

"Yeah," he said. "I stayed later than I should."

"Because it was the anniversary of your wife and baby's death," she said.

Her words stabbed him. He took a quick breath. "Yeah."

His gaze met hers. He didn't want to talk about it. He didn't say it aloud, but his expression yelled it.

"Hildie and I made a pot roast. She said it was your favorite. I reheated it just before I expected you to arrive home. I'm sorry to report that the pot roast may no longer be edible."

His lips twitched. "The toast and eggs were good."

"You would have had roast if you hadn't walked in smelling like liquor and cheap perfume," she said, still smarting over how long she'd waited for him.

"A woman sat on my lap without invitation. I left as soon as I could and grabbed a cab. The liquor was my brother's idea."

"I'm not sure I like your brother," she said.

"He's a nice enough guy," Zach said. "Just needs some direction." He hesitated a half-beat. "What made you come to the apartment to surprise me?"

She shook her head. "It's complicated. It stemmed from a discussion with Hildie. I haven't decided if it was a big mistake or not."

"What was your goal?" he asked.

"What do you mean?"

He shrugged, pouring himself another cup of coffee. "Did

you meet your goal? That's how you decide if it was a mistake or not."

She felt a surge of self-consciousness, but his gaze challenged her. She bit the inside of her lip because he wouldn't be able to see that. "I wanted to reach out to you. I was trying to make our relationship more two-way. I realized I hadn't extended myself much."

He shrugged his beautiful, muscular shoulders. "Then I would say you succeeded."

Her heart leapt at the hungry expression in his gaze.

"You wanna sneak out for a while?" he asked.

"Where?"

He shrugged again. "Anywhere. Just out," he said.

Anticipation rushed through her and she nodded. "Yes. Let's go."

A half hour later, he pressed a ball cap over her head and planted her sunglasses over her nose. He crammed another ball cap over his own head.

"Disguise," he said. "I don't want the paparazzi after you."

"I'm pretty sure they won't recognize me," she muttered, trying not to think about her now-flat hair.

"That's the goal," he said and took her hand in his. "Let's go."

He drove to a farmer's market which featured everything from fresh fruit and vegetables to jewelry and scarves. The carnival atmosphere lifted Tina's spirits.

"I'd like a few of these scarves for the nursery," she said, fingering a few of the pink pashminas.

"What are you going to do with them?" he asked.

"Hang them on the wall," she said, visualizing the nursery. "I haven't thought much about it, but I guess we need to get started."

"Yeah," he said, and lowered his hand to her belly. "How's the little princess doing?"

Her heart twisted. "Getting bigger. I think she may be a gymnast."

His lips lifted. "Busy little girl?"

She nodded. "Yes. Maybe she'll do a somersault for you soon."

He placed his other hand over her abdomen, cradling her belly. The baby jumped and kicked.

His laser blue eyes widened. "She's on the move."

"Yes, she is," she said, feeling her own kick of delight. "She must know her daddy is holding her."

He sucked in a deep breath and lowered his mouth to hers. "I've missed you, Tina. Damn it, I've missed you."

In the middle of that farmer's market, Tina kissed him and didn't care who was watching.

Later that night, Zach looked at the over-cooked pot roast with Tina and shook his head. "Now, that's a damn shame," he said. "I haven't had a good pot roast since I was at the ranch."

Tina crossed her arms over her chest. "I followed Hildie's instructions to the letter," she said defensively.

"I know you did," he said. "It's okay. Just sad in a fast-food-for-a-month-diet way," he said, chuckling under his breath. He glanced at her and chucked his index finger under her chin. "Fair payback for a stupid night of indulgence."

Her gaze softened. "You had good reason," she said.

He shrugged, not wanting to go to that dark place again. "Should we bury it?"

"Let's call Hildie first," she said.

"I dunno. She's gonna want an explanation."

"We should call her," Tina said. "She may have a suggestion."

Zach suspected Hildie would grill them on why they hadn't eaten the roast the way she'd intended. "Go ahead and call."

Tina's face fell. "I was thinking you could call."

Zach shook his head. "I don't like to get into discussions with Hildie about cooking."

Tina narrowed her eyes. "You're scared of her."

Zach reared back. "I'm *not* scared of her."

Tina lifted an eyebrow. "Then why won't you call her?"

"You brought the roast," he said.

She met his gaze and lifted her chin. "I'm Princess Valentina. I suppose I can face down anyone or anything, heaven help me," she added and punched in Hildie's cell number.

An hour later, after a quick trip to the corner market, Zach and Tina were enjoying barbecued beef sandwiches.

"Hildie is a genius," Tina said. "I never would have thought of barbecue sandwiches."

"That's because you're not from Texas," he said, downing his second sandwich.

"But you've got to admit it was inventive to turn dried-out pot roast into juicy beef barbecue," she said.

He nodded. "Hildie is first-rate," he said.

"You wouldn't want to try to replace her," Tina said.

"Hell no. I've had neighbors try to steal her away," he said.

"How did you manage to keep her?" she asked.

"Good retirement, health care and dental program," he said. "Plus, I drive her to all her dental appointments because as I said before, dentists scare the hell out of her."

"Hmm," Tina said with a nod as she nibbled on her sandwich. "So, it would take a lot for you to fire her," she concluded.

"Fire her," he echoed and shook his head. "The only way

I would fire Hildie is if she was stealing from me and that would never happen."

"So, you wouldn't have fired her for driving me to Dallas. You accepted my trade of her employment for my staying here because you wouldn't have fired her anyway," she said.

Zach's last bit of BBQ hung midway in his throat. He coughed and swallowed hard, not liking the look on Tina's face. But he took the ruthless choice. "I accepted your trade because I would do anything to keep you here. Anything," he said.

"Why?"

"Because you and our baby are very important to me," he said.

Tina set down her sandwich. "I wouldn't wish our baby away," she said. "But I wonder if I would be anywhere near as important if I weren't pregnant."

Zach's gut twisted at the expression on her face. "You can't really ask that because everything would be different," he said. "But if you want the cleanest, most honest reaction, go back to that first night we had together. That will tell you the truth." He set down his second sandwich and covered her hands with his. She felt so soft and vulnerable, yet at the same time, strong. "I wanted you. You wanted me. We both tried to take the right road and that road still led us to each other."

She took a quick audible breath. "Maybe," she finally said.

He shook his head. "Not maybe. Definitely."

That night after a long hot shower, Tina joined Zach in his bed. She fought a sliver of nervousness and smoothed her fingers over her cotton nightgown.

Already showered, he glanced up at her from the newspaper spread over the comforter. His dark hair was just starting to dry and his laser blue eyes were hooded by his thick black eyelashes. He looked like a dark panther waiting to pounce.

"I think I want some water," she said and made a U-turn for the kitchen. Tina wondered if this was a good idea. Did she really want to get so close to Zach again? *Of course she did.* Did she really want to make herself vulnerable? She bit the inside of her lip. That answer wasn't so easy.

She stared at the tall glass of water and took a sip.

Strong arms wrapped around her. "You're okay," he said. "It's not like I can get you knocked up again."

She couldn't resist the laugh that bubbled all the way from her uterus. Tina was pretty sure the baby was laughing too. "Oh my goodness," she said, turning in his arms. "You're such a smooth talker. How can I possibly resist?"

His mouth lifted in a crooked, sexy half grin. "That's what I was counting on," he said and lifted her up in his arms.

The gesture stole her heart. "I'm going to give you a hernia," she said.

"No chance. You're a lightweight," he said and carried her to his bedroom.

"I hope you have good health insurance," she whispered, leaning her head against his. "A hernia is in your future."

He laughed and shook his head. "I've lifted a two-ton tractor before. In comparison, you're a feather."

She laughed, tossing her head back. "You're full of flattery. Or as you Americans say, full of bull."

He set her down on the bed and stared at her. She didn't know what she looked like, but the way he gazed at her made her feel beautiful. He skimmed his hands over her hair, spread out beside her head, then touched her jaw, throat and shoulders as if he wanted to touch every inch of her.

He lowered his hands to the swell of her abdomen and she

held her breath as he caressed her belly. "You have no idea how beautiful you are."

His gentle possessiveness was an affirmation instead of a threat. Unable to stand any barriers between them, she lifted her nightgown and tossed it aside. Then she pushed his boxers off his hips.

His eyes darkened with need. "How am I going to hold back?"

"Maybe I don't want you to hold back," she whispered, arching toward him.

He slid his hands over her bare breasts and sucked in a quick breath of arousal. She felt his hardness against her. The obvious evidence of his need took her to a different level than she'd ever experienced.

She dragged his head downward and pressed his mouth against hers. He made sexy sounds of want and need that echoed inside her.

Zach lowered his mouth to her breast and took her nipple into his mouth. She arched upward, craving the most intimate connection they could achieve.

He rubbed his hand over her tummy at the same time he gave her a deep French kiss. "You have no idea how sexy you are. You have no idea how much I want you."

"Show me," she whispered as he slid his hand between her thighs.

And he did.

With just a little coaxing from Zachary, Tina decided to stretch her visit to his Dallas apartment for a few extra days. She enjoyed taking walks with him. Always donning the baseball cap, sunglasses and loose clothing to keep herself well-disguised, she felt more impatient than ever with her brother's resistance to making a public announcement regarding her pregnancy. She suspected he was hoping she would abandon her relationship with Zach and return to Chantaine.

Even though he was appalled that she would have a baby out of wedlock, more than anything Stefan wanted Tina back in the country. He wanted her back in charge of the royal appearances so he didn't have to deal with her younger, more difficult sisters.

On Tuesday, Zach kissed her just before he left. "Remember. Don't go out without your cap and sunglasses."

"I won't," she said, flopping onto her back and staring at the ceiling as she saw another day of hat hair and frumpy clothes in her future. Zach's reason for keeping her on the down-low was different than her brother's reasons. Zach was totally focused on her safety and he didn't want her to get stampeded by the press or an eager group of curious onlookers.

Her mutually agreed-upon captivity was starting to grate on her. Although she didn't miss the frantic pace of her schedule before she'd gotten pregnant, she needed more. She needed more of a feeling of accomplishment. At the moment, on a more superficial note, she needed a few new articles of clothing. Tina had started calling the baby Kiki because she kicked so much. Little Kiki was growing bigger all the time, which meant *she* was growing bigger too.

Tina pushed herself upward and put together a plan. Taxi to the shopping district, buy some clothes, return to the apartment, perform a quick makeover, then order takeout from somewhere wonderful. Rubbing her palms together, she could hardly wait until the stores opened.

Kicking inside her, the baby must have felt her excitement as Tina made her secret shopping mission on the windy day. She bought a couple new bras, more panties, two long-sleeved blouses, a black cardigan and a green pullover sweater, a pair of those vile maternity pants and a black dress that almost made her look sexy.

Glancing at her cell phone, she winced at the time and knew she would need to rush to not only arrive home before Zach, but also re-do herself.

Her arms full of shopping bags, she stepped outside the department store. A gust of wind caught her cap and whipped it away. Swearing under her breath, she chased it, but it slipped through her fingers. She watched in futility as it whipped down the street.

Shrugging, she raked her fingers through her hair and looked for a cab. No one would recognize her. It wasn't as if she was wearing a tiara. If she could only get a bloody cab. This was when staff came in handy. She waved her hand for a few moments, then decided to return to the department store for help.

"Excuse me," she said, lifting her sunglasses to the top of her head as she spoke to the woman at the information desk. "Could you please help me get a cab?"

The woman tore her gaze from some sort of gossip magazine. "Oh, sure," she said and stared at Tina for a long moment. She glanced down at the magazine then back at Tina.

Tina felt a terrible sinking sensation.

"You're the princess," the woman yelled. "You're Princess Valentina and you're pregnant!"

Tina gave a smile that for her was more of a cringe. "Pleasure to meet you," she said in a low voice. "Now could you please help me get a cab?"

"Oh, of course, your Highness," the woman said, quickly standing. "Would you mind giving me an autograph? I've never met a real princess before."

"A pen?" Tina asked, desperate to escape. The information clerk immediately supplied one and the magazine.

Tina couldn't bring herself to sign a copy of the rag sheet that had ratted her out. "Perhaps a piece of your establishment's stationary?"

The woman blinked. "Oh, okay," she said and pulled out a notepad with the store's logo. "My name's Lola."

Using the careful penmanship she'd been taught at a young age, Tina wrote Lola's name and her own signature. "There," she said and smiled. "Now, about that cab?"

It seemed to take forever, but a cab finally appeared outside the doors of the department store. Just as Tina walked to the door, two men walked inside the store and approached her, one aiming a camera at her.

"Princess Valentina, the official word from the palace is that you're on a well-deserved sabbatical but that you will return to Chantaine soon."

"How do you do?" she said, going into royal mode despite her casual appearance. "I wish I could talk, but I'm in a bit of a hurry. Good day," she said and walked forward.

The two men stepped in front of her.

"Begging your pardon, Princess, but you're clearly—" The man paused, waving his hand vaguely in the direction of her belly.

Bloody hell, she was going to be in trouble from all ends. "Yes, you're right. My official statement is—" She paused a half beat and smiled. "I've swallowed a watermelon seed and look how she's grown."

"She," the reporter echoed. "A girl. Who's the father? Is it Zachary Logan?"

"I must go," she said. "Please step aside. I can tell you're a gentleman. Surely you would respect a woman who has swallowed a watermelon seed."

The reporter smiled. "Let her go, Rick. We've got our scoop. Good luck, Princess. Don't be a stranger."

"Not bloody likely," she muttered under her breath as she

stepped into the cab. She wondered who was going to kill her first. Zach or her brother.

Zach pulled into the underground parking lot of his apartment and stepped into the elevator. Looking forward to seeing Tina, he leaned against the inner wall and cleared out a few text messages on his BlackBerry. Once he walked through his apartment door, he was leaving everything else behind.

The elevator doors whooshed open and Zach saw a commotion in the lobby. Several people rushed into the elevator.

"Glad I got out of that," one man said.

"Me too," the woman said, rubbing her forehead. "Did you hear what they were talking about? Something about a princess staying here."

Zach's gut knotted.

The man shook his head. "Now that could be one royal pain in the ass for the rest of us," he joked.

Sucking in a sharp breath of air, Zach bided his time until he could get off the elevator. What the hell had happened today? Was Tina okay? Had she escaped the melee downstairs? He glanced at his phone again and there were no messages from her.

The elevator finally arrived at his floor. Walking onto his floor, he held his breath, wondering if the press would be waiting outside his apartment door. A sliver of relief shot through him when he didn't see a soul. He moved quickly to his apartment, unlocked the door and stepped inside. He immediately locked the deadbolt behind him.

Jazz music played in the background. A second later, Tina stepped into the hallway, wearing a black dress and heels. As soon as her gaze met his, she shot him a huge smile. Her eyes sparkled.

"Surprise. Italian food will be delivered within thirty minutes."

Distracted by how beautiful she looked, but not quite able to rid himself of the image of the crowd in the lobby. "You look great, but I'm not sure Italian is in our future. The apartment lobby's a madhouse. I don't know how it happened, but the press has found you."

Her smile fell. "Bloody hell. I should have known that reporter wouldn't let me off so easily."

Zach blinked. "Reporter?"

Tina smiled, but it looked more like a grimace. "I had a little surprise today when I went shopping."

"Tell me about it," he said, getting a bad feeling.

"Everything went fine until I decided to leave," she said. "It was windy. My cap flew off. I had to get help getting a cab. A reporter and a camera man appeared out of nowhere, the way they always do. It all went downhill from there."

"How much did you tell him?"

Her cell phone began to ring. Even he knew that particular ring tone. It was her brother.

"Oh, bloody hell," she whispered. "This could ruin our dinner."

Chapter Fourteen

"I guess I should answer it," Tina said, oozing reluctance as the phone went into its second cycle of ringing.

"Let me talk to him," Zach said.

Tina shook her head and walked toward her purse resting on the couch. "That's not a good idea. The two of you need a proper introduction first."

She picked up the phone and punched the send button. "Stefan, how are you?"

Zach could hear the man's voice from across the room.

"Yes, I guess the news may be out. I didn't expect you to hear so quickly," she said.

The man's loud voice continued.

"Yes, I realize the announcement wasn't optimal, but it was going to happen sometime," she said. "And I didn't exactly call it a pregnancy. My official explanation was that I swallowed a watermelon seed." She met Zach's gaze and shot him a mischievous smile.

He couldn't hold back a chuckle at the image of Tina making such a statement.

She suddenly frowned. "Of course, I'm not trying to make you look like a fool."

The distress on her face put all his protective instincts on alert. He moved closer to her and gestured for her to hand over the phone.

She shook her head and lifted her hand. "Stefan, I meant no disrespect. I was caught off guard and attempted to use humor to defuse the situation."

Refusing to allow her brother to berate her, he put his hand over hers. "Give me the phone, sweetheart," he said firmly.

She took a breath and surrendered the phone. Stefan was yelling. Zach counted to ten, twenty, thirty. Finally, even the crown prince decided he needed oxygen.

"Have you said enough for now?" Zach drawled.

He heard a harsh intake of breath and a muffled oath. "I was speaking to my sister," Stefan said. "I wish to speak to my sister."

"Not right now," Zach said. "You've more than had your say. She's in a delicate condition and she doesn't need to have anyone yelling at her."

"Who in hell do you think you are to keep me from my sister?" Stefan demanded.

"I'm the father of her child," Zach said. "My job is to protect her. You're a prince. Tell your PR people to handle this. You've got better things to do."

"I don't want her reputation besmirched," Stefan said.

"I appreciate that," Zach said. "I'll do everything to protect her and the baby."

Silence followed. "You realize now that the press knows where she is, it will be more difficult than ever to protect her. How do you plan to do that? I could send over her guard...."

"Not necessary," Zach said. "I'll be packing her up and taking her to the ranch no later than tomorrow morning, and I'll assign one of my men to watch over her when I'm not available."

"The palace would be a much better place for her. We're equipped to deal with crowds and publicity, and there's a physician available twenty-four hours a day."

"Tina is staying here," Zach said firmly.

"For now," Stefan said, and those two little words raised Zach's hackles.

He refused to rise to Stefan's dig. "I think we've covered the essentials. Feel free to call me if you need anything else."

"I'll call my sister directly if I need to talk to her," Stefan shot back.

"Just don't upset her. Bye now," he said.

"Wait," Stefan said, some of the imperious tone fading from his voice. "Is it really a girl?"

Zach smiled. "Yes, it's a girl, and she's a kicker."

"That must be why Tina calls her Kiki," Stefan said.

"How'd you know that?"

"From the news," Stefan retorted, not bothering to hide his displeasure.

Zach stifled a chuckle. "I'm glad we had this little discussion. Bye," he said and turned off the phone and handed it to Tina.

"You're technically supposed to wait until Stefan ends the conversation," she said.

"Yeah, well, he technically shouldn't act like such a jerk to you."

"He really is under a lot of pressure," she said. "Most people don't know it, but my father was ill for several years. The advisers insisted we keep it secret because many people would have considered Stefan too young." She sighed. "This is terrible to say, but I wish he would get married."

Zach lifted an eyebrow. "So you think marriage can solve his problems, but not yours?"

"*I* don't have his kind of problems." She glanced at her cell phone. "The food should be here by now."

"Like I told you, the delivery guy may need a special escort to get through that lobby."

Her eyebrows knitted together in frustration. "Maybe if I put on a cap and—"

"No way," he said.

"This is my last night here. I wanted it to be...special," she said.

Something inside him squeezed tight at her admission and he rolled some solutions through his mind. "Give me the number of the restaurant. I'll see what I can do."

It took a few calls, but Zach arranged to meet the delivery man in the underground parking garage. Taking the elevator all the way down, he adjusted his ball cap and sunglasses. He walked into the garage and spotted a vehicle with the name of the Italian restaurant and walked toward it, cash in hand.

"Thanks for meeting me down here," Zach said.

The young man glanced around nervously. "I tried to lose them—"

Three men stepped out of the shadows, one armed with a camera and bright light. Zach held his hand up to his eyes, squinting. "What the—"

"Mr. Zachary Logan, we're with the *Worldly News.* Tell us, are you the father of Princess Valentina's baby? Are you planning to get married? Is it true that you kidnapped her from France? And there have been rumors she's having twins—"

"Twins," Zach repeated in alarm. "Hell, no. And the rest is none of your business," he said and headed for the elevator.

The men stepped in front of him. "Mr. Logan—"

"You need to get out of my way. This garage is exclusively for the residents of this building. Do I need to call the cops?"

"That delivery driver isn't a resident of this building," one of the reporters said.

"He brought me Italian food. Did you bring me Italian food? No. Get out," he said and shoved them aside as he walked into the elevator.

His temper rising with each floor he passed, he was ready to growl when he arrived on his floor and entered his apartment.

"I don't see how you stand it," he said as he dumped the bags of food on the dining room table. "Damn bloodsuckers were waiting for me in the parking garage."

Alarm shot across Tina's face. "What bloodsuckers?"

"The press or pretend reporters. I had to threaten them before they would let me get back on the elevator, for Pete's sake."

Tina bit her lip. "This was what I was always afraid of. Your life is totally different from mine. I knew you would find the lack of privacy a terrible invasion. To some extent, it will never change. It's a bit worse now because I'm pregnant and unmarried and Stefan insisted on trying to keep it secret, but dealing with the press and being in the public eye will always be at least a part of my life."

"Not if you spend most of your time at my ranch," he said.

She gave a sad smile. "I won't hide out forever. Although it was time for me to not be the only royal making most of the public appearances, I'm not a hermit. I crave that feeling of accomplishment I get when I can be a part of helping."

"What about the accomplishment of raising our child?"

"That will be part of raising our child. I want our child to see the joy of helping others. She won't be able to do that if I stay locked up at the ranch."

Frustration trickled through him like acid. Although he could understand part of what she said, the idea of her or their baby being exposed to the dirty paws of the paparazzi on a regular basis made his stomach churn.

She moved closer to him and lifted her hand to his arm. "I understand that this is difficult for you. You weren't raised in a fish bowl. Do you remember when I told you that I hadn't planned to tell you that I was pregnant? This is why."

His gut twisted at her words. She made an important point that he didn't want to be true. She was from a different world, and her different world wasn't just going to go away. "I'll figure something out," he said and pulled her against him. "I'm good at that. Trust me."

Tina returned to the ranch and continued to gestate. She badgered Hildie until the housekeeper taught her how to cook some of Zach's favorite dishes. Zach visited every weekend, and she felt closer to him. Then he would seem to draw away from her. Tina suspected his conflicting feelings were related to his former wife and child. The knowledge made her feel helpless, but if Tina even hinted at bringing up the subject, Zach immediately shut down. Tina felt as if they weren't making any progress.

Thanksgiving passed and she became larger than she'd ever dreamed possible. Despite the fact that she grew tired more quickly, Tina organized a charity drive for local families—parents, grandparents and children. She was thrilled with the response. So often at Christmas, only children were remembered, but Tina wanted all ages to experience the happiness of Christmas even if it was only in a small way.

"You're doing too much," Hildie said as Tina helped the

housekeeper bake Christmas cookies on a Friday afternoon while a chicken dish simmered in a large Crock-Pot.

"I told you before. I can't just sit like a hen on an egg," Tina said.

"Humph. At least it's Friday. Maybe Zach will get you to calm down."

"It's not like I'm running a marathon," Tina said as she put another sheet of cookies into the oven.

Eve sighed and munched on a cookie. "This is a great break from my job."

"You have a good job," Hildie said. "Good salary. Good benefits."

"If only I didn't hate it," Eve muttered.

Hildie whipped around. "There are much worse situations you could be in, Missy. Plenty of people would love to have your job."

"I know," Eve said with more than a trace of guilt in her voice. "I work hard, Aunt Hildie. I just don't like it."

Hildie sighed and patted Eve on the shoulder. "You won't have to do it forever. Maybe you can find someone who will pay you good money to take care of their horses."

Eve smiled, unconvinced. "Yeah, and maybe I'll win the lottery next week."

"Don't be negative," Hildie said. "You weren't raised that way."

A knock sounded on the front door. "I bet one of the ranch hands smelled the cookies," Hildie said with a knowing grin. She put a few still-warm cookies on a plate and headed for the door. "I'll feed 'em and tell them to get back to work."

Lost in thought, Tina sprinkled green sugar on the cookies. The baby was kicking and her back ached. She wondered when Zach would arrive.

In her peripheral awareness, she heard the sound of a familiar male voice. She stopped mid-sprinkle and listened more closely. Her heart jumped. "Stefan," she called and ran to the foyer, which was filled with a royal entourage.

Her brother in all his tall, strong handsomeness gaped at her. "Valentina," he said. "Oh, my God. You look like you're ready to pop."

She laughed then flung herself at him and gave him a big hug. "I've got a few more weeks. What are you doing here?"

His smile dipped. "I haven't been satisfied with our communication lately. I've been concerned that your—" He cleared his throat and frowned. "Mr. Logan has been keeping you from the palace and me."

Tina shook her head. "Oh, no. Zach has been in Dallas lately. I've been in charge of a special Christmas sharing project and I can't deny I've been very tired at the end of the day. I told Bridget I couldn't do as many e-consultations, so I think she's felt a bit overwhelmed. You may need to hold Phillipa's feet to the fire a bit more."

Stefan sighed and shook his head. "There's just no one who can replace you."

She waggled her finger at him. "There you go, flattering me. You must be desperate."

"We've truly missed you," he said. "All of us. I insist you return. The palace physician is ready to oversee the delivery of your baby."

She bit the inside of her lip, feeling pulled in opposing directions. Seeing her brother again made her homesick for Chantaine. "We can talk about that later. You must be exhausted from the flight. Let's get something to drink for you. Something to eat." She turned to Hildie. "His Royal Highness, the Prince of Chantaine, this is Hildie Ferguson, CEO of domestic life at the ranch."

"My pleasure to meet you, Ms. Ferguson," Stefan said. "Thank you for your hospitality."

"It's my pleasure, your highlyness. Would you care for some tea or apple cider?"

Stefan's mouth twitched at *highlyness*. Although Tina had attempted to tell Hildie the correct way to address royalty, her suggestions had seemed to fall on deaf ears. "Cider, thank you, and please call me Mr. Devereaux. We are, after all, in America, not Chantaine."

Hildie nodded. "And you can call me Hildie. Please come into the dining room. Have a seat and make yourself at home," she said to Stefan and the two men standing with him. "All of you."

The men moved to the dining room. "I'll help with the cider," Tina said as she returned to the kitchen with Hildie.

"You'll do no such thing. You sit down and visit with your brother," Hildie said.

"Brother?" Eve echoed, peeking around the corner. "Is this the prig prince?" she whispered.

"Hush," Hildie said.

Tina couldn't quite swallow a chuckle. "He's not all bad," she said and returned to the dining room with a plate of cookies. "How is the road construction project going?" she asked as she sat down.

"We're making progress, more slowly than I like, but it's coming along," he said.

"And the development of new business you've been pursuing?"

"Not bad. Ericka's husband had decided to use Chantaine for some more of his films and he has spread the word among the film industry that we offer excellent terms. We're also in negotiations with a cruise ship company to become one of the stops on their itinerary."

"That's terrific news. More jobs, more exposure."

"But not too much," he said. "There's a balance we're determined to keep." He smiled. "This is part of what I've missed with you. Bridget and Phillipa couldn't care less about infrastructure unless it interrupts their trip to the beach."

Tina laughed. "Give them time. They've only been doing the job for about five months."

Stefan shot her a look of doubt. "I've never been one to rely on wishful—"

He broke off as Eve served apple cider, lifting his eyebrow at Tina as a demand for an introduction.

She caught herself thinking how much fun it would be to watch Stefan try to pull his royal attitude over on Eve. "His Royal Highness, this is Eve Jackson. She's Hildie's niece, and she's excellent with horses. They call her the horse whisperer."

He rose and extended his hand. "Really? My pleasure."

Eve met his gaze and Tina could almost swear she felt a crackle of static electricity shoot between them.

"Your royal highness," she said. "I've heard so much about you."

Tina swallowed over the urge to chuckle as Stefan shot her a quick glance. "Why do I have the feeling most of it wasn't good?"

"Please excuse me," Eve said, her voice neutral. "I really need to get back to the barn."

"Of course," he said then looked at Tina again. "Was that one of your staff? You know, I need a new person to work with my horses. Is she that good?"

"Yes, Eve's that good," Tina said and rolled the idea of Eve working for her brother around in her mind. "She would love the job," she said then reconsidered. "On second thought, I'm not sure she would be interested in working for you," Tina said.

He lifted his chin, clearly affronted. "Why not? I would pay an excellent salary."

"Eve is a very modern, liberated woman. I don't think she's the kind to bow to anyone."

"Hmm," he said, rubbing his finger over his bottom lip as he wore a thoughtful expression.

Hildie came into the room with a platter of mile-high sandwiches. "I fixed you a snack since we won't be having dinner for a few more hours."

Stefan blinked in surprise. "Thank you. I wasn't planning to eat—"

"Please do," Hildie said, folding her hands in front of her apron. "And your men can have a bite too."

As soon as Hildie left, Stefan turned back to Tina. "I'm quite serious about having you return to Chantaine. My private jet is waiting for us in a small, private airport not far from here. I know the trip will be long, but the staff will make you as comfortable as possible. As you know, there will be a nurse on board if you need any medical—"

Tina put her hand on her brother's arm. "Stefan, I can't do that. I promised Zachary I would stay here at least until one month after the baby is born. He will want to be a part of the baby's life and—"

"It's not as if you're married," he said. "Or you would even consider marrying him. There are many men more suitable—"

Tina's defenses flew to the roof. "Zachary has been very protective and considerate. I can already tell he'll be a wonderful father."

Stefan's eyes rounded in horror. "You're not considering marrying him? Tina, I haven't mentioned this yet, but this is the kind of thing that could make the advisers suggest you surrender your title."

She bit the inside of her lip. The idea of losing her title was less frightening to her than losing the affection of the people for whom she'd worked so hard. From the beginning of this pregnancy, though, she'd been faced with difficult choices. "I won't be pressured into making a decision for my child based on a title. Do what you have to do."

Hearing a loud noise at the front door, she broke off. "What—"

"Who disarmed my ranch hand? Where is Tina?"

Zach's voice roared through the house. Tina stared at her brother. "You disarmed one of Zach's men?"

Stefan shrugged his shoulders. "He wasn't hurt. My men merely relieved him of his shotgun and cell—"

Zach burst into the room with two men hanging off of him, his eyes blazing. "What's going on here?" he demanded as the two men in their chairs jumped in front of Stefan.

Tina cringed. This was not the way she'd wanted Zach and her brother to meet. She took a quick breath. "His Royal Highness, Prince of Chantaine, this is Zachary Logan."

"Why is he here?" Zach asked.

Stefan slowly rose. "I'm here to take my sister back to Chantaine where she belongs."

"Over my dead body."

"That can be arranged, but it would be messy."

Chapter Fifteen

"Get off my property," Zach said, his blood pounding through his veins. It was all he could do not to go after Stefan even though the prince's guards would likely kill him. "You're trespassing."

Tina touched his arm. "Zach, he's my brother."

He sucked in a deep breath. Nothing inside him softened even one millimeter. "He came to take you away."

"I told him I wouldn't go," she said in a low voice.

Something inside him eased just a fraction. He glanced at her. "Did you?"

She nodded. "Yes. Remember, he will be our daughter's uncle."

Zach couldn't say he was thrilled with the idea. After all, Stefan's goons had disarmed his man and left the poor guy tied up on the side of the road. He gave a grudging shrug. "We were doing okay before you arrived."

Stefan rose, his eyes glittering. "For a royal, okay is never enough."

Zach stuffed his hand in his pocket to keep from punching the superior expression off of Stefan's face.

"Later," Tina said to him, squeezing his arm.

Her tone calmed some part of him and he took a deep breath, searching for some common ground. "I'm glad to see how much you care for Tina. All of us have grown to care for her too. She's a remarkable woman."

He saw a twinge of hostility drain from Stefan's face. "Yes, she is. You're lucky to have enjoyed her presence all these months."

"We have," Zach said.

"The palace wishes her to return immediately," Stefan said.

Zach's stomach twisted into a square knot. "That's her choice," he said, knowing he was taking a risk even though she'd said she would stay.

Stefan frowned. "She insists she wants to stay, but I still believe we can provide better medical care for her and the baby. We can provide a more thorough education for the child. More protection from the public."

"You can't provide the baby's father," Zach said.

"There are other men—"

"That's enough." Zach felt his blood pressure rise. Two heartbeats later, he felt her squeeze his arm again. Her gaze told him other men couldn't replace him. He took another breath, calming himself.

"Would you like a tour of the ranch?" Tina asked her brother. "Zach has a stable of beautiful horses."

"You like horses?" Zach asked cautiously.

"Like is an understatement," Stefan said in a dry tone.

Over the next half hour, Zach showed Prince Stefan his horses. Even Stefan was impressed.

"They're beautiful and well-trained. Perhaps I should steal your horse whisperer away," Stefan said.

"I'm not sure Eve will fit into your budget," Zach said. "She has an executive salary with benefits."

"But not from you," Stefan said.

"No," Zach reluctantly admitted. "But I helped her through college, so we have a deal. She takes care of my horses that need some extra attention."

"How long would she be required to pay that debt?" Stefan asked.

Zach shot him a half grin. "As long as I say."

Stefan nodded. "A smart man. What are your plans for my sister?"

Zach sighed. "I'm doing my damndest to get her to marry me."

Stefan narrowed his eyes. "You are not who I would have chosen for her."

"If there's one thing I've learned about Tina, it's that she doesn't want someone else making this kind of choice for her. You. Or me," Zach said.

Stefan regarded him thoughtfully. "True. But Tina cannot fully turn her back on Chantaine. In one way or another, she will always be our princess. She will want to return."

"Marriage is a negotiation," Zach said.

"Ah, yes, you know that because of your previous marriage. Please accept my sympathies," he said.

"You had me investigated," Zach said.

"I wouldn't be a good brother or ruler if I hadn't," he said. "The views of your former wife's parents are unfortunate. Her death and your child's could not have been prevented."

"Nice of you to say so," Zach said, the discussion turning his stomach.

"Trust me. I wouldn't say that if I couldn't find a way to

twist the story against you to influence Tina to return with me today," Stefan said, his gaze ruthless.

"Always good to know who's got my back," Zach said.

"I look after Chantaine," Stefan said.

"I look after Tina and the baby," Zach returned.

After that, they returned to the house. Tina greeted them with an anxious expression. "How did it go?" she asked Zach, then turned to Stefan. "What did you think of his horses?"

"They are quite beautiful and well-behaved. I would like to talk to his trainer," Stefan said, cutting his eyes at Zach.

"Eve will turn you down flat," Zach said in a low voice.

"We'll see. In the meantime, Valentina, I must leave. Are you sure you won't join me?" Stefan asked.

Zach's gut twisted as she glanced at him then away. "I told you I can't go back right now," she said to Stefan. "But I'm so glad you visited. Seeing you made me realize all the more how much I've missed you and the rest of the family."

"Good," Stefan said and kissed his sister on both cheeks. "I brought a gift for the baby."

"Really?" Tina said in surprise. "What?"

He waved to one of his staff who hurried to the stretch limo in front of the house. Seconds later, the man appeared with a white box wrapped with a satin bow. He gave the box to Stefan, who presented it to Tina.

Tina beamed at her brother. "What is it?"

"Open it and find out," Stefan said, laughing.

Tina removed the top of the box and her face softened. "A flop-eared bunny. You remembered."

"You had one as a child, but one of the staff misplaced it," Stefan said. "I thought your little Kiki might like one too."

Tina dropped the box to the ground and threw her arms around her brother. "Thank you, Stefan. It has been so good to see you."

Her brother squeezed her tightly in return. "We miss you, Tina. Come back soon."

She drew back and Zach watched her draw in a deep breath. Her eyes were shiny with unshed tears. "Call me about road construction and infrastructure."

Stefan chuckled. "I'll do that." He turned aside and lifted his head toward Zach. "Take care of her, Zachary Logan."

"I will," Zach promised, and within seconds, Stefan and his entourage rode away.

Thank God.

As they watched the stretch limo disappear into the distance, Zach watched Tina swipe tears from her eyes as she hugged the pink flop-eared bunny to herself. "I didn't know bunnies were your favorite," he said.

She sniffled. "You didn't ask."

Well, hell, he thought. How was he supposed to know he should have asked?

"Anything else I should know?" he asked and slid his hand around her waist.

She gave a soft teary chuckle. "Oh, Zachary, that kind of stuff takes a lifetime."

"Dinner's ready," Hildie called from the doorway. "Oh, no. Did they leave already?"

"Yes, Stefan is gone," Tina said.

Hildie crossed her arms over her chest. "Well, that's a darned shame. I made a fresh apple pie."

"If you put some ice cream on it, I bet we can talk Tina into eating a slice," Zach said.

"I don't feel very hungry," Tina said.

"I bet Kiki would like a bit of that pie," he said.

She shot him a sideways glance. "Maybe."

He coaxed her into joining him for dinner. At first, she wouldn't eat a bite, but she gradually ate part of her meal.

"So what is it about flop-eared bunnies?" he asked.

She smiled and took another bite. "My uncle gave me one before I was even born. He's passed away since. But that flop-eared bunny was the first stuffed animal I remember. He was also the first I remember losing."

"He?" Zach echoed.

"I named him Erie because of his ears," she said, her gaze growing distant.

Zach frowned. "You don't talk about your mom much. Did the two of you get along?"

Tina shrugged. "We weren't very close. She gave birth to me, then had her duties. I had mine."

"That sounds a little cold," he said.

"We weren't close," she said. "After I went away to college, I realized I would want to have a different relationship with my children. Keely and her mom are so close, yet her mom gives her space."

"And your mom?" Zach asked.

"She bred heirs to the throne and made appearances. She became ill and her health quickly deteriorated when I was in college. She died my junior year. I graduated early, so I could go home and contribute to a sense of continuity and comfort."

"What about your father?" he asked.

"He died soon after, which put Stefan under the microscope," she said. "That's why we're close."

"He's lucky that you were there for him," he said.

She shrugged. "Maybe," she said and glanced away. "What about your sister? What is she like?"

"She's strong and independent. She's in Chicago. I haven't kept in touch like I should, but seeing you and Stefan makes me want to call her."

Tina met his gaze and slowly smiled. "Do that. You won't regret it. Invite her here for Christmas," she said and leaned her head against her hand as she studied him. "What about you? Any favorite stuffed animals from childhood?"

He racked his brain. "A hippopotamus," he finally said.

She laughed. "But they hurt people," she said.

"Not when they're fluffy and stuffed full of cotton with painted-on smiles," he countered.

"I guess that's true," she said and slid her hand in his. "Do you remember your favorite childhood song?"

"If you're happy and you know it, stomp your feet," he said. "I didn't have to sit down for it. What about you?"

"Frérè Jacques," she said. "My nanny sang it to me before I went to sleep."

"Oh, a night-night song," he said. "My father tried to sing a song about the moon and me. I don't remember the words."

"What about your mother?" she asked.

"She hugged me a lot," he said.

"Did you sing anything to the baby before—" She broke off and dipped her head. "Before he passed on?"

Zach frowned. "How did you know the baby was a boy?"

"I didn't," she said. "I just guessed."

He thought back to his time with Jenny and how erratic her behavior had become later into her pregnancy. After they'd married, he'd wondered about her dramatic high and low moods and how the pregnancy had seemed to accentuate them. When they'd learned she had a mental illness, he'd kept tabs on her several times a day…except that one day when he'd been tied up with a crisis. As soon as he'd learned Jenny was in trouble, he'd scrambled to take her to the E.R.

Zach had sped toward the hospital, but Jenny had bled out. By the time he'd arrived, the doctors had been unable to rouse her and the baby was dead.

He would never forget the helpless feeling he'd experienced speeding toward the hospital. Even now, it made him break into a cold sweat. The doctor had told him they couldn't have saved her even if she'd been in the hospital at the time of her crisis. She'd lost too much blood too quickly.

"Zach," Tina said. "Are you okay?"

"Yeah, I'm okay. Not great, but okay." He forced a smile. "Do Kiki and her mom want a bite of that apple pie?"

Tina paused as if she suspected he was remembering something painful. "I can't believe you're in the mood for apple pie."

"I'll take a bite if you will," he said. "You know, we haven't talked about names."

Surprise flitted across her face. "We haven't. You haven't been around very much."

"That will change," he said, lacing his fingers through hers.

"Starting when?" she asked.

"Now."

"Really? Why is that?" she asked.

"Last week, I told Daniel I wasn't coming back to the city until after the baby was born. I wanted to stay close," he said. "And because the damned cell phone isn't dependable, I bought some two-way radios. Old school, but they should work."

"So you'll be here for a while?" she asked, her gaze filled with a combination of relief and pleasure.

"Yeah," he said. "As long as you need me, Tina. Now about those names," he began.

"I've thought of a thousand," she confessed. "Stella, Mc-Kayla, Lucia, Camille, Delphine, Martina. Of course there will be more than one name to choose."

"I think one of her names should be Valentina," he said.

Her lips lifted in a soft smile. "Why is that?"

"Because she's a busy girl and that's partly a testament to her mother. On another subject, Hildie tells me you haven't ordered any baby furniture. Even I know we need to cross that off the list."

"I hadn't really figured out where to put her. I don't think I'll need much more than a bassinet to start, especially since I'm not sure how long—" She broke off and shrugged her shoulders.

Her uncertainty twisted something inside him. "What do you need to be sure?" he demanded, struggling with his impatience.

"This is one of those areas where you and I don't share the same opinion," she began.

"You don't share the opinion that we would be better parents together than apart?" he asked, rising from his chair.

"I didn't say that, but I have a lot of things to consider. I promised you I would stay for a month after the baby is born. Isn't that enough for now?"

"No, it isn't," he said. "I want us to get married. We can work out what you need to do about visiting Chantaine and your family, but I think you know deep down that you belong here with me."

She opened her mouth and her eyes deepened with an emotion that sliced through the steel vault around his frozen heart. That was what she wanted from him. His heart. What she didn't understand was that he'd lost the ability to give it three years ago.

He watched her pull back her emotions and close her mouth, whatever words she'd thought left unsaid. He felt the twist of the knife inside him again. The feeling always surprised him because he'd felt like he'd turned into a man who couldn't be reached.

Tina and Hildie wrapped donated gifts for the elderly. Tina shifted in her chair, feeling generally uncomfortable. She wasn't sleeping well and she wasn't sure about her future.

Despite the holiday music playing in the background, she felt a little cranky.

She tied a red ribbon around the tissue paper and reached for an indoor geranium kit and began to wrap it. "Do you think Zachary will ever be able to fall in love again?" she asked.

Silence followed as Hildie tied her own bow. "That's a tough one," she said. "He had such a hard time with Jenny. She wasn't who she thought she was."

"What do you mean?" Tina asked, searching Hildie's face.

"Jenny had problems. They seemed to get worse the further into her pregnancy," Hildie said, tying a firm bow.

"What kind of problems? Other than her pregnancy?"

Hildie sighed. "I really shouldn't be talking about this, but the girl had some kind of mental problems. I don't think Zach knew about it before they got married. After Jenny died, though, it seemed her parents knew something. They blamed Zach for not watching her more closely. They even demanded that she and the baby be buried somewhere other than the Logan family burial ground." Hildie shook her head. "Heaven knows he hovered over her night and day. After she got pregnant, she would leave the house in the middle of the night. We'd all panic and go searching to find her."

"Oh my goodness. I had no idea," Tina said, imagining how trying that must have been for all of them.

"Toward the end, Zach wouldn't go anywhere. She was about seven months along and started cramping and bleeding. We called Zach and he came right away. He took her to the hospital, but it was too late for Jenny. Too early for the baby. He blamed himself. The doctor said she had an undetected abruption. She started bleeding and didn't stop."

Hildie wrapped a bundle of sudoku books and tied a ribbon around the top. "You're nothing like her," she finally said.

"Is that good or bad?" Tina asked.

"Good," Hildie said. "But you have to realize what a terrible experience that was for a man like Zachary. He's a man who prides himself on fixing things, on taking care of people. In his mind, he failed in the worst way imaginable. Thank goodness you don't have mental problems," she said.

"Oh, I don't know," Tina said, absorbing the information Hildie had disclosed. "Depending on the day, all of us can feel a little off center, don't you think?"

Hildie met her gaze and gave a sassy smile. "Speak for yourself. I'm always on target."

"Show-off," Tina teased.

Hildie just grinned, but Tina's mind was spinning with what she'd just learned. Her heart ached even more for how Zach had suffered. Was he so scarred, however, that he would never be able to love again?

Chapter Sixteen

"Is there a reason we had to stop by the barn before going back to the ranch?" Tina called from Zach's SUV after she'd finished her latest appointment with the obstetrician. "I'm hungry."

"Eat your crackers," he said as he stalled for a little more time. Grinning to himself, he killed some time talking to his beauties in the barn while Tina waited in the car. It was for a good cause. She would ultimately be pleased.

Hearing her footsteps behind him, he wiped his grin off his face and looked busy.

"You hire people to take care of your horses. Why are you doing this?" she asked.

"I may hire people, but I still check on them. It's a good practice. And it's not as if Eve has had any spare time lately," he added.

"True," Tina said. "She's working crazy hours."

"And she hates it," Zach said.

"I wonder if my brother really would—"

Zach lifted his hand, finding the possibility untenable. Eve was the equivalent of his youngest sister. He didn't want to see her hurt. "Your brother is a bulldozer."

"You may be underestimating Eve. She's pretty strong," Tina said and sighed. "Can we please go now?"

Zach glanced at his watch. "Yeah, let me check the rest of the horses," he said and slowly walked through the rest of the barn. When he was certain he'd taken enough time, he returned to escort Tina to the car.

"Are you sure you're okay?" he asked. "You seem like you're out of breath a lot."

"The baby's riding high. That's what Hildie says. Causes indigestion and short breaths," she said, wobbling into her seat.

"Sorry about that," he said.

"If she was riding low, I'd have to run to the powder room all the time," she said with a shrug. "It's just part of pregnancy."

"Would you ever want to do it again?" he asked, holding the door open.

She scrunched up her face. "I'd prefer to reserve judgment on that decision. This isn't the best time to ask."

"When is the best time?" he asked.

"Maybe a year after the baby is born," she said.

He chuckled and nodded. "I'll make a note of it," he said and closed the door.

Climbing into the driver's side of the SUV, he took his time starting the engine and putting it into gear.

"Is there something wrong with the car?" she asked.

"No," he said. "Why?"

"Because you're moving so slowly you're acting like you're doing an inspection on it."

He swallowed a chuckle. "Just being careful. I'm carrying precious cargo."

"Precious cargo that is hungry," she said.

He drove into the back garage so she wouldn't see the other cars out front, then helped her out of the car.

"I guess it's a good thing that the doctor said the baby probably won't come until after Christmas. That means we can enjoy the holiday without worrying."

"Speak for yourself," he muttered. Zach couldn't stop worrying. He was losing more sleep with each passing night.

"What do you mean?" she asked. "The doctor says I'm totally healthy. You should rest easy and let me toss and turn," she said.

Zach, however, saw the faint shadows beneath her eyes. The doctor said it was normal for her to lose sleep, but Zach wanted Tina and the baby safe and happy. He could tell Tina wasn't at all comfortable as she grew larger with each passing day.

"Even the doctor says he thinks she's a big baby," he said.

"Hildie tells me that means she'll sleep through the night sooner," Tina said, rubbing her back as she climbed the steps from the garage.

Zach opened the door and ushered her down the hallway.

"It's so quiet," she said as they turned the corner to the den. "I wonder—"

"Surprise!" a chorus of voices called.

Tina blinked in shock at the crowd of men and women greeting her. She put her hand to her throat. "Oh my goodness, what is this?"

Keely rose and embraced her. "It's a baby shower," she said and guided her to a wing chair. "We had to limit the guest list. A lot more people wanted to come."

"I don't know what to say," Tina murmured, glancing around, recognizing some of the faces, but not all.

"I'm Sienna," a woman standing in the background said. "I'm Zach's sister. Haven't been here in a while, but I couldn't miss this."

Tina automatically stood and stretched out her arms. "Thank you so much. I can't tell you what this means. Zach," she said, glancing toward the doorway.

Zach immediately stepped forward and gave his sister a hug. "Thanks for coming. I know I've been difficult—"

"You always were," Sienna said in a dry voice. "Daniel and I had a chance to talk before the party got started, but he looks a little distracted right now," she whispered.

Zach's younger brother, Daniel, appeared totally focused on one of their neighbors, Chloe Martin. Zach remembered Daniel's past with the woman and lifted his eyebrows. "That could be interesting," Zach said in a low voice.

"You're telling me," Sienna said.

"Any chance you'll tell me what this is about?" Tina whispered.

"Later," Zach said and brushed her nose with a kiss. "You have gifts to open."

Zach slipped Tina a small sandwich before she opened the shower gifts because he knew she was hungry. He counted how many times she rubbed her back and how many times she insisted she was just fine. The correlation was one to three. Tina was not a whiner.

She alternated between princess mode and sincere delight throughout the party. A few times, she brushed tears from her eyes when she received homemade gifts of quilts, crocheted afghans and painted pictures.

He could see that she was overcome with the generosity and thoughtfulness of the attendees and it occurred to him that she truly didn't realize what kind of affect she had on people.

"I don't know what to say," Tina said, her voice breaking. "Who's the baby now?" she said as tears slid down her face. "You've all been way too generous."

"You're the generous one," Hildie said. "You just burst right in here and shook all of us up."

"We have a few more gifts," Keely said. "This one's from Ericka."

Tina opened a package of a beautiful baby carrier and a bottle of French wine. "That's Ericka," Tina said, with a laugh.

"And from Stefan," Keely said, giving her an envelope.

Tina opened it and smiled. "One round trip charter to Chantaine on Stefan's royal jet."

"I'll go," Eve said, raising her hand.

"Those tickets are spoken for," Zach said and met Tina's gaze.

Her eyes welled up with tears. "You have done too much for me. I'm humbled by your generosity. Thank you so very much."

Deciding she needed a moment to gather her emotions, Zach nodded in Keely's direction. "Time for food?"

Keely took the cue and stood, clapping her hands together. "We have all kinds of wonderful food, punch and wine. Please enjoy."

Zach took Tina to a small formal greeting room. "You okay?"

She took several deep breaths, her eyes wide. "I'm shocked," she said. "I haven't even been here that long and look at what these people have done for me. Those homemade quilts and knitted afghans must have taken hours and hours of work."

"You really don't realize the impact you've made," he said in amazement.

Her eyes filled with tears. "I also don't know if I will be staying," she whispered, clearly in agony. "I feel so guilty."

Her admission felt like a hot poker in his gut, but he refused to give in to it. This night was about Tina and the baby. Not about him. "What you've given to this community has made a huge difference. Even if you left now, we would all be changed for the better."

She took another deep breath and flew into his arms. "Oh, Zach, what am I going to do?"

This once, he wasn't going to try to tell her, because he was beginning to grasp that Tina had been pressured her entire life. She deserved the opportunity to make her own choices…even if it nearly killed him in the process.

Zach thanked everyone for coming. Daniel came to his side. "I'm headed out. Taking Chloe home."

"She didn't bring her own car?" Zach asked, gently taunting his brother.

"Okay, I'm following her home," Daniel said, shooting him a quelling glance. "Don't ask because I'm not gonna tell."

Zach lifted his hands. "Good luck and Godspeed."

Later that night, Tina nestled in Zach's arms. His strength never ceased to amaze or comfort her. She gazed out the window of his bedroom into a sky full of stars. "Did your parents love each other?" she asked.

"Huh?" he asked, half asleep.

"Nothing," she said, not wanting to bother him.

He shifted and propped himself on his elbow. "No, what'd you say?"

"I asked you if your parents loved each other."

"Yeah, they did," he said.

"How do you know?"

"They were devoted to each other through thick and thin. He would have protected her with his life. She would have done anything she could for him," he said.

"How do you know that?" she asked.

He sighed. "He worked three extra jobs when the ranch didn't bring in enough money for food or heat. He traded one of his favorite horses for a diamond anniversary band for their twenty-fifth anniversary."

"That's romantic," she said.

"She made him trade it back," he said.

Tina gasped. "Was he insulted?"

Zach chuckled. "No. She was a very practical woman. He bought back the horse and got her a new refrigerator. She was a lot happier with that."

Tina smiled and relaxed against him again. "It sounds like they had a deep appreciation for each other."

"I think they did. My father held her hand when she died," he said.

Tina's throat closed up tight. "That must have been hard," she said.

"Yes, but he wouldn't have had it any other way," Zach said. He stroked a strand of her hair from her forehead. "What about your parents? Do you think they loved each other?"

"Well, they certainly procreated," she said with a laugh. "Two sons, four daughters," she said. "I always thought their relationship seemed controlled and proper until she died. Now that I think of it, her passing may have broken his heart. He continued to rule, but then he became ill. He didn't fight it."

"My mother always said to be careful about judging other people. They might be different on the inside than they seem on the outside. Same for relationships. I had to grow up before I started to understand that," he said.

Tina thought about Zach's relationship with his former

wife. According to the outside world, he was a devoted husband, she a devoted wife. They had appeared normal, but Hildie had told her the real story had been different.

She put her hand over Zach's chest and felt his heartbeat against her palm. "After Jenny, did you decide you would never marry again?"

He paused a long moment. "Yes," he said. "But you changed my mind."

"Kiki and me," she corrected. "Would you have changed your mind if I hadn't gotten pregnant?"

"That question is irrelevant," he said. "You got pregnant."

"It's not irrelevant to me," she said, frowning.

"Stop thinking about things that don't matter. You're with me. You're safe, and our baby is safe," he said.

Tina sighed. For this moment, that was enough. She closed her eyes and snuggled against him, falling asleep.

The next morning, Tina rose early to have breakfast with Zach's sister, Sienna. Sienna had already said she needed to leave today, so Tina wanted to maximize her time with her.

"Good morning," Tina said as she carefully descended the stairs. Sienna was already seated in the den with her suitcase packed beside her. "You don't have to rush away."

"Work," Sienna said. "How are you this morning?"

"Feeling my largesse," Tina said with a laugh. "Eat breakfast with me. I'm sure Hildie has already fixed something with enough calories to feed a family of bears."

Sienna smiled. "She always did when I lived here. I'm sure she'll turn up her nose when I tell her I'm on a low-carb diet."

"I think so," Tina said as the two women walked into the breakfast room. "Morning, Hildie, you devil for deceiving me about the shower."

Hildie tossed her a look of defiance. "As if you didn't love every minute," she said.

"All of you did too much," Tina insisted.

"If you say that one more time…" Hildie said in a warning tone.

"I'm going to throw up," Sienna finished.

Tina blinked.

Hildie gave a nod of approval. "Well said, Sienna. Good to see you again. You're about five years overdue. Have a seat. Scrambled eggs, blueberry pancakes, crisp bacon and fresh fruit coming up."

Sienna groaned. "Do you know how long I'll have to do the elliptical for this?"

"Get in line. I've been doing this for months," Tina said.

Despite their protests, the two women enjoyed the sumptuous breakfast. Sienna leaned back and gestured at Tina's plate. "You didn't eat nearly as much as I would have expected with a little parasite in your belly."

Tina laughed. "Charming way of looking at pregnancy. I have to eat small meals. She keeps kicking me in my diaphragm. Little bugger."

"Ah," Sienna said with a nod. "I like the way Zach acts with you. He treats you like fine china he wants to keep from breaking. Very sweet."

Tina's smile fell. "He does that because of his first wife and how she lost the baby."

Sienna gave a slow nod. "I wasn't around for that. I tried to reach out to him afterward, but he pretty much shut me out. It looks to me like things have changed with you around."

Tina was reluctant to disclose much more. "We'll see. Tell me about your life. What made you leave Logan country?"

Sienna shrugged. "I needed to get away. Made a few mistakes along the way, but I'm better now. The city suits me. I like the anonymity."

"Is there anyone special in your life?" Tina asked.

Sienna shook her head. "Just my cat and my job, and I'm okay with that. I don't want to lose touch with you, Zach and Daniel now. I'm too busy to come home for Christmas, but maybe I can visit afterward."

"That would be great," Tina said. "I haven't made definite plans about what I'll be doing once the baby is born, but—"

"You won't be staying?" Sienna interjected, clearly shocked.

"It's a complicated situation," she said.

"Zach would die if he couldn't be near his child," Sienna said.

Tina sighed. "I respect that. I truly do, but I also want my child to see an overwhelming love between her parents. I'm not sure Zach can do that with all the loss he has experienced."

Sienna reached toward her and took her hand. "Don't count him out. You haven't seen the way he looks at you. Promise me," she said.

"I promise," Tina said. "I promise I will listen to my heart and Zach's heart if he can open up to me."

"Good," Sienna said with a nod. "I'm glad I came."

"I am too," Tina said, but she didn't want to make promises she couldn't keep.

Tina was thrilled with the success of the holiday project. Now that all the donations had been collected, invitations had been sent to the families in need of help to pick up their gifts at a community center about thirty miles from the ranch.

Zach absolutely did not want her to go, but Tina insisted. Part of the reward of the project was seeing the happiness on the faces of those who received the gifts. Plus several other people in the community had worked hard and Tina wanted to personally thank each of them.

Hildie was charged with transporting her and making sure she didn't work too hard. Joining the other volunteers gave Tina a rush of excitement. She could tell she was more than ready to get out again.

"You're doing too much," Hildie warned.

"Nonsense," Tina said as she packed donated groceries into bags for the families. "I'm loving every minute of it. Look at how happy that mother is over there."

Hildie also helped load groceries and shook her head. "I never would have expected we'd see so much donated this year since it's been a rough one for just about everyone."

"The idea is to make it easy," Tina said. "If you make it easy, then people feel successful about giving and then they want to do even more." She glanced at the clock. "Look at the time. The next group will be coming in just twenty minutes. Do you mind telling Charlene to urge people to finish with their selections?"

"As long as you get something to eat and drink," Hildie said firmly, wagging her finger at Tina.

"I'm fine," Tina insisted, exhilarated by the success of their efforts. "I'm a grown woman. I know when to eat and drink. I'll get something soon."

Somehow soon turned into later, and everything turned into a blur after four o'clock. In the back of her mind, she noticed her back beginning to hurt. She was very thirsty, but with everyone working so hard, it was easy for her to procrastinate taking a break. Tina was so busy she barely noticed when a local news team entered the distribution room.

Suddenly a microphone was pushed in her face. "Princess Valentina, how do you feel about your holiday gift campaign?"

"Tina or Ms. Devereaux is fine," she said, glancing up

from her task and suddenly feeling very tired and thirsty. "It's not *my* holiday gift campaign. It's the community's gift campaign, and everyone has done a brilliant job."

"How's the pregnancy coming?"

"My watermelon seed has grown," she said, frustrated by her sudden feeling of weakness.

"Any chance for an upcoming wedding?"

"One thing at a time," she said. "Thank you for stopping by. Did you talk to Charlene Kendricks? You really should. She's kept everything moving today."

Tina's stomach turned and she felt her knees go rubbery. "Excuse me," she murmured to the reporter. "I'm going to get a drink of water," she said, moving toward the back of the room.

The room began to tilt and sway. "All I need is water and a chair," she coached herself.

"Tina," she heard Hildie call and then she collapsed.

Chapter Seventeen

Tina awakened to a crowd of people standing over her, including a cameraman, of course. Covering her face, she groaned. Of all the things she didn't want to make the news… "Oh, please."

"She said she needed some water," a male voice said.

"We'll get that," Hildie said. "Now back off so she can breathe. You, with the camera, stop that or I'll break it. Don't you doubt for a minute that I will," she said.

"Here's some water, Ms. Devereaux," a different female voice said. "Can we find a pillow?"

"How about a stuffed animal?" someone else said.

Willing the room to stop spinning, Tina rose to her elbows. A stuffed animal was stuffed behind her back and she took a sip of the bottled water. "Thank you, Chloe," she said to the woman helping her. "I really didn't want to make a scene. I'm sure I'll catch blue blazes for this from Zach."

Chloe shot her a look of sympathy. "Those Logan men

are tough as nails," she said, catching sight of Hildie giving the cameraman a piece of her mind. "Would you like some crackers?"

"What I would like is to get away from this crowd," she said.

Chloe glanced around and waved over a few men. "Can you guys help her to the back room?"

"We can carry her if you like," one of the three men offered.

"No," Tina said. "If you could just help me stand. I'm a bit like a beached whale in my current state."

"Honored to assist, ma'am," one of the men said, and Tina prayed she didn't give any of them an injury. After she took another sip of water, they helped her to her feet and led her to a chair in an adjoining room with a door, thank goodness.

"Thank you very much," she said to the men. Chloe remained with Tina while she sipped on the bottle of water.

"Are you sure I can't get you something to eat?" Chloe asked.

Tina shook her head. "I just need to get my equilibrium back. I should have paid more attention to the signs my body was giving me, but I got caught up in the excitement. Zach is going to kill me."

"If it helps any, I fainted when I was pregnant," Chloe said.

"Really?" Tina said.

"More than once," she said.

"That must have terrified your husband," Tina said.

"Different situation. We weren't married." Chloe paused. "I was very young. He wasn't really in—" She broke off and waved her hand. "Water under the bridge now. We need to make sure you're feeling better."

Tina racked her brain for what she'd heard about the lovely

woman. "Your husband passed away, didn't he? I'm sorry for your loss."

Chloe lifted her slim shoulder. "Thank you. We were separated at the time."

"Oh, that just makes it all the more difficult," she said.

Chloe gave a wry smile. "Exactly. Now what—"

"I taught that cameraman the meaning of respect," Hildie said as she marched into the room, carrying the camera with her. Her cheeks were flushed with anger, clearly invigorated from the fight.

"Oh, Hildie, he could charge you with stealing," Tina said.

"Let him try," Hildie said. "I'll give it back. I just need to erase the memory thingy. In the meantime, we need to get you to the doctor before Zach hears about this."

"But I'm fine," Tina said.

"That's what you said earlier when I told you to eat a snack, take a break and drink some water," Hildie said in a stern voice.

"But—"

"No buts. A record number of people in this community will be having Christmas because of you. You've done enough. Now you need to take care of yourself and the baby. I've already called the doctor."

Zach walked into the ob-gyn clinic, swearing under his breath and sweating blood. If only Tina had listened to him. If only she hadn't gone to the community center. She simply didn't understand her fragility. It was past office hours. Thank goodness Hildie had insisted on getting Tina and the baby checked.

He knocked on the door to the inner office and waited, counting to ten then twenty. Finally, Hildie opened the door.

"The doctor just finished the ultrasound. Your little bugger is kicking up a storm as usual."

His lips twitched at Hildie's enthusiasm. "Do you know how this happened?"

"It's my fault," Hildie said. "I asked her to take food and water twice, then everything got busy. I'm sorry, Zachary."

He shook his head. "It wasn't your fault. You couldn't force-feed her. She just got busy and ignored her own needs. Where is she?"

Hildie pointed in the direction of a closed door and Zach knocked. The doctor opened the door. "Come in. No complications. Our mother just stretched herself a little further than she should have."

Zach met Tina's sheepish gaze. "We covered this subject this morning."

"I know," she said. "I was fine until the late afternoon crowd. I started working and forgot about taking a break or drinking some water."

Zach took a quick breath, but held his tongue. He looked at the doctor. "Any professional advice?"

"She's in excellent health, but she shouldn't run a marathon or oversee a holiday Christmas charity event without breaks."

"Please tell him the rest of the story," Tina said to the doctor. "That it's not unusual for a pregnant woman to faint and that it's not necessarily a sign of anything bad."

"True," the doctor said. "Pregnancy produces a tremendous strain on the body, especially during the later months. It's not unusual for a pregnant woman to faint every now and then."

"Not my woman," Zach said and met Tina's gaze again. "I'm taking you home and making sure you get the rest you need."

Five minutes later, he helped her into his SUV. His gut was

still twisting. From the moment Hildie had called him, he'd feared the worst. He slammed her door closed and climbed into the driver's side.

Zach wasn't sure what to say. He was still terrified that something would happen to Tina or the baby.

"It could have been much worse," Zach said as he drove out of the parking lot. "You could have fallen in a way that hurt the baby."

"The amniotic fluid is supposed to cushion the baby. With all the swelling I've had, trust me, I've got plenty of fluid," Tina retorted.

"I told you that you shouldn't go. I knew you would overdo it, but you ignored me," he said.

"This was one of the happiest days of my life," she said. "Seeing all those people accept the gifts from the community…"

"Was it worth risking your health? The baby's?" he demanded. "What if you had been permanently injured? Or the baby? Would you have been able to live with that?"

She sucked in a shocked breath and he felt her gaze on him. "Is this about me and Kiki or Jenny and the baby you lost?" she whispered.

He blinked at her blunt question.

"At some point, you're going to have to realize that I'm not Jenny and this baby is not the one you lost. I'm doing the best I can to live my life to the fullest at the same time I nurture my baby. Don't accuse me of being a bad mother again."

"I wasn't," he said.

"It certainly sounded like it," she said and looked out the passenger window.

They rode several miles in silence. Zach struggled with her accusation. He wasn't sure she knew how fragile her life or the baby's life could be, and he couldn't begin to make her understand.

Zach pulled into the garage and stopped. "Thank you for the ride home. Good night," she said and stepped out of the car and away from him.

For the next several days, Tina slept in the guest bedroom and avoided Zach at dinner. After a week passed, he approached her in the hallway late at night.

"Are you still mad at me?" he asked.

She crossed her arms under her chest. "I wouldn't use the word mad," she said, lifting her chin.

"Then what word would you use? Furious? Murderous? Beyond angry?"

"Murderous is close," she said, her sexy impudent gaze meeting his.

"Why murderous?" he asked. "All I did was drive you home from the doctor."

"While you accused me of being a bad mother," she said, her own green gaze turning dark.

"I didn't say you were a bad mother," he said.

"Close enough," she retorted.

"How could you be a bad mother when you fled all your royal crap to search out what was best for you and your baby?" he asked.

She paused a long moment. "Do you realize what I turned down?"

"I have an idea," Zach said. "Even though you were pregnant with another man's child, you could have married an English earl, an Italian count or a Spanish prince."

She appeared surprised at his knowledge. "They wanted my title. They didn't want me."

"I want you," he said.

"How do I know you don't want me just because of the baby?" she asked.

"Because I wanted you before the baby existed," he said.

She searched his gaze then looked away. "I hadn't thought about that."

"Why don't you think about it some more while you sleep with me?" he asked.

"I'm not a good sleep partner," she said. "I wake up every hour, go to the bathroom, toss and turn."

He took her hand in his and pulled her against him. "Come to bed with me."

"As long as you understand there's no sexy hootchie koo in your near future," she warned.

"No sexy hootchie koo," he agreed and reveled in her warmth. "But that's not because I don't want your sexy hootchie koo."

Tina sighed. "That's good to know."

With each day that passed, Tina felt as if she must be gaining at least a pound. Her back hurt, her thighs ached and her abdomen seemed to cramp every other hour.

"This sucks," Tina said to Hildie and Eve. "If every woman felt like I did, there would be no population explosion."

"Sit down and put your feet up," Hildie said. "You need to focus on the gorgeous baby you're going to have in just a few weeks."

"Easy for you to say," Tina said. "You don't have hemorrhoids."

Eve winced then patted Tina's hand. "I have to tell you that the assistant to the assistant of your brother got in touch with me."

"Salvadore," Tina said, astonished, but at the same time not. "Stefan wants to steal you away to manage his prize horses. What did you say?"

"Two words I learned from Zach," Eve said with a wily grin.

"What's that?"

"More money," Eve said.

Tina laughed. "Good for you. You will earn every penny if you work for my brother, so make sure you negotiate a fantastic salary. Are you really willing to live in another country to work and earn your living?"

"I'm not happy doing what I'm doing. We'll see how the Devereauxs come through."

"I should warn you that my brother is ruthless when he finds something he wants. Be careful," she said.

"I'm a big girl," Eve said. "As much as I like you, I'm not at all susceptible to a royal title. In my mind, you are the amazing exception that proves the arrogant rule."

"I'll take that as one of the highest compliments I've received," Tina said.

A week before Christmas, Tina hid in her bedroom so she could wrap the gifts she'd ordered online for Zach, Hildie, and Eve. She'd already ordered gifts for her family and Zach's brother and sister that should arrive any day.

She felt more crampy than usual but put it down to bending and stretching. Crankiness went against her usual nature, but she was also still bothered about what she was going to do after her agreed-upon time with Zachary passed.

The closer the time came for her to deliver the baby, the more she wanted to be home, but now she wasn't sure where home was for her.

A cramp twisted her muscles, momentarily stealing her breath. The intensity of it took her by surprise. *Labor?* she wondered, then pushed the possibility aside. She'd been having cramps for weeks. This wasn't any different, she told herself.

But then she felt a gush of water rush down her leg.

She gasped in shock. Her water had broken. She was in labor. She was going to have her baby very soon. Her heart hammering with excitement, she didn't know what to do first. Tell Zach. Change clothes.

She decided to change clothes and told herself to stay calm. Women did this every day. Everything would be okay. Her abdomen tightened again, this time stronger. She took another breath.

In the past two centuries of the Devereaux women giving birth, none of them had done it naturally, and she didn't plan to be the first. Right now she wanted to get to the hospital to get her epidural as quickly as possible. No need fighting the contractions.

Despite her discomfort, excitement rushed through her. *Kiki was coming soon.*

She went to the bathroom to change. As she looked at her clothes, she saw blood instead of water. Alarm shot through her. She panicked at the sight of bright red. Was her baby okay?

Tina smothered a sob. She had to hold it together. Zach would be nervous enough for both of them. Quickly changing her clothes, she grabbed a towel and went downstairs.

"Hildie," she called. "Hildie, where is Zachary? I need to speak to him immediately."

Hildie poked her head out from the kitchen. "He went out. Some calves got caught in some barbed wire. Poor animals are dumber than dirt…."

She must have read the alarm on Tina's face. "What's wrong?"

Tina swallowed over the knot of fear forming in her throat. "My water broke."

Hildie's eyes rounded. "Oh my goodness. We have to get him here right away. Call him. Call him."

"I hope he's reachable," Tina said, taking the house phone from Hildie. Zach's cell rang once, twice, three times. Her nervousness ratcheted up another notch.

"Hello," Zach said, sounding out of breath. "What do you need?"

"It's time," Tina said.

"For what?" he asked, sounding distracted.

"For you to take me to the hospital. My water broke," she said. "I need to go now."

"Damn," he said. "Hell," he said, then swore again. "I'm on my way," he said and hung up.

With trembling fingers, Tina called her doctor and was put on hold. She stepped away from Hildie, who was watching her like a hawk. Finally a nurse came on the line.

"Dr. McAllister is with a patient," the nurse said. "How can I help you?"

"This is Valentina Devereaux. I'm in labor. My water has broken." She lowered her voice. "And I'm bleeding."

"Go to the hospital immediately," the nurse said. "The doctor will meet you there as soon as you arrive."

Go to the hospital immediately. As if she were planning to go shopping or get a pedicure on the way.

Hildie walked toward her, face wreathed in concern. "Would you like some water? A cup of tea?"

"Thank you, but I'm fine. On second thought, perhaps I should take a bottle of water with me."

"I'll get it right away," Hildie said as a vehicle screeched in front of the house.

"That must be Zach," Tina said, feeling a sliver of relief. She walked toward the door, feeling another trickle run down her leg. Was it water or blood?

Determined to keep herself together, for her sake and Zach's, she carefully descended the steps. Zach jumped out of the car.

"I'll get your suitcase," he said.

He was speaking of the bag she'd packed in anticipation

of this day, but Tina didn't want to wait one moment longer. "I'd rather leave now," she said.

He stopped in his steps and stared into her eyes. She tried with everything inside her not to show her fear. He gave a slow nod. "Okay, let's go."

Hildie scrambled down the steps with a bottle of water in each hand. "Here's one for both of you," she said, shoving them at Zach. "Call me the second you have any news." Hildie turned to Tina. "You're going to do great. You're going to be fine. I know it," she said and gave Tina a tight hug. "Now go have your baby."

"Thank you," Tina said, feeling a sudden knot form in her throat, but not giving in to it. Then she slid the towel under her seat before she stepped inside the SUV.

Zach got into the driver's side and put his foot on the accelerator. "Are you in pain?"

"I'm having contractions," she said. "My water broke."

"That's why you brought the towel?" he said.

She nodded.

"That's the last thing you need to worry about," he said.

She shrugged and focused on the pavement in front of them. She felt the moisture seep into the towel. Was it blood? Why was she bleeding? She steeled herself not to panic.

She cleared her throat. "Can you please go a little faster?" she asked. "Not too fast, but faster."

She felt him shoot a look at her. "Yeah, I can do that. I'll get you to the hospital."

"I know you will," she said and felt herself grow light-headed. *Oh, God, she couldn't lose consciousness.* Adrenaline pumping through her, she used her fear to stay awake and aware.

The contractions grew more intense and she struggled to remember the breathing techniques she'd learned during her two private prepared childbirth classes. Drawing deep breaths, she wondered if they would ever get to the hospital. The trip seemed to be taking years. She fought dizziness.

"We're close," he said.

She glanced over at Zach. His face was grim and taut. She could easily imagine what was going through his mind, the agony of his memories as his wife and son died on the way to the hospital.

Fear clutched at her. Please let her baby be okay. Please let everything be okay.

She saw the sign for the hospital and a spurt of relief rushed through her. Zach swerved into the half-circle in front of the E.R. entrance.

"Thank you," she whispered, pulling at her door before the vehicle even stopped.

"Whoa, whoa. Wait," he said, slamming the car into Park and running around to her side to help her out of the car.

As soon as she stood, Tina wove on her feet. Zach caught her against him, but he must have seen the towel on her seat. "You're bleeding."

"Sorry," she said, but the weakness she'd fought during the drive took over, and everything went black.

Chapter Eighteen

They took Tina away.

The same way they had taken Jenny away.

Zach had an ugly feeling of déjà vu. Why hadn't she told him she was bleeding? He would have driven faster. He would have gotten her to the hospital sooner.

Pacing from one side of the waiting room to the other, he checked with the receptionist twice. The hospital worker shook her head in sympathy. "I'm sorry, sir. She's in surgery. Why don't you go up to the fifth floor waiting room? Someone will give you information as soon as it's available."

Zach rode up the elevator, racking his brain for how he could have handled things differently. What could he have done to keep her and the baby safe? Maybe he should have kept a helicopter on call. Maybe he should have kept a nurse at the house.

"Mr. Logan?" a woman in scrubs asked.

He nodded, bracing himself for the worst. "Yes?"

She gave a tentative smile. "You have a baby girl. She's healthy and screaming her lungs out. As soon as we get her cleaned up, I'll bring her out to you."

Zach slumped in relief. "Oh, thank God. Thank God. Tina, she's okay, right?"

The woman paused. "Dr. McAllister is still working on her. There were complications."

His gut clenched. "But—"

"He's doing everything possible, but Miss Devereaux lost a lot of blood. She's weak, but she's fighting," the woman said and patted his arm. "I'll bring your daughter out soon."

His mind spinning, Zach sank onto the couch in the waiting room. Tina? Weak? Fighting? Oh, what if he'd lost her? What would he do?

His heart felt as if it was being ripped from his chest. His mind flashed through poignant images of the baby without her precious mother. How would little Kiki survive without her mom?

How would he?

The question shook him to the core. Tina had become as vital to him as oxygen. He couldn't imagine life without her.

He began to pray, awkward, begging prayers. He didn't want to lose her. Before he told her that he loved her.

A nurse brought his baby daughter to him. She was wrapped in a flannel blanket and wore a pink cap. He took her soft weight into his arms.

Staring into her little face, he was filled with wonder. She had Tina's lips and his hairline. Her stubborn chin might give him trouble. Oh, how he wished he could share this moment with Tina. He glanced away for a second, feeling his eyes burn with unshed tears.

The baby screwed up her face and gave a cry. Scared, he

surmised. So was he. Zach began to pace, trying to comfort his brand-new daughter and himself.

After a while, a nurse came and took the baby to the nursery. Zach waited. He paced and sat, turned off his cell phone because he couldn't bear to try to explain the situation. Hours passed and it felt like days.

Sometime in the middle of the night, he leaned his head against his hand as he sat on the waiting room sofa.

"Zachary," the doctor said.

Zach looked up, fighting fear and dread. "How is she?"

"She's had a rough time. Stabilizing her was a bit tricky, but she's going to make it. We've put her on a monitor for observation and moved her to a private room."

"I can't tell you how grateful I am," Zach said.

The doctor nodded. "Everyone was rooting for the princess. She's made an impression on this community." Dr. McAllister shook his hand. "You can go into her room, but try to let her sleep. She needs her rest. She fought hard. With the way she demanded an epidural the first time I met her, I would have never imagined her to be such a warrior."

Zach felt his spirits lift a bit. "She's stronger than she lets on. Can I see her now?"

"Of course," the doctor said.

Zach went directly to her room. The sight of her so pale, her skin matching the white sheets of the hospital bed, twisted his gut. Monitors beeped in the background. He tried not to give in to his fear, but she was so very, very still.

He wanted to touch her, but more than that, he wanted her to rest. She'd earned it. He resisted the urge to put his hand on her arm and took comfort in the steady beat on the monitor.

"Hang on, darlin'," he whispered. "Kiki and I need you. Kiki and I love you."

Sinking onto the chair beside her bed, he rested his chin

against his hands and watched over her. Looking at her, he realized she'd changed him. She'd forced him, kicking and screaming, out of his tomb of grief. She'd inspired him to look outward instead of focusing inward. She made him want to be different, better.

Hours later, a sound awakened him. He opened his too-dry eyes and saw Tina twisting from side to side. She gave a soft moan. Pain, he suspected. The nurse had told him they'd performed a C-section.

He rose and punched the call button for the nurse. Minutes later, a young man entered the room. "Hey," he said. "How's our little mama doing?"

"She seems restless," Zach said as Tina rolled her head. "Is she hurting?"

The man checked her chart and took her blood pressure. "I bumped up her pain relief so she'll rest a little longer. When she wakes up, though, she's going to feel like she's been run over by a truck."

"And my face will be the first she'll see," Zach said dryly. Zach sank back into the chair and watched over the woman who had stolen his heart.

The sun finally rose the next morning, peeking through the window blinds. Zach rubbed his beard-roughened face and stretched to get the kinks out of his back. His gaze automatically went to Tina. She still looked too pale.

Her eyelids fluttered and Zach stared at her in disbelief. She blinked again, opening her mouth as if she wanted to speak.

Zach jumped from his chair and gently touched her arm.

She stared into his eyes. "Zach," she whispered. "Our baby. Where is our baby?"

"She's fine. She's perfect," Zach said quietly, his eyes filled with tears.

She closed her eyes and tears ran down her cheeks. "She's perfect. I knew she would be."

She drifted off again before he could tell her how much she meant to him. He called the nurse to check on her and she confirmed that Tina was stable.

An hour later, Tina awakened and turned her head toward Zach. "I'm thirsty," she whispered.

He immediately rose to her side. "I'll take care of that, but in the meantime, I need you to know that I love you, Tina. More than anything. More than I ever dreamed."

Tina smiled and lifted her hand to his strong jaw.

"Marry me. We'll work out the visits to Chantaine. We can work out anything that comes our way," he said.

"I believe you," she said. "And I love you, too."

On Christmas Eve, Zach tucked Tina and their baby, Katiana Elizabeth Valentina Devereaux Logan into his SUV to bring them home. Since she'd gotten her strength back, Tina had barely been able to keep her hands off her new daughter. Every time she looked at Katiana, she was overcome with joy.

"She's the most beautiful baby I've ever seen," she said to Zach as he pulled away from the hospital with Katiana already falling asleep in her car seat.

"Yes, she is," Zach agreed, his lips twitching. "You've mentioned that a time or two, and so have I."

Tina laughed, because the fact was she'd said the same thing at least twenty times during the last few days.

"How are you feeling? Really?"

"Better. Moving around doesn't take my breath away quite as much," she said, although she knew she still tired easily. She'd quit most of the pain medication as soon as possible because she hated having a fuzzy head. "Have you heard anything from Stefan today?"

Zach had turned off the phone in Tina's room so she could rest. Since then, Stefan and Tina's sisters had been calling him constantly to check on her and the baby's condition.

"I e-mailed the photographs of you and the baby, like you asked. It was nice of you to share all the flowers you received with the other patients," he said.

"The least I could do," she said with a frown. "Think how miserable it would be to be in the hospital over Christmas."

Her comment didn't surprise him. He just hoped she would be amenable to the surprise he had waiting for her back at the ranch. Tina had told him she didn't want a big wedding, just a few witnesses. She'd also agreed that the sooner the better.

His palms itched with a trace of nerves, but he brushed them aside. "You should try and rest," he said.

"I'm too excited to get out of the hospital to rest," she said.

"Well, give it a try," he said, thinking about his plans for the rest of the day.

A little while later, he pulled toward the front of the house. Several cars were parked in the driveway.

She glanced at Zach. "Did Hildie do this? Don't tell me they're holding another shower for me."

He pulled the car to a stop and shook his head. "No, but you can be sure Hildie helped a lot." He turned to her, feeling his gut twist. "You said you would marry me."

Her eyes softened and she nodded. "And I will."

"Then you surprised me and said you didn't want to wait. You were ready to get married in the hospital."

"Well, I was. I want everything legal for Kiki and I feel like I waited forever for you to realize that you loved me."

"Well, darlin', love-of-my-life, inside our home, there's a minister waiting to do the job."

Her eyes rounded and her jaw dropped. "Now?"

He nodded. "Now. I knew you would be tied up with recovering from the C-section and taking care of the baby, so I asked Keely and Hildie if they would do the planning. Are you ready?"

Tina lifted her hand to her throat, her eyes turning shiny with unshed tears. "I am. I can't believe you did this. Why didn't you tell me?"

"I didn't want you to think about anything but getting better. If I'm moving too fast for you, then we can just have a holiday party and send the minister on his way."

"No," she said. "Let's do it. Let's make it real."

Starstuck, Tina accepted Zach's gentle assistance from the car. As soon as he collected Katiana from the backseat, Hildie rushed out the front door and down the steps. She gave Tina a big hug then turned to Zach.

"Omigoodness, she's the most beautiful baby I've ever seen."

Tina and Zach exchanged a knowing look and laughed.

"Let me hold that baby," she said to Zach. "You help your wife. Everything and everybody is ready and waiting."

After slowly navigating the steps, Tina walked past the foyer into the den. She immediately spotted Daniel, Sienna, Eve, Keely and Brent and her sister Ericka and her husband.

Tina gasped in surprise and extended her arms. "Ericka, how did you get here?"

Ericka laughed, quickly moving to embrace her. "The usual way. By jet. Of course I couldn't miss my sister's wedding after you took care of me during mine. And I got first dibs on seeing your baby. Stefan's pouting like mad. I promised to talk you into visiting Chantaine as soon as possible." Ericka pulled back and clasped her hands around Tina's. "Thank goodness you're okay. We were all so worried."

Tina greeted several of the others, then Keely introduced her to the minister, Reverend Wilhelm.

The kindly-faced man shook her hand. "It's my pleasure to meet you, your highness."

"Please call me Tina," she said, feeling her heart flutter. It was really going to happen now. She was really going to marry Zach.

"I told your fiancé that I don't perform shotgun weddings, but he insisted you were going along with this completely by choice."

She laughed at the notion of a shotgun wedding. "I am."

"Then shall we begin the taking of your vows?" he asked.

"Yes," she said. "I would like that very much."

Zach was at her side in a heartbeat, taking her hand in his. The minister led them in the promises to each other. The words and the small ceremony were important, but what was far more vital to Tina was the fact that Zach had totally opened his heart to her and that she knew he loved her and needed her. Just as she loved and needed him.

Six weeks later, after traveling across several time zones, Tina was excited to share Chantaine with Zach, Katiana, Hildie and Eve. Eve was still toying with Stefan's offer to manage the royal stables and had waited to take this trip before making such a big decision.

Hildie, who hadn't traveled farther away than Amarillo, was taking in every new experience with gusto, including a few cooking lessons from the chief chef.

Tina coaxed Zach into enjoying a day at the beach, just

the two of them, while her sisters and brothers fought over who could hold Katiana.

Zach closed his eyes as he relaxed under the beach umbrella. He slid his fingers through hers. "I could probably stomach visiting here a few times a year," he said and shot her a sideways glance.

Tina gave him a playful punch. "Yes, I know it's been torture being fed gourmet food, sleeping in that shack my family calls a palace and shooting skeet with my brother."

"Seriously," he said lifting up on his forearm. "Why would you trade this for Texas?"

"Besides the fact that *you* are in Texas?" she asked.

He gave a shrug of his strong shoulders. "I guess there's that," he said. "But—"

She put her finger over his lips. "No buts. My home is with you and Katiana. It was time for me to move away."

"Your brother still doesn't agree with that," he said and returned to his back.

"True, but did you see him melt when he held Katiana for the first time? My cranky brother turned into a complete marshmallow."

"Don't tell him that," he said.

"I'm glad we took this time out today," she said, inhaling the salty scent of the ocean and enjoying these moments with Zach. "With Stefan performing the public formalities, tomorrow will be very busy. You'll be meeting tons of people. Are you sure you're ready for it?"

"I'm ready for anything. I get to sleep with the princess at the end of the day," he said with a dirty chuckle that warmed her heart.

The following morning at precisely ten o'clock, Tina's brother Stefan gave his formal approval of her marriage to Zachary and presented Katiana as the country's newest princess. A huge crowd applauded and shouted their approval as Zachary and Tina entered the courtyard.

Katiana was in fine form, fascinated by the sparkly tiara Tina wore. Her little hand waved upward as she tried to reach for it. Kiki's face turned red and she gave a terrible frown. The baby opened her mouth to let out a yell that would have been ear-splitting if not for the sounds of the cheering crowd.

Tina made a split-second decision and pulled her tiara from her head, allowing Katiana to close her fingers around it.

Zach shook his head and chuckled. "Now I have two princesses on my hands," he said.

"Aren't you the lucky one?" she retorted.

"Damn right I am," he said and took her mouth in a kiss.

* * * * *

MILLS & BOON®

Why shop at millsandboon.co.uk?

Each year, thousands of romance readers
find their perfect read at millsandboon.co.uk.
That's because we're passionate about
bringing you the very best romantic fiction.
Here are some of the advantages of
shopping at www.millsandboon.co.uk:

* **Get new books first**—you'll be able to buy
  your favourite books one month before they
  hit the shops

* **Get exclusive discounts**—you'll also be
  able to buy our specially created monthly
  collections, with up to 50% off the RRP

* **Find your favourite authors**—latest news,
  interviews and new releases for all your
  favourite authors and series on our website,
  plus ideas for what to try next

* **Join in**—once you've bought your favourite
  books, don't forget to register with us to rate,
  review and join in the discussions

Visit **www.millsandboon.co.uk**
for all this and more today!

Printed by RR Donnelley at Glasgow, UK